CU00659892

"Part twisting mystery, part pure fantasy, *Renia* rattles along, leaving you chuckling one moment before punching you in the gut the next, and never sure what to expect on each fresh page. With a whole world outside the Halls still to explore, Forshaw and his creations are definitely one to watch."

— Sean Cregan, author of *The Razor Gate*.

RENIA

This launch edition paperback is one of 667 printed.

KARL FORSHAW

RENIA

LUNA RUINAM VOLUME ONE

Vortex3 LTD (UK)

A CIP catalogue record for this book is available from the British Library.

ISBN 13: 978-1-7391966-0-8

Printed and bound by CPI Group (UK) Ltd, Croydon, CR0 4YY
Illustration by Oliver Tsujino
Cover design by Stone Ridge Books

Acknowledgments

I am grateful to my wife, Kate, for so many things. To name a few: the love, and support, and encouragement throughout this process. Thank you, Mrs.

A very special thank you goes to my editor, John Rickards, whose advice and support I couldn't have done this without.

A big thank you to Emma Mitchell, whose advice and keen eye has made this book infinitely more readable.

Oliver Tsujino, your art has been a constant source of inspiration and pleasure throughout this project. The cover for this book turned out better than I could have imagined. Thank you.

To Mandi Lynn at Stone Ridge Books, thank you for your beautiful design work on the cover, your professionalism, and for coming through for me at the eleventh hour.

To my mother, Deborah, for reading every draft with as much enthusiasm as the first, but mostly for teaching me the joy of reading, thank you so much.

Also, to everyone else who has in some way contributed to the world of Luna Ruinam over the past two years, Theo, Ben, Kirstie, Sarah, Tahlia, thank you all.

But most of all, thanks to you, for picking up this book. I hope you enjoy it.

Twelve Years Ago

'It's over…I won.'

The words grated like sand in Raellon's throat. Every breath fought back, his chest ablaze, exhausted. Rainwater ran freely down his face, blocking his vision, dripping from his lips and chin. Like an overworked engine, his sweat turned to steam in the cold night air. He trembled in response to the adrenaline that rushed through his veins, spent, yet more alive than he'd ever been.

The crashing of the waves against the cliff wall beyond the roofline intensified, drowning out the sound of his breath. The wind rose and bit at his flesh through the torn remains of his uniform. His saturated cloak whipped his legs, flapping violently with each gust.

Bent double, laughing came with difficulty, but laugh he did as the cloaked figure approached.

'You win nothing,' came the voice from beneath its hood.

A Reaper. His chosen nemesis, the hand of southern justice, the silent approach of death. And yet here he stood, laughing, the victor.

'You're under arrest for murder. Stand down.' It was worth a shot. Uninjured, the Reaper outmatched him fourfold, but the limp told of an advantage he might be able to press.

His enemy edged closer, working against the injuries inflicted on them by the dead woman he'd known as Alia, whose corpse lay cooling just paces away, her head resting at odds to the rest of her body. A clean break.

He retreated slowly, edging backward toward the roofline. 'You're wrong. I've seen your face! I know what you are. I've exposed you. I've rooted you out.' He coughed and spat blood at the Reaper's feet. 'I've won.'

The assassin's head shook beneath the hood. Pursed lips tutted in disagreement. 'I have the book.'

'Do you?' He laughed heartily, then coughed into the rain. 'It's a fake, Reaper! See what it is you kill for.'

The Reaper complied, flicking through page after page of nonsense.

'The pages repeat! Look!' He laughed. 'Do you honestly believe that Sanas Inoa bothered to cipher his journals? It was a trap, Reaper. And you devoured the bait like a starving rat.'

A deception so simple, so effective. The assassin roared through the falling rain. The cry became a gargle, and then a snarl.

His lips spread with glee. The game was over.

And then came the pain.

A sound like no other erupted from the Reaper's mouth, dueling frequencies that rattled his senses. The sonic assault drove him to one knee. His vision blurred. Every fiber of his body threatened to shake itself apart. Heat trickled from his ears and his head lolled forward under the brutal weight of the vibration. Yet still he laughed. 'I've won,' he whispered. 'You can't kill me, Reaper. You have no writ. Your own laws are as clear as ours.'

The Reaper's step came closer. He tried to lift his head. He felt the hunter's grip pull tight against his tunic.

Such strength.

The Reaper's hand wrapped around his jaw. Focus betrayed him as he felt himself wrenched to his feet. The darkened figure thrust the book into his chest.

'I can't believe you fell for it.' He chuckled into his enemy's face.

'Poor choice of words,' the assassin snarled. 'Take your prize.'

Impact. Pain in his sternum.

Falling.

Breath…He couldn't breathe. The kick had paralyzed his diaphragm, robbing him of his final breath. His broken ears registered the whistle of rushing air as he fell, a dull echo of what should have been a deafening roar.

Was this it? This couldn't be it.

The building sped by him on either side, a blur of dark stonework and the purple of reflected moonlight.

This can't be it…

He looked upward, back to the ledge to see the outline of th—

* * *

PART ONE

Promises

ONE

Dust

THE PILE OF books landed with a thud, far too close to her face to be considered polite. A wave of dust assaulted her nostrils. She winced, coughed, and then tried her best to suppress the grin pulling at her cheeks.

Dust is good. Dust means old, forgotten. Or better yet—
Forbidden.

Her attention darted between the spines of the old books, probing for a hint of what might lie within. Her cheeks flushed, her heart raced, her senses grew numb to everything else.

Finally!

She barely registered the hoarse, grumbling voice of Master Petor.

'Well?' he said, his eyes fixed, furious at the lack of an explanation.

'I'm sorry, sir, could you repeat that?' She gulped, briefly meeting his gaze before returning her attention to the leather-bound wonders.

'It is beyond me, Miss Renia, how you come to be in the service of this great institution. It is further beyond my understanding that the first thing *I*—the master of this hall—am tasked with on this day, is bringing you three volumes of restricted material that you have no business knowing about, let alone scribing.' The master leaned forward, looming over her. 'So I'll ask you again: How did you do this?'

The Hall Master's gaze darted from her left eye to her right in expectation. He ground his teeth, his jaw muscles taut with restrained aggression.

Renia recoiled as slowly as she could bear, as Master Petor grasped the edges of her workstation and leaned in closer. His breath was foul—the mark of a man clearly married to his position and hopelessly reliant on the stimulation of coffee beans.

She allowed the moment to rest, watching the flicker of the light from her desk lamp as it danced over the old man's features.

Were you handsome once? she wondered absently. Perhaps, once, beneath the layers of hard skin, the lines of worry, and those eyebrows, oh those eyebro—

The moment of curiosity was quickly dashed as his fat, sticky palm slapped the desk. Another wave of dust flew up and into her unsuspecting nostrils.

She coughed again, and wiped the top of the pile of books in a futile attempt to prevent the dust from spoiling her work.

She couldn't resist; her attention drifted toward the spine of the top book. It filled her with a nervous glee.

LIGHTSTONE: A Practical Study – by Istopher Venn.

Light of the moon! Finally, finally! And written by the Lord of Knowledge himself! she gushed to herself.

Renia suppressed the thought and stifled the urge to laugh. She shuffled in her seat, and cautiously broke the silence.

'I'm not entirely sure, sir,' she said. 'I had registered my interest in the subject previously. Perhaps my personal background was taken into account when the order was processed?'

It was a long shot. The truth was that she had no idea. Her work was exceptional—though she would never express the belief aloud—but there were many scribes from other halls whose skill outshone her own. The fact that Master Petor didn't know either only deepened her anxiety. There were precious few people that outranked him. What was it that had invited their attention?

'Ah, yes,' he said, thrusting himself backward and straightening.

Master Petor showed little interest in the personal lives of his scribes, though duty dictated that he should have a working knowledge. After all, the Halls of Venn held the largest repository of knowledge—both public, and forbidden—in Luna Ruinam. Any of the latter falling into the hands of the enemy would in most cases cost him his life.

Renia considered this fact as she wiped the beads of spit from her face. She grudgingly accepted the old bastard's vicious assault on her otherwise quiet morning.

The old master let out a restrained sigh and glared about the hall in a gesture that saw the eyes of those distracted by the rare moment of drama return to their work. He shot her a stern look and started towards his office, before stopping abruptly to deliver a warning.

'See to it that those tomes are returned to my office upon every interruption to your work. If I see them left unattended, you'll be returning to the Wastes in haste.'

A grim look escaped his restraint. He snorted before departing.

Renia rubbed her eyebrow. 'Yes...Master Petor,' she muttered, pursing her lips as she absorbed the unlikely exchange.

He didn't seem very happy for her.

The expectant gazes of her colleagues met her as she surveyed the hall. It had been a strange month. Not long ago, a tremor had shaken the walls of her workplace, cracking plaster, spilling ink and freeing the bookshelves that lined the walls of their burden. The resulting halt in production had angered Petor to the point of screaming, stomping, and hurling abusive language at her and her colleagues as they hurried to fix the mess.

Everyone was tired. They had put the hours in, determined to make up for lost time, pushed themselves to the limit of endurance, and still produced exceptional work. She was proud to be part of it, she reveled in it. Despite the exhaustion and the strange dreams that came with it, she felt content, a happy cog in the machine.

And now this.

This wonderful gift from an unknown benefactor. The first chance she'd had at a project that truly inspired her, a chance to fulfill a promise made long before she stepped foot in this place.

Renia had come to be in the service of Hall Three by virtue of her aptitude in both recall and calligraphy. But it was her sheer thirst for knowledge and relentless approach to acquiring it that had seen her recommended for the role. She had been born in an unlikely place for such a future, the Moonwastes, the irradiated crater that surrounded the most mysterious and venerated feature of Luna Ruinam.

Being so close to the site of the fallen moon did different things to people. To some it inspired greed: a ruin, rich with the treasures of a forgotten civilization. It was out of that greed that her family came to be there, with her father taking a job in the Gatherers' Guild, and spending his life searching the Wastes for the highly coveted lightstones that lay scattered around the vast, desolate region.

To Renia though, the fallen moon was a source of wonder, the lightstones a curiosity, and the endless stream of visiting scholars and their stories an escape from the brutal reality of survival in the Wastes.

Sensing the coming wave of discomfort, she shook the memories away, dusting off her thighs and returning her attention to the pile of leather-bound joy that had found its way to her station.

She ran her gaze down the stack of old books, her heart racing at each title and the promise of secrets within.

Aceraceian History and Culture – by Vala Veridia

Journal 26 – by Sanas Inoa

Renia's palms began to sweat. She took a deep breath, swallowed the pooling saliva in her mouth and retrieved a clean handkerchief from her desk drawer.

Quickly wiping her hands and making a conscious effort to slow her breathing, she took another glance around the room. The appearance of material from the forbidden section was a rare occurrence, eyebrows were raised, hushed words exchanged, and envy showed its ugly colors in the eyes of other, more competitive scribes.

Her status amongst them had already changed; she saw it in the mystified faces of her peers. All eyes now fixed on her, or the newly arrived books still sitting exactly where the Hall Master had dumped them so inelegantly.

Reveling in the rush of her newly elevated position, she locked eyes with the devilishly handsome, smirking face of Dail Svelt, her friend, and occasionally—when the touch of paper became tiresome—her lover.

Turn them around then, let's have a look! she heard him think. Her cheeks flushed. She glanced around to see who else might be monitoring their unspoken exchange, before risking a quick response.

Absolutely not; you know the rules. Now stop embarrassing me and get back to work! she thought.

No words needed to be spoken; they knew each other so intimately that entire conversations could be conducted from across the hall, and often were on slower days.

Dail chuckled silently, shook his head and winked at her as he dipped his quill and returned his attention to his own mundane task.

Satisfied that the exchange had concluded, Renia lifted the first of the three tomes and ran her fingers down the opening edge.

Leather bound, gold leaf, metallic inlay in the shape of the falling moon. Impressive craftsmanship. And old, very old.

Carefully prising open the cover, she ran the tips of her fingers down the contents page, scan reading entries between short breaths.

'Manipulation of Inanimate Material, Healing and Enhancement, Atmospheric Anomalies, Elemental Manifestation,' it went on, and on.

Only sheer force of will prevented her from jumping out of her seat. Renia found herself adrift on a sea of emotion, waves of confusion and awe crashing over her, buffeting her with a torrent of unanswered questions.

Why me? Why now? Why this book? What are the others? Who is to be the recipient of the copies? It was a deafening roar in her head. She barely managed to consider any of it before a loud bang and a very real roar of frustration erupted from Master Petor's office.

'Piece of garbage!' the tirade began. 'Utterly useless, worthless piece of trash.'

The rest of it became inaudible, lost within the sound of venting steam and the tinkle of a hand-sized brass gear that almost joyously rolled down the center of the hall in a final act of defiance.

Master Petor appeared in the doorway, shoving the door against its hinges with an audible crack, his reddened face flushed with outrage, spattered with soot, oil, and coffee. He glowered at the stunned faces of the staff closest to the event, gritted his teeth, and growled.

'Service! Get me service here immediately.'

Renia sat dumbstruck, mouth agape, completely speechless at the drama of the morning. She slowly averted her eyes to her neighbor, Sundance, in a shared moment of recognition.

Sundance had seen many years, and many more pages, in this hall. She was a stickler for the rules, particularly the rule of complete silence. Her gripe with the old Hall Master had always been that for all the stick he gave out to those who broke the rule of silence, he was by far the worst offender. This tirade only further proved her point. She raised an eyebrow, cocked her head, and threw up her palms in an open display of disapproval.

Renia laughed quietly. In truth, she was almost glad of the old man's outburst. She still had four pages of *Assorted Children's Stories, Vol 2* to copy, and up until this moment, she had been starting to worry about how the distraction of this morning's events were going to affect her performance.

No longer would she be alone in the sentiment. The whole hall's production would be slowed thanks to the raging Hall Master and his broken coffee machine.

THE SCENE IN Master Petor's office was shambolic. He stood dripping with all manner of liquids, staring at the shattered pieces of his coffee machine at his feet. The broken machine let out a pop, forcing him back on his heel, and hissed its final dying breath.

He resisted the urge to smash it to pieces.

As days went, this was the worst he had suffered for as long as he could remember. To be denied his morning coffee was the tip of the spear.

That book. He grimaced. *Why* that *book?*

The machine had been the one true luxury afforded to him as a reward for his long service. Fitting that it should blow up in his face on the same day that a lowly scribe received the honor of not one, but three forbidden book projects. And, of course *that book*, the one that had almost ruined his career twelve years ago.

Petor frothed. He threw the broken cogs and gears he'd gathered up at the wall and admitted defeat, turning hard on his heels and storming out of the door.

A walk would do him good. Some fresh air.

He paused on the threshold, finding himself the focus of thirty-three gawking faces, all staring at him in mute anticipation.

'Back to work, all of you,' he barked. He projected the order with as much confidence and poise as he could muster, before turning his back on them and leaving the hall with a swiftness betraying his mood.

The walk to the Masters' Lounge was short, some five minutes through the old building, but he had tried his best over the past few years to be noticeably absent from within its walls. He was old, far older than some of his colleagues, and he found their boundless optimism tedious.

The work of the institution was a serious business; thousands of people depended on the Halls of Venn. As the only legal distributor of knowledge in Luna Ruinam, the responsibilities of himself and his peers were crushing.

These young upstarts—in most cases elevated to the position of Hall Master due to the death of a superior—were far too interested in secrets, and the revelation of the knowledge afforded to those who shared his title. Petor found it masturbatory, the height of self indulgence, a mockery of the oaths they had taken.

He paused to compose himself before entering the Masters' Lounge, willing the room to be empty in the hope of retrieving his cup of coffee without having to engage in idle chatter. To his dismay, he opened the door to find two of his fellow masters engaged in a painfully mundane conversation about the tremor and the ongoing repairs.

'Master Petor!' gasped an annoyingly youthful, shoe-headed, waste of a man.

His name. What is his damned name? Petor mused, frowning at the idea that this know-it-all piss-stain might have him at a disadvantage. He gave up, shrugged and spared the younger man a forced pleasantry.

'Yes. Behold. It is I,' came Petor's retort. It left a bad taste on his lips, devoid of wit, a loss.

'To what do we owe the pleasure?' Piss-Stain said.

Petor's patience expired long before he reached the kitchen area, where he stood pulling a mug from the cupboard.

'Coffee machine broke,' he said over the clattering cacophony he intentionally created.

'Oh, how utterly vexing,' said Piss-Stain, his thinly veiled annoyance missing its intended target.

Petor shot a stoic look at the second master in the room. She hadn't said a word, and Petor was grateful for it. Master Vedora had been in service for almost as long as Petor; she knew his ways.

She returned the blank look, noting Petor's complete lack of interest, and returned to her book with a barely noticeable grin on her lips.

The smell of the coffee filling the cup flooded the room, and Petor felt the fog of his morning lift in anticipation. With his mouth watering, he took a loud slurp, fixing his gaze on the young master, still trying to recall his name.

Petor smiled for the first time that day. 'Ahh, that's good,' he said, a grin spreading over his face.

He locked eyes with Piss-Stain and winked. It struck that him that nickname actually suited the young fellow. With a bit of luck, it might even stick.

Content at the thought, he glided past the two figures toward the door. He nodded at Vedora and then to the other.

'Have a nice day, Vedora,' he said. 'And you too, Piss-Stain.'

THE HALF-HOUR FOLLOWING the coffee machine disaster had passed uneventfully. Renia had dutifully completed her work and now sat checking it over for mistakes and imperfections. She knew there would be none, but over the years she had found such rituals could be useful. In knowing this step would come, she would be far less likely to make a mistake.

She had employed hundreds of little tricks like this over the years, some so bizarre that she had obsessed for some time about her state of mind. The fact that she had the lowest error count and the lowest number of rewrites, however, gave her great pride. 'Renia the Relentless,' they called her, a nickname that she secretly enjoyed.

It was time to submit her work for review and binding. As she stacked the meticulously copied pages into a neat pile, she steadied herself, struggling against the buzzing sensation in her limbs.

She eyed the stack of books she'd been struggling to ignore for the past hour and licked her top lip, nervous about the protocol for leaving her desk. She wasn't about to lose this project before she'd even begun.

Her hesitation hadn't escaped the notice of Sundance, who eyed her over the top of her spectacles. For the first time in all the years they'd had neighboring desks, maternal instinct overrode Sundance's rigid adherence to the rules, and she broke the silence.

'Relax, dear girl. Leave the children's book on the desk and take the restricted books to Petor's office as he requested,' she whispered with a thin smile.

Renia nodded at her senior, placed down the neat stack of pages, and followed the instruction, grateful to Sundance for making the decision for her.

PETOR HADN'T RETURNED. Renia entered the old man's office for what was perhaps only the third or fourth time in her service.

She navigated the mess, taking care to avoid any of the scattered wreckage left by the coffee machine, then placed the books on his desk and waited, fighting the urge to tidy up.

She hadn't realized that her Hall Master's office had doubled as his living quarters. Behind a screen of purple cloth lay a haphazard arrangement of furniture that almost perfectly reflected the old man's personality.

The cot had not been made, and in the wash basin, various grooming instruments and dried splashes of ointments lay neglected.

She hoped they were ointments...

A faint wash of sympathy passed over her as she stood in the musky room. She had never thought of Master Petor as a real person, with his own stories to tell. She couldn't help but wonder if the old man felt lonely in these four walls he called home.

'You have finished your project, Miss Renia?' came the voice from the doorway.

Spinning toward the sound, and making a show of looking at the pieces of wrecked machinery littering the floor, she tried to mask her prying. She braved a glance at Master Petor, who seemed to be quite pleased with himself for some reason, and not at all the man who had stormed out of the hall less than an hour ago.

'Yes, sir,' she said, keeping her head bowed slightly so as not to risk his ire.

'You may leave the books on my desk whilst you submit your work. I trust you will be returning presently?' he asked with a raised eyebrow. He kept his attention fixed on her as he rounded his desk and sat down.

His chair creaked, his mug thudded on the desk; the silence that followed was painful. Renia held as still as she could, periodically looking at the old man for a sign that she had been dismissed, but he just sat. He rocked back in the old chair, the fingers of both hands held together in an arch in front of his lips, considering her.

Just as Renia felt ready to risk breaking the uncomfortable silence herself, he spoke.

'You must be eager to get started, Miss Renia, after all the badgering I've had from you over the years.'

'Eager to serve my hall, sir. It is a great honor,' she said, happy that her delivery didn't betray her.

'Better get to it then,' he said dismissively. The old man turned in his chair and raised his hard-fought cup of coffee to his lips. He nodded toward the door with a raise of his eyebrows, and Renia returned the nod before scurrying back to her desk.

Two

Home

Eighteen years before

NOROK WAS DRENCHED. His sodden boots rubbed at his feet with every labored step. The regular squelching noise had been his only companion in the day-long journey home. The gatherer stopped to catch his breath. He straightened and wiped the sweat from his brow, squinting into the foggy twilight for the familiar hearth-fire glow of his home.

It never really rained in the Moonwastes. The immense energetic barrier surrounding the region did something strange to the precipitation. The moisture seemed to bleed through space rather than fall, resulting in a sort of haze that permeated everything, no matter how bloody much you tried to cover up.

It had been just a few days this time. But he'd done well to retrieve a couple of lightstones that he'd found in a cave while attempting to find a relatively dry place to sleep. A picture was starting to form in his mind; he was sure that he'd found an ancient track that would lead him back to a forgotten settlement. If so, a motherlode of lightstone would await him there, and help him to secure a decent life for him and his young family for at least a few years—providence permitting.

His wife was a savvy sort, and although initially hesitant to set up home here in the harsh wastelands, she'd supported him—even suggested that they build a home large enough to take in lodgers. *An extra income,* she'd said, providing room and board for the traveling scholars and historians that frequented the area in search of their own kind of treasure.

Satisfied with his short rest, Norok straightened, pulled his pack tight into his shoulder, and took a sharp breath before resuming the trudge. Half a mile or so and he would be home and dry. A hot meal would be waiting for him, and the smiling face of his little girl would lift his spirits.

THE YOUNG MISS Renia sat swinging her stubby little legs under the big chair. She liked the feeling of the air between her toes. Today was great, because she'd written out the entire alphabet without smudging or moving out of the lines. Everyone would be proud of her, even Ma.

'Very well done, little madam,' said Molan. He smiled so much you could see every one of his brown teeth. Ma said it was because he smoked too much.

Molan was her teacher, one of them anyway. Mama had said that Molan had been good enough to offer to teach Renia in return for room and board—whatever board meant. She hadn't seen Mama giving him any boards, so it all seemed a little strange. *Maybe he's getting some boards for her,* she thought, swinging her legs, and rubbing her eyebrow.

She shrugged the thought away and spread her hands in the biggest arc she could with her little arms.

'I was concentrating soooo much,' she said loudly, grinning from ear to ear.

'You'll be writing whole words soon! Maybe you could start your own journal.' Molan winked at her and did the weird smile, the one that might mean he was teasing her.

'What's a jurnle?' Renia said, scrunching her face up.

Molan just laughed. 'Renia, my love. You really are a rare ray of sunshine in an otherwise dull place.'

'Hey, stop laughing at me. I really don't know.' He never took her seriously, always laughing. She folded her arms so he would know she was serious.

'Of course,' said Molan. He put on his pouty, stern face and sat up straight, but Renia knew he was acting. 'It's like a book that you write yourself. Every day you write down the things that have happened—so you don't forget.'

'That's silly. I never forget anything. I'm very smart.' She puffed up her chest and held her chin all the way up so he could see how smart she was.

She was about to stand up on the chair, but then she heard the front door open.

Is it him?

She knew it was him; she heard the heavy boots banging together.

'Daddy!' She ran as fast as she could, knocking the chair over by accident.

NOROK DROPPED TO one knee and braced himself as the speeding child leaped into his open arms. She squeezed him as tight as her little muscles could, and he let out a sigh of relief.

'Hello, Moonpie,' he whispered. He took her by the shoulders and kissed her forehead. The look in her eyes was its own reward for the hard trudge home.

'Daddy, I wrote out the whole alphabet and I stayed in the lines and I didn't smudge it once.' She could barely get the words out fast enough.

Norok feigned shock, wishing he had his daughter's energy. '*Amazing*,' he said. 'Not even one smudge?'

'Not. One.' She waved her finger and swayed on her heel, with a serious expression she frequently borrowed from her mother. 'Daddy, did you bring me anything back this time?'

Norok chuckled to himself, and tried his best to look stern. 'Maybe, but you'll have to be a good girl and get ready for dinner first. We'll talk about it later, alright?'

'Alright.' she said with a sharp nod, already bounding across the room with her arms outstretched.

He placed his pack on the stool by the front door and looked to his wife, who had been patiently watching the exchange between father and daughter with amusement.

'You're a sight for sore eyes,' she said, grinning at her sodden husband. She wouldn't appreciate him dripping all over her floors much, but she held her complaints—he was *home*.

'It's good to be home,' he said. His voice softened, the harsh reality of the Wastes giving way to the familiar warmth and smells of his girls.

The mop bucket already sat beneath the coat hook. Norok chuckled to himself as he hung his dripping burden above it. He removed his boots where he stood, making a show of not getting any mud on the rug. His wife grinned and nodded in approval.

The hearth at the end of the room blazed, roaring its heat and light into the dining area. The smell of stew lingered around him. He filled his lungs with its aroma and swallowed his anticipation.

My favourite.

He glanced around the room to find everything pristine. The interior, as ever, was adorned with hangings. The walls were lined with images of the city in which they had met. Many of them were works of his wife. She had a way with oils.

'You're a good woman.' He grinned back at her before making his way across the room toward her embrace.

She always smelled good.

'I'll go and clean up.' he said. 'You'll not have me smelling of ash and sweat for dinner now, will you?'

DINNER LIFTED NOROK'S spirits considerably. Moyra was a good cook, and she'd made sure he'd ate his fill after his journey, refilling his bowl and pushing extra bread rolls onto his plate as he spoke.

In all the years since she'd married him, he'd never doubted her. She made sure he was always properly prepared for his work, and listened to his reports of each adventure with enthusiasm, despite her initial misgivings about him joining the Gatherer's Guild. It was a difficult life, but he'd promised her his best efforts, and a retirement that would see them comfortable in their old age.

His two lodgers, Molan and Carol, congratulated him on his find, and now sat at the table with his family, listening intently to his theories, nodding and making notes.

'We had theorized that the impending calamity would have resulted in increased movement,' Carol interjected, no longer able to hold her enthusiasm at bay. 'I mean imagine waking up one morning and seeing the moon hurtling toward you, there must have been an *exodus*. Any tribal communities would have no doubt rushed to confer with each other, undertaking long, arduous journeys that would have seen *many* dead along the way. It appears you may have stumbled upon a point of shelter, perhaps.'

Norok shot a grin to his wife.

It was a stroke of genius really, taking in the scholars. Upon his application to the guild, his lack of experience had given him many a sleepless night. The established gatherers had been working the Wastes for generations, and had a plentiful stock of light-hounds. The beasts were capable of sniffing out lightstone from miles away, but by the moon were they pricey, and the expense of building this larger homestead had left precious little in the pot for such a luxury.

Moyra had masterfully suggested offering room and board to traveling historians and scholars, knowing full well it would offer Norok a competitive advantage in his trade. It would never have occurred to him. She'd never voiced the strategy outright, but Norok knew his wife's silent brilliance, and it filled him with unspoken pride.

'It stands to reason,' Carol continued. 'That if you are able to follow the original beaten path, so to speak, you may stumble upon an old settlement, yet undiscovered.' She tapered off, nodding as much to herself as to the gathered diners. Norok finished his bread roll as she scribbled in her notepad.

Nobody knew much about the lightstones or their original source. There were old tales of potato-like faeries with magical powers, but Norok had long dismissed those as children's tales. What he *knew* was that there had been a tribal civilization here, it had been utterly destroyed by the Moonfall, and that wherever the old ones lay dead, there were lightstones.

He nodded at Carol, thanked her for her knowledge, and gestured toward a tired-looking Renia, who had been sitting patiently for an hour, awaiting her gift.

The poor girl. Her head bobbed low to the table. She held her eyes open through sheer determination.

'Right you, little lady. Let's get you to bed.' He sighed, pushing himself to his feet.

His little girl let out a yawn as he hoisted her up, and she wrapped herself around him in a slump.

'Goodnight, Carol, Molan,' he whispered, offering them a half-wave with his free hand. He smiled at his wife and carried his favorite little person to her room.

NOROK PRESSED THE blankets in tight, and stroked Renia's hair out of her face. He sat by her on the bed, watching her silent battle between patience and excitement. 'I'm sorry you had to wait all night for this, Moonpie,' he said, reaching into his pocket. Renia shot into a sitting position, instantly reinvigorated, her eyes darting from his eyes to his pocket.

'What is it? What is it?' She bounced in place.

'I found it in the cave,' Norok whispered. He beckoned Renia closer, as if about to reveal a secret. For added suspense, he brought his closed fist up slowly, turned it, and opened his hand to reveal a tiny, glittering blue stone. Its brilliance manipulated the light from Renia's night lamp. Imitated points of light moved within it, creating dancing reflections on the walls.

Renia gasped, entranced by the offering. 'It's a *lightstone*,' she whispered, her bottom lip moving silently.

'Not a lightstone, Moonpie. Just a shard. A fragment of a broken one. The Baron has no need of these and lets us keep them as trinkets. This is a pretty nice one, though, eh?'

'It's beautiful,' she said. Norok felt his heart lift at the look of wonder in his daughter's eyes. Spending so much time away from her was difficult, but he felt proud of her sense of curiosity and adventure. He saw a younger version of himself before him, and wondered where it would take her in life. He would do his best to nurture that spirit, to see his daughter leave the Wastes one day and travel the world, learning, reading, writing—all the things that he never had the opportunity to do.

'Is is magic, Daddy?' she said, still fixated on the fingernail-sized shard.

'You know what? It just might be.' He winked. 'Maybe you can figure out how to make it do things, you being so smart and all. I wouldn't know where to start.'

She took a sharp breath in, and with a determined nod she looked her father dead in the eye. 'I will. I'll learn everything there is to know, and I'll make magic—like the potato faeries.'

Norok chuckled and placed his hand on Renia's head. It covered most of her skull. She wriggled under its weight.

'Daaad, *stop it*. Your hands are rough and they mess up my hair.'

'Alright, alright. Now, get some sleep, madam.'

Three

Trepidation

THE DINING HALL was alive. Each table wrestling for its place in the audible, the volume reaching increasingly uncomfortable levels, gasps of shock and exaggerated laughter danced around the edges of the throbbing mass.

Renia barely noticed.

She sat with her eyes unfocused, pretending to watch Dail as he enthusiastically recounted his tale. His words were a distant mumble in the fog that arrested her senses.

She had a vague idea of the subject that had set the dining hall ablaze; apparently Master Petor had managed to deeply offend one of his fellow Hall Masters, resulting in a venomous tirade that had been overheard and was now being retold on almost all of the dozens of dining tables, including hers.

The unexpected events of the morning had caught her off-guard, and now she reflected on her task with dueling feelings of excitement and trepidation.

For most of her life she'd coveted the secrets of the lightstones; some of her earliest memories were colored with overwhelming curiosity for the strange objects.

As a child, she'd reveled in tales of their mystical properties, fantasized about magical powers wielded by those who possessed them. As a teenager, she'd spent sleepless nights imagining where they had come from, what kind of species had created them, only to leave them behind. As an adult, she'd considered how their distribution could tip the balance of power and mused over how much of their value lay in their perception as opposed to their actual use. Now, as Renia the Scribe, as Renia the Scholar, she found herself in conflict.

Mysteries are eternal.

She'd heard it said so many times in heated debate between Molan and Carol. It had taken her so long to put her finger on it, but here, now, sitting in a noisy dining hall, she finally understood why.

Optimism.

A mystery is a box filled with possibilities, a space where anything could be true or false. It is, by its very definition, magical, for what is magic but the unexplained, or misunderstood.

Secrets, however... Even the word evokes feelings of shame. Secrets are the currency of the dishonest, the schemer. They are singular, a shrouded truth that has been hidden to serve an agenda.

Secrets are fleeting. The thrill of uncovering a secret is intense, but forgotten too soon, like the first bite of something sweet.

She sat mute, detached, ignorant to her surroundings, and afraid. Afraid that all the magic of the lightstones, and the myriad of possibilities their mystery represented, could be reduced to little more than a secret. Afraid that the hidden world of magic, of mystery, of *possibility*, that she'd waited her whole life for a glimpse of could soon become as mundane as the lunch that grew cold on her plate.

A life's ambition reduced to mere *practical knowledge*.

Her quest for the answers to her questions had been her inner compass for as long as she remembered, and now she stood brandishing a mallet in its shadow.

She sighed and let the moment of sadness rush from her, wiping the smirk from Dail's face like the smack from a bucket of cold water.

'Don't you think?' He sat back in his chair, frowning.

Reality fell back into focus. Dail and Sundance exchanged concerned glances, awaiting an explanation.

'Forgive me. This morning has left me feeling a little...out of sorts.'

'Ah yes,' Dail teased, raising a finger toward the ceiling and adopting the tone of an announcer. 'Renia the Relentless and her stack of forbidden knowledge.' He leaned in and lowered his voice. 'You've caused quite the stir. I'm *dying* to know what you've managed to get your hands on.'

Dail quickly returned to his food, munching with fervor, only to realize that he'd left it to chill in his enthusiasm. As he bunched his facial muscles into a sight that reminded Renia of a beast chewing nettles, she laughed out loud for the first time since she'd sat down and remembered why she enjoyed his company so much.

Sundance did not share her amusement. She sat with her arms folded, scowling. Renia awaited the inevitable lecture.

'You would do well to remember your oath, young man,' it began. 'We adhere to a strict code of conduct that no amount of charisma or comedy will erode. You'll refrain from making any more comments like that, or find yourself in hot water.'

Dail opened his mouth to defend himself but was interrupted by the abrasive sound of Sundance's chair legs scraping the floor tiles. She rose to her feet, fixed Renia with a sympathetic smile, and rested a gentle hand on her shoulder.

'We're all very proud of you, my dear. I'm sure you will do remarkable work, as you always do.' She shot Dail a final admonishing look before striding from the table, leaving the two lovers alone.

'I wonder what she's like with a bottle of wine in her,' Dail mumbled through a mouthful of cold food as he watched Sundance walk away.

Renia studied his face, trying to decipher his true meaning. She felt a smirk creep over her lips. 'You're terrible,' she said.

He shot forward in his seat. 'Come on then, tell—'

Renia raised her palm before he could voice the question. 'Shush. This is the most important moment of my career and I'll not have people questioning my professionalism.'

She flashed a look around the room.

Satisfied that they were free from prying eyes and ears, she offered him a small consolation:

'I'll come by later tonight, alright?'

MASTER PETOR SWEPT his way along the eastern wall corridor, carrying a fresh mug of coffee and attempting to waft as much air up through his robes as he could. It must have been a curious sight, he was sure. There was a trick to it, walking with the legs wider apart. Here, where the sea air drafted along the tiles, it made for a few minutes of pleasant relief.

Of all the distractions old age brought with it, it was the sweating that annoyed him the most. His knees and back—fine, he'd expected them to go, but perpetually sweaty balls had been a most unwelcome and unpleasant surprise.

So it was that he trudged his way along the corridor, with young scribes, aspirants, and janitorial staff alike politely avoiding his step with a mixture of fear and confusion, all of them completely oblivious to the fact that his funny walk had nothing to do with them, and everything to do with his balls.

If he hadn't been so uncomfortable, he would have laughed at the thought.

It had been a while since he'd walked this much. He found it refreshing, and took the opportunity to remind himself of just how beautiful his home was.

Tall columns of carved stone supported ornate archways, which in turn separated windows of stained glass that faced out over the ocean, creating a dance of light and unfocused imagery upon polished marble floors. The scene was a work of art in itself. Petor found himself itching for a brush and canvas on which to paint it.

Now that was a pleasant thought.

Whether it was the increased exercise from having to fill his mug in the Masters' Lounge or the sense of satisfaction from having been the source of today's gossip, Petor was feeling particularly pleased with himself. He'd had time to think his way through the dread that had arrested him upon seeing the book that had almost cost him his career. It had been years, after all. A rational man couldn't live in fear of the past. Despite himself, he started to hum—an old fisherman's song that his grandfather had taught him in simpler times.

With a slosh, and a sudden flash of pain, he looked down to find his coffee dripping from his torso.

'Honored Master, it appears you have disgraced yourself.'

Regaining his footing, and pausing to check the level of coffee that remained in the cup, Petor lifted his attention to the smirking waste of air that had broken his stride and robbed him of his moment of pleasure.

'I'm glad to have bumped into you, so to speak, as it seems that your earlier attack on my character has caused somewhat of a stir amongst the staff.'

Petor knew exactly what the young brief-sniffer was referring to, but decided to play along, wiping down his tunic with an old handkerchief.

Piss-Stain, he laughed internally, relishing the simplicity of it. *Piss-Stain. It's brilliant. He'll be trying to shake it off for years.*

'Your character?' Petor enquired, determined not to show his annoyance at being physically assaulted.

'Indeed.'

'That would be a rather juvenile attempt at character assassination wouldn't you say? No, I don't imagine that's the issue here.' Petor eyed the figure of youth and naiveté standing in his path. 'What is it that I can do for you, uh…' The young man's name still escaped him.

'A full public apology, before the entire staff,' Piss-Stain said, barely allowing Petor time for a single breath.

The young man loomed more than a head taller than Petor. Beads of sweat collected on his brow. Petor fought the urge to laugh as the idiot periodically spat air upward in an attempt to blow his fringe out from in front of his eyes.

What a stupid haircut for a Hall Master. How does he read?

Making a show of looking his aggressor up and down, Petor sighed and swatted the young man to the side gently with the back of his free hand. He paused to look his adversary in the eye sidelong. 'It is my opinion, dear boy, that those who can be offended *should* be offended.' Petor concluded the exchange with a smile, leaving the outraged youth rocking from side to side, his jaw agape in incredulity.

Relieved of his superior demeanor, Piss-Stain flew into a raging torrent of expletives and barely comprehensible attacks on Petor's age, position, and professionalism.

Petor however, continued to walk away, slowly, enjoying the moment, savoring it like a delicious meal.

Mere feet away from the tirade, an unassuming member of the janitorial staff looked on in horror, mop in hand, knowing what was about to happen, eyes darting from Piss-Stain to the freshly cleaned marble floor.

With a loud thud, the grand doors at the far end of the corridor juddered on their hinges, thrown open by the guard standing watch on the outside.

Startled onlookers stared in unison toward the figure advancing from the opening. The guard was Mohruscan, a gastropod, a humanoid slug. It charged into the space, plates of golden armor rattling, flecks of slime spattering the floor and clothing of unsuspecting scribes. Petor covered what remained of his coffee instinctively, watching in sheer delight, almost unable to believe the scene unfolding before his eyes.

Brilliant, flawless.

Piss-Stain continued to rant even as the guard reached him. He barely noticed until he found his arm seized and twisted by the armored figure. Mohruscans were strong, and resilient, smart enough to follow orders, dumb enough not to question them.

Talk your way out of this one, boy.

'Hall Master,' the guard said in the typical Mohruscan slime-rattling gargle. 'You are in violation of code. This outburst will cease and you will accompany me to a relaxation room.'

Spots of off-cast peppered the raging young Hall Master as he struggled against the guard's grip.

'Get your hands off me, you disgusting slime-glider!'

'Please come with me, sir…' The ruckus trailed off as the idiot boy was dragged away. Petor stood grinning from ear to ear. Justice served.

Perhaps I should leave my office more regularly, he pondered as he turned and walked away to the sound of mop-slap.

THE SOUND OF pages turning far too regularly disrupted the hall. Eyebrows were raised, heads shook, and throats were cleared. Renia rubbed her eyebrow, hunched over her desk, oblivious to it all.

Lost in her inner world, her thoughts raced with each paragraph. Revelation after revelation leaped from the page.

She was *reading*.

The workflow of the scribe was a well-established thing. You copy each character on the page, precisely, methodically. You do not skip ahead, you do not read. You do not allow your personal feelings to cloud the task at hand.

Renia was now in open breach of protocol, and she hadn't even noticed.

The magical properties of the lightstones, it was written, were well known, and had been for many decades. It was all here, within these pages. Forbidden knowledge locked away in a vault for none to hold. The rush of being one of the few people permitted to *know* was overwhelming. She charged through the words now with no thought spared for anything, or anyone else.

The chapter she now devoured detailed the various healing abilities offered by lightstones of a certain type. There were studies on miraculous feats of healing demonstrated during the Great War.

The healing stones, it was written, appeared to grow in their potency in proximity to acts of compassion. The effects compounded over time. A particular point of fascination for Renia was the study on the extended lifespan of the users of the healing stones, some of whom were recorded as living well beyond their years, and appearing younger than they had before.

After what, for her, seemed like no time at all, she became aware of the pain in her neck, and stopped to stretch and take a breath.

Imagine how much you could learn with unlimited time.

In shock, she cast her gaze around the hall. It was empty. How long had she been reading? She was sure it hadn't been that long. The color of the light bleeding through the windows told her otherwise. The sun had long since set. She had forgotten herself.

She gathered up the little work she *had done* with care, and crept toward Master Petor's office.

She found him sat at his desk, reviewing the day's progress. The old man held up a palm. She halted, and stood in silence, awaiting his attention.

When he did look at her, she was surprised not to see anger in his eyes. Instead she saw pride, a gentler side of the Hall Master she had not seen before.

'Intoxicating, isn't it?' the old man said. He carefully placed his glasses in their case and rose to his feet before making his way toward her.

Renia found herself disarmed by the old man's demeanor. 'Entirely,' she said. She held out the book, expecting him to store it away, but he dismissed the gesture with a wave.

'I have something for you,' he said. He reached into his tunic and produced a small key. 'I have a feeling one of these nights you're going to walk in here and find me sleeping.' He turned and gestured toward his cot. 'This will open the cabinet over there. You may come and go as you please.' The old master lowered his gaze and chuckled once. 'You're going to need to, if you're going to catch up on the work you missed today.'

A flush of embarrassment painted Renia's cheeks in crimson. 'Sir, I—'

'Oh hush. Come, child.' Master Petor's robes dragged across the stone floor as he made his way toward the window. He turned and beckoned Renia to join him and pointed out into the night. 'There. See?'

Beyond the gates, and out into the borderlands beyond Venntown, a caravan approached in the distance. Lanterns danced back and forth, illuminating the large insectoid beast pulling its load toward the Halls of Venn.

Walking alongside the caravan, a dozen heavy-set men were visible, holding torches and laughing amongst themselves.

The Baron. Coming to deliver his latest haul.

They stood side by side at the window, both lost in thought in a moment of silence.

'Many years ago, before you were born, I copied that book.' He pointed at the dusty old tome she held to her breast. 'The copy was given to the man that leads that caravan.'

Renia's attention returned to the advancing convoy. Suppressing the hatred rising within her, she considered its cargo. She imagined the sacks full of lightstone, the rattle of glass as the caravan rocked gently to and fro.

She'd seen the sight before—it was a regular occurrence—but now she saw it in a different light. The sheer power contained within, the potential.

Beyond the caravan and back toward the Wastes, the fallen moon sat in its eternal seat. The celestial invader, bringer of the shade, ever present, casting its purple glow deep into the darkness of the night, up and into the heavens where the airship could be seen bobbing on the wind, away and to the west.

What a sight it must be from up there.

'It would be difficult for me to chastise you for reading ahead. After all, it had the same effect on me.' Master Petor winked at her. 'Goodnight, Miss Renia.'

Taking the old man's cue, she dutifully locked away the book. Petor didn't move. He stood with a noticeable hunch, fixated on the scene beyond. Renia opened her mouth to wish him the same, but faltered and made for the door.

Light of the Moon…Dail.

BY THE TIME she'd reached the door to Dail's quarters, the hour was late. Renia half expected to find him sleeping. She hadn't eaten, or bathed, and now found herself sniffing at her armpits, worrying about what he would think of her.

She tapped out their shared code on the door, loud enough that only he would hear it, and the door cracked open.

She pushed her way through and carefully closed it.

'I thought you might have passed out at your desk.' His tone was cold, devoid of the usual cocky manner that she knew so well. He stood with his back to her at his workbench, filing away at what sounded like a piece of metal.

Dail hadn't entered into the service by his own choosing. He'd been forced into the role by his father, who had served as a chef up until his death. Dail had been a well-loved mascot for the institution as a child, and had found friends amongst the practitioners of the arts and crafts. He was incredibly creative, skilled in writing, painting, and jewelry-crafting. Renia often wondered whether his mischief stemmed from his boredom. Copying third-rate books must have been torture to a mind like his.

Was he angry with her? Why wouldn't he turn around? Each passing second drew on, mounting pressure in her chest adding to her anxiety. He had to understand. It was an eventful day. How could he not understand?

'There,' he said, finally. He turned to greet her with a smile she found hard to read, looked her up and down and shook his head. 'Good day, was it?'

She looked to the floor, blushing. 'Time got away from me.'

Striding toward his modest dining table, he lit a candle placed at its center and pulled out a chair, motioning for her to sit. He moved with an almost forced pleasantry, an undertone of aggression.

'Perhaps I should go. You seem busy,' she said, hesitant to sit.

They locked eyes. 'Don't,' he said. He smiled, and placed his hand on her shoulder. 'Please, stay.'

Dail uncovered a plate of bread and cheese, and poured her a glass of water. He shrugged. 'I figured you would be hungry.'

'Thank you,' she said. 'You're so good to me.'

He straightened, wiping his hands clean with an old rag. 'Eat up, then. You'll have to do it all over again tomorrow.'

Four

Innocence

RENIA SMACKED THE table with both hands. She smiled at Molan, and showed her teeth just like her ma had said, but the tingles in her hands made her frown.

Molan jumped back; she must have surprised him. But then he laughed and scruffed up her hair.

'You scared me.'

They laughed together. Renia thought her tummy would break.

'Tell me more about the lightstones.' she said.

'You're a demanding little bugger sometimes, you know.'

What's a bugger?

It was the time after breakfast and before lunch, and it had stopped *raining*. Renia wasn't sure why everyone said *raining* in that funny voice, like it wasn't real. It annoyed her that she didn't understand the joke.

Anyway, it had stopped *raining* and the light came through the window in four thick bars that tingled your skin like when you first put your foot in the bath tub. Her ma said not to let the light rest on you for too long, that it would steal the color from your skin, but Renia didn't mind. She didn't like being the odd one out anyway.

Her ma was roasting meat in the kitchen; she could smell it. It was one of the smells that made your tongue prickle and your mouth water, but lunch could wait, this was the best lesson ever.

Molan sat back in his chair with his legs crossed and lit his pipe. 'You know the Praelatus?'

'Of course I do.'

'It's said he has the biggest lightstones in the world.' Molan stopped talking so that she could think about it and she felt her mouth opening wider and wider.

'How big are they? As big as a house?' she asked, grabbing at Molan's hand.

Molan laughed really loud. He coughed away the pipe smoke that got stuck in his throat and started waving. 'No, no. Not *that* big. About as big as your head, I think.'

'Whoaaa.' *Imagine that.* She wondered how the Praelatus carried his giant lightstones. Did he have a big sack? He probably had his own cart.

Molan stopped talking again. He was being a tease. Renia knew that he was about to say something even better.

'Do you want to know the best part?' he said.

'Yes! Yes!'

'He doesn't even walk. He sort of floats above them—glides around.' He showed Renia how, waving his hand around like a bird.

She gasped. 'He can fly?' She nearly fell off the chair, but luckily she was fast and moved quick to stop it falling over.

'Just between you and me, I bet he can do a lot of amazing things with those stones, don't you think?'

So many things, she couldn't think of all of them at once. She imagined the big Praelatus flying in the sky, throwing wishes and kisses and flowers at everyone below. He could stroke the birds in flight, or even go wherever he wanted without getting tired or scared.

'I wish I had a giant lightstone head,' she said. She jumped from her seat and whizzed around the room with her arms stretched out like a giant bird. She could feel the wind blasting her face and hair, and how her dress would flap around behind her. She could taste the clouds, she could—

Her ma came in. She gave Renia a funny look but Renia didn't care, she already had that rushy feeling in her heart.

'Lunch is served, you two,' her ma said. 'A good lesson, was it?'

'The best, Ma. Look at me—I'm the Praelatus.'

LUNCH TOOK FOREVER. Molan and Carol had gone off into the other room. They were talking about soil samples or something really boring like that. Her ma was cleaning up, banging pots and pans and making it difficult for Renia to think.

'Ma, I'm trying to pack my things. Could you keep it down?' She used her dad's voice for that part so her ma would know she was serious. It was a very serious thing, going on an adventure.

'And just what is it that you think you're packing for?'

'I'm heading out to find a giant lightstone.'

Her ma chuckled. 'Just like your father. I see. Did you remember to pack water?'

Renia nodded, putting her thumb and finger on her chin the same way she'd seen Molan do it. 'Yes. That's what I'm missing.'

Ma went to get some. When she came back, she had a waterskin and a serious look on her face. 'Renia, stay where I can see you. Do you understand?'

'Yes, Ma.'

'Off you go, then.'

THE AIR TASTED sour. It was like that sometimes after the sun came back. Renia put her hands on her hips and stretched. Her back hurt.

She'd been digging holes for an hour or so with a trowel she'd borrowed from Carol and found nothing. Not even a small lightstone. She shook her head and rubbed at her brow, sniffing because her nose was running.

Everywhere around her were empty holes. It was a mess. All that work for nothing, and now all the dust and sand was making her itchy all over.

'Bugger,' she said.

Her face was covered. Sand and dust had found its way into her mouth and dried it out. Looking around to check that no one was watching, she spat into the dirt; she wasn't allowed to do that, but her dad did it all the time.

She wasn't going to give up. Her ma always said that you either happen to life, or life happens to you. So she got to work thinking up a new plan whilst rummaging around in her pack for the waterskin.

If I'd made a giant lightstone, where would I hide it? Not here. How would I remember where I'd buried it?

She tightened her lips and took a good look around in a slow spin, squinting like a real gatherer. 'There.'

A rock formayshun—that was what Molan called it, anyway. She could just see it on the edge of where the sky touched the land. Jagged stones cutting up from the earth like the teeth of a mighty beast. It was quite far, a little way away. Her ma's voice rang in her ears: *Stay where I can see you.*

It wasn't *too* far.

After all, if Renia could see it then surely her ma could still see her…

You either happen to life, or life happens to you.

She pressed on. *Time to find a lightstone.*

THE HOUND WAS thirsty and tired. Whimpering and breathing heavily, it lapped at the water cupped in heavy hands.

'Good boy. There you go now.' Terrick had been sweeping the Wastes aimlessly for the better part of the week. His hound, Dagga, hadn't had much in the way of food. He was starting to wonder if he should call off his sweep and return home.

Dagga was a good, solid beast. Hardy enough to withstand prolonged exposure to the harsh environment, obedient, and just the right side of brave. Terrick reassured him with a good tummy rub, rustling the scales on his hide with a clack.

Terrick was a tough, stoic man. He'd been raised by gatherers, taken on his first sweep at the age of nine by his father. They worked in larger parties back then, and they had been accompanied by his brothers, uncles, and cousins. He'd learned all too well the dangers that lurked in the Wastes and knew never to take its lack of activity for safety. Over the years, most of said uncles and cousins had lost their lives to it, and he'd even lost one of his brothers.

He preferred to work alone now. After his father retired, he thought twice about bringing his sons into the business. Competition grew more fierce with each passing year and it wasn't uncommon for feuds between rival gatherers to become fatal. No, his sons were better off at home. He'd secured apprenticeships for them with the local blacksmith, a skill he thought would be more useful in the days ahead.

The supply of lightstone was starting to dry up. The gatherers had been hard at work for decades now, scouring the great dust bowl for anything that sparkled. Really, the only way to have any luck these days was with a light-hound, and he was glad of his.

Slapping the beast on its rump, he stood and surveyed his surroundings. An hour or two more wouldn't hurt.

RENIA SKIPPED BETWEEN the two huge teeth. They weren't really teeth, but they did look like them. She was panting. The jog had been longer than she thought, and she took a look over her shoulder to make sure she could still see home. Sweat dripped from her nose, and she took deep breaths because her throat was burning and needed some cool air.

'This is perfect.'

Throwing her pack to the ground, she set about looking for a good spot to dig before taking her trowel out of her pack. '*I* would def-nitly hide something between these two rocks,' she said, strutting over to her new spot.

She squatted in the crack between the rocks, and smashed at the ground, throwing dirt over her shoulder like an animal. After a few minutes, she heard a loud clink as her trowel hit hard rock. She growled, all her blood rushed to her face and she stood up, shaking her fists.

'Bugger!'

She threw herself onto her bum, crossing her arms in front of her knees, and sulked. 'This is so hard! I need some kind of dutector or something—' That was it. The lightshard her father had given her. Maybe, just *maybe* she could use it to find more.

She pulled the thimble-sized gem from her breast pocket and stared at it really hard before waving it around in the air. She thought some magic words might help.

'Mighty lightstone! Show me where to dig!'

Renia whipped around, imagining currents of magical energy pulling her from one place to the next. She imagined her fingers tingling like a fly when it does the buzzing thing. Her focus shifted from her outstretched arm to the rocks beyond.

Two hugging boulders, one resting under the other in an A-shape. She moved toward them.

'This is it,' she said. 'This is the place!'

TERRICK SWORE. HIS shoes were full of stones again. He'd have no bloody feet left if he didn't get the soles fixed soon. He found a rock to park his arse on whilst he rectified the problem. Dagga sniffed around nearby, unimpressed by the latest distraction.

'Alright, you grumpy sod. Give me a minute.' The beast grew impatient. He'd have to make for home soon before he started to consider Terrick as a meal.

He reckoned he probably had about twenty minutes or so before the sun began to set properly. He'd fix his boot and head back to avoid the worst of the cold.

Dagga snorted abruptly and the beast's neck jerked up, grasping at something on the wind. A scent. He'd caught a scent. Bugger the cold, this was the first chance he'd had to find something he could use to feed his family in a week; he wasn't about to ignore it.

The beast continued to sniff, leaping up into the wind periodically to get a better sense of it. Terrick tied his laces in a makeshift knot, rushing to prepare himself for what was about to happen.

He shielded his ears as Dagga let out a deafening howl and burst off into the approaching night.

RENIA WAS HACKING away at the dirt, spitting and avoiding bits of chipped stone when she heard the howl. Her blood felt cold, and she bit her lips as her little legs began to shiver. When she'd entered the cave it had been light. She hadn't noticed the sun setting behind her as she sat digging in the dirt.

She clambered to her feet, keeping an eye on the gap in the rock.

What was that?

Her dad had warned her never to go too far at night, told her stories of stray hounds that skulked around the Wastes in packs, looking for a meal. She didn't know what to do. Half of her wanted to run home as fast as her legs could go, the other half told her to stay there and hide.

She took a step toward the opening. She only had the trowel as a weapon, so she held it out in front of her. Her step was shaky. She was really scared. It felt like a cold, wet blanket.

She couldn't stop the shaking now. She stepped out from the cover of the rocks, darting left to right.

Then she saw it. She locked eyes with it. A snarling purple beast twice her size, with long, dripping fangs. Its mouth was watering like Renia's did before cooked meat.

The beast looked like it was going to sit down, resting on its back legs, but then it shook itself. It made a clattering sound that echoed through her bones.

She leaped as fast as she could, back into the opening, stumbling at its mouth and losing her footing. She scrambled and pushed her body into the dirt as her ears registered the flurry of thuds she knew must be its footsteps. She pushed herself as far into the crack as she could, wriggling and writhing, crushing herself into the space.

A thud, followed by a whine and the clattering of claws. She could smell the thing as it lashed into the opening, sweat, and rock dust, and dirt, and slime.

Keeping her eyes clamped shut, she could feel the tears rolling down her face. Renia screamed. The sound rattled her ear drums, and shocked the beast for a short moment, but not long enough. It carried on its gnashing and clawing, unable to reach her. Beads of sweat ran over the backs of her knees.

There was no way out.

Renia groaned and sobbed. She had wet herself.

'Please. Please, help me. Daddy, please find me. Please.'

TERRICK WHISTLED.

'Dagga, away,' he told the hound. He'd heard the scream, and wasn't exactly sure what he'd find next. He shooed the beast away, and looked into the crack.

A child. A girl, no less, stood trembling against the stone.

The hound sniffed around his feet in frustration. He booted him, ignoring the yelp he let out in confusion. Hunger was one thing, but to hunt down a *child*; that was quite another.

Terrick cursed himself. What if it had been one of his sons?

Leaning into the crack, he spoke in the softest tone he could muster. 'What are you doing in there, love?' The child didn't respond; she just continued to tremble, trying to disappear into the rock.

'Sorry about the dog. He must have thought you were a lightstone. He's usually very friendly.' More trembling. 'I should take you home to your parents. Are they nearby?'

The little girl turned to look at him. She looked scruffy, face covered in dirt that had been streaked with tears.

'Bloody hell,' he said. 'You can come on out now, I won't let him hurt you. I promise. We'll get you cleaned up and I'll take you home, alright?'

She just stared at him, tears rolling down her face of their own volition. But after a moment, she yielded and reached for Terrick's outstretched hand.

He scooped her up, and she went limp. She looked exhausted, the poor kid. She'd wet herself too. Terrick grimaced, wondering how he would explain this to the girl's mother. 'Alright. You're alright now.'

Dropping to one knee, he cleaned her face with a rag. 'Where do you live, sweetheart?' Still the girl said nothing, but he caught her looking to the north, where he could see a dwelling on the horizon. The faint glow of hearth-fire and smoke rising from its chimney told him it was inhabited. He pointed towards it. 'Is that home? The house over there?'

The girl nodded before closing her eyes. Terrick rose to his feet, lifting her with ease. 'Come on then, little one.'

HE FOUND THE mother outside, pacing with a mixture of fear and fury. Her eyes widened, jumping from the hound to the limp figure of the girl he carried.

'Renia! Renia, where in the world have you been?'

Renia, is it? Nice name.

'Oh no! Renia?' The child's head shot up, and she leaped from his arms like a grasshopper before charging into her mother's arms.

'I told you to stay where I could see you.' The mother held the child at arm's length, checking her over for signs of injury. Terrick was glad she wouldn't find any; there wasn't much more dangerous than a woman with an injured child.

He smiled and turned to leave.

'Good sir. Good sir, what has happened? I thank you for returning the child.'

'There's no need to be so formal with me, ma'am. I'm just a gatherer. The child—Renia was playing in a rock formation where she happened across my hungry hound. I owe you my apologies for frightening the girl, but she came to no harm.'

'I see.' She shot her daughter a disapproving look before continuing. 'Please stay for dinner, and allow me to feed your hound. We wouldn't want it hunting down anyone else, would we?'

Terrick hesitated, noting the veiled telling-off he'd just received. He chuckled and glanced at his guilty-looking hound. 'Aye, very well then.'

He tethered Dagga to the arch that supported the gate, and followed the mother and child into their home. The heat hit him like a furnace, forcing him to remove his coat.

Two soft-looking folks stood in the kitchen area to his left, preparing food and seeming very relieved to see the mother carry the child to bed. 'Well met,' said the male one, apologetically waving toward the food being prepared. 'I am Molan, scholar of the Halls of Venn. This is Carol, my colleague.'

The woman smiled at him. She looked fairly young, cropped hair, very nice. He nodded in response. 'Terrick. Gatherers' Guild.'

'Ah, another gatherer.'

'Beg your pardon?' Had he wandered into the home of a fellow gatherer? This might not end well; gone were the days of welcoming rivals into your home.

'This is the home of Norok of the Gatherers' Guild,' Molan said. 'His wife Moyra you just met, and his daughter Renia you just saved, by the looks of it.' The scholar chuckled at him in disbelief. 'You'll eat well tonight, I fear.'

Terrick smiled and nodded, still standing in the doorway. The mother returned and looked at him confused. 'Sit. Sit,' she said. 'How long have you been out?'

'A week or so, ma'am.'

'Call me Moyra, please. My husband is a gatherer, Norok. Do you know him?'

Terrick did know Norok, had met him at least twice. He was the outsider; his skin still had some red in it. Terrick didn't know whether to respect the man, or think him a bloody fool. The folk still gathering this late in the game were born into it. To come from the outside into the Wastes willingly—it was unusual, to say the least. 'Aye, we've met once or twice.'

'He's been out for a week or so himself.'

'The weather has been kind to us this week.' He tried to be as polite and noncommittal as he could. He was not enjoying his imposition on another gatherer's home. Had the situation been reversed, he would probably set his hound on whoever sat in his home making small talk with his wife.

There was a commotion outside. The fencing creaked as Dagga pulled on his tether, howling and barking like a wild beast. 'Bloody dog. Excuse me a moment. I'll see—'

The door opened.

THE TWO GATHERERS stood staring at each other in a silent stand-off. Norok seemed rightly confused at returning home to find a hungry hound tied to his gate and a rival gatherer sat at his table. It was he that broke the tension.

'Terrick.'

'Norok.'

Terrick shifted slightly, looking around at the confused faces that surrounded him. Norok shot a look of distaste at his wife before addressing him again.

'What has happened here?'

Terrick adopted a conciliatory tone, and attempted to explain. 'I happened upon your girl playing about a mile out in a rock formation. The hound chased her, frightened her a bit, but she's alright. I carried her home.'

Norok looked slightly surprised, and a flash of worry escaped him. He seemed to be nervous about something. Terrick surveyed him and a picture started to emerge. He carried a large sack, and his pack was full. Either he'd been gathering rocks, or he'd been a very busy boy. It was small wonder Dagga had been losing his mind moments earlier. Terrick's pulse raced at the thought. He hadn't seen a haul like that since his father's day. Had this outsider found a store of lightstone that had evaded his guild for all these years? Better yet, had he proven that there was still plenty of lightstone to be found?

Catching the rival gatherer eyeing his loot, Norok attempted to redirect his attention. 'You'll be staying for dinner then, no doubt. I'll go and check on Renia and be back with you shortly.'

'There's no need, Norok, honestly. I have to get home myself. I just thought I should make sure the girl was safe.' He gave Moyra an apologetic nod and made ready to leave.

An awkward moment passed whilst he pulled on his coat. He was glad to feel the open air on his face when he pulled open the door.

'Terrick,' Norok said. Terrick turned to face the man. 'Thank you for looking out for my daughter.'

Terrick nodded and left, his mind racing with what he'd just seen. It would be risky with his hound in the shape he was in, but he could track it. Track the scent Norok had left right back to its source. A haul like that and he'd be set. The Baron would make sure his family ate like royalty for years to come. He quickly untethered the beast and started out into the night, before having his thoughts interrupted.

'Terrick! Terrick.' He turned to see the woman, Moyra, running towards him. He stopped, confused, and turned to her.

'Here,' she said. Dropping bag of wet meat into his palm. 'For your hound.'

IN THE DEAD of night, Renia stands staring at her father's pack. She's struggled to sleep after the day's events, adrenaline still rushing through her.

Just one look. Nobody will know.

She unclasps the flap. Awe fills her as she stands in front of the most beautiful sight she's ever seen. Dozens of glowing orbs the size of her fist, all different colors, shimmering in the dim light.

A blue one grabs her attention. It's calling to her, begging her to pick it up. She bites her lip, looking from left to right to check she's alone, and takes it. She closes the pack.

'What have you got there?' A whisper from behind. She turns, startled, and stumbles back a few steps. It's Molan. He must have gotten thirsty in the night.

He sits cross-legged on the stone floor next to Renia. She's looking at him with a mixture of guilt and fear.

'A blue lightstone, eh,' he says, smiling. 'Let's have a look.'

He takes the stone from Renia, and places his glass of water down between them. He winks at her, and closes his eyes. Renia doesn't understand; she thinks he's making fun of her.

Suddenly the water starts to dance. Pencil-thin columns rise out of the glass and twist into the form of a double helix. They begin to spin and a ball of water pools at their head. It's so beautiful. Tears form, breath grows shorter. The hairs on the back of her neck stand on end.

And then it's over. The water sloshes back into the glass. Molan hands back the stone, rises to his feet, and grins at her.

'Not bad for a teacher, eh?'

Renia stares at her tutor as if seeing him for the first time, completely speechless, wondering if she's dreaming.

'Renia,' he says. He's looking down at her. 'This is not for you to keep. It's very important that you put this back where you found it. Do you understand me?'

She nods.

He turns, and walks away as silently as he'd approached.

* * *

We shared a womb.

I don't claim to remember it; that would be a lie. But I know that the first thing I touched was you, that yours was the first hand I held.

I often wonder which of our hearts beat first.

But I know it was yours.

Always first. That's how it's always been.

Did you think me weaker?

You felt every lash of the whip as it split my skin, my every pained cry, my every torn muscle, my every miserable tear. As I did yours.

Because the bond we share is more than blood. It is more than name, or doctrine, or allegiance to a higher power. Our souls are bound, forever. Two halves of the same.

Was it fated then that I should live half a life? That we should live half a life?

There was a time that I would have endured it in silence, for you. There was a time that we were all we had, and we fought, and we endured, and we persisted to prove that we belonged.

Even when the training became too much, when we were broken, we endured. We drew strength from each other, fed off each other's resolve.

Like parasites.

You are a parasite.

Did you still think me the weaker when you brought this shame upon us? When you condemned us both to this festering existence? Did you feed off my strength when you made the choices that led us here?

Once in a generation, they said. A gift from the shade-bringer. The twice-born.

A gift for whom? Not for us.
Half a life, half a soul.
I wonder…
If I take your life, might I know for once how it feels to be whole?

FIVE

Confidence

RENIA WOKE WITH a start, shooting up in the bed and tearing the covers from Dail's naked body. She was drenched, sweat soaked the sheet beneath her. A dream. Just a dream.

She hadn't dreamed about the day with the hound in years, but whenever she did it was the same. Embarrassment flooded her as she watched her lover start to stir, confused and slightly annoyed.

'What's going on?'

'A bad dream, that's all. I'm really sorry about the sheets, Dail.'

Dail pulled himself on to his side, peeling his torso from the saturated sheet. He rubbed his eyes and frowned. 'They were due a wash, anyway.'

By twilight they lay together. Gentle purple beams of light leaked through the curtains, casting long shadows where they met their naked forms. It was a warm night, and both welcomed the cooling effect. Dail yawned, rolled onto his back, and clasped his hands behind his head. 'Are you alright? I would have thought you'd be ecstatic about this new project, but you seem…nervous.'

'Of course. It's an amazing opportunity. I'm just…well, why me?'

'What do you mean?'

'Dail, I'm a junior scribe. The books I've been trusted with, they aren't only forbidden, one of them was written by Istopher Venn himself. It's just so irregular. Why not Sundance? Or someone from Master Vedora's team?' She frowned into the gloom, trailing off.

She didn't move as Dail sat up; her thoughts had her tangled. Why now? Ever since the tremor—the dreams, and now this.

'Venn himself.' He rubbed at the stubble on his chin. 'Well that does seem a little irregular, but you're taking it at face value.'

She broke her trance, turning to look him in the eye. 'Meaning what?'

'You're by far the best calligrapher in the hall. Not only that, you're virtually unstoppable—they don't call you "Renia the Relentless" for no reason. Did you consider that they might be testing you for a different role?'

'No,' she said.

'It's no secret that Petor is losing his marbles. I've heard he sleeps in his office now. He's also taken to stirring up drama with the younger masters—it's like he's regressing. Not just him, but Vedora is old too. At some point they are going to need new Hall Masters.' He pointed at Renia, looking directly at the cabinet key she'd tied around her neck. 'Younger masters, with energy, who can lead from the front.'

Renia's eyes widened; she hadn't considered any of this. 'I'm no leader,' she said. She didn't want to be a Hall Master, not one bit. It was the knowledge that drove her, the work that soothed her. The idea of standing on the sidelines cracking the whip made her feel sick. *Moonspit! Anything but that.* 'I don't want that kind of responsibility,' she said.

'I doubt there are many that do. But it's a duty. The whole of the north depends on the work we do here.'

'I'm not that kind of person, Dail. I can't lead anything, let alone from the front. I'd make a disaster of it.'

'What are you talking about?'

'I just know it. Something would go wrong and I would be responsible, and—'

'Shh.' He looked deep into her eyes. 'I don't know why you're so afraid of yourself, Renia. Sometimes I really do wish you would get out of your own way. You love this place. The work we do.'

A glassy look came over him. Renia knew he loathed his job. It bored him silly—such a waste of his talents.

'One of the books is a misfit.' She attempted to draw him from his melancholy. 'It's a scholar's journal.'

'Oh don't *tease*, woman.' Seeing him piqued made her smile. It was only a small breach of protocol after all, and they were alone in the dead of night.

'Oh yes, I'm sure you'd find it quite interesting. I can't talk about the details of course, but I had a quick glance through it and I can tell you there are quite a few things that were left out of the public record.'

Dail sat bolt upright. 'Truly? I knew it. There are so many things that don't ring true, details that just don't align. You know, I was discussing it with the guys in the club and they agree with me—'

'Club? What club?'

'I'm sure I mentioned it. I joined a book club with some of the scribes from the other halls. A sort of thinkers' circle. There's nothing strange about it, just a few guys throwing ideas around, really.' He waved her question off and continued to plug for information. 'So tell me, does anything else stand out?'

His revelation that he'd joined some kind of club made her feel a little defensive. Renia didn't like the idea that the things she told him might end up being a talking point at some kind of boys' club. She knew Dail was prone to intrigue, that it was a side effect of his creativity and boredom. 'Not really, not yet anyway.' Seeing his face drop, she offered a little more. 'It's very strange. It seems to document a voyage or exodus, but it doesn't sound like the Great Exodus. It was written after the Great War. I didn't recognize the author. Inoa, or something.'

'Sanas Inoa?'

'Yes, that's it,' she said.

She watched something wake within him. He darted to his writing desk, rustling through notebooks and torn sheets of paper. 'Here!' He pulled out a few pages and shook them, tripping as he rushed back to present them. 'Sanas Inoa: a defector from the south. He was a real piece of work. He acted on the Praelatus's behalf to bring the Mohruscans to our side during the war, but there's been a lot of rumor and conjecture about how he did it—underhand stuff. They still begrudge the arrangement to this day.'

'Alright, alright. Come back to bed, will you. It's too late for this sort of thing.' Politics bored her. She saw it as a giant tangle of roots. The desires of a thousand souls vying for recognition. Too variable, too unknowable; Renia preferred order to chaos. Why question a system that had brought their world to relative peace for decades?

Dail groaned, mocking her. 'Aren't you just the slightest bit curious about how we came to be in this mess?'

'Mess? How could you possibly consider our society a mess?' She rubbed her eyes, stirring in the saturated sheets, trying to find a dry bit.

'Seriously? Does it not bother you in the slightest that this is the only place on the continent allowed to publish books?' He was looking at her incredulously now, animated as ever, employing his boyish charm.

'I'm tired, Dail. You're out of luck on this one, I'm afraid.' She lay back down, making a show of appearing exhausted. Perhaps an expectant look would keep him quiet.

'Oh fine.' He sprang over her, throwing himself on the bed as if in protest. He lay on his side next to her, toying with her hair, his gaze lingering on the small key resting on her clavicle. 'Just think. Some of the greatest secrets in the world are tied around your neck.'

Renia hoped they didn't choke her.

PETOR HAD ONLY slept for a couple of hours. The sound of rustling pages echoed out of his office door and through his hall. A dim flicker of light from the single candle by which he read, shone through the windows of his office.

He sat at his desk, lost in his own world. He preferred the night. It was the only time he could concentrate, free of the responsibilities of his position, the only time he could truly be himself. Nobody bothered him, nobody interrupted his thought process. It was just him, perfectly focused, an echo of his youth.

He whispered to himself between sips from a glass of water. He would have preferred coffee, of course, but he wasn't about to start stalking the corridors in the dead of night. It would only raise more questions as to his state of mind.

'Ah yes. Remarkable work as ever, dear girl.' He chuckled and mewed, taking extreme care not to damage her work in any way.

Reading through the pages of the old book had reminded him of the time he'd undertaken the same task. He was much younger then, and the recall provoked a sensation of youth. He started to remember the naive young lad that stood rod-straight, cocksure, just the wrong side of arrogant.

He'd paid dearly for that.

Petor had long let go of the desires he once had: *What it would be like to spend a month in the restricted archive, to have all the world's secrets laid bare.* He scoffed. What a foolish boy.

Some things were best forgotten. But he had to admit to himself in some small way that he did miss the excitement. He envied Renia her innocence and had no desire to rob her of the sensations he'd had as a much younger man in the same position.

She would probably replace him one day. Renia was the young woman who *could*. Intimidating by merit of her ability to overcome. He didn't enjoy belittling her, it was simply part of his job. *Dull well the brightest shining star,* he mused. It was important to humble the ones that inspired by example, lest they reached too far too soon. Important to temper the mettle.

He realized then that he was not alone. 'Jeff. How long have you been standing there?'

'Moments. Your reflexes are keen enough, old man.' The steely chief of security regarded him inquisitively, looking presentable enough for the hour.

'Been paying a nighttime visit to some starry-eyed young woman or other, have you?'

He was rewarded with a blank stare for his comment. 'It's beneath a man of your station to judge people based on hearsay.'

Jeff took the measure of the room before sitting down on a small couch beside the door, rubbing his knee.

'It always does well to give rumors a good poke, I find. Still having problems with the knee, I see?' Petor said.

'It worsens at night.'

'Not the worst problem a man of your station could have.'

Petor actually liked Jeff. He was a man of duty. And he was right; Petor had not judged him based on the rumors. *Judge a man by what he shows you*; that was his way. He'd seen nothing that gave any life to the flapping of lips. It was the way of folk to forcibly humanize figures like Jeff: stoic, unmovable. Petor hadn't decided yet if that was a consequence of his job or the reason for it. 'I suppose you've come about the restricted books?'

'Aye, that's the short of it.' He sighed. 'Every time one of those bloody things finds its way out into the halls, it means a headache for me,' he said, rubbing his knee.

Petor found the contradiction amusing, but said nothing.

'I have your assurances?' Jeff paused; he knew Petor knew the consequences of mishandling the things and would be wishing he didn't have to ask. 'I know you remember well what happened last time *that book* was checked out.'

Petor waved the comment away. 'I had nothing to do with that. Surely you read the report.'

'It's not you I'm concerned about, old man.' Jeff shifted, uncomfortable in any position, it seemed. 'I have no idea what's in the thing. I don't care to know. What I do know is that I'm only here because my predecessor died holding it. I wish I could burn the bloody thing and be done with it, but I can't, so duty dictates that I be on my watch, and unfortunately that means bothering you with questions I needn't ask, and you needn't answer.'

'Quite,' Petor said. It always pleased him to hear Jeff speak. He was a man of few words, but he chose them well. 'The books only leave this office when they are being used. They will be stored in *that* cabinet, over there. There are two keys. One is with me, one is with Renia.'

'Is that wise?'

'Believe me, she'll die before she loses the opportunity to devour every word of every book in that cabinet.'

A HOODED FIGURE swept through the darkness. Graceful, silent, unseen. An enigma. Unknowable, unstoppable. He checked himself there, and fought the urge to grin.

It was a dance of deception, a theater played out before no one. He danced to no tune but his own, as it would always be, for none knew better than he. In his brilliance he stood apart, and yet still he suffered the ignorance of those too dull-witted to recognize it. But the day would come. It *was* coming. He felt it in his guts.

Swooping around the corner, cutting the air with the edge of his robe, he stopped before a nondescript section of wall. A theatrical look to the left, a swing of the head to the right. *All clear.* It was all too easy.

He ran his fingers over the coarse block work, smiling inwardly as two of the bricks gave way to his touch, and the wall began to move. The mechanisms that worked the stone operated in silence. He nodded his approval and wondered at the level of engineering, whilst the darkness of the hidden void revealed itself.

The musk enveloped him as he strutted forth into the gloom and made a show of depressing the flagstone that would close the hidden door behind him. He bowed to empty space as the last of the light slid away, and imagined the applause of a crowd as the curtains closed on his grand theater.

The scrape of a match, the illumination of flame. He lit the candles in order, meticulously, counting each step so as to leave the exact same amount of time between each. The flames cast a ritual glow across the space.

The room was perfect for his purpose: a stepped, round chamber, suitable for seating a dozen people comfortably. Tomorrow it would play host to a carefully selected group of young scribes, sitting in hooded robes, masked and speaking in whispers so as not to reveal their identities.

He sighed and removed his cloak, folding it neatly, and allowing his thoughts to settle on his recent disgrace.

Piss-Stain. How dare they mock me. Mock my name! 'Dull well the star', indeed. He'd grown sick of the old saying. Sick of people who didn't even know the poem—or its true intent—using it, misquoting it, celebrating their ignorance at the expense of the blessed. He'd had his own brilliance *dulled* countless times in his life: by his father, his brothers, schoolmates—all of them jealous of his charm and wit, his ability. He'd been denied the opportunity to fully excel in his talents, held down for most of his torturous childhood. He snorted. *Childhood, indeed.*

He was the third and youngest son of the ruling house of the great city of Verda. The brightest son, though he had long given up his titles and inheritance in a glorious act of defiance—something his dullard brothers could never understand.

Verda, the vibrant, energetic heart of Luna Ruinam. Where the sun rose over the ocean and set behind the moon. Where the light of the Praelatus shone from his palace in the north, like a beacon, inspiring the people with the spirit of trade and cooperation—an image of home he would likely never see again.

No matter. His past was past and his designs were above the prattle of heirs in waiting, above the mere quill-scrapers who mocked him now. The time had come for a new age. An age of reason, of ingenuity. Luna Ruinam's reverence for sorcery had led the country into a state of stagnation, anyone with a brain could see it. The people were happy enough to allow a machine to make them coffee, or allow them to accurately measure time, but dare to create a machine that challenges doctrine and watch how fast they turn. *How dare you? How dare you challenge the teachings of the Light? Teachings that were written over a century ago, in a time where our kind barely understood how to create the sharp sticks they used to kill each other.*

Moronic.

The people deserved progress—new leadership, new ideas, and it would all begin *here*, in the Halls of Venn, with him in the Grand Master's chair.

In the first step on the path to his ascension, he would sow the seeds of revolution, nurture his ideals in the hearts and minds of the future inheritors of this institution. He would build for himself a platform on which to shine, stand apart from his name. His own man. His own vision. When the time was right, he would take his rightful place as Grand Master, and from there, there would be a reckoning. If that cancerous old fart Petor was still alive to see it, *he* would be the first to fall under his hammer.

Then he could effect *real change*. Wield his influence to illuminate the masses to the backwards thinking and injustices of his time. He could raise the common folk from ignorance and petition the great Praelatus to reform the institution, to shake off the bonds of tradition that hampered their ascent, and leap boldly into a new era. Of reason. Of compassion. Of respect for the minds that carried the heavy burden of progress.

With precision, he laid each hand-bound booklet at regular spacing around the ridge. The title: *The Price of Peace.* Pride filled him. It was his greatest work yet. A question piece on the impunity with which the Reapers were permitted to operate within their borders. Sanctioned murder by writ—no trial, no justice, just cold-blooded deletion. It was a law that sat at odds with the culture, a holdover from a war that ended long ago. A child would question it, yet none did. For those unlucky enough to have their name in writ, only death awaited; there was no escape, no aid, no choice. For the writ represented the consent of the Praelatus, and who could question the will of the protector? How could the Praelatus have sanctioned this? What hidden force bound his hands?

From this seed, my influence will grow. Fear is the sharpest knife in the politician's war chest. Where it lingers, it breeds doubt, it demands change, it creates a void in the heart ripe for suggestion, for solution, that is where my power will be found.

They would lap it up, feast upon his work, and, over time, he would inspire them to question everything they took for truth, until *his* solution became the obvious course of action and *not* the nagging of dissent.

After preparing the room for the following day's meeting, he left the scene set to perfection. He donned his hooded cape once again and pressed his ear to the cold stone wall. No footsteps, no sign of activity.

He recessed the correct slab, and the door opened into the cool night air once again. After ensuring the coast was clear, he sealed the chamber and glided from the scene.

Thump.

Leather, blood. He staggered backward, reaching for the tang of copper where his tooth had punctured his inner lip. He had collided with the shoulder of the chief of security. His heart leaped, his ears burned. *Breathe normally, keep calm,* he told himself.

'A bit late for prancing around in the dark, Hall Master.' The voice was gravel, and thick with the moronic drawl of the Wastes.

'Ah. Quite so, Jeff. I'm afraid I find myself rather unable to sleep. In fact, I have a grievance to report to you.'

'Is that right?' The gruff figure folded his arms and cocked his head.

'Would you believe that I was verbally assaulted by none other than Master Petor? He referred to me in a rather unfortunate manner, well, my name that is—'

'Piss-Stain, wasn't it?'

'Ah, yes… That was it. I was hoping—' He found himself cut off.

'You're going to have to grow a thicker skin than that, young master. Losing sleep over playground insults won't do you any good in this place.'

'You're refusing to prosecute my complaint?'

'Just so.'

Anger bubbled in his stomach at the look of disdain on Jeff's face. Such blatant disrespect, arrogance even. It took concerted effort to suppress his outrage.

Jeff said nothing as he strode past him, indifferent, with little regard for his personal space.

I'll be coming for you, too, he thought. They would never suspect, or see it coming. *He* was the shadow in the dark, the *true* agent of justice. They would know his *real* name, and he would be remembered.

Six

Consequences

It WAS A noisy night. Renia sat with Molan and Carol. Nobody said anything, they just sat there, watching the lamp flicker.

She looked from Carol to Molan and then back to Carol again. They smiled at her, but they weren't real smiles, they were the fake ones you gave when something was wrong.

The shouting in the kitchen made Renia's heart hurt. She hated it when her ma and dad were angry with each other. Why couldn't they just say sorry and stop it? Didn't they love each other? The thought made Renia want to cry. She loved them; they should all just be happy.

From outside came howls and muffled voices. She didn't understand that either. Her home was for them, and Molan and Carol. Who was outside? And what did they want? Was that why her ma and dad were fighting? Maybe they had come to take them away, or take her away.

She was confused, anxious, and scared.

She tried to listen, but what little she could hear she couldn't really understand. She wasn't used to hearing her father in anger; it made it difficult to take in.

Carol was trying to write. She huffed and puffed as the noise got louder and gave Molan funny looks where she made her eyes big, but he didn't seem to notice, just sat in the corner watching Renia with a serious look on his face. He lit his pipe and leaned back in the rocking chair. It creaked. Carol didn't like that much. She looked even angrier, and was staring straight at him.

Then the banging started. The first one made her jump. She bit her lip and ran to Molan, before climbing on to his lap.

NOROK SLAMMED HIS palm on the counter top. Dishes and cutlery jumped as if in surprise. He was furious, his face burning so red it almost looked as if it had returned to its original color.

'And just how could they have known exactly? It was Terrick, that's how! The bastard left here and that bloody mutt tracked the scent all the way back to my dig.' His breath came heavily as he struggled to control his rage. 'You let that sneaky rat in here, and now I've nothing to show for months of work!'

'Don't you dare blame me! You should have stayed clear until he left. How was I to know you were carrying a cart load of lightstone?' Moyra battered back the implication with ferocity. 'The audacity!'

'Oh yes, just sit and wait whilst some other bloke sits cozy in my house.'

'What's that supposed to mean?'

'You know damned well, woman!' He didn't mean that one. But they were beyond the point of reason. He'd been venting his frustration for an hour or so and Moyra wasn't the type to put up with it.

The heat in the kitchen was fierce. Norok's return and subsequent tantrum had resulted in dinner being well and truly neglected, fires raged higher than they should, and the smell of burnt food filled the room.

Outside, the noise grew louder. Whoever was out there was getting closer. Seething at the interruption, Norok yanked the window open and yelled out into the darkness. 'Shut those bloody dogs up!'

THREE FIGURES STOOD in the night, dimly illuminated in the purple glow of the fallen moon. Around them, hounds circled in a restrained dance of frustration. They had the scent, but gatherer code prevented them from advancing further.

The ragged cohort of women eyed each other. A rougher vision of the Gatherer's Guild, clad in leather armor and brandishing weapons fit for putting down invading zealots from the south. It was unusual for the three of them to venture this far north, but this is where they had been led, no less than three times in the past week.

'We can't just roll up there.' Mo had a hard face. The braided hair pulled tight to her head only added to the aesthetic.

'What choice do we have? The hounds are confused. We're going around in circles. Whatever is going on here, it's wasted a week of our time.' Ever the voice of reason, the eldest sister, Bara, spoke with her usual commanding tone.

The third and youngest sister stepped forward, dusting down her armor. 'We could just head south. Take the hounds out of range and forget this whole thing.' Eva was the only sister who didn't braid her hair, preferring to tie it up in a bun. She was the smallest of the three, but arguably the most deadly. She was nimble, fast, and preferred daggers to swords.

'That's a breach of code too,' Mo said. She shook her head and sighed. 'We'll draw in a little further, see if we can entice them out with the hounds.'

RENIA BIT HER lip so hard the skin broke. She covered her mouth. It tasted like cooking pans.

'What have you done, child?' Molan said, standing up as he said it. He pulled a handkerchief from his pocket.

'I didn't mean to.' The words came out in a gurgle. Wide-eyed, she tilted her head back as Molan dabbed at the wound. Her eyes started to water again.

'It's alright, love. It's only a bit of blood.'

She sobbed. 'I'm not crying because of that.'

'I know.' Molan looked at Carol when he said that. Renia didn't understand why, but it was like he'd said something else to Carol. She nodded and sat on the floor. She took Renia's hand and asked her if she wanted to play a game.

THE SCENE IN the kitchen escalated. Norok had unconsciously been banging the flat of a saucepan on the worktop for the past minute. 'Laughing! Laughing! Like a pair of bloody chickens. I rocked up expecting to find it as I left it! Months.' Another bang of the pan. 'Months of my life I've been working on this.'

Moyra had gone from defensive to mute. She regarded him with a mixture of disbelief and concern. This marked a low point in their relationship, one that would not be forgotten, but the rage had him now.

'We could have retired! You should have seen all the holes they dug, hundreds. They must have swarmed the place, laughing and joking with their bloody hounds.' The noise outside grew louder still, the hounds howling. Norok flipped. He charged to the door and wrenched it open with enough force to crack the wood around the hinges.

AN ENRAGED MAN marched from the open door towards the gate, growling audibly, ready to fight. The three sisters were gathered a dozen yards away, holding their ground with their hounds in tow. Eva silenced the dogs with a clap.

Bara took a step forward. 'Ho! Gatherer. Name yourself.'

The man took in the sight of them, glowering and cursing. 'Norok,' he said. 'Of the Guild'. *Norok* was in no mood to talk; it was obvious that they had just interrupted an unpleasant conversation.

'I am Bara of the Guild.' She gestured towards her sisters, standing sentry. 'My sisters, Mo and Eva.'

Norok said nothing. Bara looked to her sisters, the silence sat between them, pregnant with the threat of violence.

Finally the man spoke. 'What do you want?'

'The fair chance to make a living, as anyone else.'

'Speak plainly.' Norok seemingly had little patience for tact.

'Fair enough. Our hounds have brought us to this property no less than three times in the last week. You're holding lightstone here. You know the rules as well as we all do. One night with family whilst you're laden, then the stones need to be turned in to the Baron. Exceptions only when you're sick or injured, and you, sir, are clearly neither.'

Norok stood visibly confused by the announcement, shaking his clenched fists and grinding his teeth. This was not the way gatherers dealt with each other; something was off.

'Your hounds are wrong,' he said. 'There's nothing here. I turned in my load five days ago.'

'Our hounds are the finest in the Wastes. They never miss the mark. Perhaps you mislaid a stone or two.'

'As I just said, there's nothing here. Don't take me for a fool.'

Bara looked to her sisters again. The younger of the two, Eva, avoided her gaze, thoroughly unimpressed with the situation. She turned to Mo, who spoke in a low tone. 'Rules are rules. We have to inspect.'

A harsh wind blew between the two parties. Norok stood tall, defiant and ready to defend himself.

Bara had to shout over the rising wind. 'We respectfully ask that you vacate the property so that we can carry out an inspection.'

'You can fuck off,' he shouted back. The response was less than welcome.

Mo sighed, clearly bored of her sister's diplomacy, and stepped forward herself. 'Look here, you idiot. This is a serious issue, do you think we want to be here? Vacate so we can sweep the place and then we can leave. If there's nothing to find then it ends here.'

'No.'

Mo shook her head, laughing in disbelief. 'Right then, you know the rules. We have to report this to the Baron.'

Norok shrugged. 'Go ahead. Be sure to let him know that the stockpile of stones he's sitting on is thanks to me. And that I have a bone to pick with a good few of my colleagues who chose to ignore my claim post.'

Bara had no idea what he was talking about. It was Mo that spoke first.

'He's an outsider, still has some red in him. Give him one more chance.'

Bara looked Norok in the eye. 'This is your final warning. Submit to inspection or be reported.'

Norok stood fierce, staring down the armored woman. 'I heard you the first time. Now get off my land.'

She shook her head. 'Have it your way,' she said, though it was unlikely that Norok heard her over the wind. She turned her back on him.

'Looks like we're heading home, sisters.'

CAROL TURNED TO Molan and sighed. 'That was incredibly stupid,' she said. 'We can't stay here.'

Renia stood between them by the window. They'd heard most of what had been said, but she didn't know some of the words.

'It doesn't make any sense,' said Carol. 'Norok wouldn't make a mistake like that. What were the hounds picking up?'

Renia felt Molan's eyes resting on her. She tried not to look up.

NOROK SAT SLUMPED in an armchair by the hearth, one fist holding his chin up, the other nursing a long-emptied tumbler. He'd been sat there long enough to feel the sun rise. Its probing first rays had crept over his legs like treacle.

The weight of the situation pinned him in place. He sat locked in a battle with himself, desperately looking for a solution but plagued by flashbacks to a man he didn't want to be.

He'd spent most of the night turning the house upside down, searching for the stone, or stones, that might or might not be in his possession. He'd retraced his steps, carefully re-enacted his actions during the day he'd been at home with his haul. He'd thought about every place and every movement the pack containing the stones had been and made. There was nothing.

This was not a situation he had ever wanted to be in. A complaint had been levied, and now, in no small part due to his rash actions, he was housebound, a prisoner in his own home until a resolution could be made. Such was the law of the guild. If he was not present when his jury came to call, his life would be forfeit. The consequences would also be dire for his family, not to mention his house guests.

He cursed himself and his behavior. Moyra had barely said a word after the incident and gone to bed alone after checking on Renia.

Renia… He must have scared her half to death.

His thoughts were interrupted as his house guest approached. Neither spoke, the two men regarding each other with delicacy. Norok considered Molan a friend. It had brought him comfort to know that his family were under Molan's watchful eye during the time he had to spend away, and despite his scholarly appearance he looked like he could handle himself if the need ever arose.

The scholar indicated toward the empty armchair that lay between them. Norok nodded.

'Find anything?' Molan said, sitting.

'No.'

Molan emptied his lungs through closed lips. 'There's something you should know.'

Norok raised an eyebrow. A flicker of annoyance crossed his brow. *Did you have something to do with this?*

The scholar fixed him with a severe look. 'The night Renia went missing—the night Terrick was here, I woke with a thirst. I found Renia awake about the house…She was playing with a lightstone.'

'What?' He sat forward in his chair, suddenly wide awake.

'I saw little harm in it. But I did warn her that it was important she put it back where she found it.'

'Did you see her put it back?'

The scholar looked to the floor.

'Molan, did you see her put it back?' Norok probed the man, learning forward in his seat.

'No,' he said.

The two of them sat back in their chairs, looking opposite ways, shaking their heads, saying nothing.

'What happens now?' Molan said.

Norok sighed, resting back into a slump and eyeing his empty tumbler. 'The women register their complaint. Whether they do it in person, by messenger, or by bird, it's up to them.' He cast his palm aside. 'The Baron will come, he will blow the horns and summon any guild members in the area to bear witness. They will inspect the property, and then the complaint will be resolved.' His frown deepened. 'If they are satisfied the complaint is invalid, apologies will be made, compensation agreed upon, and life will return to normal.'

'And if they are not?'

'I'd rather not think about it.' The response invoked another moment of reflection. 'We could be sat here for a week, two if the Baron is otherwise engaged. Molan, you may be tempted to leave, but I have to warn you that if you do, and they find something here, it could be very bad for you and Carol.'

'The Baron has no jurisdiction over us,' he said.

'It's a risk I'm not sure I would take in your position. I will do nothing to stop you, but it wouldn't sit right with me if I hadn't warned you.'

Molan nodded. 'I understand.' He looked around briefly and then concluded his thoughts. 'We will stay. Carol won't like it. But it wouldn't sit right with *me* if we didn't do everything we could to help you. I've grown very fond of you all during our time here.'

Norok nodded and locked eyes with his guest. 'The feeling is mutual, friend.'

The two men sat regarding each other for some time, respectfully, allowing the other time to think and plan for the events to come.

'I've spent most of my life suppressing my temper,' Norok said. Inviting a curious glance from his friend. 'You might not believe it now, but it's gotten me into some difficult situations. In my youth, of course.'

'I'm sure there's a saucepan or two over there that would understand better than I.' The men chuckled, a moment of comedy to lighten the dour mood.

'I feel shame at my behavior, I should apologize to you both. Had I controlled myself better, we wouldn't be in this—'

'Please,' Molan stopped him with a raised palm. 'It was frustrating for all of us. We were all invested in the project.'

'Another fact I neglected to appreciate last night.'

'Norok, you're a passionate man. I respect that quality in people. Please do not apologize for it. We would not be here were it not for your passion.'

'Passion is small comfort to a corpse.'

'But the lack of passion makes a corpse of any man, does it not? Passion is one half of what drives people to greatness. Passion and discipline—the twin faces of progress. Passion without discipline leads to chaos, discipline without passion leads to stagnation. Occasionally one overpowers the other. All that really matters is that the balance is restored.'

Norok sniffed. He was sure that Molan meant well, but he had little energy left for philosophy.

'Let's hope I live long enough to find this balance that you speak of, then,' he said. He nodded at his friend, and raised his empty tumbler.

THEY SURROUNDED HER. Renia sat at the table across from Ma and Daddy. Carol and Molan were stood at either side of them. They were all so big, looking down at her, she felt like an ant. Her daddy looked tired, not tired like he usually looked, but like he was sick; he had rings under his eyes and he wasn't sitting straight.

'Renia, are you listening?' her ma said.

'Mm-hm.'

Her ma looked cross again. She was always cross with her, always telling her she was doing things wrong.

'Renia, we know you were playing near Daddy's pack, and we know you were playing with a lightstone.'

Renia looked at Molan. Why had he told on her? She thought he was her friend. She scowled at him, but he didn't seem upset by it.

'Renia!'

It startled her. 'What?'

'Did you put the lightstone back in the pack?' Her ma looked right at her. She was doing that thing where she said she could smell a lie.

'Yes, I *did*. Molan told me to put it back, and I put it *back*.' She looked at her daddy. Something was upsetting him. She wanted to give him a cuddle. She felt naughty. They were all ganging up on her and making her sad. Tears started to creep from her eyes and she felt her lips getting wobbly.

'I put it back,' she said. 'I did! I put it back!' The tears came faster. Everything was all blurry and her mouth felt sharp at the back. She wiped her eyes and coughed, sniffing back the snot that had started to run down her nose.

Her daddy stood up. 'Enough,' he said. He came over and knelt next to her. He rested his big, rough hands on her cheeks and wiped away the tears with his thumbs. 'I'm sorry, Moonpie,' he said. 'I believe you.'

Seven

Warnings

THE HEARTHFIRE IN Petor's office burned low. Its glowing embers throbbed behind his eyelids as he drifted between sleep and waking. He came to for a moment, aware that he needed to clear his throat, but fell back into a dream shortly after.

He only dreamed when he drank, and he'd been particularly busy in that regard; a glass of whiskey hung loosely in his grasp, threatening to make a mess of his night robe.

A noise, a presence. Was it real or was it a dream? He wanted to know, but he couldn't seem to cross the threshold. Was he dreaming now? Or was he sitting in his armchair by the fire?

A shuffling. He felt the tingling sensation of consciousness returning to him. He woke.

Petor turned with a start, directing his gaze directly at the door. His vision hadn't caught up with him yet, and he saw a hazy black figure, a ghost, or a hooded witch, or...

'Vedora?'

It was Vedora. He looked down to inspect the wet patch on his crotch, annoyed that he had wasted good whiskey, but relieved he hadn't soiled himself.

What in the name of the moon is this bloody woman doing skulking around my office in the middle of the night? How dare she invade my privacy like this. Standing there with that smirk on her face like she's better than me. Really.

'I had heard you'd taken to sleeping in your office. But I didn't realize it was this bad,' she said.

'What's bad about it? I was happily pissed-up before you came rolling in here like the wife I never had.' He grunted, relieved that such a thing had never happened. A *terrible* distraction that would have been.

'You don't fool me with your grumpy old git routine. I still remember you when you could stand up straight *and* hold a conversation.' She loitered around his space, picking up oddities and the half-written notes strewn around the room as she spoke.

'Yes well, better keep that to yourself. I quite like being left alone.'

'I'm sure you do.'

She stood rooted in place, making it clear that his thinly veiled request for her to leave had been denied.

'What is it you want, old friend? It's been a lifetime since you've visited me in the night.' He smirked into his almost-empty glass and drained the few drops that remained.

'A different life,' she said.

'Indeed.' They shared a smile. 'Drink?'

She nodded.

Between them, they represented the old guard of Hall Masters, but for a time they had been the youngest, fresh blood in an arena of veterans. The shared experience had meant that they had been close, but the demands of the job, and the secrecy, had rendered the whole thing short-lived. They had grown apart after that; only a silent, knowing respect had remained.

As he shuffled back to the fire with the drinks, he looked at her, now seated. He could still see that fiery young woman who had turned his head all those years ago.

'These walls have seen more than a few visitors recently,' he said.

'How unusual. Nothing to do with the restricted books you're keeping in here, I take it?' She smelled the glass, seemingly impressed with his choice of drink.

'Word travels fast.'

'Always did.' She took a swig and fixed him with a serious glance. 'Are you worried?'

'About spilling this glass as well?'

'Don't be glib, you know what happened the last time that book was out and about.'

He waved the comment away. 'Yes, well, things were different then.' He winked. 'Were they not?'

'Petor, *someone died.*'

The memory was a dark cloud he'd rather not stand under, although he would have been lying if he'd said it hadn't been on his mind since Renia's project had been commissioned. He'd certainly drank more; the almost-empty bottle of whiskey spoke to that. He'd been saving it for his retirement—oh, well.

A part of him that should have been long dead stirred. By the hot coals and the smell of good drink, he felt affection for this brave and worn woman who had come to him in the dead of night out of concern. For the first time in a lifetime, his eyes softened, and he smiled deeply at his old friend.

He raised his glass. 'Let us hope then,' he said, 'that nobody dies.'

'I'll drink to that.'

RENIA'S APARTMENT WAS—on most days—a place of serenity. It was south-west facing, with two windows that allowed for the enjoyment of the sunset and the multitude of interesting colors it painted on her walls. She had taken advantage of this property by using a dry brushing technique she'd learned from some of the artists. With some pigments she'd been given by them, she'd lightly dusted the two stone walls in her apartment with white, bringing extra light and reflectivity to the space. It was a pleasing offset to the dark oak wall paneling that also graced her apartment, along with almost every other space within the Halls of Venn.

Her quarters had their quirks and imperfections. None of the apartments in this tower had originally had running water, and as such, a network of pipes lined the walls in odd places, making strange shapes as they snaked their way toward areas of the stonework that had been easier to drill through. The pipes were often a source of distraction, making bizarre noises as they expanded and contracted in the light of the afternoon sun. Renia, though, had learned to love them, cyan-colored oxidation stains and all, thinking of them as a living thing, a companion and comfort to her in her occasional bouts of loneliness.

There was no serenity to be found this morning. Layers of dust rushed from corner to corner like jellyfish suspended in tidal currents. Rugs had been flipped, bedding stripped bare, and furniture upturned. Renia's frustration hit its peak as she slammed a drawer closed with such force that her ears rang.

'Where is it?' she huffed, rubbing furiously at her eyebrow. It wasn't like her to misplace things. Renia had always believed that a tidy house is a tidy mind. *A place for everything, and everything in its place,* her mother used to say. She frowned at the memory.

The dreams had shaken her awake again, and she'd reached for her lightshard as soon as she'd awoken. Her heart had almost stopped when she found it missing from its usual place in her bedside cabinet.

She frantically tried to remember the last time she'd taken it out. She didn't wear it, she rarely ever looked at it. She just enjoyed knowing it was close. How could she have been so absentminded as to have misplaced her most precious possession? She couldn't have been, she wouldn't have been. Her thoughts turned to darker possibilities. She had refused housekeeping service and no maintenance had been carried out here in months. Only two people had been here: herself and her lover.

Renia's hands shook as she raised a glass of water to her lips. She paused, allowing her imagination to run away with her.

Is Dail capable of this? Did he betray me? Her thoughts raced as she saw this man, this boyish man, this bored and strange man who visited with his secret club to discuss conspiracies in the dark, in a new light.

He must have taken it, a trinket to show off to his new club. Her stomach turned at the idea that this gift, this gift from her father, was being paraded around like some bauble to impress. She saw her father again, felt the weight of his palm on her head. She remembered the way he smelled and the way his cheeks creased as he smiled. She imagined Dail and his club gawking around the lightstone shard, pawing it, cheapening it with their touch, sullying the memory of her father.

Her fists shook. She clenched the glass so hard that it cracked and then broke. Water slapped the floor. Glass shards fragmented and bit deep into her palm.

She barely registered the pain, or the blood dripping to the floor. She would have her answers.

She would have them now.

RENIA CHARGED TOWARD Dail's apartment with such aggression that people leaped from her path in fear. Her eyes were glazed, darkened with anger, and her gaze lethal, predatory.

I'll have him.

She hammered the door with the side of her fist, spattering it with the blood from her palm.

No answer.

She hammered and hammered until the blood streaked and began to run down into the grain of the wood. Then there was a click. The door cracked open an inch and the eyes of her target met her own through the crack.

'Renia?'

She spoke through gritted teeth. 'Let me in.'

He broke her gaze momentarily, looking into the room. He had that stupid grin on his face like it was a joke. 'Now's not a good time.'

Not a good time... Not a good time? She was at a pivotal moment in her research—no, *project*—and he had the nerve to tell her *this* was not a good time? Her rage became infernal, her temper reaching boiling point like she'd never experienced before. She hammered her hand on the door. 'Let.' Thump. 'Me.' Thump. '*In!*'

His grip on the door held. He stood aghast, laughing nervously and barring the door with his foot. Renia screamed in frustration, while confused onlookers gathered around, whispering from a safe distance.

Footsteps and the sound of platemail came from the end of the corridor. Her heart raced. How had she lost control this quickly? Confused, she started to see the situation for what it had become. She was standing in a puddle of her own blood, yet she felt nothing save the throbbing of her pulse. She was breathing heavily; following the blood trail up from the floor to the door, it looked like the scene of an assault. This was bad.

Her head whipped to the left to see the charging armored slug bearing down on her with determined pace. It slowed and came to a stop neatly, dripping mucus from its armor, a mirror of her leaking hand.

It spoke:

'Citizen, you are in violation of code. This outburst will cease and you will accompany—' Its gaze moved from her to the door, following the trail of blood to her hand and then to the steaming visage of Renia. The gastropod stopped mid-sentence, now entirely alarmed and looking at what appeared to be a woman on the verge of passing out.

In a deft move, the creature grabbed her and threw her over his shoulder like she weighed nothing at all.

The world was bouncing, and she was moving away from the door, from her lightshard. She locked eyes with the shrinking image of Dail as he stood outside the door.

She screamed. 'This isn't over!' The shriek left the gathered crowd dumbstruck. Dail looked at the door, seeing the mess in full. 'This isn't—' The words died in her mouth as her limbs grew weaker. She felt her eyes close, and faded into nothingness.

Dail clicked the door shut and let out a long, forced breath. He realized he'd been holding it for most of the debacle.

'I think this might blow up in my face,' he said.

'You think she suspects?' Tannis sat in shock, looking thoroughly uncomfortable in his surroundings.

'Are you deaf, mate? She's going to end me.' They shared a nervous laugh before Dail's face set, dour. Had he blown it?

He flashed a nervous smile at his guest. On the bed where he sat lay a booklet, *The Price of Peace* written on its cover.

WHEN RENIA CAME to, she found herself lying in a bed she didn't recognize. Cold sheets wrapped her tightly, and her head was awash with vague memories of blood and raised voices. Her throat felt like it had been shredded.

She was confused. As her eyes focused, she noticed the sun was fading. It had been morning just a moment ago. She must be dreaming. But she wasn't, the pounding in her head told her that. She knew this place—the medical wing. *Oh moon, no.*

On a table to her left, a jug of water glistened in the evening sun. An empty glass next to it. It called to her, inviting her to quench her thirst.

'That's far enough.' The voice came from the other side of the room. The doctor caught her as she'd been leaning over for the glass. He dashed to her side, poured the water for her, and handed it over with an inquisitive look that made her feel like a test subject.

'Do you remember your name?' he said.

'Renia.'

'And do you remember what you were doing before you woke up here?'

She frowned. It was hard to tell how old the doctor was, but the indifference he showed toward her was unsettling. He was a short man, with black hair tightly tied behind his head. His sharp nose gave his voice a somewhat nasal edge.

'Do you remember what you were doing?' he repeated, impatiently.

'Sorry, doctor. Yes. I was in a disagreement with a friend. Uh…he—'

'And the wounds on your palm?'

Renia was not accustomed to being interrupted so dismissively. She flared her nostrils out of instinct. 'A glass…It must have broken in my grip.'

'Are you prone to fits of rage, Miss Renia?'

She recoiled at the accusation. 'I'm sorry?'

'Answer the question, please.'

'No. I haven't lost my temper like that in a very long time, actually.' Dark memories threatened to surface. She suppressed them.

'And is there any particular change in your lifestyle? Some new stress, or trauma?'

She sighed. Until this point she hadn't realized the change in her behavior. 'There's a new project. It's fairly stressful.'

The doctor peered over the top of his spectacles. He didn't believe a word. 'You're a scribe, yes?'

She nodded slowly.

'Do not attempt to write for a few days. You'll have to stay here while security figures out whether or not you're still a risk to your *friend.*'

'Doctor, I really need to leave. I'm sorr—' He cut her off with a surgeon's precision.

'If you try to leave, that large Mohruscan fellow by the door will stop you. He can go for up to thirty hours without sleep, so good luck.'

'Aren't you supposed to be nice?'

Again, looking at her over the top of his spectacles. 'No. I'm supposed to fix you, and get you back to work. I suggest you take steps to relieve your stress, or pass the project off to someone else. I don't want to see you in here again, Renia.'

Words delivered at the temperature of a glacier.

Charmed.

SHE'D BEEN LEFT alone with nothing but white walls and a window for company. The image of her past stared back at her through the glass. The Wastes looked no different. They never did. Just the same old purple tinted orb. Ever present, silently judging her in her lofty haven.

The book on lightstone had stirred so much within her. At first she'd seen it as an opportunity to keep a long-forgotten promise, but what came with it—the dreams, the memories—was overwhelming. She couldn't help but draw parallels between now and then. Another time, another stolen lightstone.

The dreams would not relent. Even as she had lain unconscious in the hospital bed, they had plagued her. The taste of smoke, the sound of rope rubbing on stone, the sobbing.

The whispers… The whispers she could never make out, that drifted around her like ghosts, only this time she could understand them, and they sang their ghostly accusation to her loud and clear.

Dail, Dail, Dail. And her fury had risen to them in response.

'I don't like hospitals.' The voice interrupted the moment of inner darkness. Sundance stood in the doorway, looking at her with concern. 'So very boring, don't you think?' She smiled and nodded down to her hands, which held a cake tin, two saucers, and two forks. 'At my age, you do your best to avoid them. You start to feel like they are chasing you.' She chuckled.

'Hello, Sundance,' Renia said, pleased at the interruption.

The two women sat for some time, eating cake and exchanging pleasantries, but Sundance was not the type for idle chatter and changed the subject to more serious matters when good conduct had permitted it.

'Now then, dearest. What's the matter with you? It's not like you to lose your temper so.'

Renia looked at her lap, ashamed at the observation. There was something about Sundance that made her feel like a child again. The feeling wasn't entirely unwelcome.

'Come now, don't be shy. Is it your young gentleman? Has he been playing the field?'

'No. It's not that.'

'You can tell me all about it, lovey. I've dealt with my fair share of immature men over the years, let me tell you.' Sundance pursed her lips in disapproval. No doubt she had, and Renia doubted they had fared well for it.

Renia hesitated, but then felt the words start to flood from her like a dam bursting. 'Something precious to me, a gift from my father. It's a lightstone shard, a tiny piece. I woke up this morning to find it had gone missing. I know I didn't move it. I didn't. I keep it in the same place all the time.' She met Sundance's gaze in anger. 'Only one person knew it was there, knew I had it, Sundance. And I knew he'd taken it the moment he saw me through the crack in the door. Standing there smirking like a naughty little boy.'

She looked out through the window into the Wastes, feeling like a caged bird. 'And now I'm stuck in this room, like I'm the guilty party, unable to do anything about it.'

Sundance shifted in her seat, listening intently. Renia continued, 'I allowed this man-child into my life through boredom, perhaps loneliness, some degree of pity. I found his boyish charm entertaining. I *trusted* him. And he repaid me by stealing from me. Running off to his stupid boys' club in the small hours of the night, doing moon knows what.'

Sundance raised an eyebrow. 'Club?'

'Some sort of thinkers' circle. Honestly, I think he's so bored of his job that he needs to fantasize about great conspiracies and injustices just to keep that part of himself alive. Since I've been given this new project, he seems to resent me for it, like he's trying to have something for himself too.'

Cogs turned inside the mind of the older woman. Renia knew recognition when she saw it, and she knew she'd said something that her mentor had found interesting.

Sundance packed away the impromptu picnic she'd brought with her at a speed bordering on impolite, and rose to her feet. She paused, and a look of sympathy passed between them. 'Don't you worry, my dear. I'll do some digging for you whilst you're stuck in here. Keep your chin up. Things always come right in the end.'

And then she was gone.

That's the problem, Renia thought. *They don't.*

EIGHT

Reckoning

THEY HEARD THE approach long before its arrival. Assembly horns had been ringing out across the Wastes for the last day. The Baron was coming.

It had been over a week since the conversation by the fire. The longest week of their lives, and by far the quietest. Silence had settled over the house like a veil, a bubble of dread, ripe for bursting.

The first few days had passed in a flurry of systematic searching. Each room of the house methodically probed for the missing stone. After that, floorboards had been lifted, eaves explored, storage un-stored. Then the search had moved to the grounds. Bushes had been parted, ground scanned for signs of recent burial. A shaking head had become the most common gesture in the household, much to everyone's dismay.

After the searching had ended and the accusing looks had stopped, the young Renia had been pleased to see a wave of confidence return to her parents' faces. The four adults had concluded that the stone was not there, that they would be vindicated, that the Baron's wrath would be leveled at their accusers for their mistake. But still the dark veil loomed: *what if?*

So as the horns bellowed out across the Wastes, and the gatherers came to their master's summons, the young girl stood by her bedroom window, staring at the rock she had buried her treasure beneath.

SHE WAS SCARED. They were coming now, coming for her treasure. She'd hidden it as well as she could, wrapped in a blanket in a mug full of water, and covered with stones. She thought that the water would hide the smell, so the hounds wouldn't know.

She must have hidden it well, because nobody found it when they were all searching. They wanted to take her treasure, and it was hers.

Her daddy would send the Baron away and then she could keep it safe. Her daddy was going to be so mad at him. The Baron would be scared.

Her daddy was really scary when he was mad.

NOROK PACED BACK and forth in front of the hearth. Concerned eyes followed every step. Nobody spoke. Moyra, Molan, and Carol watched, silently, knowing nothing they could do would alter the course of events about to unfold.

Ultimately, this was Norok's call to answer. It was his membership under attack, his reputation and position that hung in the balance. This dream had been his sole focus for most of his adult life, and now it stood on a knife edge, threatening to slit his throat.

He trained himself, talked himself into a state of calm. His temper would not betray him today. He would not rise to baiting, he would not disrespect his peers, the Baron. *Stay calm*, he repeated to himself over and over with each step.

Out of the three onlookers, Carol was the most nervous, and showed the least faith. She'd spent considerable time loading a cart with her research materials, and packed her work in a way that it would be easy to search through without damaging it. She'd got it out of the house. Norok didn't like the implication, but he couldn't fault the woman for taking the precaution, nor for making her priorities so distastefully obvious.

He looked to Molan. The man sat in an armchair, smoking his pipe, watching him intently. Norok wondered if smoking might help him to calm his own nerves too, though he'd never had a taste for it. The two men shared a nod, and Norok's gaze turned to his wife.

Moyra stood as still as stone. The metaphorical rock holding him together. She didn't need to say anything; she knew him so well that even a look could convey what she was thinking. He smiled at her. *Thank you*, he thought.

He'd sent Renia to her room. He didn't want her to feel the tension, or see him like this. A man was supposed to be an example to his child, larger than life, something to aspire to. Trying to maintain that facade at this point in time would be too much to ask of himself. This was a memory that would likely stay with her as she grew. He wasn't going to let that memory paint him in the wrong light.

The footsteps beyond his walls ground to a halt. The scouts had arrived. Horns blasted. A pause. Two more horn blasts.

A voice boomed in their direction. 'Norok! You stand accused. You have ten minutes to prepare yourself for the Baron's arrival.'

The words washed over him like a cold wind. His blood froze. In that moment he knew, however slim the chance was, that this might be the last chance he had to speak with his child.

He looked to his wife. 'I need to talk to my daughter.'

WHEN HE ENTERED the room, his child span to face him. He saw his own eyes looking back at him. He saw his drive, his ambition. He wanted so badly to see this child rise higher than he could ever reach himself. This wonderful creature of his own making.

She ran to him. He dropped to one knee and held her tight. 'Hello, Moonpie,' he said, smiling at his greatest achievement.

'Daddy, they are here.'

'Yes they are, love.'

RENIA LOOKED INTO her daddy's eyes. He wasn't mad. He wasn't going out there to shout at the people, to send them away. He just looked sad. She didn't understand. She took his big hand in her own, not knowing how to feel.

'Will you send them away, Daddy?'

'I'll do my best, sweetheart.'

Renia didn't understand. She had never seen this look on his face before. There were tears covering his eyes, they were shining in a way that made her heart ache.

That's when she knew, she knew that *she* had done this. If she hadn't taken the treasure, he wouldn't be sad. Her little heart hurt so much she started to tremble, and tears of her own started to roll down her cheeks.

A thick thumb wiped them away. Her daddy's voice broke as he spoke. 'What's the matter, my love?'

'Daddy, it's all my fault. It's my fault, Daddy.' Her knees gave way and she fell into his arms. 'I took the lightstone, Daddy. I hid it outside, so nobody would ever find it.'

She felt his breath stop, his body start to shake. She rushed to answer it. 'I'll take them to it. I'll show them where it is and then we can go back to normal.'

He pushed her back, to his eye level. 'It's too late for that, Moonpie.'

She'd never seen this, never seen her daddy scared. She didn't know what to do. She let out a groan and started to cry.

'Renia, listen to me now. Listen child!' He shook her gently, breaking her cry. 'You must remember this for the rest of your life.' He shook her again. 'The rest of your life.' Her lip quivered, her whole world started to collapse. 'This is *not* your fault,' he said. 'It's my fault. I was careless. It's my fault. Do you hear me?'

She nodded.

The big voice from outside came again. 'Norok! Stand and face your accusers. Stand in submission to the authority of the Baron and the law of the Gatherers' Guild.'

Her daddy rose to his feet. He looked like a giant. Their eyes met.

'I love you, Moonpie,' he said.

A GENTLE BREEZE washed over him. Dark figures bathed in torch-flame glow surrounded his home. The scene was silent, save for the huffs and sniffing of hounds, tens of them. They howled and mewed at the scent of the stone he now knew lay hidden within the grounds.

It was difficult to say how many now stood before him, to bear witness to his fate. Who knew what that would be now. He saw faces he knew, the three women who had brought this upon him, also Degna, Stov, Barros—these were men he'd shared camp with, broken bread with. Terrick was there, standing apart with his hound beside him, the source of the rage that had been partially responsible for the situation he now found himself in.

The Baron was an imposing figure, shoulders like boulders surged from beneath a cloak of deep crimson, trimmed with gold. His massive jaw clenched as he approached the waiting man like a titan, each huge step slow and measured, dragging out the inevitable. Everything in the Wastes happened to the ticking of this man's clock, lord protector and judge alike.

'Norok.' The voice was as harsh as the land it commanded. 'You stand accused of theft. Kneel now, before the authority of the Gatherers' Guild.'

Norok dropped to one knee and lowered his gaze.

The giant spoke again, this time to the gathered crowd. 'Inspect the property. Start with the grounds.'

Dozens descended on his home, gatherer and hound alike. Sniffing and howling, torches illuminating every corner of his modest holding, all passed around the kneeling man as if he didn't exist. He closed his eyes as he felt the world close in on him.

TERRICK WAS ONE of the first to begin the search, heading for the rear of the property. His brow sat heavy with concern over this incident, as unusual as it was; it was not the first such event he'd been part of.

When the horns sounded, you came. It was a matter of duty, to bear witness to the resolution of disputes between gatherers. Matters of gravity were best seen with many eyes, such was the way of the guild. It had always been like that.

He couldn't help but wonder at his part in this. He'd rationalized what he'd done to Norok's claim by considering him an outsider. Part of him still believed that the gifts of the gravel were the birthright of those born in this harsh place, but he couldn't shake the guilt that had grown stronger with every bite of good food he'd found on his table as a result of his betrayal.

His concern now was not lightstone, or finding the ones that had gone missing. His thoughts were with the girl. The weeping mess that his hound had almost eaten. If they found the stone, she would be in danger, the whole family would be in danger.

He wouldn't have that on his conscience.

He established a mock perimeter for his sham of an inspection, close to the windows at the rear of the house. He ordered Dagga to take large sweeps, to keep wandering feet as far away as he could.

Howls, barks. Shouts of declaration came from behind. Gatherers ran to the position to bear witness to the find. They held the stone high for all around to see.

Terrick sighed. 'Fuck me,' he muttered, shaking his head. This was it. He'd have a very small window of time to get this right.

The opportunity came shortly after, as the gathered party returned to the front of the house to present their find to the Baron.

He tapped at the window pane. Then again louder, eagerly.

It opened.

'Terrick?' It was the scholar, Molan. 'What are you doing back here?'

'No time.' He raised his palm, shaking his head. 'The girl. Out of the window. Quick!' He looked in. The child shook visibly, protesting at the idea.

'Absolutely not,' said Molan.

'Listen to me, man. They found the stone. Things are about to get very, very ugly. Do you understand me? Give the girl to me and I'll get her to safety. You can retrieve her when you talk your way out of this mess. Which you *will* do. Do you understand what I'm telling you, Molan?'

The scholar nodded, the grim realization creeping over his features like a ghost. He took the girl by the shoulders. 'Renia, listen very carefully. Remember when we used to play hide and seek?' The child struggled to concentrate; panic held her in its snare. Molan shook her. 'Renia! Do you remember, child?'

She nodded.

'That's what you need to be like now. Go with Terrick. No matter what you see, or hear, you stay unseen and as quiet as the sand. Just like the game. Do you understand?'

Another nod.

Terrick took the child under the arms as Molan guided her out of the window. She recoiled at the sight of Dagga and threatened to bolt, but he held her tight. 'Hush now, lass. He won't hurt you, I promise.'

The man and his hound disappeared unnoticed into the darkness, carrying Renia over his shoulder, wrapped in cloth like a sack.

Unseen. Quiet as the sand.

THE BARON TURNED the stone over in his hands, regarding it with respect and disappointment. Rings of silver and gold sparkled in the glow of torches. He looked directly at Mo and raised his palm, silencing the assembled gatherers.

'The house—bring everyone out.'

Three of his honor guard led the search, followed by a handful of gatherers. Moments later, the wife was dragged from the house by her arm, protesting at the disgrace. The muffled sound of protest could be heard as the interior was torn apart. Hounds were at work, showing little to no respect for the owners, or their belongings.

They positioned the wife to face her husband side-on. Still on one knee, pleading to the assembly with his eyes.

Moments later, two scholars emerged from the house, one with grace, the other in a rage.

Mo met the Baron's gaze with a sinking feeling in the pit of her stomach. She bit it back. She'd be dead before showing weakness in front of the Baron or her sisters. The eyes of her older sister bore into her skull. She knew what was coming, what would be asked of her.

The Baron spoke. 'Mo. Your complaint is justified. Your party will be rewarded for your service to the guild.' He turned to Norok before continuing. 'Norok. You have been found in possession of lightstone. This is high theft. To steal from the Praelatus is the highest crime of the land, therefore your entire household stands with you in this disgrace.'

The scholar, the female one, burst into protest. 'We are scholars of Venn! You and your guild have no authority over us, Baron.'

A flicker of annoyance crossed the Baron's jaw. He curled his lip at the woman. 'Present your credentials,' he said.

The honor guard released her, and she strode towards him in defiance, proudly presenting her papers. The Baron inspected them, nodded, and beckoned over the other scholar, who did the same. 'Stand aside. This matter will be brought to the appropriate authority in due course.' He rounded on Norok once again. 'Norok. Speak now on this matter or take it to your grave.'

The kneeling man looked around for something, wincing into the night. 'These lodgers had nothing to do with it. They pay for room and board, and a place to conduct their research. They are not members of my household.' He looked to his wife then, and something passed between them, unspoken. He nodded.

'Very well.'

Less paperwork for the Baron, then. Mo felt her chest tighten as her lord looked her way. He turned to one of his honor guard, nodded, and spoke again. 'Norok, the penalty for theft is well known. Do you have anything to say?'

Norok looked up into face of the Baron, cold defiance burning in his eyes. A brave man, to face his death with such courage.

Two men emerged from the crowd with a block. They placed it before Norok. The Baron turned to Mo. 'Mo. As the registrant of this complaint, it falls to you to carry out the sentence.'

The time had come. She felt her stomach knot and churn. She shook away the dizziness that crept into her. Unclasping the ax cover at her belt, she looked down at the man, looked into his eyes, and shared a moment of intimacy with him that no two people should ever share.

She could not defy the law. This was her burden to carry. For her sisters, so that they never had to.

She pulled the ax free, walked the longest three steps of her life, and once again met the eyes that she would see in her dreams for the rest of her days.

'I'm sorry, Norok.'

She took a sharp breath, and time stopped for her, for the longest split second of her life.

The ax fell, severing Norok's hands at the wrists. The scream was harrowing. Onlookers stepped aside as blood shot at their legs. His wife shrieked, but Mo couldn't hear it fully, the blood rushing to her ears made everything seem like it was underwater.

The guilt. Unbearable guilt. Her knees trembled under the weight of it. She fought it with everything she could muster as she stared open mouthed at the bloody stumps she'd created.

THE MAN, TERRICK, held her still, muffling her cries when the ax came down.

She saw the glint of it, and the spray of blood. She heard the sound of her parents screaming.

Her heart splintered, fractured, and then broke. It took with it her innocence, and her sanity.

Daddy.

The floor rose to meet her. She fell, lifeless and limp into Terrick's embrace.

NOROK LAY IN a heap in the dirt, coughing and heaving. His life source poured into the earth beneath him, churning sand and gravel into crimson soup.

The Baron nodded again, and his honor guard knelt to tie a rope around the severed hands. The lord of the Wastes looked out into his domain, face set hard, stern, devoid of emotion, unaffected by the horrific scene.

'Take them inside,' he said, and Norok and his wife were dragged back into the home they had built for themselves.

The Baron turned to the two scholars. 'Where is your research?'

The male realized what the Baron was planning to do next and opened his mouth to protest, only to close it again as he looked to the blood in the dirt.

'The cart, around the back,' said the woman, eager to ensure its preservation.

'Pull the cart away to a safe distance,' he commanded his remaining guards.

The Baron cleared his throat and addressed the crowd. 'Assembled gatherers of the guild. All those who bear witness to justice today, say aye.'

A muted chorus followed the command. Saddened eyes looked on at the scene. Mo looked to her younger sister, who wept openly. She knew it would disturb her dreams forever.

A heavyset guard swung the severed hands over the archway that gated Norok's home, and left them swaying, dripping their warning for all to see.

The Baron waited for his guards to return, raised his palm, and the building was set ablaze. As the flames began to rise, the Baron spoke again, his grim visage lit in tones of red and orange.

'Take this image home to your loved ones. Let it serve as a reminder that there is no step I will not take to protect you and your honorable service from thieves and deceivers. Let no one, outsider or moon-born, test the letter of our laws. The will of the Praelatus is absolute. May he protect us until the end of time.'

The assembly was dismissed. The gatherers turned and walked from the horror they had witnessed, in silence, in mourning.

Her sisters pulled at her, whispered to her, implored her to leave, but she couldn't move. She stood transfixed, bathed in firelight, staring at the bodiless hands swinging in the wind.

* * *

I remember the box most of all, my twin.

There are nights when I wake, sweating and shaking in this hole, convinced for minutes that I am still in that box.

With you.

I remember the way it swayed, how we heaved and retched and wiped our watering eyes for those first few days on the sea.

How I longed to see it.

The only light we saw came from the occasional stab of orange through the planks of the crate we festered inside.

Naked, dirty, starving.

How relieved we were when the box hit solid ground. How foolish we were to think that it might soon be over. What an eternity it was.

I remember the noise—when we were shipped like meat through the town, the whoops and cries of the people, the laughter. How I held my fingers to my nose, terrified that the faintest smell of roasting meat might make its way into our wooden prison. I remember when it did, I could barely smell it because we stank.

I remember seeing that look in your eye, on the long road. That glint. I wonder if they intended us to consider each other food.

What a sight we must have been.

When the lid finally came off, how blinding was the light that burned our eyes.

I'll never forget his face. The way his gaze passed over our foul, naked bodies, how it lingered on our ribs, our hips, how his lip curled as we reached out to him.

How could I ever forget?

NINE

Crisis

PETOR'S NIGHTS WERE getting later. He'd procured another bottle of whiskey for the first time in a year, which concerned him, but there were good reasons. He had become fairly adept at justifying his behavior—after all, he'd been doing it for decades.

His wrinkled hands trembled around his third glass. The clear brown liquid rippled in the firelight, giving it an infernal quality which it matched in taste. The last of it burned its way down his throat, causing him to cough, narrowly avoiding spoiling Renia's masterpiece.

He pushed his chair back a step, realizing his error and relieved at the near-miss—a mistake that could have ruined his reputation. Worries about his drinking pawed at his thoughts. He would stop soon, lest it become habitual, moon forbid.

Petor wobbled over to his armchair. Limbs like heavy sacks pulled him down into a slump in front of the fire. His eyes closed for a moment, and he allowed himself to slip into the realm of odd shapes and colors that defied logic.

A sense of peace leaked through his forehead, his skin tingling like static as his limbs let go. Adrift. Small waves splashing against the edge of a rowboat. The familiar coughing of his grandfather. The smell of fishing bait.

He was back in his armchair. The crackling of charred wood. His vision blurred, his feet were hot…Slipping away again.

Water splashed in his face, and he struggled with the fish. It slipped around in his hands, evading his grip. He couldn't get the hook out. His grandfather laughed.

He was back in his armchair, bile in his throat. He cleared it. The room span. Something grazed his elbow, but the sensation felt delayed. He was falling. His eyes felt wet. The grass at his feet swayed gently in the wind. His mother was crying. His father delivered a eulogy.

He was back in his armchair. He had been snoring. The fire burned low. A twinkle of light from the whiskey bottle caught his eye. A shadow, but his eyelids were anchors.

Adrift again. Lying face up in a lake, floating on his back. There was a mist on the water. He wanted to die.

He woke. His brain throbbed, locked in a vice. He leaned forward in his seat as his vision adjusted. The movement sent a wave of nausea up from his stomach. As he struggled to focus, he wondered how long he'd been unconscious. The smell of embers told him it had been far longer than he thought.

Petor jumped to his feet in a panic. Heat rushed through his esophagus as nausea threatened to put him back in the chair.

The book. I left the book out.

It was still there, laid bare on the desk where he had left it. He cursed himself for his carelessness and glared at the empty glass that had allowed him to make such a moronic lapse in judgment.

He groaned as his body protested at the movement. He carefully gathered up the manuscript and made his way to the locked cabinet. The key was in his breast pocket where he'd left it, and he sighed in relief as he opened the cabinet door. At least he'd remembered to lock the bloody thing this time.

These incidents were becoming far too frequent. He was getting sloppy. The drinking had to stop. He eyed the half-empty bottle with contempt, and vowed that his next act would be to pour it down the sink. He would be buggered if he was going to end his career in disgrace after all these years of impeccable service.

He placed the manuscript on the top of the pile, as Renia had left it there before her *incident*. Terrible business, that. The pressure, no doubt. Perhaps it was more than she could take. Still, the indiscretion had caused tongues to flap, and that wouldn't be good for his hall. Nor would it reflect well on him if this high-profile project had to be reassigned to someone of more stable mind, probably from another hall altogether.

He locked the cabinet door and turned away.

Wait.

He frowned. Something didn't feel right. It didn't feel right at all. Petor suddenly found himself very sober indeed. Cold beads of sweat leaked from his pores. Had he mis-seen?

He prayed to himself, unlocking the cabinet again and taking a sharp breath before revealing its contents.

Two books and a manuscript. He counted them again—two. He reached inside, patting at the woodwork to see if the back may have come loose, to see if one might have fallen through, but it was solid.

The Inoa book was missing. The same book that had already almost cost him his career once was missing again. That same old, damned, bastard of a book was missing once again.

Petor fumed. She hadn't even finished her first book before sneaking off with the next, to get her reading in. He would have her guts. She would feel his wrath. *When the Hall Master gives you an order, you bloody well follow it!* But there was something else, a doubt, a niggling feeling he couldn't shake. When had it gone? How had he not noticed its absence earlier in the evening? Surely he would have noticed. *Has someone been in here? Is it possible? Surely not.*

Petor found himself pacing before the open cabinet, thoughts racing, calculating, deducing the possibilities. He had been a bloody fool, a careless, complacent old fool, and as his thoughts followed the issue to its logical conclusion, his blood ran cold. If he wasn't cleared of this crime, it would be his life. He would lose his position. He could spend the last years of his life staring at cold cell walls, useless, old, and waiting to die. At the very least his position would be forfeit, but only *if* he could prove he had nothing to do with it—again.

Would anyone believe that a second time around? The book had to be returned, and quickly, before anyone realized he was unaware of its location.

The bottle of whiskey stood tall, laughing at him, mocking his lack of character. With a stomp, he yanked it from the desk and launched it into the sink, grimacing at the shards of glass bouncing around his office.

Sundance had found the perfect spot to observe her target. A seated corner of the corridor with a direct line of sight to Dail's apartment. It was busy enough that she wouldn't stand out, and quiet enough that she would be able to see any activity.

She sat in front of a coffee table with three open notebooks, a quill and ink pot, and a crime novel she'd only read three times.

She loved detective stories. The thrill of a mystery revealed slowly, like peeling an onion, *so satisfying*.

Her father had been a book dealer, and as such she'd been one of the luckiest children in the city of Verda, with almost unlimited access to novels, one of the highest luxuries in the land. In that sense she'd only ever really had two career choices: the family business, or the Halls of Venn.

As a scribe, she had access to the library, which contained almost every novel still in circulation, except, of course, the ones that had been deemed restricted. She'd read all of them during her long years of service, most of them more than once, and out of frustration, she'd decided to try to write her own.

All she needed was an idea. The desk in her apartment had drawers stuffed with unfinished manuscripts, bits of chapters, plot outlines. But none of them had ever truly satisfied her, given her the hunger to take to the page. The problem was a lack of inspiration. Typically, her workplace was entirely dull, tensions were usually petty affairs, nothing juicy enough to draw in an audience. There had been an incident with a missing book once, but awful as it had been—a man was splattered all over the courtyard—she wasn't about to start stirring up memories that many would still find painful. She needed something new. Something fresh.

And then young Renia had done it, she'd lit the spark. She'd reminded Sundance of something she'd caught a glance of, something that she'd dismissed: a booklet that had been discarded, bearing the title *Who was Sanas Inoa?*

The name was not unknown to her. There were references to Inoa in some of the history books she'd copied over the years. But from the public record you would have thought that the character was a fairly dull diplomat who assisted with unification towards the end of the Great War. This booklet, however, painted a different picture, a picture of evil, scheming his way toward unification through bribery and intimidation. It would have made for an interesting story in itself, but she didn't fancy being strung up for trying to publish it.

What she did find interesting is who would care enough to distribute this sort of information illegally. If there had been any truth to it, that would have to mean that the information came out of the restricted library. If there hadn't been any truth to it, it meant that someone thought highly enough of themselves to attempt to bend the hearts and minds of others, which, in her experience, never ended well.

Now that is a good character to have in your book, she had thought.

Alas, the booklet had been a dead end. It had been discarded; smelling it hadn't given her anything, other than a sneeze. She didn't recognize the penmanship either. Whoever had written it was skilled enough not to give themselves away. She'd simply filed the idea away in her inner library until another clue presented itself. And then Renia mentioned this *club*.

'*Some sort of thinkers' circle,*' she had said.

The image of the booklet had flashed into her mind's eye immediately. She knew there had to be a connection. Dail was the one who could lead her to her inspiration. Of course she would be looking for clues about Renia's missing piece of jewelry too.

So now she stalked. She'd been around this building so long she'd become part of the furniture. She could move unnoticed, feigning indifference. She would spend her spare time here, working on ideas, jotting down notes, and watching. Watching like a hawk.

Movement: two young girls gossiping, and the head of security. She put her head back down and watched with her peripheral vision.

Jeff approached. She liked Jeff. The man inspired a lot of gossip.

'Sundance,' he said. 'Funny place to work.'

'Hello, Jeff. Well, one can't help where they find inspiration, I suppose.'

Jeff studied her. Professional curiosity, no doubt. 'What is it you're working on?'

'My debut novel. It's a romantic thriller about an irresistible security chief.'

The blankest of stares. The man gave away nothing, and he was obstructing her view of Dail's door.

'I don't think many people would read that,' he said.

'Oh, you'd be surprised.' She gave a little chuckle and looked at the young man properly. She could see how the rumors about him might be true; he was strong, attractive, in a position of authority. Had she been younger, she may have been tempted. She wondered where he got the slight limp he managed to hide rather well, though.

Still blocking her view.

'You're familiar with the girl, Renia, are you not?'

Sundance blinked in surprise. 'Yes, dear, very much so. I mentored her.'

'There's been an incident reported. I have to make a character assessment. I'm told she had an outburst here and threatened another member of staff.'

'Yes, quite unfortunate. As I understand it she was provoked, and the timing was bad. She'd been under a lot of pressure with a new project.'

Jeff rubbed his chin and nodded. 'Ah. She's the one with the restricted books. Master Petor's girl.'

She could just make out Dail's door opening down the hall. Jeff was still in her way; she'd have to move. She had to do something, quick.

Sundance rose to her feet and rounded the table toward Jeff, smiling. He seemed genuinely concerned at her approach.

Does he think I'm about to make a pass at him? Oh how fun.

She stopped in front of him, close enough to make the man look uncomfortable, and to be able to see Dail fumbling around in his pockets—he must have lost his keys.

Jeff straightened slightly and cleared his throat. 'In your opinion, is it likely she'll endanger anyone if she's returned to work?'

If she wanted to follow Dail, she had to get rid of Jeff quickly, and she couldn't resist toying with him a little more. She reached over, gripped him at the triceps. *Well, well. Very nice.*

She had him. He recoiled, visibly uncomfortable. Sundance laughed internally.

'It is my considered opinion,' she said. 'That she was just caught out by an immature comment at a stressful time. I *hardly* think you'll have any issue with her in the future.' She followed up with a wink, for good measure.

He pulled away, stumbling backward, putting weight on his bad knee. It gave way and he fell backward towards the table. With a thud, his elbow smashed into the hardwood before his backside rebounded off a plant pot and hit the floor.

His face was a picture, utterly priceless.

Sundance looked to Dail's door. He stood staring at the scene in surprise, key still in the door. She feigned embarrassment, helping Jeff to his feet. 'Oh, Jeff, I'm so sorry. Are you alright?'

'Yes, yes. I just lost my footing.' He jumped to his feet and looked around to check for witnesses. Sundance balanced on the verge of laughing out loud. It took every ounce of strength she had to keep a straight face.

Jeff nodded at her sternly.

'Thank you for your assistance,' he said, before hobbling away at speed. This was her chance. She quickly gathered up her things and set off in pursuit of Dail.

RENIA WINCED AS the door flew open and bounced on its hinges. Master Petor burst into her room, flush-faced and veins bulging. He must have found out the doctor had signed her off work. *No, that can't be it. He's too angry.* He glared at her, breathing heavily. *What is going on here?*

'I gave you very specific instructions, Miss Renia.'

She shook her head, dumbstruck. 'Sir?'

'You cannot simply take a restricted book home for a bit of bedtime reading.'

Renia froze. She must have heard him wrong. He couldn't mean what she thought he meant, surely.

Master Petor paced at the foot of her bed. A nurse's head appeared in the doorway briefly—a quick inspection before deciding she wanted nothing to do with it.

'Where is it?'

She said nothing, she couldn't find the words. A series of unintelligible noises escaped her.

'Where is the Inoa, Renia? Is it here?' The eye contact was intense.

Renia could barely process the new information. 'Sir, I have no idea what you're talking about.'

He started to growl, charging toward her bed. 'Where is the key?'

She thrust herself backward as he pulled at her gown in an attempt to remove it.

Renia grimaced at the invasion of her space, she pushed herself sideways off the bed, landing with a thud. The floor collided with her coccyx, taking her breath away and giving Petor a chance to get around and drag her up by the lapels. He pulled them apart, exposing the key still tied around her neck, and then shoved her backwards. 'Do you understand the gravity of this situation, girl?'

She did. Her thoughts returned to the smoke, the fire, the guilt. The childhood that had been robbed from her flashed behind her eyes. She saw the woman with the ax, the hound.

She found herself kneeling on the floor by the bedside table, numb. She didn't know what to say. Another flash of memory hit her.

'Did you say the Inoa?' Her eyes widened. The whispers returned, chanting *his* name. Through the fire and the smoke of her memories, she saw *him*, waving the papers. *'Sanas Inoa?'* he'd said. *'Underhand stuff.'*

The words echoed over the sounds of her parents screaming, the roaring of flame. The betrayal sliced at her like a cleaver, bleeding her of any doubt. Her rage returned. She met Petor with a savage gaze. The two outraged figures stood coiled and ready to pounce.

The old man snarled at her, his lip curled in a venomous expression. 'You mark my words, girl,' he said. 'If I find out you did this, I'll have your hands cut off.'

She found herself growling. A growl that turned into a scream as she launched the glass she'd unconsciously picked up toward Petor's face.

It struck him with enough force to rock his head back on his neck. The glass rebounded, shattering on the wall as Petor staggered back in shock, clutching his eye and making guttural noises.

He dropped to one knee, screaming in agony as the stem of the broken glass bit into his calf muscle.

Blood had been spilled, but Renia was oblivious to the consequences. She watched him with the intent of a predator as he shuffled backwards on his rump, flapping and fumbling in an attempt to move away from the glass, pricking his hands on stray shards and crying out as they tore at his skin.

His brow bled freely, covering one side of his face in dark crimson streams.

Jeff stood in the doorway with a look of sheer incredulity plastered across his face, rubbing his elbow, switching his gaze back and forth between the two panting animals. She met his gaze, sweating and exhausted. He laughed in disbelief and shook his head.

'Fucking weekends,' he said, pulling handcuffs from a pouch. 'Come here.'

TEN

Aftermath

IT WAS A sight Molan would never forget: the first rays of the sun colliding with a smoldering ruin, framed in a sea of nothing but ash and gravel. Between himself and what was left of his home of two years, two huddling figures sat in a pack cart, swaying gently.

Carol had done her best to console Renia, but the poor girl wouldn't speak. Barely responsive, despite Molan's best efforts.

Molan thought he could make out the charred remains of her parents, locked in a final embrace. He hoped he was wrong for Renia's sake; the girl had seen enough.

They had found Terrick and Renia after everyone left—true to their word. The girl had been unconscious at the time. Nobody had known what to say or do. Renia had slept in Terrick's tent with Carol, and as horrific as it was, Terrick and Molan were glad of the heat from the burning house to keep them warm as the night drew on.

None of them really slept. Molan had spent most of the night staring into the flames without a thought in his head, a trauma-induced trance that still lingered behind his eyes.

'They are still here.' Terrick spoke from behind him; he'd been keeping an eye on the women since first light.

'Why? What's left to look at?' said Molan.

Terrick grunted. 'Us. It's going to be hard to explain why we have a catatonic girl sitting in a cart who wasn't present last night.'

'They are a ways away. I doubt they have seen the girl.'

'Well, they aren't staying there for the view.'

Molan nodded slowly, considering the situation.

MO FIXATED ON the puffiness of her sister's eyes. Eva had spent most of the morning sobbing, an appropriate soundtrack for the images that lingered in her thoughts.

They had made camp where they stood, unable to move Mo from the site of her ordeal. Her sisters would understand what she had done for them, they might even think they could understand how she felt, but she doubted it was possible.

Norok's hands still called to her. She tried not to look, to tell herself they were just hands, but she saw them whether she looked at them or not. They were a limp reminder, suspended in eternal submission, pointing down into the dirt, to the underworld that awaited her soul.

How could they ever understand?

She'd killed before, many times—it was a hazard of working in the Southern Wastes, but there was a difference between killing a man who wanted to kill you, and mercilessly dismembering a man in front of his screaming wife.

Nothing would ever be the same. Her sisters would never look at her the same way again. She'd become something else, a warning to the guild, a story to be told to naughty children to keep them in check. It wasn't a reputation she'd carry with pride. She'd become a pariah, the whispers in the room, the awkward silence of halted conversation.

Bara frowned at her, searching for the right words to say. Mo knew she had none, so she answered her unspoken question. 'We can't leave yet.'

'What do you want to do?'

She looked out towards the cart. The cart she knew held the orphan daughter of the man she'd just killed. 'Something,' she said.

Eva piped up for the first time since they'd woken. 'I suppose you'll want to report the child to the Baron too, will you?' The barb was delivered with intent, crafted to provoke a reaction.

'Child, Eva? I don't see any child. Do you see any child, Eva?' The rebuke stunned Eva into silence, but the glare remained painted on her puffy face.

Mo took in a deep breath, and looked to the sky. 'I can assure you I don't want to see *that* kind of justice served ever again. Much less be a part of it.' Her sisters exchanged glances, already noticing the change in her.

'Pack up your tents.'

THE TWO MEN stood side by side, witnessing the women's exchange from afar. Terrick tried to make out what was being said, but the ax wielder had her back to him. 'What will you do with her?' he said.

'I'm not sure.' Molan turned to face him in concern.

'You're going to have to think fast. The longer you linger here the more chance you have of being discovered.'

'I can't help but think on my part in this.' The memory of dancing water and the misty-eyed child had tormented him as the ashes fell. He was responsible. How could he consider himself not to be?

Terrick grunted in agreement. 'I have wondered at my own,' he said.

The butcher approached their position, slowly, with palms raised at her sides. Terrick eyed her with suspicion. Had it not been for the exhaustion, he might have taken a more defensive stance. 'She wants to talk.'

Molan murmured his assent, and the two men walked out to meet their fate.

THE TRIO STOOD on neutral ground, a respectable distance from the cart and its precious cargo. They eyed each other in a deflated triangle of shame, each feeling the weight of their part in the night's dreadful pantomime.

Mo spoke first, feeling the suspicion of the two men bear down on her. 'You have to leave—leave the Wastes.' Her usual confidence was absent.

'That's not as simple as it sounds,' Terrick said, pointing toward the pack cart. 'They can't exactly *pull* that thing out of here.'

Mo rounded on Molan. 'If anyone finds out about the child, it will invite another round of...*justice.*' She delivered the word with care, making her feelings on the matter known.

Molan shot a concerned look at Terrick, who shook his head, exhaling hard.

'Do you have a plan?' she said.

Molan sighed, nodded, and surrendered his reservations. 'We'll take her to the Halls of Venn with us. I'll say she's an orphan I've taken as an apprentice. The child has the right mind for the place, but I worry that she may never recover it.'

Terrick nodded. 'It's a long way to go with a full cart. You'll need supplies, tents, weapons.'

'Carol wasn't thinking of that when she packed the cart, unfortunately,' said Molan.

'Can you not leave it?' Terrick said.

'I'd have to leave Carol too. You're looking at years' worth of work. Plus the law is clear on the distribution of knowledge. It would be best if we didn't return empty handed—'

Mo spoke over them. 'You'll have everything you need.'

The two men looked at her with a mixture of suspicion and surprise. She threw her pack down at their feet. 'Food for a week. My sisters are packing their tents. We'll leave you with two of them.'

Terrick frowned at the offer. 'And what of the cart?'

Mo removed a belt housing a dagger. She cast it to the ground next to the pack. 'A few hours from here, there's a stable. The owner owes us a debt. We'll have him pick you up and pull you to Venntown.'

They stared at her, silently questioning her intentions, hesitant to trust the motives of a killer. She sensed it all, a feeling she would have to get used to.

She drew in a deep breath of charred air. 'I did what I did out of honor. Believe me, it gave me no pleasure to carry out the sentence. I'm not telling you this to ease my conscience in any way. I'm telling you so that you understand that I am a woman who understands duty. I feel a duty to this child. I'm not a fool. I know Norok didn't steal the stone. I saw it in his eyes before I—' She looked to the ground. 'He told me as much with his eyes. I'm willing to pay the price for letting the girl escape, should it come to that. We're trusting you as much as you're trusting us.'

Terrick nodded at the pair of them. 'I made my choice when I pulled the girl from the window.'

Molan stared at the ruined house, and the blackened hands swinging in the wind.

'Very well then.'

THE TWO PARTIES separated to make preparations. Molan approached the cart. A concerned-looking Carol awaited him.

'What are they going to do?' she said.

'Help us get out of here.' He placed his hand on Renia's head, the child that had given him so much joy over the years. He prayed that some part of that girl would survive.

'Pack up, Carol. We're going home.'

PART TWO

The Missing Book

Eleven

Duty

Home.

Jeff ran his palm over the windowsill and allowed the day's heat to permeate his flesh. He stood in the security office, apart from his team and oblivious to their conversation.

Deep within the fog that lay heavy over his thoughts, he found himself comforted by the echoes of his past, the familiar grinding of metal on stone, the snorting of pigs, the calling of market tellers, and the trudge of well-trodden dirt.

Southgate.

Home.

He returned to the nagging concerns about recent events. The tremor that had shaken the earth and resulted in minor damage from Aradinn to the palace had set rumors flying: tales of betrayal in Verda, gatherings of cultists fleeing the Wastes, skirmishes fought over food. His sources told him of the burrowing moon cultists, and how their behavior had changed, become more organized, less reckless.

He should write to his father, but he wouldn't. *That* life was over, denied him. His *new* life had him removed from such concerns, a glorified mediator, hobbling through the Halls of Venn with a leg that defied his every movement. His *new* calling was to be bound in service to a place he didn't understand: the realm of the learned, the clever, the cowardly.

He ran his fingers along the grain of the wood absently, both cursing and embracing the numbness behind his eyes. The blur of the view beyond the glass a fitting metaphor for his memories. Southgate lay distant and invisible on the horizon, obscured by the purple glow that clung to the fallen moon like a bubble, lost behind shifting winds of sand and ash and gravel that cut through the irradiated fog of the Moonwastes. Unnatural, unsettling, dangerous, beautiful.

To work, then.

He turned from the window and feigned distraction, avoiding the inviting stares of Bobb and Jinger as Bobb recounted his latest tale. They all ended the same—with a bar brawl, and Bobb as the unlikely hero, showered with free ale and lauded for his deeds. Jeff spared not a shred of interest as he left the room and made for the attached cellblock that housed his latest guest.

Renia the Scribe. Barely known to him, quiet, professional. Now embroiled in a matter that might or might not be of great import. How quickly life could change.

Jeff came to a slow halt outside her cell door and peered at the sleeping woman through the viewport. Was this *her* low point? The pivotal moment in her life? Would she find herself looking back, wishing *she* had behaved differently?

How depressing it is, he thought, *that more often than not, it's our weaknesses that direct the course of our lives, and not our strengths.* How many could say the inverse, in honesty? If he had been stronger, denied his desires, would he be home now? Preparing for battle?

What purpose did he serve here, really? Any man could find purpose in defense. It was a calling, something primal, the instinct to shield the weak from harm. It was their way in Southgate, to protect the Wastes from the interlopers that dared to venture north. As it should be. As it had been since the day the Praelatus had charged the Sothgard family with the protection of Luna Ruinam's southern border, generations ago.

It was *Jeff's* way. *A man protects, he works, he provides. A man creates, or destroys, for those who need him, who give him purpose.*

What is a man without something to carry?

He is nothing.

What a thing it would be, to count the moments of his life in battles won, in protection of his home, his family, his land. How was it that he should count the time here, in this foreign place? In squabbles mediated? In days since the last petty theft, perhaps? In patrols? Or perhaps in needless reports filed away for none to ever read.

He flared his nostrils, annoyed at his procrastination. *Is that what I am now? A lost man, wondering at how to mark the passing of time?*

'Tick, tick, tick, Jeff?'

What?

The voice carried down the hall, alone but for the dripping of leaking pipes. He padded toward it, toward another of his guests. 'Tick, tick, tick, Mako.'

The old man looked up from his cot, raising his bushy eyebrows as if hearing the greeting for the first time. 'Good, good.'

Mako Aranomo, first among his peers. Legend among engineers from the Halls of Venn all the way to Aradinn. At least that's what he *had* been, years ago. His cell had no door, just a wide gate of barred iron struts. By virtue of his genius, he was still permitted a small workshop, and occasionally materials with which to work. The bars helped his supervisors ensure nothing illegal happened.

Jeff gave the man his best smile, despite himself. Mako had been steadily losing his mind for as long as Jeff had been chief. A tragedy, and a waste he was sure, though it wasn't Jeff's place to judge the laws of the Great Protector – they had been compassionate enough not to leave him to rot beneath the North Wing.

'Keeping busy, Mako?'

'Roundabouts, Jeff, roundabouts.' He scratched as his unkempt mane, no doubt infested with lice. 'Tick, branch, tick.' He had a habit of doing that. Total nonsense. Jeff attributed it to his work. For a long time Mako had made timepieces, the finest in Luna Ruinam.

The old man grinned. 'Not as busy as you, I bet.'

'Oh?' Jeff raised an eyebrow. 'What makes you say that?'

'Tingles in the wake, lad. Lots of branches budding. Taro-tarotaro says things are afoot.'

His imaginary friend. Jeff chuckled, almost envious. 'Next time you see Taro-taro, you ask him if he'll tell me what those things are.'

'Oh no, he doesn't like that. It's Taro-taro*taro*.' Mako looked down, his voice shifting to a grumble. 'I suppose I could. Hmm. Perhaps…I would need chocolate,' he said, locking eyes with his captor in determination.

Jeff tried to imagine the train of thought that had led to that statement, and quickly thought better of it. 'Leave it with me then. I'll see what I can do.'

'Good lad!'

'I have to go. I'll see you soon, Mako.'

JEFF SHUFFLED BACK toward the main office, conflicted. He entered the room again to hear Bobb reaching the peak of his story.

'Oh I did, lass. You should have seen his face.' Bobb fumbled around to catch the crumbs falling out of his mouth. Half of his biscuit fell on the floor. Jeff winced. Did the man ever stop eating?

Jeff started to turn away as the door swung open. A small, spring-loaded bell fixed to the frame rattled to life.

A young man stood sweating in the entrance, heaving and bent double in an attempt to catch his breath. He held an envelope out toward Jeff.

He took it, and felt the blood drain from his face with every word it contained. 'A Reaper? Is this a joke?'

'No, sir. You're being served with advance notice from the palace. She'll be here within the week.' The messenger was a scraggy youth who clearly took his job too seriously, panting and dripping all over the place, though Jeff wondered if he just resented the boy's ability to run.

'Wonderful. Off you go, then.'

The nightmare that had become Jeff's week had reached its crescendo. The missing book would be a pivotal case, perhaps the most important in his career. The consequences of not recovering it—well, in honesty, how was he to know? The book was a restricted piece. Jeff had no knowledge of it other than its title and designation. Recovering it would be akin to running a marathon with lead weights strapped to his ankles.

And now, this.

Bobb eyed him from his desk across the room, a mixture of curiosity and frustration on his rotund features. Jinger, Jeff's assistant, would also be watching, although not directly.

He held his breath, closed his eyes, and counted to three. It didn't help.

'Are you going to tell us what's going on, then?' Bobb, of course, always the first to break a silence.

'Well,' Jeff said. 'We have an assault to deal with, a missing book from the restricted archive, and now we have a Reaper coming.'

Bobb let out a whistle and rolled his eyes. The gesture smacked of self-satisfaction. Bobb had passed on the promotion to chief, and taken every opportunity to point out that he was right to do so. His primary concern had always been how long he got to spend in the pub each evening. That was the way he liked it. 'You're going to be a busy boy, then.'

'As are you, Bobb.'

Bobb snorted in response, grinning in a way that clearly said, *good luck.*

Jeff pulled out a sheet of letter paper and began to write a notice for the Grand Master. It filled him with dread. In the few years he'd been doing this job, he'd rarely had to deal with the man, and he would have liked to keep it that way.

AO: Grand Master Venn-Dor
Priority Matter: Missing asset. Request attendance.

That was all it would take. He marked the note with his seal and handed it to Jinger on his way to the door. He looked to Bobb but thought better of inviting him to join. It was doubtful he'd be of any use.

Bobb swung around on his chair to face him. 'Where are you off to?'

'I have to see a man about a book. Keep an eye on things here.'

As JEFF MADE his way to the hospital ward, his thoughts were cast to the missing book. He began his usual ritual of thinking of what he *could* know about the case. He knew it was being kept in a locked cabinet, he knew that two people had a key, he knew that his knee ached—*focus, Jeff*. That meant starting with the two people who had the keys and finding out who had access to them, and cataloging their movements from the approximate time the book disappeared.

A young scribe winked at him as he walked. He kept his gaze low, looking forward to the day that he was old enough for this persona he'd acquired to fade. Luckily, the rest of the journey passed without embarrassment.

JEFF FOUND PETOR sitting in an uncomfortable position in the same room he'd been attacked in. The hospital bed creaked in protest as Petor tried to find a pose that didn't pull at his stitches. His leg had been raised for him, presumably because the old git refused to sit still. It was a nasty gash.

Jeff's signature step on the tiled floor had given him away before he'd entered the room.

'Jeff.' Petor nodded at him, squinting, with a bandage covering the eye that had been struck by the glass.

'Hall Master.'

'I take it the girl is in chains?' Petor still refused to sit still. He twisted to face his visitor, grimacing.

'She's locked in a cell, awaiting questioning.' Jeff positioned himself at the end of the bed to save the old man moving around too much. 'I need to ask you some questions about the book.'

The old master grunted, as if knowing as much.

'Let's start with who could have had access.'

'As I said, only two people had keys: Renia, and myself.' Petor was staring out of the window. *Evasive.*

'And who had access to *you*?'

The old man's face wrinkled as he expressed his distaste at the idea. 'I have no time for such things, Jeff. I'm not a teenager.'

Jeff nodded. 'When did you notice the book was missing?'

'Yesterday, in the early hours.'

'Up late, or waking early?'

Petor thrust his chin backward and crossed his arms. 'What are you suggesting?'

'I'm trying to establish a time line, old man. I needn't remind you that your neck is closer to the chopping block than mine is here.'

Petor's gaze returned to the window, a malaise falling over him. Putting the old man on the defensive wouldn't work. Jeff moved to his bedside. He positioned himself between the disgruntled master and the window, and poured him a fresh glass of water.

Petor looked at the glass and snorted, with a quick glance to his injured calf. He fixed Jeff with a look of regret. 'The truth is, Jeff, I don't know when the book was taken. I fear my neck is already on the block.'

THE SOUND OF dripping water was a welcome companion in the cell. Without it, Renia feared the silence would have driven her insane. She sat on the edge of a cot more suited to storing barrels—rough and sturdy, but not suitable for sleeping on. Dim light bled in through the barred slit that was her only connection to the outside world, but only through another void which seemed to her to be some kind of access corridor. Between that, the iron door, and the small hole in the floor for waste, escape would have been impossible.

She replayed the moment of impact in her mind, the glass colliding with Master Petor's eye socket with a satisfying thud. Horrific, shameful.

Does he live?

Her erratic behavior was as much of a worry as the consequences of the battle with Petor. She couldn't understand it. The events of the past few days almost felt external to her, like watching someone else through her own eyes.

The dripping continued. She wasn't exactly sure how long she'd been locked up, or how long she would be. Would they leave her here to rot? Doubtful, the questioning would come soon. The search for the missing book would be well underway.

Something had changed in her. She'd disgraced herself twice in as many days, and word would spread. She mused over what new nickname they would think up for her: *Renia the Wicked, Renia the Wrathful?* She shook her head, then let it loll on her shoulder.

She felt a drip on her wrist and frowned. Another leak must have started above her new bed. Only it hadn't. It had come from her. Without so much as a sob, she laid down and fell asleep with the tears pooling around her cheeks.

JEFF CURSED. THE knee was getting worse by the minute. The pain seemed proportional to his anxiety: the Grand Master would no doubt be on his way for a briefing, and Jeff had nothing.

He supposed he should be grateful that neither of his prime suspects were a flight risk. Renia was locked up in the cells and Petor couldn't walk if his life depended on it. As for what he'd managed to learn from the old man—well, it didn't look good for him. Between his heavy drinking and his general forgetfulness, Jeff worried about the consequences for Petor. He didn't consider him a suspect; he had nothing to gain, already in his twilight years and with no family or friends that would benefit financially. Was it time for the old master to hang up his robes? Jeff wasn't sure the choice would be his. Not after this.

He was considering his line of questioning for Renia as he approached the corner that was the site of his embarrassment the previous day, and saw Sundance sitting in exactly the same spot, eyeing him in anticipation. He picked up his pace and flashed her a non-committal wave, hoping it would be enough to prevent another painful encounter.

AND... THERE HE goes. Sundance smiled as her plan to avert the attention of the security chief succeeded. After having spent the better part of the last twenty-four hours in this exact spot, she stretched and cursed her aging joints for letting her down. Nothing of interest had occurred during her watch. Dail had not left his apartment since she'd followed him to the canteen, where he'd spoken to no one and sat with a withdrawn, miserable look on his face.

She was gathering up her things when she noticed a janitor approach in her peripheral vision. Seeing him rant to himself at the bloodstains that still decorated the floor by Dail's apartment pulled at her heart. *Poor girl.*

After watching the erasure of Renia's outburst, she stood to leave, satisfied that the incident would be forgotten as soon as the next drama came. As she turned, she caught the janitor check his surroundings, reach into his pocket, and pull out a small slip of paper. Sundance pretended to busy herself, patting down her dress pockets so as not to make a show of watching as the janitor slid the note under Dail's door.

The plot thickens!

What was this mysterious note? What clandestine events were occurring beneath the surface? The dull ache of age was forgotten in a heartbeat as this rare moment of excitement swept it aside.

Sundance had a lead, and she intended to follow it. And follow it she did. Over the next hour Sundance stalked her prey with the grace of a mountain lioness, passing unseen from corridor to corridor in the janitor's wake. It was with a sense of accomplishment that she returned to her apartment that evening with what she believed to be the address of another member of the thinkers' circle.

HE'D KEPT HIM waiting... One does not keep the Grand Master of the Halls of Venn waiting.

Jeff stopped mid-step over the threshold of the security office at first sight of the Grand Master.

Venn-Dor was a hard-faced man, a powerful man, a man with a direct connection to the Great Praelatus. He was a figure of slight build, but unusually tall. He stood adorned in crimson robes, trimmed in silver, and a black, high collared over-cloak. A single brooch of pure gold representing the fallen moon held the cloak fast around his chest. Jeff winced as his superior frowned at his arrival.

'Jeff.' The tone of his voice was smooth, as neutral as lake water in spring. The Grand Master inclined his head. 'Let us speak in your office.'

JEFF DIDN'T USE his office; he preferred standing to sitting as a rule, on account of his knee. When he did sit down it was out in the main office with his team where he could keep his ears open. So it was with some embarrassment that Jeff blundered around his *so-called* office while attempting to clear a suitable place for the frowning Grand Master to sit. Jeff cursed under his breath as the room full of boxes of dusty files and confiscated items protested at his intrusion. The Grand Master moved his robe as a pile of long-forgotten papers fell on Jeff's head as he attempted to move some of the clutter to a high shelf.

'I do hope this is not a reflection of your state of mind, Jeff,' Venn-Dor said.

'Not at all, sir. I prefer to be in the thick of it.'

'The thick of dust, apparently.'

Jeff bowed his head, thinking better of trying to justify his surroundings.

'Enough delay. What is the missing asset?'

Jeff couldn't prevent himself from gulping, finding his throat dry at the question. 'It's the Sanas Inoa book, sir. *Journal 26.*'

Venn-Dor's gaze was molten.   He stared Jeff down, unblinking. 'How?' he said.

'Stolen from a locked cabinet in Master Petor's office.'

'When?'

'It was reported stolen yesterday, sir.' Jeff's lie of omission sat wrongly with him, but it would reflect poorly on himself as well as Petor to admit that he didn't know exactly *when* the book had been taken.

The questions continued to come in single syllables. 'Leads?'

'One at this time, sir. I've concluded my enquiries with Master Petor and I am on my way to question the scribe who was charged with it.'

The Grand Master looked up to the ceiling, taking in a deep breath and wrinkling at the dust content in the air. 'I don't like the timing, Jeff. No Reaper has darkened these halls for a decade and yet one appears just as this particular book is misplaced.' He leveled his gaze on Jeff again, looking over his nose. 'Find it, Jeff. Find it before the Reaper arrives.'

'Yes, sir.'

Venn-Dor scrutinized the disarray of his surroundings. He curled his lip in distaste as he left, without so much as a glance toward Bobb or Jinger on his way out. Jeff followed at a safe distance, stopping to rub his knee in front of Bobb's desk.

'That was intense,' said Bobb, stuffing his face with some sort of pastry.

Jeff grimaced in response. 'Come with me. We have a suspect to question.'

THE INTERROGATION ROOM was hot, sweaty. Renia hadn't bathed in days and she was acutely aware that she didn't look her best. She sat with her arms at her sides, staring at the bloodstained table in front of her. Images of interrogation rushed through her mind, worries of what she might endure in this sticky, forgotten hole of a room. The gas lamp in the center of the table ebbed, illuminating her two interrogators from below, painting them in a ghoulish light.

'Let's start with where you were on the night before the book was reported stolen.' His name was Jeff, chief of security. He was the one that had wrestled her to the ground after her attack on Master Petor.

She heard the question, but it didn't quite register. It got lost somehow, caught in a tangle of wrestling thoughts that wouldn't allow her to focus. She frowned, casting her gaze to the floor in frustration.

The chubby one stood up. Renia flinched, expecting violence, but the man gave her an odd look before fetching her a glass of water. She gulped it down to the last drop before he could reclaim his seat.

The two men looked at each other sidelong before pushing on. 'The night bef—'

'In the hospital wing, under guard,' Renia said. The rush of hydration had lifted her from the fog, and her wits returned.

Jeff made a note. 'To your knowledge, who had access to the cabinet?'

'I am aware of two keys. One is with Master Petor, the other is here.' With sweaty hands, she opened the first two buttons of her blouse, and revealed the small key she wore around her neck.

'Do you ever take that off?'

Renia shook her head, keeping her tone steady. 'No,' she said. 'Never.'

Jeff let out a sharp breath, still making notes. The other one just sat there ogling her. Renia ignored him.

'You were arguing with a young man before you were taken into the hospital wing, a Mr Dail Svelt. What is he to you?'

'A lover. Occasionally.' The other man's reaction disgusted her; she chose not to register it.

Jeff made another note. He spoke as he wrote, with a casual indifference.

'Did Mr Svelt show any interest in your project?'

Renia felt her pulse quicken. Memories of slammed drawers and bloody palms flashed through her mind. She focused on Jeff.

'Yes. On one occasion he spoke of a club. A place where thinkers could gather to discuss curiosities in the public record. He had notes on his desk about the true identity and deeds of Sanas Inoa.' She couldn't help herself. All the injustice she'd suffered in the past forty-eight hours bubbled like molten lead in her gullet. She wrestled to maintain her composure.

Jeff raised an eyebrow and looked up at his colleague. 'A club?'

'He referred to it as a *thinkers' circle.*' She flashed a mocking smile.

'Did he mention any of the members by name? A location of where they meet?'

'No, he didn't,' she said flatly.

Jeff closed his notebook and placed his palms on the sweating slab of wood that separated them. 'Renia. What were you arguing about outside his apartment?'

Her vision cleared. She locked eyes with her interrogator as a cool grin escaped her restraint. 'I was confronting him,' she said. 'A family heirloom—something that only *he* knew about—is missing from my jewelry box.'

Jeff cocked his head in wait as she paused for effect.

'I believe he stole it.'

Twelve

Revenge

GRAND MASTER VENN-DOR hadn't seen the inside of a Hall Master's office in a long time. He stood by the cabinet from where the book had escaped Petor's watch...again.

Journal 26. Inoa's final bloody gift to them. How benign it must have felt under his pen. He wondered how it would feel to have a piece of your legacy draw blood, not by its content but by the gravity of your choices. This was not the first attempt the south had made to lay their hands on it, nor would it be the last. It refused to be forgotten. As did Inoa.

Painful memories began to surface, and the Grand Master allowed himself a small moment of despair as the gravity of his own choices pulled him closer to the events that followed the first theft of *Journal 26*.

He looked around Petor's sanctum, at what had become of the once legendary master. Ruined machinery, cogs and screws kicked into corners and forgotten. Dishes and glasses thick with old grime, unseen, unnoticed. The makeshift cot, sheets unmade and stained with sweat. Shards of glass, pieces of a broken bottle slick with the oily residue of whiskey, an act of frustration, of failure. This was the example set for the next generation? Or

Inoa's legacy, plaguing the poor soul as it had plagued all those entrusted with its care.

Saddened, the Grand Master shook his head and left, leaving no sign of his presence behind.

'TICK, TICK, TICK, Mako.' Jeff greeted his favorite captive with a smile.

The old man stared at the wall, deep in thought. Consternation covered his features, searching for a memory perhaps. Lead poisoning could be cruel. Jeff's words took a few moments to pierce the effort.

'Tick, tick, tick!' Suddenly animated, Mako sprang from his cot, bounding toward the bars of his cell. 'I was just thinking about soup. I loved carrot soup.'

Jeff winked at the old man. 'Here.' He passed the bar of chocolate through.

'Wonderful, wonderful!' Mako shook the chocolate, holding it in both hands like a captured rodent. 'Now we can get to business!'

'Mako, you were here at the time that *Journal 26* was stolen, were you not?'

A glassy look colored the old man's face. His eye twitched. 'Yes, yes. Terrible business. It was dark, as I remember it.'

'Do you remember any details? Particulars of the case?'

Mako rubbed his clump of chin hair, nodding, brows furrowed in concentration. 'Well...I remember it was dark.'

Oh, well. It was worth a try. Jeff tapped the bars in resignation. 'Enjoy the chocolate, Mako.'

'Jeff?'

Jeff stopped in his turn, looking back over his shoulder. 'Yes?'

'Where did you get it? The chocolate?'

Jeff started to laugh. 'I stole it from Bobb's desk. Don't let him see you eating it.'

Renia didn't look good. She'd spent most of the time in the cell sleeping, and even now, as Jeff had come to release her, she slumbered, unaware of his presence. Her hair had knotted and hung heavy with grease. Her clothes were sweat stained, and clung to her like wet paper as she tossed and turned. He couldn't help but feel pity for the girl. He couldn't shake the feeling something was amiss.

He'd read Renia's file. She was an orphan, found roaming the Wastes like a stray by two traveling scholars who ultimately took her as an apprentice and taught her how to read and write. How she'd survived that environment was a mystery to Jeff. He knew the Wastes well, and what they could do to a person over even a short amount of time.

He'd have to wake her now if his plan was to work. He cleared his throat. Her eyes shot open, pupils adjusting instantly to focus on her invader.

The words came out in a whisper that echoed around the damp space like the voice of a ghost. 'It's time to go,' he said. The old blanket he'd brought along served to cover her modesty as he helped her get to her feet and ushered her out of the cell toward the main offices.

Bobb manhandled young Mister Svelt in as Jeff escorted Renia out. Dail protested physically, twisting in Bobb's grip. Bobb just laughed, dragging him towards the cells by his elbow. Dail's eyes widened at the sight of his lover and his anger dissolved into sadness in an instant.

'Renia? Renia, what have they done to you?'

She stared at him without emotion, like she didn't recognize him.

'Renia?'

Renia drew herself to her full height, standing tall for the first time since she'd been arrested. She set her stare on her lover, scorn plain for all to see.

Jeff nodded at Bobb and the young man was dragged away toward the cells.

'Renia,' Dail cried back at her in desperation. In that moment Jeff saw in the young man what he had expected to see: genuine concern. 'Don't worry. Everything's going to be alright. We're going to be alright!'

She grinned at him venomously. It was unnerving. Dail's face paled visibly as he started to realize why he'd been brought here. She leaned forward and her cracked lips parted in a sneer. 'I told you this wasn't over,' she said.

Dail pulled at Bobb, thrusting at him, trying to wrestle free as he was dragged away. Dail's protest rang through the offices. He shouted her name, over and over.

Jeff had seen all he needed to see. Betrayal, revenge, perhaps a misunderstanding amplified by intimacy between them. But he hadn't read anything lurking beneath their reactions, no conspiracy, no fear of reprise over a deeper crime.

Dail had nothing to do with the missing book. There was more to this lover's tiff than met the eye, but he knew love when he saw it, and Dail loved Renia. He wouldn't do anything to jeopardize her position.

Jeff's trail had gone cold, there were other motives at play here, but he was still hesitant to submit to the Grand Master's theory that agents of the south were making a move. Something else pawed at him, like an itch that he couldn't seem to scratch. Who would benefit from disgracing Master Petor? Who had a grievance with him?

And then it hit him. A chance encounter in the dead of night with a painfully egotistical Hall Master who wished to register a complaint. A Hall Master whose petition he had dismissed. *Could he be that petty?*

Renia shivered. She'd resumed her weakened stance and stood staring at the door leading to the cells. Jeff wrapped his arm around her shoulder. He steadied her, and led her toward the exit. Jinger watched him; she would be waiting for instructions. 'Prepare me a search team for Mister Svelt's apartment. Inform the doctor that I wish him to inspect Miss Renia. Then send notice to our Master Piss-Stain and tell him I want to see him.'

'RETIREMENT?' PETOR SHOOK his head uncontrollably. 'No, no. There's no need for that. My wounds are healing. I will get to the bottom of this myself.' The bed creaked and rattled as Petor desperately tried to pull his injured leg out of the sling that suspended it.

The Grand Master laid his hand on Petor's leg, and looked him in the eye with a severity that told him to stop. 'The decision is mine, Petor.'

Petor's eyes glistened. He struggled to catch his breath as the news filtered through his psyche. *This can't be the end... Not like this.* He wrestled with himself, darting from point to point, each half-finished thought overlaying the next as he struggled to accept what he'd heard. 'A leave of absence, yes. I have been burning the candle at both ends. Perhaps now would be a good time to rest, to recover fully before returning to my duties.'

The Grand Master shook his head, standing sentinel over Petor, the grim harbinger of his fate. 'You've served this institution longer than many. It's clear that it has worn on you of late, Petor. I believe you to be the victim of this plot, an easy target to be thrown under the cart. I've seen the conditions in which you're living. We both know it's time for you to step down.'

Petor was struck dumb by the blow. Had he been so blind as to not realize that he'd become an unsuitable candidate for the role he'd played for so many years? *No, no. He just caught me at an inopportune time. It's the book—the book has driven me to this.*

Venn-Dor looked at his employee with compassion, and whilst Petor appreciated his attempt not to erode his dignity any more than was necessary, bile rose in his throat at the pity in it. 'In recognition of your long service, I've made arrangements for you to take possession of the Mandor cottage. You'll be within the grounds and retain the title of Master, and all its associated perks. Your active service will end as of today.'

'C—cottage? Me?' Petor trembled, gripping at his sheets in disbelief. Mere minutes ago he'd been Hall Master Petor, fearsome, respected, useful. To become what? A figurehead? An example of retirement for younger employees to aspire to? No. Not him. He would die at his desk. This must be some ploy, a tactic to draw out the thief. They couldn't just replace him.

The Grand Master took his hand in response to his disbelief. 'Petor, I leave you with a warning. Do not take this act of compassion as license to defy me. You will not interfere with this investigation. You will not attempt to return to the halls or involve yourself with the transition of your responsibilities. You will retire to the cottage and stay out of the way. Do you understand, Petor?'

'Y—Yes. Yes, sir, Grand Master.'

'Good. I'll arrange to have you escorted to your new home when the doctor discharges you. Everything will be prepared.' The Grand Master spared him a last look over his shoulder as he left. 'Enjoy your retirement, Petor.'

SUNDANCE FELT THE prickling of nerves as her fist hovered over the door. She had no idea what she would say; the thrill of the hunt was all that drove her. She hesitated, finding herself out of her depth, and above her station.

There's nothing wrong with asking, is there? A friendly chat, that's all it has to be.

She knocked three times and took a deep breath, allowing her chosen persona to come to the fore. The part she played well—the stern teacher, the disappointed mother.

The doorknob rattled before turning.

'S—Sundance?'

Nervous, scared even. Who had he been expecting?

'Hello, Tannis. Can I come in?'

TANNIS'S APARTMENT WAS the very image of a young man's mind. Dishes were piled high in the sink, crusted with week-old grime with no sign of getting any attention in the short term. Scattered literature of an indecent nature decorated the floor. Towels and dirty laundry were draped over every vertical surface, and the rotting remains of half eaten meals filled the rest of the available space.

Tannis scratched at his scraggy hair as he looked for somewhere Sundance could sit. He was clearly unaccustomed to entertaining guests, particularly female ones.

'I'll stand,' said Sundance. She tried her best not to look judgmental.

Tannis gave her an embarrassed smile as he dabbed at the flop-sweat that had enveloped him since her entrance. 'Wh—What can I do for you?'

It was rare that Sundance found herself lost for words, but in that moment she genuinely didn't know what to say. She had no intention of making improper accusations. Protector forbid she should attract a reputation for herself as a meddler. But how was she to uncover any more of this mystery without digging a little?

She eyed the young man as she considered her options, inviting a silence that seemed to make him increasingly uncomfortable. Perhaps she didn't need to say anything at all.

She slowly unclasped her satchel, being sure to maintain eye contact. Tannis's eyes darted from hers to the bag in anticipation, the suspense mounting. As she pulled out the booklet, his eyes widened. He stood in slack-jawed horror at the sight of his connection to the thinkers' circle. He froze in place like a cornered rodent. His breath quickened. Panic set in.

Sundance watched as he slowly backed into his desk, stumbling as he looked from door to window, considering escape. She stood between him and the door, and the fall from this height would surely kill him. Still she said nothing, but her own heart began to race as she felt her disadvantage.

He started to heave, each breath now labored. His hand fumbled around behind him, probing for something.

'Tannis, what are you—'

She saw it. A letter opener found its way into his grip and in an instant was between her and the younger man. Sunlight glinted off the edge, teasing its lethal potential.

Shock arrested her from the diaphragm upward. She felt a lump swell in her throat as she wrestled with her body over what to do. The sting of salt threatened her eyelids, but she held firm, grimacing at the blade.

'What have you gotten yourself into, Tannis?'

Seconds drew on like the flow of treacle as they held each other's gaze. Sundance stood determined, Tannis shaking, desperate, child-like.

He wavered, blinking rapidly as his tears began to roll.

'Please. Th—They took Dail. They know, I—'

She kept her eye on the blade. 'Put it down, Tannis. Please.'

He looked at the letter opener in his grip, regarding it like a stranger. Realization crept over his face and he dropped the blade in alarm.

Exhale. She straightened herself in relief. 'Who took Dail, Tannis?'

The young man started to sob. 'The chief, and the fat one. They dragged him...I—'

'Tannis, calm down.'

'Please, please don't tell anyone. I'll do anything you want. I don't want to be a part of it anymore. Really, I don't!'

Sundance said nothing; she didn't have to.

'I can't do this,' he said. He dropped to his knees, speaking through his hands. 'Look, in the beginning it was just poetry and book reviews. Just a group of us enjoying good literature, bonding. That's all. I always thought it was strange that we had to wear cloaks, and masks, and to speak in whispers. I just thought it was part of the experience.'

She continued to stare at him in silent accusation. He trembled, waiting for her to speak.

'I have the other booklets. Look. You can have them,' he said, darting to his desk to recover them in a panic. 'Here, here. Take

them, please. I don't want them anymore. I don't want anything
to do with any of it.'

She took the booklets, a dozen of them, and placed them into
her satchel without inspection. Tannis waffled on.

'And then there's the location, I mean, how did they even
find that place? It's so odd. Honestly, I can't believe I've allowed
myself to become a part of it. It's getting really political. Not at
all my thing. Not my thing, no.'

Sundance placed her hand on the weeping man's shoulder.
She looked to the window, curiosity piquing. Masks? Cloaks?
The secrecy of it. What could possibly warrant such measures?
And what hidden *odd place* could he be referring to?

She spoke in a low, neutral tone when she finally opened her
mouth. 'Take me there.'

WHEN THEY REACHED their destination, Sundance wondered if
she'd misread the young man.

'This is it,' he said.

'This is a wall, Tannis. Are you quite well?'

'No, no, you don't understand. When we arrive for the
meetings the wall isn't here.'

He stood shaking, still looking over his shoulder for some
invisible threat.

'Not here?' She wasn't sure whether he was mocking her
or not. His demeanor suggested *not*, but things were growing
stranger by the minute. Sundance had never heard of, let
alone seen, a secret door in the Halls of Venn, though it wasn't
inconceivable that such a thing might exist, given the history.

'It's like a secret door. I don't know how to open it. I just
know that when we come for the meetings, it's open.'

She nodded thoughtfully, placing a hand on the stone. Nothing remarkable, but there wouldn't be, would there?

Tannis jumped in his skin. She snapped around to face him. The sound of plate armor became apparent, and the young man paled visibly.

'Oh no, oh no. They're coming, they—'

'Tannis, wait.'

'I did what you asked, please—'

'Tannis, listen to me. They took Dail because he stole something from Renia. It has nothing to do with you. You—'

He blinked. 'The stone?'

'Yes, do you know whe—'

'No!'

The sound of the guards grew louder. Not far now. Sundance watched as his desire to flee intensified. He shuffled uncomfortably, unable to accept her reassurance.

'He didn't steal it, he—'

Two guards rounded the corner. Now in full view, Tannis lost his train of thought and shot her an apologetic look before bolting down the hallway. She watched him scramble away, perplexed, and turned back to the wall.

What are you hiding?

Another visual inspection gave away nothing, so she probed gently at the stones for any indication that this was, as Tannis had said, a secret doorway.

'Madam.'

She span around. The guard spoke through slimed lips as he peered down at her. The fact that she looked like a silly old woman caressing a wall made her flush with embarrassment.

'Is there something wrong? The young man seemed to be in distress.'

She found herself nodding, staring in disbelief at the situation she had found herself in.

'Madam, do you need assistance?'

Snap out of it, Sundance. She blinked, smiling gently as if remembering something. 'My apologies. Nothing to concern yourself with. I'm afraid I had to deliver some bad news. He didn't take it well, but I'm sure he'll be alright.'

The guard turned his head with a squelch and shared a glance with his partner, who shrugged, disinterested.

'I should be about my own business,' she said. 'If you don't mind.'

The guard replied in a gargle, standing aside. 'Of course.'

She felt his eyes on her back as she scurried away.

JEFF AND BOBB stood in the aftermath of a thorough and methodical search. He'd instructed the team to be respectful of Dail's work and belongings, and they had been true to their word. As Jeff stood at Dail's workbench, he looked over countless pieces of unfinished jewelry, wondering if any of them could be the stolen heirloom Renia had mentioned. The surface was strewn with delicate stars and floral charms so tiny they would be difficult to pick up, each discarded for some imperfection Jeff struggled to see. He wished Renia had been more specific; he could be looking right at her lost treasure and not notice it.

'This is worrying.' Bobb was flicking through a collection of unlicensed booklets that had been found in Dail's desk. Jeff wasn't accustomed to seeing the man so serious. Perhaps he would have made a decent security chief after all.

'What are they?'

'Looks seditious to me. Whoever is writing these is clearly trying to incite some kind of revolution.'

Jeff frowned at the thought. He saw a web of possibilities and realized that he had more than one problem, or one very large problem; neither was welcome. Petty disputes usually lay at the heart of the issues he'd dealt with during his service. He hoped that this was the case here; he wasn't sure he was properly equipped to deal with the alternative. 'We'll take them back to the office for further inspection. No doubt one of the Hall Masters will recognize the penmanship.'

'Aye, I'd expect so. Do you see any real connection between this club and the missing book?'

'Not yet. Do you?'

'No.' Bobb looked at the clock. 'We'd better get back and question the lad.'

Jeff nodded, taking one last glance around the room for signs of the missing piece of jewelry.

* * *

I've tried to forgive you.

Truly, I have.

It's not as if I didn't see the appeal. That raw, animal strength, charisma, prestige. Every woman saw it.

But despite what you thought, despite those heated, dreadful nights spent arguing, despite everything you accused me of—

I never had eyes for Hosst.

Never, Vera.

I never felt the tang of jealousy, sitting watch outside the door to the sound of your lovemaking. I felt only concern, fear.

Fear of what I knew would come.

Fear of what I knew you would do when it did.

You claim that I will never understand. But I do understand. I do.

It is you that doesn't understand.

Do you think I will sit and watch idly while you destroy what it is that I have chosen to love?

Have you even considered that I love at all?

I have tried to forgive you for the things that have passed, for they brought us here, but I know now that I will not forgive you for this.

I will never forgive you for this.

Thirteen

Torture

Pregnant. That was what the doctor had said. At least two months along. The news had hit her like a brick to the face, sapping at her ever-diminishing energy reserves and bringing her to a slow halt. Tears collected in small puddles between her crossed legs as she sat with her back resting on her apartment door. She'd collapsed into this position upon thanking the doctor for his visit and hadn't moved in what must have been hours. She had no desire to move, to read, to clean, to do anything at all other than sit, and cry.

Renia had never seen herself as a mother. Never possessed the maternal instinct, or drive to reproduce, to nurture. She'd never fantasized about the fairy-tale life: the big, strong husband to provide for her and her young, the beautiful home with the kids running around, playing hide and seek. She'd never wanted any of it. The images always reminded her of shattered glass, fire, loss, fragility. She always felt the urge to flee from the idea, to keep it at a safe distance. If she kept it there, out of her mind, she couldn't hurt it—she couldn't destroy it.

The tears burned, her throat ached. She wondered how there could be any water left in her after the week she'd endured. The urge to drink was strong, but still she did not move.

Thoughts instead turned to the life inside her, the growing shard of her that she feared so much. She feared its innocence, its ignorance. She feared its father, and his betrayal. What would become of them now? Would she have to forgive him? To allow him to play with her, take from her?

And what of her career? Was it over? How could she possibly continue to work in the halls and maintain her reputation with her attention split so rudely? She might not have the energy to finish her current commission and have to pass it off, in which case she would likely never be offered the same opportunity again.

Renia despaired, gripping at her hair and growling into the gloom of her apartment. It was impossible. Her life would never be the same. The world had dealt her another crippling blow, derailed her, and eaten her aspirations. Her curse had returned to keep her in her place, struggling and suffering in a never-ending cycle of frustration and pain.

She didn't want to be a mother.

Had the dreams been a warning? The spearing intrusions into her inner fortress had been unwelcome. Had her body been trying to tell her, to remind her of the consequences of her carelessness? Of course she had revisited the horrors of her childhood in dreams before, but not like this. They had been so vivid, so *real*. She'd experienced them as a passenger, dragged along by some faceless puppeteer, the whisperer in her thoughts.

She found herself lost. Lost like the little girl she had been, riding in a cart, heading away from the life she loved toward a darker future. Lost and helpless, a slave to the path laid out in front of her.

Finally, she moved, rolling onto her side and curling into a ball to let the darkness take her again into the realm of dreams.

She didn't want to be a mother.

Jeff lifted the note from his desk:

> *Jeff, I need to see you. It's important.*
> *Sundance*

He turned it over in his hands, frowning, reliving the embarrassment of his last run-in with Sundance. His elbow throbbed in sympathy, still sore from the fall.

A veiny-looking man of indeterminate age stood in wait in front of his desk. He was dressed in robes of dark purple, holding on to the handle of a wheeled chest, the contents of which Jeff did not want in his space.

'You were ordered here?' Jeff asked from his chair, struggling to hide his distaste.

'Oh yes, the Grand Master was insistent.'

Truthseer, torturer, mind-butcher, universally despised and feared. His very presence seemed to paint the air with filth, to sour the palate. Jeff would never have sent for their sort, no matter the circumstances. Experience had taught him that some things were better left alone.

The truthseer continued, the words dripping off his tongue like slime, 'It is my understanding that the matter demands expediency. My expertise can meet this demand.'

Bobb was watching. He snorted through the ice pack he held to his jaw, rolling his eyes. Dail had been less than cooperative. From the start of the interview he'd been defiant, responding to questions with dismissive gestures and nonsense. He'd given them sod all, and laughed when presented with the illegal booklets found in his room. The whole debacle had lasted roughly fifteen minutes, and ended when Dail struck Bobb squarely in the jaw before spitting in his face and calling him a pig. The tussle that followed saw the two men on the ground. Somehow Bobb had found himself with the upper hand, pinning Dail to the floor and smashing his knuckles with the heel of the boot he'd lost during the struggle.

Jeff shook his head in dismay. He had started to long for the simple life, finding himself envying the shoemaker who made the boot. 'Expediency my arse.'

The unwanted guest stuttered in surprise. 'My orders are clear!'

'That they are. But this is my investigation and it proceeds on my time. Mr Svelt is currently with the doctor, and I have another interview to conduct. I suggest you find somewhere to kill an hour or two. See to your *pets*, or whatever it is you call them.' He stood and held his position, staring down the protesting truthseer long enough to see the back of his robes storming out of the room with his sickening cargo in tow.

'Foul,' Jeff spat.

'Aye. No argument there, lad.' Bobb's face had swollen to at least four thirds of its usual size.

'You look like a spud.'

Bobb laughed until the pain in his jaw stopped him, and slapped his belly. 'You are what you eat.'

Jeff continued to glare at the door, his memory conjuring the smell of burning slime, and the shrieking of a woman who did not deserve her fate. 'Keep an eye on him,' he said.

JEFF LIMPED TOWARD Interview Room Two. His knee throbbed in time to the pain in his head. *Just fucking kill me and get it over with.* It wore on him, the weight of the investigation, the drama.

He was waiting for the other shoe to drop, feeling it might as well have been his head under Bobb's boot.

He closed the door behind him and opened his notebook without looking his guest in the eye. 'Right then, Piss-Stain.'

The Hall Master flared his nostrils in anger; the barb had caught hold. Jeff would have to prod at it, if his suspicions were well founded.

'Why am I here?' He glared at Jeff, furious at the imposition.

'You're here because I have questions, young man.'

'How dare you address me so? I am a Hall Master!' He rose halfway to standing, threatening to leave.

Jeff took the measure of the man. Self-important to the point of nausea, standing there as if his presence were optional, as if the moon had fallen just for him. The weasel could barely keep his hair out of his face. 'How dare I? Do you think your position intimidates me? I bet I could walk these great halls all day and find not a single soul intimidated by you. You're here because I have questions for you. Now sit down before I'm forced to show you just how little your position means within these four walls.'

The Hall Master hesitantly sat with as much decorum as he could muster, curling his lip as the words ate into his ego.

Jeff carefully laid the series of booklets from the thinkers' circle on the table, examining the Hall Master's face for micro-expressions. The response he gave felt rehearsed, flat. 'What do you think to these then, Piss-Stain?'

Slam.

Enraged, the Hall Master hit the table with the flats of his palms and jumped from his seat. 'My name is Pistorious Staine!'

Jeff grinned. *Gotcha.*

'Pistorious Staine.' Staine's nostrils flared against the rushing of breath, veins almost burst from the pressure. 'I am a son of the ruling family of Verda. I will not stand to be berated by you, *Sothgard*. Take your schoolyard jibes back to the Wastes, back to that pig-pen you call home. You don't belong here.'

The young Master Staine waited for his comments to register, until confusion broke his anger. An ocean of calm met his rage.

Jeff sat with his feet up, rocking slightly on his chair, his face unreadable. He winked at Staine and motioned toward the booklets with one finger. 'And these?'

'I've never seen them before in my life.' Staine was still spitting words.

Jeff rose to his feet, and started to pace, dragging each step out momentarily. 'Terrible business, this missing book. It's creating all sorts of discomfort. You know, sometimes I wish I had stayed in Southgate, raised a few pigs. Hard to believe some of the stuff people will do over a missing book. Did you know, before I came in here I was having an awkward conversation with a truthseer who's insisting on reexamining everyone I speak to?'

Staine shifted in his seat, his forehead glistening with the sheen of nerves. As a son of Verda, he would know, and perhaps even have witnessed, the truthseer's craft, though the threat failed to deliver the impact Jeff had hoped for.

'And now,' Jeff sighed, 'I have a Reaper to welcome into our home.'

'A Reaper?'

'Oh yes, I'm sure you can imagine how uncomfortable that will be for us all.'

Staine was visibly panicked. The mention of the Reaper drew his attention to the booklets on the desk.

He had to be involved.

Jeff retrieved two glasses and a water jug, and placed them on the table without breaking eye contact. Staine's eyes flickered from left to right, calculating. Jeff had him where he wanted him—off balance. The sound of pouring water filled the empty space of the room as the water itself filled the first cup. Jeff lingered over the second glass before he began to pour. The jug loomed over the booklets still spread out in front of Staine.

He poured, and the glass began to fill. Staine looked at the glass. His alarm began to show as the water passed the mark.

Jeff continued to pour. Staine shifted in disbelief as the water crested the lip and began to run down its side.

'What—What are you doing?'

Jeff continued to pour, continued to look Staine dead in the eye. The water pooled around the base of the glass. Still he continued to pour.

Sheer panic escaped the Hall Master's restraint. He reached out to gather the booklets like a protective father and pulled them close to his chest.

Jeff grinned, and placed the jug down on the table before sitting. 'Here's what I think. I think you're behind these. I think you're playing a petty little game of "look at me". I think you honestly believed that you could fool everyone. I also think you took the Inoa book. I think you did it because Master Petor shattered your delusions of grandeur. He dared to humble the great Master Staine, and you wanted him to pay.'

'No.'

'You wanted him to pay by losing the only thing that really meant anything to him, his job.'

'No.'

'You might not even care about the book, or its value. *You* are actually petty enough that you would utterly destroy a man's career for daring to make fun of your name.'

'No!'

'No? I think you have some serious problems, Staine. You know, I've been wracking my brain, thinking why on Pulvis anyone within these halls would attract the attention of the Reapers. Sedition seems like a good enough reason, doesn't it? After all, it wouldn't be the first time someone with your name was erased under similar charges, would it?'

'How dare you?'

'Oh yes, you're not the only member of a noble house. And whilst you might consider Southgate to be a den of pigs, we pride ourselves on our intelligence, especially when it comes to the movements of dissidents. We heard all about it.'

'This is nonsense, utter nonsense.'

'We'll find out soon enough, won't we? Because I have a feeling that our Reaper friend is coming here for *you*, Master Staine.'

Staine stood. 'This is outrageous. On what grounds do you level such accusations at me? What proof do you have of these claims?'

'None, yet. But I don't doubt that I'll have plenty after I send Bobb to search your apartment.'

'Wh—What?'

'That's right. Make yourself comfortable. You'll be staying here for a little while.'

Indecision poured from Staine as he stood in disbelief. He sat slowly, searching his thoughts.

Jeff smiled fully for the first time that day. 'I'll be sure to send for refreshments befitting a man of your position.'

HALL MASTER SUNDANCE. She wasn't sure she liked it, it didn't ring right. Although it might not be a permanent posting, she'd been asked to fill the position until a suitable replacement for Petor could be found.

The room was bare, not the office she remembered it to be, or the place she'd endured both praise and censure over the years. Petor was gone, not only in form but in spirit. It saddened her. The man was many things, but he had been an anchor, and a mentor. Stepping out of his shadow under these circumstances didn't feel right, and she felt further justified in her efforts to get to the bottom of this situation for Petor's sake as much as her own.

She'd been offered a new desk as a gesture of gratitude for taking on the extra responsibility at such short notice, and expected delivery of it within the day. Beyond that, the only objects of note in the room were her old chair, the fireplace, a newly installed safe, and the window, which was very much a welcome change.

The first thing Sundance had done with her newly found authority was request samples of work from the other Hall Masters. The story she'd spun had been one of quality control, that she'd wanted to compare the output quality of her own team with that of the others, to help maintain consistency. It was a half-truth. She wanted to study the penmanship of every scribe she could to find a match for the illicit booklets she had in her possession.

In *her* possession. She frowned at the thought. It would not look good if she was found to be in possession of the complete collection. She desperately needed to speak with Jeff, to tell him of her discovery. If it meant being instructed to stay out of the investigation, then so be it; nothing was worth being implicated in this scandal—not even an acclaimed novel with her name on it.

It would not be easy to get his attention after their last encounter. He would be extremely busy, extremely distracted, and probably trying to avoid her entirely. She would have to find a way, one that didn't see her losing her new job before she'd started it. She hoped that the note would be enough.

'GET YOUR DAMNED hands off me.' Dail writhed in Bobb's grip, an echo of their prior bout. In the dim light of the interview room, the truthseer's features painted grim shadows over his face, his unnatural grin betraying any sense of professionalism.

Jeff stood away, putting as much distance between himself and the procedure as possible, both physically and mentally. This practice was considered brutal to even the hardest of men, and he wanted no part of it.

'This will be far less painful if you submit to it willingly, Mister Svelt.' The truthseer's grin gave no hint of the compassion in his words. 'This *is* going to happen. Resistance is futile.'

'Fuck off! You can fuck off!' Dail's words became a cry, his voice breaking with every sentence. The rumors of the method of extraction used by the truthseers were horrifying, shielded from the ears of children for as long as they had been spoken.

'Strap him to the chair, please.'

Bobb swung his weight, his elbow taking to Dail's jaw with a crack. A single bloodied tooth bounced off the table, narrowly missing the truthseer.

'*Without* damaging his head, if you will.'

The blow almost knocked Dail out. He murmured and groaned as they strapped him to the chair. The look of malice on

Bobb's face left a sour taste in Jeff's mouth. This was not a side of his colleague he enjoyed.

Jeff grumbled, glaring at both the truthseer and Bobb. His gut argued against the unfolding trauma, disproportionate, unnecessary. 'This needs to stop,' he growled. 'I won't have it.'

'Your hesitancy will be noted.' The truthseer barely registered his withdrawal. He bent over the table, leering into Dail's face as if appraising a piece of art. The seer stood, cocked his head. 'I'm afraid you do not have the authority to rescind my orders.'

Jeff huffed. 'And what happens when this goes wrong?'

'Wrong?'

'I've witnessed what these things can do to a person. I watched a woman burn.'

The seers lips curled in a display of condescension. 'Failure is to be expected in all emerging arts.'

'Art? Is that what you call this?'

'Oh yes, yes.' The seer returned his attention to Dail as he groaned in his chair. 'Worry not, Mister Sothgard. We no longer conduct the procedure on women, and anything left behind in this subject will quickly die and be discarded by the body.'

It's still wrong.

The Truthseer knelt before his travel case and retrieved his cargo with all the care of a nursing mother: a single glass jar, large enough to hold a human head, filled with sea water and containing a monster from the ocean's depths.

Dail returned to his senses in time to see the lid being removed. His eyes widened in terror as his bladder released its contents to seep out onto the tiled floor.

The thing emerged slowly. Black tentacles made of more tentacles, swirling and writhing in impossible motions, seeking release into the open air.

A xentt. How anyone could bear affection for such a disgusting creature was beyond Jeff. He stood repulsed in the corner, fighting the urge to vomit. The thing resembled a jellyfish, jet black with a slimy bulbous orb for a head. It had no eyes, or ten thousand eyes depending on the light.

The truthseer inched the jar toward Dail's head, as Bobb held him in place at arm's length. The creature slowly slithered toward the broken face, hungrily, as if smelling the blood. Tentacles started to feel their way toward nostrils, ears, eyes, while a larger bundles of tendrils bunched, poised to propel its sickening body toward its target. It leaped and landed with a slap, rapidly jerking into an optimal position covering Dail's eyes and forehead. Dail's scream curdled, rattling the eardrums and bones of everyone present, and ending in a muffle as the creature plunged its appendages into every hole in Dail's skull.

Jeff could bear to see no more. He snarled at the truthseer and closed the door behind him.

The noise. Pistorious Staine listened to the scene unfolding in the adjacent room in horror. He gulped, feeling his stomach knot, sweat beads burning on his skin.

I have to get out of here.

He stared at the plate of cakes that had been left on the table in front of him, forcing down the threat of vomit that they inspired.

What should he do? Would they try him for sedition? *No.* At the most, his works could be considered controversial. He had been careful, though they might try. *No.* Unlicensed publishing would be the worst thing they could pin on him, a stretch in the cells, perhaps demotion?

But they have no proof.

They had no proof. And the search of his apartment—they would find nothing. He wouldn't have been so careless as to leave anything incriminating there. Still he plundered his memories, retraced every step, ensured it to be the case.

No. I'm fine, it will be fine.

Another gurgled scream traveled through the wall. Staine winced, and his leg muscles fired, forcing him to his feet. His heart began to race. Every thread of logic disappeared in the involuntary urge to flee.

I have to get out of here.

He bolted toward the door and clasped the handle before his higher function gained the upper hand. *Wait!* He held his ear to the door, then positioned himself by the opening before turning the handle.

The door wasn't barred. The underling must have forgotten after bringing the cakes. *Fool.* He pulled it open slowly, and checked the hallway before emerging.

Now! It has to be now. But how would he transit the security office on his way out? What would he sa—

'Boy.' The hushed voice came from down the hall. 'Boy.'

He turned, his heart leaping. A face he hadn't seen for what felt like a lifetime. His mentor, his only friend.

'Mako?'

'It's me, boy.'

Staine started toward the cell and then froze in his tracks as the sound of the interrogation intensified.

'Do they have you, boy?' Mako's voice had aged, coarse tones bounced off the damp brickwork that surrounded him.

'Yes—no. I'm not sure.'

'Then go, boy. Go, before they take everything from you.'

He turned, and started to jog toward the security office.

'They take everything from you!' Mako's cry stirred in Staine's breast. The walls of the hallway seemed to close in around him as he fought to control his breathing.

He found himself standing with his hand on the door to the office, panting like a strained hound.

Compose yourself.

But his heart would not slow.

Compose yourself.

He took a sharp breath. He turned the handle and pushed himself into the office, back straight and head held high. The space was empty, bar the wench who ran Jeff's errands. She raised an eyebrow at him from behind her desk.

He turned from her, masking his panic with disdain. 'I will not listen to such barbarism.' It came out well. He continued, 'Inform your chief that I will be at my post, should he wish to continue our *conversation.*'

The woman's face creased, indecision pouring from her.

He threw in a sniff and straightened himself for good measure, and then stormed from the office, appearing as impatient as he could, slamming the door behind him on his way out into the corridor.

And then he ran.

Fourteen

Blind

Jeff stood before a great double door, hardwood, thick as your leg, and reinforced with iron. Decorative rivets trimmed the outer edges—for art, or intimidation? *Both*, he thought.

Though muffled, and impossible to make out, Ferron's voice battered its way through the barrier. Quite a tirade. By the sound of it, someone was in trouble. He shifted his ear to the left in an attempt to make sense of it, but to no avail. It wasn't his business anyway.

Things were different in the North Wing. They had to be. A fortress within a fortress, the real heart of the Halls of Venn, where the lightstone and its handlers festered beneath the surface of their world. Very fitting.

'Sir?' He'd forgotten she was there. 'Sir, did you hear me?'

He turned to Jinger and blinked. 'He just walked out?'

Jinger's gaze dropped to the floor, her face flushed with embarrassment. 'I'm sorry, sir. I don't know what I was thinking, he just seemed so—'

'It's not your fault.' He placed his hand on her shoulder. 'No sign of this "Tannis"?'

'No, sir.' Jinger shifted uncomfortably.

She wasn't to blame. In fairness, he was as much at fault as Bobb. He'd reacted badly to the xennt debacle. A cooler head might have thought to check the door that kept Staine within their grasp.

'Tannis hasn't been seen for days. He didn't authorize the absence with Master Vedora, nor did he leave a note.'

'And Staine?'

'Bobb is still on the hunt.' She looked at her shoes again. 'I think he's feeling a little guilty.'

Jeff took a sharp breath, and a moment to contain his frustration. For all the *progress* he'd made with Staine, he'd given them the slip at the first opportunity. Furthermore, the truthseer and his disgusting method of interrogation had resulted in a single name. *One name*: Tannis Rutger. There was a case there, surely. This 'thinkers' circle' would have been an interesting one at any other time, but to assume a connection to the missing book was a stretch. And a dangerous, potentially distracting one.

'Thank you, Jinger.'

'Sir.'

He didn't watch her leave, instead he returned his attention to the wooden barrier and the argument he couldn't hear.

'Back to work!' He heard that.

He checked his pocket watch. *Fifteen minutes.* The Mohruscan guarding the door risked an uncomfortable glance in his direction.

'I've been here for fifteen minutes,' Jeff said.

'The chief made it clear that none be admitted.'

Jeff looked to the other solider, and back, making a show of his disbelief. 'What's your name?'

'This one...'

Is slow, Jeff thought.

'This one carries the name Gorhrulage.'

'Gorhrulage,' Jeff repeated. Mohruscan names were not easy to pronounce. 'Are you new here?'

'Yes.'

The second guard stifled a laugh. Jeff didn't share the joke, tilting his head toward the comedian as neutrally as he could. The guard straightened.

'Do *you* know who I am, guardian?'

'Sir. Chief Sothgard.'

'Are you going to tell Ferron I'm here or shall I ask Captain Garamond to deliver the message for me?'

Gorhrulage certainly took that to heart, judging by the gurgling noise from beneath his plate. He shuffled over and pulled on a heavy chain. A bell chimed. A viewport opened in the door.

Jeff was admitted at a glance. One of the doors opened wide enough to allow him to pass. He spared the guards a disapproving look before leaving them at their post.

He arrived in the North Wing's entrance hall to a cacophony of activity. Carts skidded on their small wheels, grating on the stone floor as menials rushed about and crossed paths. Small arguments were breaking out throughout the hall, fingers were pointed, commands protested, a group of robed figures hit the deck as one of them dropped a lightstone, resulting in a flash and a discharge of energy that stunned the closest worker and left him twitching, face down on the ground. The event inspired little interest, seemingly a common occurrence, an occupational hazard.

All around the circular space, guards watched silently. Equidistant around the hall's outer rim, they observed, towering over all, clad in black, the mark of the elite.

Jeff caught a look at Ferron through the mass, poking his deputy's shoulder in a harsh exchange. His counterpart stood at the head of one side of the grand, sweeping stairway that led down into the underways. He thought it best not to interrupt and waited for Ferron to return to his clipboard.

'Do you have a moment?'

'Jeff, welcome. Of course.' Ferron waved away his deputy dismissively. 'What can I do for you?'

'I'm sure you've heard by now. About what's going on,' said Jeff.

'Missing asset, and a Reaper inbound. Yes.' Ferron cast a critical eye over his domain, no doubt taking names. 'Any idea who the target is?'

'How could I?'

Jeff's equal in rank, though not in responsibility, Ferron had the cool stare of a man used to feeling the weight of command. He regarded Jeff for a moment before speaking.

'I've been told the Reaper is falling under your jurisdiction. It would be nice if that meant I didn't have to double security around here, but that's not the case.' Ferron shook his head, and blinked. 'Double shifts and missed birthdays. This lot acts like we're not at war.'

A strange comment. Jeff didn't know what to make of it. 'But we're not.'

Ferron laughed. 'If that's what you think then you're in trouble.'

'That's why I'm here.'

'You've come for advice.' Ferron nodded.

'You've been here for a long time, you have experience I'm lacking...'

Ferron sighed. 'What's the asset?'

'Sanas Inoa, *Journal 26*.'

The chief of the North Wing briefly made eye contact, blew out his cheeks, and then looked away. 'Moonshit,' he said, shaking his head. 'I'm sorry.'

'What for?'

Ferron turned his body toward Jeff, perplexed. 'You read the file, right? The chief—Raellon. He died for that book. He was a secretive bastard, but he swore blind that these halls were infested with southern agents. Kept claiming he was going to embarrass me by weeding them all out.' He paused, mulling the statement over. 'Didn't work out very well for him, did it?'

Jeff frowned, assuming the question was rhetorical.

'The whole thing stank of Reaper involvement. It was too quiet, too tidy. Were we supposed to believe that the book sent him insane and he threw himself from the roof, or what? One minute he's bragging about exposing undercover Reapers and the next he's dead.'

'So you think there's a connection?'

'Isn't it obvious?'

'I tend not to think the worst without good reason. Disputes here are often petty, ego, or career driven. I suspect that someone is trying to ruin Petor.'

Ferron turned away again, nodding. 'A good way to do it. The same book goes missing on his watch twice... There's no coming back from that. It implies knowledge of the past, so that narrows it down some. I hope you're right, Jeff. But I would prepare for the alternative.'

'What would you do if you were me?'

'Quit?'

'That doesn't help.'

'I'm not joking. Look, Jeff, I mean no disrespect. I know you're capable and well trained. But Reapers aren't like us. And if that Reaper is here under false pretenses—for *that book*—then you are the primary obstacle to their goal. Of course if you quit now, it would all fall to me, so I'd rather you didn't.'

'I'm not quitting.'

'Then be smarter. The investigation around *Journal 26* was rushed, and incomplete. Start there.' He paused, lifted his clipboard and tapped it with the edge of his hand. 'One hundred and seventy-two lightstones. What am I supposed to do with that? The Baron must be laughing his way back to the Wastes. Do you know how long it takes to process that many? I'll lose most of my stone markers. And now, with this Inoa mess, the gates will no doubt close. Bringing in fresh blood will be out of the question. I was a soldier, for moon's sake. Look at me now—bean counter.'

Jeff did his best to change the subject. 'Didn't you assume Raellon's responsibilities after his death?'

'No. Venn-Dor took command personally. Closed the whole thing up pretty quickly. Bobb sat in your seat when required but we both know that doesn't mean anything.'

'The Grand Master suspects the south.'

'Well, what does that tell you? Venn-Dor isn't as absent as he seems. You should heed his words, prepare yourself. But if he is right—I'm telling you, Jeff, be careful. You will not fight a Reaper and win.'

'You've seen one fight?'

Ferron looked out over the hall, rubbing the scar that ran from his forehead to his cheekbone. 'Two of them. Once,' he said. 'Two of *them* slaughtered their way through three squads of men. Well trained, mountain-hardened soldiers.'

'I haven't heard that story.'

'You never will.'

The two chiefs regarded each other silently. A shared respect, or perhaps mutual appreciation for the gravity of the situation passed between them.

Ferron spoke first. 'I can't spare any men. But my thoughts are free, if you need them.'

'Thanks.'

'Good luck.'

He'd need it.

THEY HAD REPAIRED his coffee machine. *Bastards.* The detail with which they had prepared the cottage was breathtaking. Petor's whole life sat before him in welcome. Each piece of furniture, both from his office and his long-abandoned apartment had been restored, fabrics renewed, cleaned to perfection.

He spat, disgusted. *How dare they? Bastards.*

The far wall of the cottage was lined entirely with books. A huge display cabinet dominated the surface. At its center stood Petor's desk. His latest journal sat patiently on its top, next to a selection of new writing materials and art supplies. One side of the unit contained his entire book collection, categorized and set in alphabetical order. To the other lay his collection of journals, decades' worth, ordered by date ascending.

The adjacent wall housed a generous fireplace. His favorite chair, both familiar and unfamiliar due to its restoration, had been positioned at the exact angle to the fire as it had been in his office. The name plaque from his office door had been polished and put on display as a centerpiece. Dated with the start and end years of his service.

Bastards.

He limped to a glass cabinet in the corner. It must have stood nine feet tall. Within, an enormous scroll hung from top to bottom, listing every volume of text Petor had supervised through his long career, the scribe's name and date accompanying, thousands of entries.

His fists trembled. The audacity of it boiled him.

This is it? This is how they forget me? With a smile and a pat on the back?

He had everything a man like him could want. Spacious bedroom with a large four-poster bed, en suite privy with running water and sewerage, a well-stocked kitchen, room to entertain guests, a beautiful, well-maintained garden. In Petor's eyes, an utterly disgusting gesture. He thought of his office, and whoever might now be fouling it with their own belongings, wiping their feet on the doormat.

'Petor?'

He span, almost losing his footing and wincing in pain as the movement pulled at his stitches. 'You?'

Staine had emerged from the shadows, hunched and nervous, repeatedly looking over his shoulder for some unseen threat.

'What are you doing in my home? Skulking around like a snake in the dark.'

When the young master spoke, his voice cracked. He looked unkempt and exhausted. 'I—I need your help, Petor.'

Petor laughed out loud, his belly rocking with the force of it. Staine shushed him in panic.

'My help? What in the fuck have you gotten yourself into, Piss-Stain?'

'They are coming for me, Petor.' Staine's voice trembled. 'They—They think I took the book—to get back at you. Th—'

'*You?*'

'They took the Svelt boy. Oh moon, the noise, Petor. The sound of it, what they did to him—'

'*You.*' Petor's voice turned into a growl.

'You don't understand, I didn't take it, Petor. I don't have the book.'

'Get out!'

'They're going to *kill* me, Petor. There's a Reaper here!'

'And why should I care? They can eat you for all I give a—' Petor raged. The young master stood in shock as the old man charged at him. 'You arrogant, self involved, weasel. You deserve everything you get. Who's going to believe you? Me? For all I know, you did steal the book, you were behind all this, and you've come to rub my face in it. Come to laugh at the career you destroyed, have you?'

'No, Petor, I—'

'Get out! You stupid sack of turd! Get out, before I kill you myself.'

Staine was sobbing, weeping openly for the old man's mercy. He tried to protest as Petor slapped at him and shoved him out of the door. He turned, but fell as Petor's boot slammed into his backside, sending him sprawling into the dirt.

Venn-Dor bared his teeth to the wind that gnashed at his side, and welcomed the aching cold. Lactic acid ate into his bones. His legs protested every step, pleading for rest. Sweat ran down his calves as he climbed the palace stairs. Block after block, breath after breath, he drove himself onward, upward toward his summons.

Light burst from the tower, a hundred feet above his head. He grimaced up at it as it seared its afterimage into his retina, painting the featureless gray stone of the palace walls in prismatic chaos.

He pushed on, around the spiral stairway that wrapped the tower's outer wall. Around, and around, like his life, the same song, different players, different times.

The Grand Master paused to catch his breath after the long climb, just out of sight of the Praelatus's private guard that stood sentinel at the door to the throne room.

The two towering soldiers tipped their heads toward him as he approached, each adorned in armor of the finest artifice. Somewhere between ceramic and pearl, each plate shimmered in brilliant white, colors dancing over the contours as if gifted from the broken cloud cover. Lightstones were recessed into their shoulder guards, breastplates, and thighs, emitting a soft glow of shimmering hue.

'Venn-Dor.' The guard to his right unclasped and removed its helm, revealing a face of incredible symmetry and flawless crimson skin, masterfully painted over androgynous bone structure. The face was hairless, featureless but for the three perfect circle scars that glowed red, white, and blue upon its forehead.

Doratus bowed his head before its brilliance. 'Sahralla Nodiri Shallaila.' Each name carried three syllables, as with all the Exalted. The language was their own, the meaning known only to themselves.

'Your presence has been announced, Grand Master,' Sahralla said.

'My thanks.'

The Exalted tilted its expressionless face in response. 'You may proceed.'

The Grand Master regulated his step. The cavernous space enveloped him. High vaulted ceilings swept by, humbling him with their majesty. Each archway was simultaneously featureless and a work of art, appearing organic in mathematical precision.

The crack of static startled him as the huge doors sealed behind him, and he paused to draw upon his wits, steeling himself against the coming pain, before approaching the dais.

Dim light illuminated the space, though its sources were as elusive as the being that it served. The room had a nullifying quality to it which was exaggerated by the lack of adornment, from the flawless marble pillars to the impossibly large tiles that served as flooring.

Venn-Dor stopped, and bowed his head before the dais.

A throne room without a throne. It spoke to the character of their lord and protector that the Praelatus had never required worship, or engaged in acts of aggrandizement. His veneration was simply a product of his deeds, his legend, and the peace that had been enjoyed by the people of Luna Ruinam since the end of the Great War with the motherland.

He grunted. The fabric of reality compressed slightly—the precursor to *his* entrance. The temperature in the great space rose in anticipation, tasking the Grand Master's lungs. The sensation was familiar to him, though mastering it was no small task.

Light gathered, swirling into coalescence before him upon the dais. Venn-Dor tried to focus on it, but it burned his eyes, forcing him to avert his gaze. Sound rose in chorus, resembling the chanting of monks, low, both soothing and unsettling, rattling his teeth.

At once, a blinding flash of light filled the cavernous space, effortlessly, with the brilliance of a star. It drove him to one knee in supplication. Out of respect, out of pain.

The barrage on his senses calmed, but the light remained intense. He did not dare to lay eyes on the great being before him for fear of going blind. He spoke with what little strength he could gather.

'Great Praelatus. My lord and protector.'

The Praelatus's tri-tonal voice came from within, speaking to his very soul.

Grand Master. You have come to discuss your misgivings.

'I have, Your Light.' His breath caught in his throat, his well-rehearsed speech lost to him in the face of such power.

Then speak.

'Your Light. *Journal 26* has been stolen. I fear history is repeating itself.' The Grand Master gulped in an attempt to reclaim some moisture with which to speak clearly. 'I fear we find ourselves haunted once again by southern agents hiding in the shadows—and that other, unfortunate events are being orchestrated in an effort to create chaos.'

You speak of the girl.

'Your Light, the girl is clearly unsuitable for the position. The loss of *Journal 26*, and then two separate violent outbursts, one of which resulted in the hospitalization and subsequent retirement of Master Petor.'

You do not suspect the girl of the theft?

'No, Your Light. I do not.'

The pause that followed hurt. Energy pulsed, resulting in waves of pressure that compressed the Grand Master's consciousness.

What is your plan, Grand Master?

'I propose the total isolation of the Halls of Venn. We have supplies enough to last for three weeks, during which time we will conduct a search of the entire grounds.'

And the Reaper?

'A great concern, Your Light. I intend to have her movements monitored if possible, though my intention is to recover the book before she arrives. I don't presume to know your thoughts, but I would be remiss if I didn't note the coincidental timing of her arrival. I believe we are in a race to find the book…I humbly ask you to reveal to me the subject of the Reaper's writ.'

Another silence. Venn-Dor winced into his blurred vision.

The name is Pistorious Staine.

Staine. Unsurprising. A family of schemers and despots. What had he been up to to draw the ire of the Five? Under his nose no less.

What of the girl, Grand Master?

He blinked, torn from his train of thought. 'I believe she should be prosecuted to the full extent of the law.'

No.

The word rang in his ears, delivered like a barb through the skull.

'My Lord, I don't understand. There are many scribes of equal or greater ability who would be honored to finish the work—'

No.

Venn-Dor deepened his bow, ashamed at his presumption.

You believe I chose this girl to replace an aging Hall Master. This assumption is false.

Our fragile peace creaks under the weight of recent events, Grand Master. As we speak, my world-weavers struggle against the song that arose from the tremor. You have heard it. It is chaotic, malicious. It inspires rebellion. In the cities of Verda and Aradinn, greed pulls at those in power. It will lead them into darkness and threaten our way of life. It suggests change in the Moonwastes, in those dark places beyond my sight, where the cultists dwell beneath the surface.

'Forgive me, but what does this have to do with the girl?'

News of the Shepherd's suicide has travelled to the southern continent. Our position is weakened. The Five will seek to press their advantage. We must not allow Daralar to exploit the chaos that we face in our own lands. We must not be pushed on two fronts. We must uphold the letter of the treaty. A Shepherd must be present. We must replace him, and soon. Precious little time remains before the next generation awakens.

'The Shepherd? This girl? Molan's stray?'

Pressure erupted from the dais in a wave of sickening light and sound, knocking the wind from his chest.

Compose yourself, Grand Master.

'Fo—forgive…me.'

You may take whatever measures you deem necessary to recover Inoa's work, but equal measure to protect and nurture Renia Collis. Ensure that the work is completed, Grand Master. Prepare the girl. We will have a great deal more to worry about than Inoa's legacy if we delay.

He panted with confusion, every minute of the exchange taxing his body. A part of him wanted to protest, to demand more of his lord, but the overriding need of his body to submit held his tongue in restraint. The throbbing continued, as if in punishment for his insubordination.

'Forgive me, Great One. Your will is not mine to question.'

With a flash, and a sudden energetic release, the room fell into darkness and rang with the echo of Venn-Dor hitting the floor. He panted into the gloom and wiped away the tears welling in his eyelids. Shell-shocked and violated, confused, he rested on all fours, with his master's words ringing in his skull.

A HOODED FIGURE watches from afar, standing atop a formation of broken earth that should not be. For hundreds of metres, waves of shattered ground are frozen in time like a snapshot of rough sea suddenly set in stone.

The Last Stand: a monument to the sheer destructive power of the Praelatus. The doorstep of the world, watched over in perpetuity by the great palace, eclipsed by the light of the beacon shining from its highest tower. None dare to linger in this place. It is a mass grave, a haunting reminder of the last days of the Great War.

The Reaper kneels for a handful of dust. She inhales, strokes at the pyramid of sand in her palm, feeling for the tiniest remnant of her ancestors. How many of them died here? Thousands? Tens of thousands? What must it have been like to bring such a force to bear against such godlike power, to fight alongside a legion of her countrymen.

Each wave of rock represents the death of dozens. Such power, such a brutal display of force. The futility is comical. She laughs. She sees what it must have been to march against tsunami after tsunami of cold, inanimate stone, and she feels the cold shadow of it creep over her, she feels the hopelessness of their historic endeavor.

Between the waves, there are statues. Huge stone golems, twice the size of anyone of her kind. They had been animated with a singular purpose: to prevent the approach. Even now, rusted suits of armor bearing the sigil of her cause are held in place by the golems, trapped and smothered in a crushing embrace that will last for all eternity. The sight reminds her of her own calling, the gelid embrace of death.

She dances around man-sized spikes of ice that refuse to melt, touches the vapor that swirls around them, eternal candles of finality to deter the invaders. She pauses and squats by an empty suit of armor impaled on an impossible icicle. Its wearer is long dead, eaten away piece by frozen piece over the decades. She strokes its sweating helmet, tastes it. It burns her tongue. She grins.

The Reaper sings as she reaches out to stroke invisible threads of vibration, affectionately pawing at them like a child. She sings, but it is not song—she plays with the notes in mimicry of discordant frequencies, the song of the world, the song of the moon, she feels them. From the base of her spine, the vibrations emanate through her being, animating her, playing her like a marionette. The sensation is ecstasy, and she gasps in pleasure as the duality of force rocks her in a microscopic dance that only she can feel.

A crack in the land vents a stream of latent energy, not of heat, or gas, but of light. It's an echo, the cry of the dead released from its tomb, welcoming her with a beam of impossible color swirling and writhing like snakes in a basket, racing to escape into the open sky. She hears the cries of her fallen progenitors follow it on the wind.

She does not feel sorrow or pain. She is not affected by this place as others of her kind are. She is a tool, sharpened to perfection, poised in wait. The wind avoids her, she is nothing. She is the darkness that awaits all, the watcher, the fear of what lies between worlds. She waits.

She eyes the tower that eyes her back, challenging it, grinning from ear to ear in defiance. Does he watch her now? Does he weigh her purpose against his desire to protect his people? Does the great and powerful protector care at all for the pitiful desires of lesser beings? She waits.

She waits for his confirmation of the writ—the Reaper's writ. For with his approval, the writ becomes law, and the hunt can begin. She will bring death's embrace with her into the Halls of Venn, to her unsuspecting target.

The hooded figure pulls her death mask over her face and watches from afar. Fashioned after the skull of a great reptile, long extinct, it serves dual purposes: to intimidate, and to dehumanize the wearer. She sniffs for her prey through the beast's nostrils. She listens for his heartbeat in the great symphony of life. She sees his outline in the great sea of thought, and licks her lips.

A hooded, skull-masked figure watches from afar. She watches and she waits.

FIFTEEN

Intent

THE GRAND MASTER awoke with a start, lurching upright with the silk sheets clasped between his fingers. He held a hand to his throbbing temple and replayed the words of his master.

Compose yourself, Grand Master.

Harsh morning light blinded him through a slit in the curtain. He shielded his eyes and rose to begin his morning ritual.

The previous day marked the first in a lifetime that he had not completed his definition ritual. The lack of discipline wore heavily on his mind. For all he'd achieved in mastery over himself, the basic Daralarian weaknesses of grief, shame, regret, fear, and doubt were no less ready to assault him on this day than any other. These were battles that were never won. Such mastery was never attained, merely borrowed. The prayer of definition was only the start of each battle in the long war.

He washed, dressed, and knelt before the window in his study: a marble arch with double, oak-framed glass doors. The view swept out over the Last Stand and to the palace beyond. A daily reminder of the conflict that had taken so much—a conflict that was as much a threat to the realm as it ever had been—and the fragility of the peace that his society balanced upon.

'I am the master of my fate,' he began. 'I steel my soul against the darkness and stride boldly into the light. In this moment, and the next, I am unwavering. My purpose is definite. My focus is true.'

Venn-Dor opened his eyes and held his right palm in the light.

'Today I carry out the wishes of my lord.'

He smiled, and rose to his feet. His gaze passed over his desk, at the neglected work that had sat idle since the girl had been chosen for advancement. To his left, a glass cabinet loomed. Within it, his staff lay, untouched for years, a daily test of his humility. He cast his heavy gaze up its length. A fine example, carved from a tree that died during the Moonfall. At its head, a white lightstone cast its glow, held in place by a finely carved depiction of the tree itself, its miniature branches wrapped around the stone.

He opened the case and reached out toward the staff, but his hand faltered. An oath to oneself is sacred. He would not break it today.

As VENN-DOR MADE the journey toward the dorms, he flicked through the day's messages. The most concerning note was that his presence had been requested in Hall Two, Staine's hall. As the request had not come from the Hall Master himself, he was probably absent. Which suggested he knew that his fate had been sealed. Perhaps his family had ears in the palace. He frowned and placed the note back in his robes, nodding politely at passing staff who fell silent, surprised at his presence.

He knocked three times and took a step back, before the girl opened the door and blushed, bowing before him.

'Miss Renia.'

'Grand Master, I am honored. Please enter.'

The girl stood in an apron, flushed, cleaning equipment scattered around the space. He nodded approvingly.

'Tidy house, tidy mind?'

She kept her gaze from him. 'Just so, sir.'

He smiled, attempting to disarm her. 'Do you remember the last time we spoke?'

'Not well, sir.'

'You were just a girl, barely able to speak when Molan brought you before me. I have to admit, you surpassed my expectations.'

He saw fear in her eyes when she eventually looked up. Fear and frustration.

'I have failed you, sir.'

He gave her a slow nod. 'How so?'

'I lost track of a priceless work. I lost control of myself. I injured my Hall Master.'

'Two of those things are true.'

She flashed surprise. Hope perhaps. He continued. 'Which book are you currently working on?'

'*Lightstone: A Practical Study*, sir.'

'How do you find it?'

The girl beamed, animation incarnate.

'Fascinating! It's a dream come true. The sheer number of practical uses for lightstone—it's awe inspiring. And to think of all the possible applications that we are yet to discover—'

She continued on for several minutes before Venn-Dor held up his hand, grinning.

'Yes, yes. I'm starting to understand why Molan pressed so hard to have you school here.'

Renia blushed at him.

'Do you feel ready to return to your work?'

She began to remove her apron. 'Absolutely. I would have returned already had the doctor not insisted I rest until tomorrow.'

Eager too. That was fortunate. The Grand Master waved her off. 'Tomorrow will be fine.'

She looked at him expectantly, her frustration held at bay by a hair.

He made to take his leave, turning back to her before he reached the door. 'I had a safe installed in Petor's old office. Here is the key. From now on the only two people with access are in this room. There can be no more distraction, no more loss of control. Do you understand?'

She nodded her thanks.

'Good day, Miss Renia.'

JEFF'S WALK TO the Gatehold did nothing for his knee. The road was uneven in places, creating all manner of hazards that threatened to unbalance his limping approach. Still, the fresh air was a nice change.

The grounds of the great halls were large enough to house the majority of the academic and administrative staff, but small enough to be defensible. The Halls of Venn held enough lightstone to turn the tide of a war with the south, and as such, its outer limits looked more like a bastion than a place of learning. This meant that the message he carried held enough weight to disrupt the lives of many of the menial staff that moved in and out of the Gatehold on a daily basis from their homes in Venntown. It was not a step he took lightly, but one he understood, and had expected, given the circumstances.

He entered the hold and presented himself to the Mohruscan guards on watch.

'Need to see your captain,' he said to the closest, who nodded and trudged away down the corridor.

The entrance hall was functional, sporting strong stone walls adorned with enough ceremonial armor and weaponry to deter bad behavior, but welcoming enough for Jeff to sit on a bench by a small fire and enjoy a moment's peace.

He pulled his pocket watch from his jacket idly, regarding it with indecision. The ornate piece had been with him for a long time and showed signs of wear. He'd kept it in his quarters for most of the past year out of worry for its condition, but recent events had drawn him back to it. It was a comfort to him, a reminder of his past life and of his weaknesses. He stroked the scratches in its bronze casing with affection, drifting between memories.

'Chief.'

Jeff stood. 'Captain Garamond.' He hadn't noticed her approach. The captain stood before him, armored in full plate, freshly crusted with salt from ocean spray. She sniffed, and wiped her reddened nose with a rag. She had enough purple in her skin for people to see she'd spent time in the Wastes. Jeff had been grateful for that when he'd arrived years ago; it meant she probably knew how to hold a wall.

She adjusted her white, braided hair, looking him up and down. 'Wasn't expecting you,' she said.

'You're not going to like it.'

She shrugged. 'More cultists come to throw themselves on our spears?'

Jeff's frown deepened. 'Worse.'

The captain rolled her eyes at him, and released an exasperated sigh. 'You know I hate being a tour guide, Jeff. Get someone el—'

'You have to close the gates, Garamond.'

She straightened, nonplussed, before placing one hand on her hip, rattling her armor plates. 'Come again?'

'Lock it down. Orders from on high.'

The captain looked up at the ceiling. 'Wonderful. How long?'

'Could be weeks. We're doing a full sweep of the grounds. We're going to need you to call back troops from Venntown to assist.'

'How many?'

'Half, maybe.'

Garamond paced, jaw clenched in frustration. Jeff allowed her the moment. He respected the captain and had no desire to do this to her.

'Orders are orders,' she said. 'If the cultists or the raiders get wind of this, they will have a field day with the peasants in town. I hope you're ready.'

Jeff nodded—nothing he didn't know already.

'We're trained to defend this place from the outside, Jeff. Not from within. You get a riot situation here and I'm not confident we'll be able to deal with it cleanly.'

'What can I do? I have no say over this.'

She stared at him flatly. 'What about the Reaper? I don't have the authority to detain her.'

'Let me worry about that. You'll have to make an exception to let her in, but have her sent directly to me.'

The pair shared a moment of bemusement before she started barking orders at her soldiers.

'Looks like we're in for an interesting few weeks,' she said. 'I'm glad you came, saved me sending for you.'

'Something else for me to deal with?'

She looked to his knee. 'It's a tricky path, but you should see this for yourself.'

THEY WALKED TOGETHER toward the cliffs on the eastern side of the grounds. Armored as she was, Garamond walked with purpose, each stride expressing her rank. Jeff admired her confidence. She wasn't overly tall, or brutish, but she carried an air of ferocity and discipline that left no doubt of her battle prowess. He had walked like that once. Proud, competent, fierce.

The winds rose, and salt water misted Jeff's face as they descended the cliffs. Each step sent a wave of dull pain up through his thigh. He grimaced into the gray crashing waves, breathing heavily.

'There,' Garamond shouted over the rush of the surf. She halted and pointed toward the rocks below.

A broken body lay face down on the stone. One leg twisted backward at an unnatural angle. Its shoulder was a bloody mess, shattered into scraps of meat. It wouldn't be long before the crows removed the arm entirely and took off with it. Garamond had her soldiers rigging a pulley system to retrieve the remains. Two of her guards stood by the body, waving the rope down toward it.

'Do you know who it is yet?'

The captain grave a grim nod. 'The one you told us to watch for. Tannis Rutger.'

'Shit,' he muttered.

'What?'

Another dead end. Jeff sighed, wiping the spray from his brow. The wind whistled in his ears. He raised his voice over the noise. 'What happened?'

'Looks like a nasty fall. As for why he decided to go for a climb, that's for you to figure out.'

He stared into the captain's eyes. As gray as the sea that assaulted them. She smiled in apology, and offered her wrist to pull him up toward the rocky path they'd descended by.

Something must have seriously spooked the lad; nobody tried to leave by the cliff route unless they were terrified, highly skilled, or just plain stupid.

'Garamond, did he have anything on him? A book?'

'No,' she shouted. 'A bag of coins and a few items of clothing.'

'Tell your men to keep an eye out for anything in the surf. A book, specifically.'

'Right you are, chief.'

They struggled back up the path, Garamond offering her help where she felt he needed it. Jeff said nothing else. Tannis had been his only lead, his only hope of discovering the identities of the rest of the circle members. His head reeled. Another closed door, another answer denied him.

DAYS HAD PASSED since Dail's encounter with the xentt. As he understood it, it had taken twelve hours to remove the creature from his head. He felt as if they had done so with a hammer.

The doctor had given him a salve for the bite marks, though his eyes would remain bloodshot for a while and the internal wounds from the tentacles would take time to heal fully. More worrisome were the larvae it had pumped into his system. He felt them fluttering and pressing around his organs, and though he'd been assured that they would die within days and pass through him normally, the sensation brought panic, and shame—sullied him.

It had taken a day or so for him to recall the event. He spent hours in a fugue state as his brain fought to hold his sanity intact. There was a numbness to it, like it had happened to someone else. He had no memory of what he'd said under the disgusting creature's influence, no idea how much he had given away, who he'd implicated. He felt guilt, but only in anticipation of what he could have done. It was a complex feeling. The experience had left him violated, scooped out like rotten fruit.

Bed rest for a week, they had said. Like that would stop him. He knew who was to blame, who'd implicated him. *That bitch.* All that hard work, all the love and affection he'd shown her, the care he'd given when she was too preoccupied to look after herself. What was his reward? Suspicion? To be thrown to the wolves, to be head-fucked by a monster?

That bitch.

It was time for her to hear a few hard truths. Dail's breathing labored as he limped toward her door.

That bitch.

TWELVE HOURS.

The scraping of brush bristles was Renia's meditation, a distraction from inaction. The doctor had insisted on bed rest, but staring at the ceiling between bouts of nausea had done nothing for her mental state, so she cleaned. She cleaned everything. Entire cupboards had been emptied and wiped down, every surface dusted and polished, ornaments inspected, and then she'd turned her attention to the floors.

Twelve hours. Twelve hours and she would be back at her desk. Back to her work. Its absence had gnawed at her like an itch she couldn't scratch, each hour away from it driving her further into a state of irritability and restlessness. Even sleep had become a chore.

She wiped the sweat from her brow and stood, stretching to ease her seized muscles.

She'd resolved to finish the entire assignment before her pregnancy rendered her unable to work. It hadn't been easy to accept that this might be her greatest and last project—that she'd reached her peak. Renia was not the type to give up in the middle of a journey. The greater the obstacle placed in her path, the more her desire to push through it, not because she felt a desire to prove herself to anyone else but because in order to believe in herself she had to do battle with that part of her that told her to give up, let go.

She would finish. She would finish, or she'd die trying. It was that simple. Sheer force of will would make it so.

In twelve hours she would be back at her desk, delving into long-forgotten mysteries, letting the tension flow out of her quill with each stroke. Renia paused to enjoy a moment of satisfaction, casting her gaze around the flawless space she'd created.

A dull banging on the door snatched her from her thoughts. Then again, banging, more insistent.

Words died in her mouth as she opened it. It took her a moment to recognize the man stood before her. His face was different; it was more than the cuts and bruises, the swelling had misshaped him, placing his eyes and nose at offsets that fooled her memory. He stood smoldering with murderous intent at the threshold.

'Dail?'

'Bitch!'

She stumbled back into the room as he forced his way in, twisting her ankle on the brush she'd been using to clean the floor. The pain shot through her leg like a spike.

'How could you?' Dail raised his fist as he loomed over her. She backed away in shock, regaining her footing.

'Do you have any idea what they did to me, Renia?'

She looked at him. His left hand was bandaged tightly, bloodshot eyes glared at her from a head wrapped in gauze, traces of cracked blood present near every orifice.

Dail shook, pain leaking out of him through gritted teeth. 'They *ruined* me—' Momentary confusion split his train of thought. 'They—they—' He shook his head as if unable to grasp his thoughts.

'Dail—'

'Don't you *Dail* me. Why, Renia? Why did you do this to me?'

She reset herself, refusing to feel compassion for the man who'd betrayed her. 'What choice did I have? You *stole* from me.'

Dail paused, disbelief turned into laughter that rose from a chuckle to mania.

'That's what this is about? The lightstone? You threw me under the cart for *this?*' He pulled at her hand and slapped something into her palm.

Illuminating her hand and pupils, light danced around the shard, the only connection she had to her childhood. It had been polished to perfection, and seated perfectly and deliberately into a beautiful pendant. Minuscule golden leaves and vines held the shard in place where it hung on a necklace of gold, each ring in the chain had been handmade. The craftsmanship, breathtaking.

Pain shot through her back as she collided with the shelf. The dull ache of new bruising told her that he'd shoved her into the wall.

'Do you like it? Do you know how long I worked on that? A fucking year.'

She fought to breathe, winded.

'A year. Do you know what's hilarious? I was going to return it to you the very same day you came marching up to my door like a lunatic.'

She hit the wall again, wincing as the shelf hit lower, dropping her to her knees.

'That's how much you care about me, isn't it. All you had to do was ask.'

She wheezed. The words wouldn't form. '*Dail.*'

'I'm a thief now, am I? How could you think that I would ruin your career? Do you even know me at all?'

She dizzied as the lack of oxygen robbed her of her senses. She was rising. Dail had her by the lapels, pulling her off her feet. She cried out as he slammed her into the wall.

'Dail.'

'Shut up!'

Stars, her head. What was happening? *Get a grip Renia. He's bouncing your head off the wall.*

She screamed. Instinct took over and she swung toward his face with the pendant in an effort to gouge his eyes.

Time slowed.

Her movements became fluid, each moment stretched out like elastic as an energy ebbed in her gut.

Every hair on her body sharpened as the air around her contracted, pushing in on her senses. A tingling sensation snapped into a stream of energy that manifested itself as arcs of lightning that danced their way through her arm, clutching at Dail's disfigured face. His head jerked, caught as if by a magnetic force as bolts of rage seared his skin, bubbling and blistering as he struggled to open his jaw. Dail started to scream as his eyes boiled in his skull, and every hair on his face evaporated as the gauze erupted in blue flame.

The smell.

Charred flesh flooded her senses. She watched, horrified, as Dail's convulsions turned his scream into a jabber. The lightshard in her hand pulsed with the brilliance of a star, heaving and churning energy from the space between moments as it channeled her intent through the meat of his body.

Energy drained from her as water rushes from a hole in a bucket. Her eyes began to sag at the exertion. The power, the overwhelming force of her will battered his flesh as it held him helpless in her grasp.

She released him.

Dail fell to the ground in a smoldering heap, wheezing and dry-heaving, groaning in agony.

She watched, dumbstruck. He clawed at the floor, pulling himself away from her. She felt the pain in her knee through a filter as she dropped, delayed, as if she'd been wearing armor. Every part of her felt numb. Every breath amplified tenfold.

He wept, clutching his smoking head, lying in the fetal position.

'Dail.'

The word echoed, dull, muted, as if underwater. Her vision blurred, blackness drew in from the corners of her awareness. She felt her consciousness escaping her grasp.

'Dail.'

Floating now, the word came from somewhere else. An invisible thread tethered her to her body from the top of her head, it bristled and waned as she slipped away.

'I'm pregnant.'

The blackness smothered her vision. Invisible tides pulled her away. She let go.

THE REAPER RETURNS to the palace, striding along the dusty esplanade that runs from the edge of the Last Stand to the palace gates. Dust, rich with bone, salt, and ash announces her arrival. She makes no attempt to mask her approach. It is a slow, stalking march, measured, undaunted.

The sentinel that awaits her stands in a haze of distorted reflection, its armor a brilliant white pearlescent barrier, a vision of superiority. She cocks her head, bubbling with mockery, hungry for an opportunity to sharpen her blade on its flawless finish.

'Halt.' The creature speaks. She stops before it. It stands over her, seven feet tall, immovable. It looks out into the distance, with no regard for her or her mission. Its face is unreadable, hairless, unnatural. She looks upon the glowing scars that decorate its forehead, the massive lightstones that sit recessed into its armor.

'The Praelatus accepts your offer,' the thing says.

She hefts the pack from around her shoulder and holds it out before the *Exalted*. The stones within clink, but lie at rest.

With only a short inspection, the soldier takes the trade. It looks down at her at last, and returns to her the writ: approved, marked with a drop of glowing blood.

And so it begins.

Sixteen

Between

Hands. The swing of her father's detached hands wakes her. As regular as a clock. The grinding of rope anchors her mind. Her vision clears to purple and she finds herself in the last place she felt whole. Home.

Winds whip at her skirt. The last light of day is upon her as she stands before the ruin of her childhood. Jarring fragments of sound lash at her and threaten to unravel the scene manifested around her. The roaring of flame, the muffled discontent of a crowd, the stony proclamations of a warlord.

A sobbing rises, her own voice but not her own, a voice she used to know. A weakness she used to know. She is caught between sympathy and scorn.

Still her father's hands swing in the wind, harassed by insects and fine sand, they decompose. She feels them slipping away.

A snap, the sound coming from her inner ear. Grinning faces make their entrance, only to flee at her scrutiny, never quite there, but never quite absent—whispers from the place between sleep and waking.

The echo of a scream alone without its source draws her attention back to the hands. The sound of her father in his final moments. It tears at her, wrenches her innards. Her father's hand is moving, forming a fist, index finger pointing down. She follows it. A puddle of mercury lays beneath. She drops to her knees to look within. Her reflection awaits her, riddled with sorrow and self doubt. She looks on in horror as her skin begins to sag. Gravity exerts itself on the flesh under her eyes. She is rotting.

She is standing again. The movement happened in a blink. She is frozen in her step. Her father's hands are no longer pointing. They continue to swing, uncaring. The sobbing returns. There's a pull at her dress. Something is tugging at her dress. She turns.

Her own face looks up at her. The child she was, a face she's forgotten. She tries to understand but she already knows, and doesn't know. It doesn't matter. The child is looking up at her through welling tears.

'Why are you crying?' She kneels to her own eye level.

The child touches her head, and the world disappears from beneath her as she's pulled through an open window into the night, and into the embrace of a man who regrets his part in it.

His name...She can't remember his name. She doesn't struggle anymore. She knows that he will save her.

He is in her face, she cannot move, she feels his breath, he's so close. 'You have to leave this place behind.'

She is in his arms again. They are moving.

Her awareness is spinning; she is in two places at once. Half of her is pushed back. A gust threatens to hurl her into a canyon so deep that she cannot see the bottom. She feels his grip. He's still holding her. She's not supposed to be here.

There's chanting from below. Waves of purple light dance within the canyon. They sing to her, 'Away, away.'

The man's voice is inside her. 'You can't stay here. Fly away, little one.'

He lets go.

THE GRAND MASTER steeled himself against the pressure of his lord's presence. 'She has lapsed into a coma.'

She will wake.

He gritted his teeth hard. The throbbing only intensified, compressing his brain.

Why do you suffer, when you need not?

He did need to. It was his penance, his anchor. Without it, his disease would multiply. He would lose his humility. More would suffer, or die.

'It's important to me, my lord.'

Echoes of a dead man bounced from the chamber walls. A voice he had almost forgotten. Youthful, determined, words of encouragement, hubris. A request to launch an operation that would purge the halls of southern agents.

Raellon.

A tear rolled down his cheek. He felt the pressure subside fractionally as the Praelatus considered him. A welcome relief.

You have punished yourself for long enough, Doratus. It was his will. You are not responsible.

'I would not have allowed it, had I abstained then as I do now.'

And you believe he would have listened?

'Perhaps not.'

Venn-Dor let his head sag. All the years that had passed, he'd wrapped his grief in stone, believing he could master it, that he could ignore its call. The book had undone that. It had opened the door, and allowed every unresolved thread to loose itself.

Mastery of one's self is not an exercise in denial. You know this much. You believe your gifts invite hubris, endanger you and those around you, cloud your decisions. You deny them as you deny your guilt over Raellon's death. We no longer have the time for self-indulgence, Doratus. The girl will need your help. When the time comes, you must pick up your staff.

RENIA.

She is falling. She closes her eyes in anticipation of the end. She feels the prickling of light at her fingertips. Power courses through her veins. She can hear screaming. Burning flesh fills her nostrils. The sensation of laughter is in her throat, though she does not laugh; she hears it from somewhere else, a venomous laughter that taunts her, tempts her. She opens her eyes.

Purple phantoms dance in free fall with her, faces she is yet to know: an old man glaring at her over a stack of books, the disapproval of a mentor, the lecherous gaze of a pervert, the measured appraisal of authority, the jabbering form of a man aflame.

The visage of the burning man falls through her and she feels the heat. The laughter returns.

Renia.

She is falling. Falling faster and faster into the gaping maw of the world, the great scar of the Moonfall. The whispers slap at her: *Away, away.* The power inside her builds. Currents of force, an impossible vibration paralyzes her. It is not pain, but something else entirely. It is a blockage, a held breath.

Release.

She is somewhere else. Shapes resolve around her, familiar pipework, boards of old oak. The chair creaks in complaint, her back aches. The familiar scent of paper and ink greets her. Before her lies an ancient tome. She reveres it. It holds the secrets she promised to uncover. She rubs her eyebrow in frustration. She is distracted.

This isn't her desk. She isn't in Hall Three, she's in an apartment.

This isn't her apartment.

An infant is crying. It's her responsibility. A man is shouting now.

'Renia, Renia.'

She turns in anger. 'I'm working.' The words are hollow; she doesn't feel them.

The cry becomes a scream. She needs to feed the baby.

Renia.

SHE BLINKS. IT's dark now. Her back aches. The infant suckles. It's difficult to write with the baby at her breast.

The urge to sneeze threatens her. She doesn't want to bang the baby's head or ruin her work. She bites her tongue so hard it bleeds, and the feeling passes. Her eyes strain against the lamplight; everything aches. The man is shouting again, 'Renia. Toilet!' She squeezes the quill to the point of breaking it.

SHE BLINKS. SHE's standing in the twilight at the foot of a bed she doesn't recognize. The man is Dail. His voice has changed on account of the burns.

She did this to him.

She is trapped in a prison of her own guilt, watching the sleeping figures of her dependents: her infant child, her invalid partner. She sobs silently, desperate not to wake either in this rare moment of peace and independence.

Renia.

She turns. There's nobody there. Curious, she steps into the study, to the desk that has become both her cage and her escape. She squints into the room. The book is glowing from within. Odd reflections of green and gold highlight the space from the wrong angles.

Renia.

She's aware of something calling to her, but she can't hear the voice. She winces at the creak of the floorboards as she approaches the desk. The page dances, words ripple outwards from the centerfold like water. The hissing of a thousand voices rattle her, *Away, away.* A face is forming on the page, ancient text reforming into frown lines. Ink pools into breathing holes as it fights against the surface from the place between places. It's a face she knows, a face she's forgotten.

It breaks the barrier. A phantom of green mist envelops her, its mouth agape. She screams into nothing. All is black.

VENN-DOR KEPT his head bowed, fixated on the wisps of steam that reached from the stone he knelt on. 'She broke the law.'

He grimaced, feeling like a petulant child questioning a parent. The girl offended him. Though he hadn't realized it until this moment. It wasn't her age, or her thirst for the secrets that his order held dear—he actually appreciated both. It was the lack of restraint, the wanton abandoning of control, the disregard for consequence. It made her unreliable, and therefore unfit to replace the Shepherd.

'She's impulsive, reactionary,' he continued. 'Unlicensed use of magic is punishable by death in such cases. Forgive me, Your Light, but what gives this girl the right to continue, to thrive, where so many brilliant minds lie in the ground or rotting in our cells? Minds that have enriched the lives of our people in ways that we could never have foreseen.'

Silence fell, and for a long moment the Grand Master expected the wrath of his lord and protector to come.

You are right.

He staggered, flicking his eyelids as he dared to look upon the face of his master. The glimpse, however short, seared the image of the Praelatus's saddened face on his retinas.

You see clearly enough. But fail to look beyond the wall of grief you have erected. Renia is not Raellon, Doratus. See the truth of your misplaced anger.

Venn-Dor tucked his head to the left, enlightened yet ashamed.

You do not see as I see, Doratus. For I have watched this girl from the moment she was born. And her mother before her. And her grandmother before her. She is no stray, Doratus. Molan did not come across her by fate. It was by my order that he should watch over her, and bring her back to us.

His hands began to shake. His body was starting to crack under the strain of the energy that buffeted him. Who was this girl? What did she mean to them?

I have no doubt, Doratus, that you would not suffer before me now if you had your staff. Because you would have already sensed who Renia is. You would hear the song that imprisons her mind even now, and understand that her impulses are not entirely her own. Now take my hand, and I will show you why she is important, why she is the only candidate to become Shepherd, and why it is necessary to allow her to complete her journey—no matter the cost.

Home. Blades of grass tickle her ankles as she stands naked in the Wastes. Only it's not the Wastes, not as she knows them. The air is sweet, ripe with the scent of life. Insects chatter and bustle, running their errands. The absence of the purple illumination that she knows so well is a relief, like the first breath out of water. She is free.

Where her home should be there are creatures at play, swimming in a watering hole. Giant leaves shield them from the brilliant golden light of the sun. She's never seen plants of such proportions, and stares, aghast at their majesty. A pack of hounds laps at the water. It is clear, free from contaminants.

She shakes her head. *This is all wrong.*

The rumble of a thousand tiny feet from behind draws her attention. She stands in awe as a titanic snail casts its shadow over her. The sheer scale of it drives her back in shock as it passes her without care.

You're here.

She hears him. He's here.

She whips around in anticipation, desperately searching for the source. 'Dad?'

She runs for the tree line. The dancing creatures pay her no mind as she disturbs the long grass. The earth is like carpet beneath her, soft and welcoming with every step. The cool air bathes her naked body as she bounces toward the voice.

Renia.

'Dad.'

She stops. The voice comes from over her shoulder.

'Hello, Moonpie.'

She drops to her knees, a child again, caked in dirt. Her dress is filthy. Her mother will be furious.

She feels her father's arm around her shoulder. She knows he is there but she can't bring herself to look at his face. Her stomach turns. Hot tears burn her cheeks and she shudders into the nook beneath his arm.

'Now, now. It's alright.'

'I'm so sorry, Daddy.'

'Sorry?' He chuckles. 'No. I don't think you have anything to be sorry for.'

She wraps her arms around his waist. The familiar smell is a rush, a release from all that burdens her. She feels safe for the first time in an eternity.

'What's the matter, love?'

She laughs. 'I don't know where to start.'

She feels him kiss the top of her head. 'You're not having the best time at the moment, are you?'

She shakes her head.

'Feel like the whole world is trying to break you?'

She nods.

'You have to learn to ride the waves, sweetheart.'

'I don't understand.'

'The waves…'

The scene dissolves into nothing and the two disembodied voices are cast adrift in a sea of time. Memories, moments, and emotions ebb and flow around them.

'Don't move,' he says. All is still, and for a moment all is calm. The silence is deafening. She waits. Seconds stretch into minutes, minutes into hours, hours into eternity.

It's crushing her. A silent scream. She yearns for activity, for life. She thrashes out.

'Dad, come back.'

A rush of memory, visions of moments that have happened and will happen that send her spiraling deeper into the sea.

'Do you see, sweetheart?' The voice is all around her. 'A life without action, without will, is no life at all.'

Waves of fire, screams, anguish, and regret thrash at her.

'These things aren't happening *to you*, Renia. You are happening *to them*.'

'I don't understand. How do I make it stop?'

'You can't make it stop, Renia. It's who you are.'

She starts to cry. 'No!'

The vision stops. The smell of pollen leads her awareness back to the watering hole. Her father pulls her in tight.

'You will understand, sweetheart.'

They pause there for a while. The sound of running water comforts her.

'You were never going to stand still, love. You have your mother's blood.'

She's older again now. She looks down at her hands, turning them over. 'Sometimes I just want it to stop.'

'To stop is to die.'

'So what am I to do, Dad?' She frowns, still reeling from the images of her future, the apartment, Dail, her child. 'Accept life in a box? Become a nursemaid? The best parts of me are dead in that place.'

'In that place, yes.'

'What does that mean?'

'Look around you, Renia.'

The view spins from one place to another. A clearing, large enough for a small village. Children play, laughing and chasing, dancing in the glow of the morning sun. She sees a people at peace, a nomadic type, no writings or complexity adorn their homestead. A sense of peace rolls through her, and she yearns to stay here, to learn.

The children surround her, they are stroking at her skin, confused. They aren't like her. They resemble plant life, skin of green, bark covering patches of their bodies. Renia kneels to inspect what appears to be a little girl's third eye, but it's not an eye. It's a lightstone. They all have one. Renia laughs; she understands.

The elders are shouting. There's a disagreement over something. She listens but the language is strange to her. She can't make it out. One of them is pointing at the sky, yelling at the others. She follows the vector of his arm upward. She sees what it is that troubles them.

The ball of flame in the sky. She's seen it before, in the wreckage of this place. It's Luna.

Geysers burst from the earth around her, bleeding light upward into the sky. The hiss of a thousand whispers accompanies the eruption. She is unmade, her skin breaking into shards that splinter and float in the wind. A single shard becomes stone, the gift from her father. It glows with the light of a star, a storm in a shell. She feels the power again. It reforms her.

'Dad. Are you there?'

Always.

She stands on the roof of the Halls of Venn. The air dock. She's dressed in clothes fit for an adventurer. The palace looms beyond, a sentinel in the dead of night, its beacon ablaze in the darkness. She looks out over the scarred landscape toward it and feels its gaze upon her.

'What am I supposed to do?' She roars into the light. 'What choice do I have?'

There is always a choice.

'There is no choice. I can't escape it.'

The light bursts into an orb around her. Petals of starlight spiral in dance, pouring into the lightstone shard necklace.

Every choice has its price, love. The time will come for you to decide.

'Decide what?'

Whether or not you are willing to pay it.

Her father's voice begins to fade, back into the place within her, where he lives forever. She panics.

'Dad, don't leave me again. I don't understand.'

You will…up…pie…is…coming.

'What?'

Wake up!

VOICES CLAMOR OVER each other in a cacophony of emotion as night falls on Venntown. The Reaper hears laughter, lust, rage, the whooping of hounds, a chef calling out table orders.

The air is rich with the scent of life—smoke, food, ale, sex, waste. The Reaper takes a deep breath and inhales all. She smiles and licks her lips as below her lookout a griddle hisses with the sound of searing meat.

The bell tower affords her the perfect spot to drink in the chaos of the scene. The narrow streets that border the stone walls of the Halls of Venn are packed with poorly built terraced houses that lean precariously inward toward the muddy roads that carve into the town. The people lout about below, oblivious to her presence.

She removes her death mask and casts her gaze over the scene. A traveling merchant curses and kicks the wheel of his cart. She laughs as he cries out, hopping to and fro. In a window across the street a woman screams at her half-naked husband, waving undergarments in front of her that are clearly not her own.

Before the great gates of the Halls of Venn, a crowd gathers. Merchants, servants, and a troupe of whores wave papers and shout into the faces of the guards barring their path.

The gates are closed.

The guards point away, and wave off the complaints of the mass, shaking their heads and barging those who dare to press too close. The Reaper nods, and casts her gaze up toward the watch tower of the southern wing. The signal fire there flickers, once, then dies briefly, before turning a shade of green.

She grins.

It is time.

SEVENTEEN

Arrival

RENIA, RENIA, RENIA. The rhythmic chanting of a madman. Over and over it came. She woke slowly, allowing dream and reality to settle their differences.

'Welcome back,' said the Grand Master.

Her head throbbed with the dull ache of reality. Despite the pain, she was glad to be back in the relative safety of the hospital wing. Renia felt at her abdomen for some trace of the child within. She didn't know how, but she sensed its distress.

She eyed Venn-Dor in confusion at the rush of unfamiliar sound. A ruckus echoed into the space, a distant protest or commotion of some sort. She tried to speak but found her voice hoarse. 'Water...Please.'

Her name still rang through the wing. Dail. Visions from her dream flashed back at her. She pushed them aside as she accepted the glass.

'Quite a display. I wasn't sure you'd be brave enough to return to us.'

She detected the disdain in the Grand Master's tone, but felt nothing. The time she'd spent unconscious had left her numb. She tried to move her legs and found them weak. 'How is he?'

The Grand Master simply frowned at her in response.

Her hands shook with effort as she pulled the sheets away.

'What are you doing, Renia. Sit down.' His attempts to restrain her were halted by the fierce look she gave him.

'Help me up. I need to see him.'

Reluctantly, he took her weight as they struggled to the room they'd left Dail in. The sight of him hit Renia in a gust. She gasped at the broken figure strapped to the bed, blistered and bandaged, a hairless, charred husk.

'Renia! Renia! Renia!' He rocked back and forth against the restraints, screaming in pain.

'That's all he does,' whispered Venn-Dor.

It was her fault. She reached for the necklace that had allowed such devastation only to find it missing. She blinked away the tears, and rounded on the Grand Master.

'Where is it?'

'Where it should be, with the rest of the unmarked light-stone.'

She flickered annoyance. 'It's a shard, no larger than a pebble.'

'And look what you were able to do with it. Where did you even receive such training? You're a scribe, not a magician.'

She didn't know. She looked back to Dail, sadness pooling in her gut.

'Will he recover?'

'The doctors aren't sure. He should have died.'

Renia shot a look of venom at her Grand Master for the remark. She hobbled to the father of her child, taking his hand and shushing him.

'What will they do with him?'

'What would you have us do with him? He has no living family, save you and your unborn child.'

Some family. She wiped the sweat from his blistered chest as the guilt bit into her. 'Why are you giving me a choice? I should be tried for this crime.'

The Grand Master sneered. 'Oh I agree.' He stood unmoving at the foot of the bed. 'You have work to resume.'

'I don't understand.'

'Neither do I. But unlike you, I don't let my personal feelings cloud my judgment. Despite the fact that you show blatant disregard for our laws, and seem to be ignorant to the consequences of your actions, I've been ordered to ensure that you complete your work. It irks me, Renia. Many have died for less, or suffered worse. I don't believe you deserving of the opportunity you've been given simply because of who you are.'

'What is that supposed to mean?'

Venn-Dor blew out his nostrils.

Renia gritted her teeth as she returned her attention to the quivering man she'd mauled.

'Do you hear the chaos outside? That's the sound of people protesting at being trapped here, unable to return to their families. This project of yours, that blasted journal, it's affected the lives of every soul working for this institution. Before long we'll be searching the whole complex, room by room, the unrest will leave a bad taste in their mouths for years.'

Renia didn't care. Nothing he could say would make her feel worse than she already did. Dail didn't deserve this, nobody did.

'Are you listening, girl?'

She nodded.

'You're being moved. A suitable apartment has been prepared for you, somewhere you can live and work without presenting a threat to anyone else.'

She nodded again. What did it matter now?

'I'll give you a minute to say your goodbyes. We may have to move Mister Svelt to an institution more suited to his condition.'

'No,' she said.

'What's that?'

'No. I'll take care of him.'

The Grand Master looked over his nose at the young woman, and inhaled sharply.

'I'm not accustomed to repeating myself, Renia. You have a job to do.'

She looked up, undaunted. 'I'll finish the work. He comes with me.'

PISTORIOUS STAINE HELD his nose against the gap in the planks that made up a large packing crate. He'd lost track of how long he'd spent inside it with no sunlight to measure time by, and the apparent panic of the menial staff making it impossible to judge the changes in their shifts.

Paranoia had become his friend. Entrusting his safety to an ally he didn't know he could trust wore on him, fresh doubts assaulting him by the hour. How had he been foiled so early in his plan? Had Jeff been watching him all along? Had their chance encounter been by design?

He'd lost count of how many times he'd reached up to push the lid off the crate, to make his own escape, only to allow thoughts of being hunted, captured, and killed to override his fleeting bravery.

Only one person could protect him from a Reaper. There was only one place in Luna Ruinam where the laws of the Great Protector did not apply. He had to take his chances here, to trust in fate.

Staine flinched as the crate lid slid to the side, allowing a pillar of light to burst into the tiny space he inhabited. He squinted into the open air of the basement.

'Relax, it's me.'

He snatched a tray of food from the man and began to savage its contents, while his ally replaced the bucket of filth from beside him.

Staine mumbled, his mouth full of bread, 'What's happening?'

'Shh. Keep your voice low.'

He blinked, still waiting for his eyes to adapt. 'How long must I stay here, Londo?'

'They've closed the gates. No cargo may pass. I'm not sure if that includes airship. But I doubt we could use that to get you out of here.'

'I'm a sitting duck here. The Reaper will surely find me.'

'Trust me, these crates have been here so long they're part of the furniture. Nobody comes down here, and no one expects to find anything valuable in them.'

'You still believe *he* will take me?'

'Why wouldn't he? You're a Staine. And with your brother's death and your father's ambitions growing, who knows what will occur over the coming years.'

'My brother?'

'Yes.'

His heart leaped. Dueling feelings of guilt and elation wrestled to the fore. 'Which brother?'

'Dorian.' Londo frowned. 'You didn't know?'

Images of his brother's laughing face shifted through his thoughts. He shook them off. *Good,* he thought. *Let him be dead.* His father too; they deserved it. 'My father cares not for my life.'

'Perhaps not. But he does care for power. Suppose the Praelatus falls. Who do you think the people will turn to to protect them? Your father will have need of his remaining sons then. And the Faithful will be there to provide what he needs.'

Staine tweaked at a distant sound. He pondered the man's words. How could the Praelatus fall? 'You truly believe that the Faithful have the power to dethrone the Earth Breaker?'

'Our leader is strong and wise. He has foreseen the death of the Great Protector, your sleeping king. They call us cultists, savages, but we are Faithful, we are everywhere. The Praelatus *will* die, and *we* shall rise from the depths and spread the truth across all of Luna Ruinam. And *you* will be part of that.'

'Yes.' He nodded. 'Yes, I will.'

Londo held his finger up and looked to the left. 'I have to go. I'll be back when I can. Try to stay sane.'

The crate lid began to slide back into place, and with it the thin sliver of light died, leaving Staine to his thoughts, and the hope that he would survive to see the vision of the world they had discussed.

A new world.

JEFF GROWLED AT the scattered papers he'd recovered and laid out on the main table of the security office. He stood hunched over them, mumbling to himself. Tannis dead, Staine missing. Dail had been unceremoniously fried by Renia, rendering him effectively useless, and Renia's days were numbered.

It had taken Jinger a considerable amount of time to wade through the boxes in his office and piece together the fractured report of Raellon's death. Why had it been scattered? Out of all the paperwork that littered his space, this report was not the one he expected to be treated with such carelessness.

He straightened and made for the cells, straight to Mako. The report he held in his hand was a witness statement. The jabbering old man had been there. Raellon practically fell at his feet. Something else had happened here. Something that the report failed to mention. He couldn't believe for a minute that the great Venn-Dor would close the book on this incident with so many holes in it.

He padded into the dimness of the cell block distracted and without autonomy, willing his mind to make a connection, to show him something he had missed.

Mako sat on the edge of his cot, counting his fingers.

'Mako?'

The old man had a distant look in his eye. He mumbled about threads, and missing time.

'Mako?'

Focus slowly returned to the old man. With it, came enthusiasm. 'Ah, Jeff.'

'I need to ask you some questions, Mako.' He waved the paper in front of the bars. 'Why didn't you mention that you had filed a witness report after Raellon's death?'

'I did?'

Jeff kept his gaze firm.

'I did! We saw it, the lad and I.'

'You were with Staine, the night of Raellon's death. You saw him fall from the roof.'

Mako winced at the memory. He nodded once, grinding his teeth.

'Terrible mess, it was.'

'What else can you tell me about that night? Did you see anyone else? On the roof?'

'It was dark. And raining.'

Jeff sighed, and made a conscious effort to keep his frustration in check.

'Taro-tarotaro said there was another. But I didn't see them. He swore by it though. Said I was too distracted by the body parts. I can tell you who he saw if you like.'

Jeff raised his eyebrow. The man's imaginary friend knew something about the case that he didn't. Was this Taro-taro some remnant of the mind that Mako had once possessed? A part of himself he'd broken off to protect it from insanity? Jeff couldn't afford to ignore anything at this point.

'Can I see it, Jeff? The watch.'

Jeff looked into the eyes of a madman, at the total lack of coherent thought behind them, and felt a pang of sadness. He pulled the pocket watch from his pocket and handed it to the poor fool.

Mako affectionately ran his fingers over the metal casing, like a parent remembering a lost child. He flipped the cover open and stared in wonder at its face, smiling back at his own name, his maker's mark on the faceplate. For a brief moment, Jeff caught a glimpse of the man that was—the engineer, the scholar. He grinned and met Jeff's gaze, before handing the watch back.

'I can give you a name, but I want you to do something for me, Jeff.'

Jeff tensed, taken aback by the transformation. 'Are you bribing me, old man?'

'Not a bribe, a bargain.'

'What is it that you need, Mako?'

'Release me.'

Jeff scoffed. 'Come on.'

'Let me go, Jeff. We'll make it look like an accident.'

Jeff paused, questions running through his skull. Had it all been an act? All this time, had he been duped? 'You know I can't do that, Mako. I won't. My duty is to the law.'

'A law that prohibits progress, leaves its generation's finest minds to wilt in cells for daring to challenge it?'

'Law is law, Mako. It's not my place to challenge it, nor to question it.'

He felt alone in that. The more he dug into this case, the more he seemed to be the only one who felt that way. The broken case notes pointed to conspiracy.

Jeff sighed. 'Will you help me, Mako?'

The old man nodded, dropping his head. 'Something else then, perhaps.'

'Something legal, please.'

'I'd like to see my wife, Jeff. Can you do that?'

That was a surprise. Mako had made no mention of a wife before. 'You're married?'

'I was. Her name is Sundance. Tick, branch, tick!'

A rattle from down the corridor caught Jeff's attention. Bobb stood in the doorway, a serious look on his face. His voice bellowed through the block toward him. 'Jeff. She's coming, the guards are escorting her in now. A few minutes, tops.'

Mako moved toward the bars, imploring. 'Can you do that, Jeff?'

Jeff flashed his gaze from Bobb, to Mako, and back. 'I'll send for her. I have to go—the Reaper is coming.'

The men shared a nod and Jeff strode away toward the coming storm.

FOOTSTEPS RANG THROUGH the corridor, leaving a trail of hushed conversation in their wake. The Reaper approached with purpose, flanked by two of Garamond's finest Mohruscan soliders. Her presence unnerved them, unnerved all. The Reaper halted as she passed the waiting benches outside the office, casting her attention toward Sundance, who sat with her hands in her lap. The older woman paled visibly.

'Have I met my end, Reaper?'

The Reaper leaned in, uncomfortably close, and sniffed at her, pupils dilating in curiosity. 'Not today, friend.'

With that, the Reaper resumed her stride as if nothing had occurred, leaving Sundance feeling violated.

'CHIEF, MAY I present Bandack of the Reapers.'

Jeff rose from his desk, rounding it to stand before the grim representative. He dismissed the guards with a nod, and addressed the source of his stress.

'Have I met my end, Reaper?'

Bandack the Reaper rolled back on her heels, stretching as if released from a cage.

'What is your name?' Her voice was soft, almost soothing.

'Jeff.'

'Not today, Jeff.'

Bandack bounced toward him like a child. Squatting at his side, she poked at his bad knee.

'How'd you get the limp, Jeff?' She sniffed at it.

Jeff recoiled in horror, lifting his leg protectively. The Reaper stood and cocked her head. 'I'd rather not say,' he said.

She pouted, mocking disappointment. Jeff shook his head in shock. Was this normal behavior? He'd seen Reapers before but never interacted with one.

He cleared his throat. 'I've prepared luxury accommodations for you. We hope that you'll find them acceptable.'

'Oh I'm sure they will be fine.' She waved away the courtesy.

'Do you have any idea how long it will take to uh… conclude your business?'

'You should know better than to ask questions like that, Jeff.' She stood rocking on her heels, looking around the room like a bored toddler. Jeff cast a questioning look toward Bobb, who refused to look up from his paperwork. *Typical*, he thought.

Bandack's face suddenly appeared in front of his own, leaving them almost nose to nose. 'Are you going to take me to my room then?'

'Uh, yes,' he said, backing away. 'Follow me please.'

He shared a bemused look with Jinger, who spoke as quietly as she could. 'Sir, Sundance is outside again. She says it's important.'

Again. What had he done to give this woman the impression he was interested? He nodded. 'I won't have time today. Could you take her to see Mako, please?'

'Sir?'

'Please, Jinger.'

He nodded at her and led Bandack toward the door, avoiding her attempts to link his arm.

JEFF COULDN'T HELP but wonder at the mental state of the Reaper. He'd expected to find her cold, her movements deliberate and measured. As he walked, he found his preconceptions shattered. Numerous times she stopped to sniff at nothing, or stroke at mundane objects like curtains or lamps. He swore he turned to catch her licking at a brick, but she moved so quickly he wasn't sure of it. He started to wonder if it was a practical joke.

Bobb would be behind it if it was, but Jeff wasn't sure even he would dare to go this far.

'Here we are.'

They arrived at the door to the room he'd had prepared. It was on the upper floor in one of the wings dedicated to older staff who liked their peace and quiet, hopefully far enough away not to cause too much paranoia, or disruption. He unlocked the door and handed her the key.

'Very nice.' Bandack threw herself onto the bed and lay with her arms folded behind her head. 'Not what you expected, Jeff?'

'I'm sorry?'

She gave him a discouraging look; clarification was not required.

'You could say that,' he said, rubbing his knee.

'Why don't you come and sit?'

The very idea of it repulsed him. 'I have urgent matters to attend to.'

The Reaper rolled her eyes.

'On that topic…' He paused, unsure of how to broach the subject. 'There's an issue I'm investigating, stolen property. It's a high value object. It may be necessary to lock down the inner grounds. Anyone coming or going will likely be subject to search. I know that you operate outside our jurisdiction, but I was hoping that you might willingly submit as a show of faith.'

'Don't trust me?'

'Should I?'

Silence followed. She regarded him playfully, making a show of her consideration.

'Well, I suppose that could be fun.' She winked at him. 'But I will insist that you carry out the search yourself, Jeff.'

Jeff resisted the urge to grimace. She continued, 'And if you should conclude your business before I conclude my own?'

'Then it will not be necessary. I sincerely hope that will be the outcome. As such, I would consider it a personal favor if you would give me some time before you do.'

Bandack sat up in excitement. 'A Reaper's promise? You would ask a personal favor of me? Be in my debt?'

'Within reason. I am bound by the law of Luna Ruinam.'

'Of course.'

She removed her dagger from its holster at her thigh. Light danced around the lightstone in its hilt, illuminating her in a brilliant yellow glow as if in response to its unsheathing. Jeff winced at the weapon as she played with it. 'I wonder what you could do for me.' She took on a serious tone for the first time since their meeting, her words delivered with steel. 'My work, my movements, are my own. I do not expect to meet with resistance during my stay.'

Jeff pulled his attention away from the dagger. 'As is law.'

She smiled at him. 'I like you, Jeff.'

JEFF MADE HIS way back toward his offices, scratching his head and wondering what he'd gotten himself into.

He paused after stumbling over a brush, apologizing to the janitor who busied himself by a wall. The man frowned at the graffiti on its surface. A mark, left in chalk. He looked at Jeff, startled.

'Everything alright?' said Jeff.

'Ye—Yes, chief, fine.' His gaze flicked from Jeff to the wall.

Jeff inspected the graffiti. The mark was familiar to him, and filled him with dismay. With everything going on, this was the last thing he needed. He moved closer and laid his hand on the spiral glyph. 'I've seen this before. It's a cult marking.'

The janitor blinked. 'Cult marking?' His eyes widened. 'No, no. I'm sure it's just the mark of some misguided youth.'

The janitor doused his brush in soapy water and began to scrub away the omen.

Jeff stepped aside, taking care not to let the water land on his shoes. 'Have you cleaned these markings up before?'

'I'm not sure, sir. Perhaps. Vandalism does happen.'

Jeff turned to leave, then took a look back to the glyph as it smeared its way to the ground. 'What is your name?'

'Londo, sir.'

Londo.

He watched as the man nervously erased the mark with unsettling pace.

Cultists, he thought. *Wonderful.*

SUNDANCE STOOD STARING into the gloom beyond the bars, at the jibbering form of the man she'd put there. He sat with his back to her, chuntering to himself, a barely audible series of broken sentences and interrupted thoughts. His hair had grown long and shaggy, with missing patches and reddened traces of scratched skin beneath. Mako burst into a laugh that lasted for half a breath, then shouted at the wall. 'Tick! Branch!'

What am I doing here?

She curled her lip and turned on her heel. Half of her wanted to leave. What did Jeff hope to achieve by parading the shell of this man in front of her? What had this disgusting fool promised him in return for this reunion? It could have been possible Mako was involved in the situation. Even from this cell, he probably still had influence. His lackeys had always followed in his wake, keen to suck up any of the man's discarded genius and claim it as their own.

She cleared her throat.

The face that turned to her had lost most of the steel that had turned her head as a young woman. Deep frown lines had taken root around his eyes, skin had leathered, teeth been neglected. His slow smile turned her stomach.

'Sundance,' he said.

She couldn't bring herself to speak. She'd buried her husband long before she had him arrested. She backed away as he bounded toward the bars.

'My wife! It's so good to see your face. So long, it's been—tick. Branch.' He twitched with the words, before turning back into the cell as if expecting someone behind him to speak.

'What happened to you, Mako?'

He shook his head. 'What's happened is happening, and what is to happen has happened.'

Was this an act?

'Why did you ask to see me?'

He hunched and cocked his head to the side. 'It's important. Do you remember? Do you remember the missing moments? Nobody seems to remember.'

'I remember a lot,' she spat. 'My jaw still clicks when I eat.'

A look of sadness fell over him, before abruptly ending in another tick, branch, episode. 'No, no. Not that. The missing time. Do you remember things that didn't happen?'

'You have lead poisoning. You're losing your mind.'

'Ha!' He straightened and blew out his chest in a display of pride. 'That's what I thought. But then I realized I'm not losing it, I'm finding it! Listen to me.' He hunched again in a conspiratorial gesture. 'There's a pressure in the unseen, something huge is about to happen. Things are already shifting.'

She cocked her eyebrow. 'And you just happen to know about this, from whom?'

'You don't believe me.'

'Oh, I don't doubt you've continued your scheming, somehow. You and that rat Staine. How is your little whipping boy?'

'He doesn't come.'

'Oh, really? I don't suppose it pays to be seen with the man who tried to make us all redundant.'

'The printing press would have changed the *world*.'

'It's forbidden. Who are you to usurp the teachings of the Praelatus?'

'Oh yes, oh yes. *In writing there is art, in art resides the sublime. The quill is the conduit. Let it always be so.* Rubbish. You never understood, always so righteous, dear wife. You wasted no time in putting an end to that did you? You might as well have thrown me in here yourself. Tick. Branch. Tick!'

'I wish they had let me.'

'You only delayed the inevitable. Even as we speak, the war between magic and technology rages on. The people of Luna Ruinam will not cower before lightstone and its gatekeepers forever. Aradinn grows in wealth with each passing year, they build machines that will change the very fabric of our society.'

'You think that's why I reported you? The printing press?' She laughed. *What a fool.* 'The first time you beat me,' she said. 'They came. They saw what you'd done, they shook their heads, they checked me over, but what did they do? "*Give over with the poor girl now, Mako.*" Nothing. Not even a slap on the wrist.'

She shook her head. 'And then there was the time after that, and the time after that, and the time you broke my jaw—the doctor had a few words for you then. Oh, he had a few words. And then, when I dared to finally question all the late nights, the drinking, the whoring, the conspiring with your little friend, what did you do? You broke my arm. You took my work from me. Did they arrest you then?' She leaned toward him. 'Of course not.

'You should have stayed in Aradinn, dear husband. With your whores and your worshipers. Your little project just gave me the weapon to put you where you deserve to be.'

The broken man shrank into himself, sobbing. 'I did…I did do those things.' He fell to a slump on the floor. 'I'm sorry.'

'You can stick your apology where the sun doesn't shine.'

Mako turned again, a movement so abrupt it should have hurt. He whispered into the dark, sobbing and shaking his head. 'Sundance, please listen. Branch! You're going to find yourself in the position to release me. When that happens, you must set me free.'

She turned to leave.

'This is all going to end soon. Branch. A man came to me, Sundance. He has seen all that is to come. The Praelatus is going to die. He's going to die and the world is going to change.'

She walked away. He shouted after her.

'Sundance, I can't be here. I'm supposed to be there. I'm supposed to help change the world. You have to get me out.'

She didn't look back. He could stay where he should be: in her past.

Eighteen

Isolation

RENIA WIPED AWAY at the mulch collecting on Dail's chest. He'd forgotten how to eat, which meant a considerable amount of time had to be spent mushing up his meals.

Dail slumped, propped up by pillows on their new bed as she spoon-fed his broken, bandaged head. She sat facing the window, allowing the morning light to fall on her face and blind her to the results of her sorcery.

She hadn't reacted upon entering the apartment for the first time. She gave no indication that she recognized the space, that she'd been here before, seen hints of what was yet to come. She'd never had a vision before, and the sensation was, in fact, a welcome one. It gave her a sense of reason, some comfort that there might be a greater purpose to the chaotic existence she'd created.

She had explored the space with curiosity, looking for discrepancies between the dream and the reality, examining the details, the desk, the equipment she'd been left. It was all there, everything she'd seen in that strange place had been a gift, a warning. One she now pondered as she shoveled slop into Dail's mouth. She paused, and shook her head at just how much she could relate to his position.

The first night had been difficult. Between bouts of vomiting and the constant interruption of Dail's night terrors, she hadn't found much in the way of rest. Not that it had bothered her much. She had little desire to dream, to return to that dark place and its cryptic symbolism.

She had chosen work instead, spending the early hours preparing her workspace and materials, refamiliarizing herself with the book she'd been working on. Only things were different now, she had context. Whether intentional or not, the book had taught her how to use her lightstone shard, how to channel its energy to devastating effect, and the hunger to explore her newfound skill grew with each page. She wondered if she'd ever see the shard again, and the thought saddened her.

In the face of despair, work again became her anchor. She pressed on, despite the distraction, despite the guilt, relentless once more.

A SIGHT FOR sore eyes. The sunrise brought with it the silhouette of Master Vedora. Petor had been gardening when he noticed her approach.

'Vedora!'

She smiled at him warmly as she halted. 'Hello, old friend. Gardening? You?' She chuckled, embracing him.

'Trying to keep my mind sharp with a bit of exercise, that's all.'

She gave him a mocking nod. He paid it no mind; it was good to have a visitor he didn't despise.

'On that note, dear,' she said, 'would you like to join me for a walk? I managed to slip the guards and I fear we may not get another chance for some time. Rumor has it they're locking the whole place down.'

'Are they now?' Petor leaned in, exaggerating his concern. 'Well then, let's. I had been hoping to speak with you anyway.'

'Oh, really? Finally decided to make an honest woman of me, have you?'

They laughed at the ridiculous thought as they headed away from the cottage.

She was kind enough to link his arm as they walked, visibly aware of his leg injury. The grounds wouldn't allow for a hike anyway. They strolled together at a leisurely pace, recounting stories of days past, laughing and sighing at where their lives had led them. After a time, they stood in sight of the gates, and commented on the speed at which preparations and barricades were being erected to prevent people from leaving. To the younger eye it would have been a daunting sight, but the two veterans were unmoved by the spectacle, secure in the knowledge that all things pass.

'It shamed me greatly to be the cause of this.' Petor turned to Vedora with the weight of the world on his shoulders.

'You still believe yourself to be at fault?'

'In part. I fear I became complacent, lax in my duties.'

Vedora nodded, careful not to interrupt her old friend's train of thought.

'It might surprise you to know that I've spent time reading my old journals,' he said.

'You? Self-indulgent? I would never have thought it!' More laughter.

Petor clutched at her arm. 'I'm learning, Vedora. Learning from the man I was. Whatever drove that man, that thing that I have lost, I seek to reclaim it.'

She cocked an eyebrow, confused. 'To what end, old friend?'

'Understand, Vedora, this incident—it cannot be my undoing. I might be old, but I still have my wits, I still command respect.' His attention faltered, scattered thoughts wrestled into alignment. 'It's a lesson, that's what it is. A reminder of the weight we bear as Hall Masters.'

'Petor, forgive me, but you no longer hold that title.'

He clutched her harder. 'But I can hold it again, Vedora.' He felt the threat of emotion in his aging eyes. 'If you could just speak to the Grand Master on my behalf. Inform him of my determination and resolve. You could help me return to my duties, reinvigorated!'

He detected sympathy in her eyes. Her lips parted repeatedly as she tried to find the right words, but none came. He shook her. 'Please, Vedora! In all these years I have asked you for nothing. I would do it for you.' Petor sobbed. Only the wound in his leg prevented him from dropping to his knees.

'Petor.' She turned to face him. 'Sometimes things happen that affect our lives in terrible ways, and there's nothing we can do to reclaim the past.' Vedora became distant, looking out over the walls toward Verda. 'Have you asked yourself why it is you became disillusioned in the first place? Have you considered that perhaps you allowed this to happen out of a desire to be free?

'Use the time you have to ask yourself what your life would have been like had you not taken this assignment. It's a luxury that I'm not sure you have seen the value of. I must admit, I envy you that.' A solemn silence passed as Vedora looked back toward the Halls.

'Vedora, please, I—'

'Listen to me, Petor. Ask that young man you're working so hard to reanimate: what was it that his heart desired that his pride robbed him of? What passion died in the pursuit of respect and status?'

She tapped his hand, rousing him from his self-pity.

He laughed. 'I wanted to paint.'

She smiled and nodded with warmth. 'Then grant me this favor—paint. Be the best painter you can be for three months. If you're still intent on returning to the Halls after that, I'll speak to Venn-Dor on your behalf.'

Petor smiled as he looked into the face of the woman he'd done his best not to see throughout the decades. He realized in that moment that in doing so he'd robbed himself of her kindness and guidance, her point made. 'Thank you, old friend.'

'Let's get you back home,' she said. 'Before they notice us.'

THE CAPTAIN'S LIPS moved, her frown lines deepened, and her armor shook with the force of her frustration. Venn-Dor saw all of this, but didn't hear a word. His attention lay elsewhere, trapped in a memory that refused to sleep:

'What are you doing in here?'

The boy was only twelve, caught in the act, afraid, yet still confident in his ability to evade capture. Ever the adaptor. As sharp as the knife he had attempted to steal. That he had made it past the guards at all was impressive. Doratus fought the urge to grin as he studied the youth. Clad in rags, yet not dirty. Thin, yet not hungry. Resourceful, self-sufficient, yet missing two fingers. Too stupid to learn from his mistakes, then? Or too determined to allow them to stop him?

'I wonder,' he said, lifting the knife from its display. 'Do you even know what this knife is?'

The boy flinched as he took his hand, and faltered under his gaze. He placed the knife in the youth's awkward grasp, and watched as his thumb and first fingers sought to find a balance that could never be.

Doratus watched the youth as he battled his options. His immature features creased and flickered with indecision. Would he strike? Attempt escape? Or would he be smart enough to recognize his disadvantage, even with the knife in his hand? 'This knife is bound to me.' He smiled at the boy. 'You could not hope to steal it, for I would always know where it is. Do you understand?'

The boy gulped, and nodded once.

'What is your name, child?'

'Stubs.' The boy thrust his chest out.

Had the other children given him that nickname? Or had he claimed it for himself? No cursory glance toward the missing fingers—the latter then, pride.

'Did someone send you to steal this knife, Stubs?'

The boy's lip twitched. Annoyance, pride again. 'I don't work for nobody.'

Such defiance. And while the statement later proved to be false, the spirit never left him—

'Sir…Sir? Are you listening to me?' The captain had lost any sense of decorum.

He fixed her with a stern expression, and patted down his robes. 'Have you forgotten your place, Captain Garamond?'

Her jaw clenched.

'I have given you an order. Carry it out.'

He held her in his gaze throughout the silent battle of wills that followed, careful not to reveal any concern at his order's lack of weight. His position should have afforded him her unwavering support. The captain's salute came true enough, though, and he continued to watch her as she turned on her heel and strode away.

Renia smiled at the sound of her footsteps. She welcomed the opportunity to stretch her legs, even if it meant another unpleasant conversation with the Grand Master. The light rattle of armor plating accompanied her, her two guardian escorts following a few steps behind.

In the early evening the halls were more or less empty, with the majority of the staff either dining or running errands in Venntown. It spared her the embarrassment of being frogmarched from her apartment to the Grand Master like a criminal.

What could he possibly want with her now? She'd proceeded with the work at a respectable rate, despite the constant distraction and everything that came with broken sleep. Perhaps she had made a mistake, mis-seen something.

No, I would have felt it. She shrugged away any doubt.

She paused at an intersection, unfamiliar with the layout in the masters' wing. A scribe of her level would not usually be permitted to enter, let alone walk freely here.

'This way, please.' One of the slug guards took point, the smell of mucus and oil wafting her as he passed. Was it a *he*? It was almost impossible to tell. She held back long enough for the guard to reach a respectful distance before continuing on, still puzzling over the reason for her summons.

Perhaps it's Dail.

Renia's work rate had suffered. Not by a wide margin, but surely enough to be noticed by the Grand Master. Caring for Dail took its toll—accepting help with him had been difficult at first, but she'd accepted it eventually after realizing just how difficult it would be to work with him constantly demanding her attention.

A distant slam registered in her mind, followed by heavyset footsteps and rattling armor. She moved aside instantly. Captain Garamond stormed past and away from them, chuntering and reddened with frustration. Renia frowned, and returned to her thoughts.

An office would be nice. Somewhere quiet I could work for a few hours during the day. She nodded to herself. It was the most likely explanation – no need to get worked up.

They arrived before double doors of oak, highly ornate. Carvings of books, quills, vines, and trees had been chiseled into them. It must have taken months of work. She jumped slightly as one of her escorts rang a bell, announcing their arrival.

'Come,' came the voice from inside. Her guards positioned themselves to either side of her, turning their backs to the doors before parting them. The low light of the afternoon hit her, blinding her for an instant as her eyes adjusted from the gloom of the corridor. She held her hand up to shield them as the most beautiful scent rushed at her from the doorway, a pleasing mixture of rose and honeysuckle.

'Come in, come in, before the heat escapes.'

Renia took a step forward as her vision returned. The silhouette of the Grand Master stood before her in wait, arms outstretched. She stepped into the room, hesitant, and wary of his change in mien since their last exchange.

She bowed at him briefly before her curiosity took control. She cast her gaze over the chamber, lingering over works of art she'd never seen, display cabinets containing artifacts from a time long past, shelves full of books that she had never heard of. Even the structure of the room humbled her. The detailed patterns in the floor, the carved pillars that reached for the ceiling, and the windows—oh, the windows.

'Welcome,' said Venn-Dor.

She turned to him, suddenly aware that her jaw had slackened. He motioned for her to look around. 'Please,' he said.

She wandered over to the grand windows and paused before a cabinet that sat between them. A small note sat in a frame. The writing was scratchy, childlike.

> *To Daddy, I love you so much!*
> *Love you, love you, love you.*
> *From Peya.*

Renia's eyes flickered in surprise. 'Oh, you have a little girl?'

The Grand Master approached slowly, his eyes fixed on the note, a solemn smile on his face. 'Had. Once.' He held her gaze. 'She died.'

'I'm so sorry.'

Venn-Dor smiled in response.

'Your wife?'

She watched as the pain tried to claim the Grand Master's expression. He pursed his lips and nodded. For the first time she saw something in the man that she hadn't expected—humility. She looked back at the child's scratch, remembering her early lessons with Molan and Carol, how the quill had felt unnatural in her grasp. She almost felt her father's hand on her shoulder as she remembered the pride he'd shown when she'd written him a similar note.

Renia found herself looking out of the window and toward the Wastes.

'You're thinking of your parents,' Venn-Dor said. 'Your father? I'm sorry, no child should have to see what you saw.'

She looked at him with a mixture of fear and surprise.

'You know about my parents?'

'I know more than I did.' He gestured toward a modest dining table, one she'd neglected to see when she had walked in. A meal had been prepared and sat cooling upon its top. 'The food grows cold. Shall we?'

They ate in silence for a short time. Renia was surprised to find that the Grand Master ate the same food as the rest of the staff. Nothing special about it. It took her a while to find something to discuss. 'Captain Garamond didn't look very happy on my way in.'

Venn-Dor raised an eyebrow, and exhaled through his nose. 'It's understandable. The lockdown vexes her. She's spread too thin, Venntown is largely unprotected due to her men being required here to conduct the search.'

'The lockdown?'

'Yes.' He flashed her a quizzical look. 'You didn't note how quiet things are on your way here?'

She flushed, embarrassed. 'The missing book.'

'Indeed.'

She frowned and placed her cutlery on her plate. 'I have to say...I'm confused.'

'About what?'

'What it is that makes this one book so special. An antique journal? What could it possibly contain that would warrant such chaos?'

The Grand Master raised his head, wiping his face with a napkin. 'It's not so much the *what*. It's more the *who*.' A moment of silence passed. He continued, 'Do you know much about the exodus, and the war that followed?'

Renia nodded, recalling all that she'd read. 'That our ancestors fled from Daralar to the northern continent after the Moonfall blotted out the sun, that they founded the country of Luna Ruinam here in the north. That there were remnants of a civilization here that taught us a new way of life, and that many turned their back on both Daralar and its culture, resulting in a war that raged for years.'

Venn-Dor nodded in return. 'All true enough.' He turned his palms up and inspected them. 'Out of all those that turned against Daralar during the war, Inoa was the most puzzling. He was one of the Five, you see, the council that rule the south to this day.' He sat back in his chair. 'Inoa was an interesting man, an adventurer at heart, I think. His treachery was a tremendous blow to Daralar and their plan to take Luna Ruinam. What do you know of the moonstones?'

Renia hesitated. 'I know that they are large lightstones, that the Praelatus has three of them, and that they grant him unimaginable power.'

'Indeed. The power to rule continents, to shake the very earth that we stand on. There are nine of them, you know.'

Her heart raced. 'Nine?'

'Nine.' He nodded. 'Imagine what lengths Daralar would go to to capture, to wield the remaining six. We know that they have at least one.'

'They used it to fight the Praelatus?'

'No, they cannot.'

'Why?'

'It refuses them.'

Renia shook her head. What did he mean?

'The moonstones choose their companions. And only one man from Daralar has ever been chosen.'

She understood. 'Sanas Inoa,' she said.

'Just so.' The Grand Master smiled at her. 'A weapon that could be used to end the war, in the hands of one of their own. To reclaim Inoa would be to turn the tide. To give them a chance, at least, of achieving their goals. This peace that we enjoy is merely perceived. Daralar has not forgotten. We will always be *the enemy* in the eyes of the Five.'

'But Inoa is long dead.' Renia frowned. 'Those events took place over a century ago.'

The Grand Master shook his head slowly. 'Gone, yes. Not dead.'

She tried to hide her shock, but failed. In a moment she felt the cool march of realization pass over her. Her hands trembled. Her heart raced. 'You're saying that the moonstones can grant immortality?'

He laughed. 'Hardly. An arrow to the heart would do the trick, certainly. No... *Longevity* perhaps would be a better word.'

Venn-Dor's scrutiny fell up on her. Her head swam with new information.

'Inoa turned his back on the Five,' he said. 'He was instrumental in ensuring the independence of Luna Ruinam. The Five would stop at nothing to find him. They call him "the Arch Traitor". There is a blanket reward in place for anyone who recovers a work of his that they don't already have. It makes protecting the journals we have here... Challenging.'

Renia detected a hint of sadness in the last word. 'So they seek his journal for clues to where he went, or perhaps for instruction on how to work with a moonstone.'

He nodded. 'Certainly, but still your thinking is limited. The original works of Inoa, Venn, Vala Veridia, any of the old Grand Masters, are charged with energy. You're working on the Venn book now. You will have noticed its words leaving their imprint on you. The books are imbued with power. They connect you to the author through threads in the ether that you can not begin to imagine. You are barely scratching the surface of the truth that hides within these walls.'

She *had* noticed. Beyond a mere meditation, the words had bound to her. It was the best explanation for the sorcery that left Dail scorched and broken. She felt her skin pale, and looked down at her hands. 'You're grooming me,' she said.

'Not exactly.'

'Then what is all this? Why the pressure to complete my work?'

'An initiation. Your body and mind must be prepared before you are able to make a choice.'

'What choice?'

'Whether or not you want to accept an invitation. To take a position amongst the bearers of the world's secrets, and play your part in maintaining the fragile peace of our land.'

She laughed. 'Why, by the moon, would I decline?'

He looked away. 'Because such knowledge, and the means of acquiring it, comes with a cost.' His brow furrowed as he laid his palms in his lap.

Renia stifled the humor with which she had spoken and considered his warning.

'Some of the books,' he continued, 'Venn's work in particular, they change you. I courted his knowledge, accepted the tether to his spirit, and now I find myself a haunted man. Tragedy tends to follow those who chase secrets.'

'Your family?'

He shook his head. 'The war claimed my wife and daughter.'

She inhaled a sharp breath, studying his face, intent on his features, his youthful skin, his bright eyes, his sharp bone structure—'How old are you?'

He met her gaze, and pursed his lips.

'I HOPE YOU have a strong stomach.' Ferron half-smiled, absentmindedly jangling his way through a set of keys.

Jeff returned the look, puzzled.

Mako had made good on his promise and provided Jeff with a name. The validity of this endeavor, however, felt questionable. He realized that he might be making a fool of himself, and involving a respected colleague in a fool's errand at the whim of a madman.

Ferron placed the key in the door. 'The stonemarkers might live like kings, but towards the end…Well. The poor bastards in here are all but decomposing.'

Jeff wasn't sure whether to laugh, so he settled for raising his eyebrows. He'd heard stories, of course. It was known that to mark a lightstone was to invite pain, and that the ones responsible for registering and marking the stones traded their lives in service to Luna Ruinam. Each mark wiped weeks of their lives away. Out of honor? Jeff doubted it. He'd always imagined the stonemarkers traded the years away in exchange for a life of excess, debauchery, and who knows what else. He knew the type that would jump at the opportunity, the type to live fast, die young. The back streets and underbelly of Verda were littered with them, lost souls that knew nothing beyond the next hit, the city's outcast cancer. For them, trading a short life of risk, poverty, and decay for a short life of opulence, luxury, and pleasure would be akin to discovering gold in the privy.

Should he feel sympathy for them? Was their approach to life invalid, misguided, or just different?

It was necessary of course, lightstone being the most tightly controlled commodity in the world. To allow its unregulated use would be to invite chaos, anarchy, war.

They entered the stinking chamber, welcomed by dim light. Thin curtains of loosely threaded material covered the windows. Squinting eyes focused on them as they approached. Three beds, three barely living husks, each roughly facing each other in the triangular room. Jeff couldn't help but curl his lip in distaste. What a warped idea, having them watch each other die slowly.

Of the three, only two showed any sign of life. One of them lay deeply unconscious and didn't look capable of waking up. Another gave them only a sliver of attention before closing his eyes in hollow annoyance. Jeff's gaze settled on the last, a withered shell of a man, pitted with purpling recesses of sagging skin, all bone and sinew. The flesh around his mouth was scored with heavy creases, making it hard to see where his lips ended. His fervent eyes watched him as he approached, lips parted, revealing a perfect set of white teeth that sat at odds with his condition.

The old man looked at Jeff and Ferron and rasped, coughing up whatever blocked his airway. 'Well, well. Honored,' he said, wincing. 'Both of you, no less.'

Jeff took a seat by the bed. He couldn't help but stare at the state of the man's body. 'You know me?'

'I know—'another coughing fit'—a lot of people, Jeff. Eyy, pour me a glass of water, will you?'

He did. Taking care to hold the bottom of the glass while the old man drank his fill. Spittle rolled off his chin as he smiled appreciatively. Jeff moved to wipe it away but found himself brushed off.

'Pack it in, it's only water.'

'My apologies—'

'Treat me like your elder.' He laughed, coughing again. 'I'm younger than you, you know.'

It was hard to believe. Jeff shook his head, unsure what to say.

'Jakub Araman. Nice to meet you, Jeff.'

'And you, Jakub.'

Ferron stalked around behind him, impatient. Jeff heard him move to the window and sigh.

'Jakub, I'm sorry to disturb your rest. I was told you might be able to help me with an investigation. I'm trying to understand what happened to my predecessor. Do you know something about that?'

Jakub sat back with as much momentum as he could muster, and inhaled slowly, drawing out his response. 'Oh yes, I should think so.'

'What can you tell me?'

'Well.' Jakub strained forward. 'Formally, nothing. I should lie, you see. Sit here and rot in silence with nothing but the occasional moan from these two wretched bastards to entertain me.' The old man looked to where Ferron stood and grinned. 'Imagine my excitement, both chiefs of security, here in need of me. I beat you both, you know, both of you.'

Jeff shot Ferron a glance, and both reeled in shock at what they had heard.

Jakub laughed. 'Ah, the looks on your faces.'

Jeff looked back to the laughing husk. 'Who are you?'

'Jakub Araman,' he repeated. 'Order of the Unseen.'

The blade moved impossibly fast. Jeff barely had time to react as it crossed his face, leveled squarely at Jakub's throat. Ferron growled, 'I should kill you where you sit.' The old man simply laughed, his amusement plain.

'Oh, please do.' His laughter died in his throat, replaced again by a coughing fit. He wheezed at Ferron, sneering with impatience. 'I'm already dead. The next stone they bring me to mark will be my last. Just look at that poor bastard over there. It's not quick, you know. And believe me, *it hurts.* You would be doing me a favor.'

Jakub turned back to Jeff, imploring. 'Water, please.'

Ferron loosened his grip and sheathed his blade. 'Talk, traitor.'

'Alright, alright. Calm down.'

Jakub composed himself to the sound of water filling the glass, never taking his eyes from the pacing Ferron.

Jeff opened his mouth to speak. He'd lost his train of thought, so many new questions probing at him.

It was Ferron who broke the silence. 'How many more of you are there on my staff?'

'On your staff? I don't know. I'm not exactly in a position to mingle.'

'In the Halls, then?'

'Oh many, many. We've been here almost as long as you have. Surely you knew that, deep down.'

'Give me names.'

'I'll give you some, the dead ones. I have no wish to be responsible for the deaths of others.'

'Speak then!'

'So impatient.' He grinned. 'Very well, let's start with this one: Alia.'

Ferron paled.

'Oh yes, you remember that one, don't you? She was a sight, Jeff. What a body. The sight of her in leathers...mmmph. Enough to raise the wood of even these two vegetables, let me tell you,' he said, motioning to his roommates.

'Do not speak of her like that.' Ferron seethed.

'Oh, but she had you fooled too, Ferron. She was a Reaper, you see. One of the best.'

Jakub looked squarely at Jeff before continuing. 'Eyy, I think he knew that too, but nobody wanted to say it out loud. Venn-Dor probably knew. He never told anyone, though. I think he had other reasons for keeping things quiet. Guilty conscience, perhaps.'

Jeff shook his head. 'I'm lost. What is the "unseen"?'

'Oof, you are lost.' Jakub nodded to Ferron and shook his head. 'The *Order* of the Unseen, Jeff. The eyes and ears of the great country of Daralar. Everywhere and nowhere.'

'You're a Reaper?'

'Ha!' Jakub's eyes glistened as the effort pained him. 'No. No, we are not. Reapers are...tools. They have a singular purpose, limited autonomy. Their training is tailored to create a certain mindset. That mindset would not be suited to the task of gathering intelligence, the task of subtle manipulation.' He tilted his head. 'A different tool, for a different job.'

Jeff swallowed the pooling saliva in his mouth. He did his best to recall the old—young man's earlier comments, cursing himself for being overwhelmed by the situation. 'Who is Alia? Why was there no mention of a Reaper in the report?'

'Because we are an imperfect species, Jeff. Lover boy here couldn't bring himself to investigate his missing girlfriend out of fear. Fear that if he uncovered evidence of her being a Reaper, it would shatter his fantasy, or perhaps fear for his position when admitting he'd been sleeping with an agent of the South. And Venn-Dor closed the investigation quietly out of shame, and grief.'

Ferron stepped forward in confusion, his eyes glistened with pain. 'What do you mean *shame?* What did he do?'

'Well now, *that's* the question, isn't it.' Jakub nodded, his eyes unfocused, seemingly relishing the opportunity to unburden himself. 'They think themselves so superior, Jeff. You know? All their secrets. They carry them around, day after day. They have no idea how much we know, that our eyes see, and our ears hear *everything*. This story is well known in these halls. Just not by your side. They think they know it—Venn-Dor, Ferron here—but they don't. They were so quick to hide from what they did that they never asked why, why did Alia fail to retrieve the book? I'll tell you.'

Jeff watched as Jakub tried to grin and the flesh around his lips cracked.

'Alia failed, and died, because she wasn't the only Reaper here who wanted to take *Journal 26*.'

'She's dead then.' Ferron shrank into himself. Jeff struggled to contain his frustration at information he'd been denied. Did he not need to know these things? Did Venn-Dor and Ferron not take his position seriously?

The sound of Jakub farting interrupted his train of thought, followed by a smell so foul that he retched. He reached for a nearby towel and held it over his mouth and nostrils.

The dying man merely shrugged in apology. 'They caused it, Raellon, Venn-Dor. They tried to play the game, and it cost them dearly. You know what the problem is with you Northerners? You're arrogant. You're so sure of your superiority that you never think to question it. In truth, what are you? A civilization of cowards hiding under the cloak of one incredibly powerful man. You mistake his power for your own.'

Jeff filtered out the rotting man's appraisal, slowly piecing together the story. 'Wait. You said another Reaper wanted to take the book home. Why would they be working against each other?'

Another grin, another chance to dance around the truth. 'Do you know why they assign Shadow-Reapers to this place, Jeff?' Another question answered with a question. Jeff thought it best to play along.

'Go on.'

'When a Reaper needs to be punished, it's best to punish them in a way that benefits the Five. Let's say a Reaper does something naughty. You ship them off to the Halls of Venn and tell them that the only way they are ever coming home is if they provide something valuable to the Five. Must be torture for a Reaper, being cooped up in this dusty hole, eyy?' He chuckled. This time without hacking up phlegm. 'So say something really juicy comes out of storage, like for example the journal of the most wanted man in history, but one Reaper wants to deliver it to the

Five in exchange for reassignment, and the other wants it for her own purposes. That's something that would cause some conflict.

'Alia was ambitious. She came here of her own accord, you see. She wanted to earn her place among the Five by delivering *more* than Inoa's journal. She had no intention of taking the book south.'

Jeff nodded, following. 'But Raellon's body was found with the book. So neither got what they wanted. If Alia died, then that means that one of the—'

'One of the Reapers is still here, yes. And has probably been waiting for a decade for another chance to buy their freedom.' Jakub's features creased in disappointment. 'So eager to protect, this one. So preoccupied with the now.'

Ferron's fingers twitched by his blade. 'You are a liar,' he said. 'Why should we believe any of this?'

'From the bottom of my heart, dear chief—I don't care if you do.' Jakub's body rocked with the rasp of his laughter, a wheezing, rhythmic squeal.

Jeff shook himself. 'You.' He pointed his finger. 'You speak of these events as if external to them. But you were not.'

Jakub smiled.

'A tool of "subtle manipulation" would not stand by during something like this,' Jeff continued. 'You orchestrated this. Not Venn-Dor, not Raellon.'

'Eeeeee!' Jakub squealed in delight. 'Not as dense as you look! Well done, Mister Sothgard.' He coughed. 'If I could clap, I would.' The marker's face contorted into a sickly grin. 'Smart. Yes. Though not as sharp as Raellon. You know, I've missed him, I have.' He nodded toward the water once again.

Jeff sat back, and folded his arms. Jakub merely shrugged.

'He liked to have a good time, Raellon. It wasn't difficult to befriend him. And he was useful. Wine and pussy have a way of loosening the lips.' He chuckled to himself. 'Of course, he started to suspect. I could see it. I felt his calculating gaze watching me. It was a fun little game for a while. I had something he did not, however. And ironic as it might sound, that was *patience*. He needed a catalyst, something to alter the status quo. So he released the book, and watched closely. I delighted in it.'

Jeff watched as a glaze covered the marker's eyes. 'You saw an opportunity.'

'Of course. When your exiled Reaper came to me to help her notify the Five of her achievement, I relished it. She refused to allow me to take the book—only another Reaper could vouch for her.' Jakub laughed. 'Oh how the dice fell. So yes, I arranged a little gathering on the roof. I told them all where to be, and when to be there, and I watched from the shadows as fate unfolded.'

Something stirred within Jeff. He started to understand what it was that drove the unseen agent. 'If the exile succeeded, you helped to make that happen. If Alia succeeded, she owed you. If Raellon succeeded, he would accept you as a double agent and put you in an even stronger position.'

Jakub sat back, and nodded once.

'But that wasn't why you did it, was it?' Jeff studied the man's wrinkled face as it twitched. He became vaguely aware of Ferron's discomfort at the foot of the bed. 'You did it for your own reasons. You did it not for status, or recognition. You did it because it amused you. Because you were bored.'

Jakub turned his face toward Jeff in a slow fluid movement that betrayed his condition and broke into a grin once again.

'It's the same reason you're telling us your story, here, now.'

The stonemarker hissed through his teeth. 'Perceptive. So what is it that is preventing you from seeing the bigger picture, Jeff?'

The words washed over him. He didn't know. His mind's eye was locked in place, an inch from a wall.

'Why didn't Venn-Dor tell you any of this, Jeff? Why didn't Ferron here tell you his version of the story? You're not a player in this game, you're a pawn. Venn-Dor and his little lord Raellon baited the trap, then made their move, and they embarrassed themselves.' He raised his skeletal arm with concerted effort to point directly at Ferron. 'This fool fell in love with a Reaper. He actually believed she felt the same way—'

Ferron snapped. He freed his blade. 'You dare?'

'He actually *believed* that she loved him. That that fine little arse was his and his alone.'

'Lies!' Ferron spat, he charged the bed, gripping Jakub's collarbone with an audible snap. Jakub screamed in pain, his head rolling euphorically before he locked eyes with his attacker again.

'Oh we laughed, Ferron. We laughed as we smuggled unmarked stones out, right under your nose. We laughed so hard my cock fell out of her—'

Slice. The sound of tearing meat. Ferron's blade sat lodged to the hilt in the wretched man's chest. Jeff staggered backward, frantically looking from one man to the other in disbelief. 'What did you do, Ferron?'

Ferron stepped back, muttering to himself. 'Liar, fucking traitorous, lying bastard.'

Jakub looked down at the sword handle at his breast and smiled. 'See how easy it is, Jeff?' His voice became a hoarse whisper. 'Pawns.'

Jeff leaned in, holding the towel to the gushing chest wound. He locked eyes with the fading man, and watched as he relinquished his role as antagonist. He saw relief, a release of a burden. He listened as Jakub whispered his final words.

'I once chose to give my life for my country. Do you know what strikes me? It's all just a silly game. Honestly, Jeff, what difference would it make if the Five ruled Luna Ruinam? We're all the same. There is no good cause, there is no bad cause; there is only the game, and those who choose to play it. The only good in this world is that which we carve out for ourselves. The difference between you and me is that you have the time left to choose... What will you choose, Jeff?'

Jeff's lips moved, but he could not answer. He watched as the light began to fade from the stonemarker's eyes. Ferron paced, shaking his head, still muttering inaudibly.

'Thank you,' Jakub said.

'What did you do, Ferron? What did you do?'

* * *

How quickly you forget, Vera.

How short your memory.

Do you feel, as I feel, the swell of the chaos that approaches?

Of course you do.

Only this time, I will not be there to stitch your wounds and nurse you back to health as I did after you killed Alia.

You forget how close you came to giving us away, leaving a trail of blood drops through the halls that you're lucky I saw first.

I'll never forget. The sight of you, your pleading eyes as you bled through my bed. The cold, stubborn body of our supposed ally, lying with her neck broken on the floor. The body I had to dispose of while you lay with your fever.

I knew nothing. You told me nothing. That betrayal seared deeply.

I feel it always, like cold fingers wrapped around my heart, shackled in place whilst the world continues to turn without me.

I suffer you. You and your notion of what is best for us.

What is best for you…

You will lose again, and this time you will lose alone.

Nineteen

Allies

JEFF STOOD BEFORE the door to Petor's new home, listening to the rapturous, drunken singing that came from inside. A fisherman's song by the sound of it. It didn't bode well. Jeff felt a pang of guilt for not checking on the old man sooner. He wished that he hadn't come for answers; part of him wanted to forget everything and join the drunkard in his song.

Thanks to Ferron, Petor was the only person left that Jeff could trust to tell him the truth about what had happened all those years ago. With it now being clear that Venn-Dor attempted to hide the details of the case and its grim resolution, how could he trust the man? Let alone work for him. All this, and the constant, nagging suspicion that he was being followed had put Jeff on edge. He envied Petor's revelry.

Knocking didn't seem to work. If anything, it encouraged Petor to sing louder. Jeff laughed to himself and rapped at the door as hard as he felt he could without denting it. 'Petor!'

'Fuck off! It's my house and I'll sing if I want to.' He continued to sing: 'Euweeeghhh. Don't take your missus to sea. For the xentt take the wives of men and make a trull of what they beee.'

Jeff tried the door, it opened without complaint. He entered to see Petor standing astride two chairs, a paintbrush in one hand and a bottle in the other. He appeared to be naked under a painter's smock, staring wide-eyed at Jeff in confusion.

'It's me, you old fool,' Jeff said.

'Jeff. Come in, come in.' Petor staggered from his makeshift stage, almost falling into a glass cabinet in the process. The old man pulled a chair toward him. 'Sit, my good man. Drink?'

Jeff sat, attempted to change the grim look on his face, and nodded. 'Sod it. Why not.'

'Good, good.' Petor retrieved a glass from the kitchen and returned to sit across from him, grinning like a child. 'What's the matter, lad? You look like shite.'

He couldn't help but laugh. The drink seemed to bring out the common side of Petor. It was a stark contrast to his Hall Master's persona.

'I wouldn't know where to start, old man. I'm running this case blindfolded and bound at the knees.'

Petor screwed his face up in a drunken frown. It could have been the whiskey, or Jeff's explanation.

'I've been investigating the old case, Raellon's death.'

The old man paled visibly and smacked his dry lips. 'Oh, *that* case. You know I had nothing to do with that, don't you?'

'I know, Petor.'

Petor nodded his appreciation. 'Go on.'

'I found a witness—a stonemarker by the name of Jakub—'

'Never heard of him.'

'That's alright.' Jeff took a swig of his drink and let it burn his throat. 'He's dead, anyway. Ferron cut my interview short with his blade.'

'He's a twat, that lad.'

Jeff laughed again. 'So after I put together the report that Venn-Dor so kindly scattered all over the place, I found that I have four witnesses: Mako Aranomo, Pistorious Staine, Jakub the stonemarker, and you. Staine is missing and Jakub is dead, which leaves me with a raving lunatic or a drunkard for answers.'

'I am *not* a raving lunatic.'

'I was referring to Mako, Petor.'

'Oh.'

'Jakub stated that a woman called Alia wanted the book, that she was a Reaper, and that she died. But I see no mention that her body was ever recovered. He also said that another Reaper was present and fighting with Alia over who got to take it south. It stands to reason that this other Reaper is still here, and that they would have been waiting for another opportunity to take the book.'

Petor's eyes began to glaze over, he peered into the brown liquid in the bottom of his glass.

'Petor...Petor, the only common thread between these two cases is *you*. Tell me, did Vedora visit you while you had the book in your possession?'

'Eh?'

'Master Vedora, did she visit with you, roughly around the times the book was stolen.'

'Well, yes. But she didn't do it.'

'How do you know that?'

'Well the first time, we were young,' he said, leaning in. 'We were, well, eh, you know...exploring each other.'

'That doesn't mean she didn't take it, Petor.'

'You don't understand. We were, uh, well… The book was on the desk you see, and we went into the back room for a bit of rumpy-pumpy, and when we came out it was gone. After that, we both voluntarily imprisoned ourselves. We spent the whole time together in the same cell. It was the best way we could think of to clear ourselves.'

'So there's no way she could have been on the roof—'

'She couldn't have killed Alia and Raellon while being locked up with me, could she?'

'So she's not the Reaper.'

'She doesn't look like much of a Reaper, does she, Jeff?'

Jeff sighed. He noticed blood pooling around Petor's chair. 'You're bleeding, old man.'

Petor snorted and drained his glass. 'I'm always bleedin' bleeding.'

What now? Nothing left from the past to hint at the present. Had he just wasted valuable time chasing a dead end that might have only had a coincidental connection to his case?

He needed more than a drink.

He took the time to clean and dress Petor's wound, despite his protests. The old man drank his way through the ordeal and eventually passed out. He didn't weigh much. Jeff carried him to his bed and covered him, before leaving him to rest.

'RENIA! RENIA! RENIA!' She cursed the interruption. Between the outbursts and the toilet breaks, she'd only managed to commit to a couple of hours of work.

Luckily, at Venn-Dor's insistence, a maid had been assigned to take care of Dail during the day. She'd been with him for a while, but between the two of them they had yet to find a way to calm the broken man.

She sighed heavily as she entered the bedroom, inviting a sympathetic look from the maid.

'I'm sorry, dear, he won't settle.'

Her name was Alice, an older woman, gray haired and heavily wrinkled. Renia recognized her from her time in the hospital wing. She'd always seemed like one of the kinder ones.

'No need to apologize.' Renia removed her shirt, bundled it, and placed it in the one hand Dail still had use of. 'I'm here, look, I'm here,' she said, raising it to his nose. She prayed he still had a sense of smell, and another pang of guilt seared her.

Replacing her shirt, she turned to the maid. 'Don't be hard on yourself. It will take time. I have to go, I'm sorry. The Grand Master is expecting me.'

Alice waved her off without protest. 'Go, dear girl. Don't keep him waiting.'

Sundance had resorted to eating her lunch alone outside the security office. It was a worry that she'd had to resort to commandeering an escort. She was sure that some would question it, accusing her of abusing her newfound power. Hers was one of only three halls that had been kept open through the lockdown, and she knew that she should be grateful for the opportunity to stretch her legs at all when so many were confined to their rooms.

She frowned at the clock outside the office. She didn't have long before she'd have to resume her duties, and Jeff was still dodging her. It was enough to make her regret her moment of fun.

'Dreamy, isn't he?' The Reaper's voice came from beside her. She almost jumped out of her skin. How had she been able to approach and sit without Sundance noticing? Sundance coughed up the chunk of sandwich lodged in her throat and managed to drop the rest of it into the Reaper's lap. She watched in horror as the Reaper picked up the offending snack and licked it tentatively before handing it back.

The Reaper looked at her expectantly, oblivious to her disbelief. 'Jeff, that is. Very handsome.'

Sundance rejected the urge to ask the Reaper if she'd met her end, knowing it would be impolite to ask again.

'Are you mute?' said the Reaper.

She might as well have been. Sundance had heard much about the Reapers throughout the course of her life, but never had she heard them described as she found this one. The Reaper looked roughly half her age, and still possessed all the playful charm of a child, despite the fact that she killed people for a living. The duality of that made her even more disturbing.

The Reaper extended her hand. 'I'm Bandack.'

Sundance blinked in surprise, and reciprocated the gesture. 'Sundance.'

'A strange name,' said Bandack. 'Not of the mother tongue, nor of the north.'

Sundance nodded. 'My father was a writer and a poet. He believed in the power of words.'

'I see. Well met, Sundance, a pleasure.'

The two women sat side by side on the bench, eyes forward in mute suspense.

Bandack started swinging her legs. 'You're not here to seduce him, are you?'

For the first time in a long time, Sundance laughed out loud. 'No, dear, I am not.' She smiled at the younger woman, spotting something in her that her reputation would prevent most people from seeing.

'Why is he ducking you?'

'A mistake on my part. A moment of mischief. I embarrassed the poor lad.'

'Ahhh,' the Reaper said, swinging her legs again. 'Got a lot on his plate at the moment, I imagine.'

'It would appear so, dear. Yes.'

Another moment of silence passed before Bandack spoke again.

'Perhaps I can help.'

Sundance turned to the young assassin, confusion plastered across her face. 'Forgive me, Reaper. But don't you have more... *pressing* matters to attend to?'

Bandack sighed. 'Gave my word to the big man that I would wait a little, until he's finished his investigation.' The Reaper feigned boredom, Sundance suspected for entertainment purposes.

'So you're... bored?'

'Well yes. But I like you, Sundance. You smell nice.'

Sundance wasn't sure about the legality of involving southern agents in northern affairs, but they were technically allies. And she wouldn't be able to absolve herself or contribute anything to the investigation sitting on a waiting bench. And then there was the fact that Bandack was—as unlikely as it might seem—a Reaper. It couldn't hurt to have that sort of an ally.

She turned to the younger woman excitedly. 'You know, I adore stories with unlikely allies.'

The Reaper beamed.

'COME, GIRL.' THE Grand Master lit a candle on the sconce by the heavy oak door. It had swollen with time. He shouldered it open.

Swirling dust marked their entry into the darkness. Venn-Dor navigated the room with familiarity, lighting candles as he went.

Renia squinted as the space came alive. Dust sheets covered the furniture. The smell of disuse filled her nose.

'What is this place?'

'These are the private chambers of Avantus Venn,' he said.

He began to remove the dust sheets. She watched as he neatly shook and folded each, with care and respect. Each covered a work of beauty. Hand-carved furniture, statues of heroes past, paintings of incredible realism.

She nodded appreciatively. 'It seems a waste to hide these from the public.'

'I agree. I believe he would have wanted it this way, however.'

The Grand Master moved toward a hanging painting. A depiction of the Last Stand, a celestial being suspended hundreds of feet from the ground, wrenching the earth free of its bounds with his sorcery. Thousands of onlookers stood frozen in disbelief, some ecstatic, others running for their lives. Venn-Dor smiled at the scene. 'He wasn't one for recognition, nor unwanted attention.'

'You knew him?'

'He was my friend.' He smiled. 'I found him hanged from the rafter, over there.'

'I'm sorry.'

The Grand Master nodded. 'It was his wish. The only feasible heir of the great Istopher Venn. He was a tortured soul, his father cast a large shadow, but doesn't all great art find its root in suffering?'

Renia allowed the moment to rest. Why was she here? Her work called. 'Forgive me, Grand Master, but why are you showing me this?'

He turned to her, eyes widening in recognition. 'Light of the moon. You don't know, do you?'

'I'm not sure what you mean.' She flushed as she felt him studying her, wrestling with something that needed to be said.

'Renia Collis—born Renia Stone. Daughter of Moyra Veralon, the girl who shunned her birthright for a simple life in the Wastes. Granddaughter of Laira Veralon, wife of a Hall Master, daughter of Lordon Venn.'

She felt her blood run cold. Her jaw opened involuntarily as the Grand Master continued to run up her family tree.

'Lordon Venn was the son of Avantus Venn, and born in this very room.'

He motioned around the space.

'Then Istopher Venn was my—'

'Great-great.' He paused, chuckling. 'Great-grandfather.'

She stood mute, her mind as blank as stone. She mouthed words that wouldn't come. Venn-Dor stood before her, grinning wide.

'I never met my grandparents. I was very young when my parents died.'

Venn-Dor nodded, regretful. 'They were good people. Do you need to sit a while?'

Her legs felt numb. She realized the instability that the Grand Master had seen. She fell backward into his arm as he ushered her to an armchair.

Her mother... Her mother and her secrets. Why did she never mention any of this? She'd always seemed a simple woman, sharp, but simple, to the point. It all made sense: her familiarity with academia, her encouragement of Molan and Carol's theories, her insistence on Renia's learning. She had been one of them. For all she knew, born here in the Halls of Venn. Scholar's blood ran in her veins.

Renia laughed as she wiped at tears that fell freely from her face. She'd always been her father's daughter, crediting everything she loved about herself—her curiosity, her work ethic—to him. She loved her mother, but never felt any special kinship with her. Not until this moment.

She took Venn-Dor's hand, at once realizing the gift that he had given her. A mother she could understand, who she had more in common with than she had ever thought possible.

'Thank you,' she said.

He nodded once. 'I have something for you,' he said. The Grand Master reached into his pocket and retrieved her lightstone pendant. Its familiar glow lit her face. She felt the tears return.

'I had it marked and registered,' he said. 'It's legally yours now.'

She stared at it, complete once again.

He gave her a wry smile. 'I would show you more. If you would like.'

'I would.' she said. 'I really would.'

SUNDANCE AND BANDACK... no, perhaps Bandack and Sundance. Yes, much better. Sundance reveled in the inspiration that would come from this little adventure. They had arranged to meet again after nightfall, allowing Sundance to finish her day's work and fulfill her duty to the hall. She'd told the Reaper of the book-

lets, Dail, Tannis, everything she'd learned so far. The younger
woman had listened intently, nodding and making mental notes
at key parts of the story. She had insisted they seek out the janitor
that posted the note under Dail's door, and so they prowled the
basement levels, hunting their prey.

The two of them moved through the labyrinthine series of
corridors and maintenance tunnels, ducking guards tasked with
keeping people confined to their quarters with ease. Steaming
pipes ejected their built-up pressure, bathing them in sweat
as they went. Bandack went out ahead often, moving with
feline grace from mundane feature to mundane feature, sniffing
pipes, brickwork, and steel. Sundance watched with fascination,
catching her breath as her older body protested at the exertion.

Bandack stopped on the corner of a flagstone at an intersection, standing on one foot and singing a strange note that flapped
oddly in Sundance's ear. So much of what the Reaper did seemed
alien to her, yet she conducted herself with such confidence, it
seemed almost rude to question it.

'My dear, are you quite well?'

The Reaper blinked at the question, and looked at her
unlikely companion with concern. 'What do you mean?'

'What in the world are you doing?'

The Reaper span in glee, arms outstretched in a theatrical
pose. 'Sampling,' she said. 'You're struggling to keep up?'

'I'm getting old. Sampling?'

The Reaper approached her curiously, unbuttoning the
sheath of a dagger that set Sundance's teeth on edge. 'Yes,
sampling. You'd be surprised what you can read with a properly
tuned sense of smell, of taste.' She licked her lips as she stalked
toward her, brandishing the dagger. The lightstone in its hilt

lit the walls, casting a yellow glow that filled her with dread. The approaching Reaper grinned, devoid of the childish charm she had displayed moments earlier. Was this it? Had she been fooled, lured into the depths of the building where she could be dispatched without alarm?

'For example, right now I can taste your fear. I can smell the lingering excitement that filled you before I unsheathed this weapon.'

In a blink, the Reaper was upon her. Bandack turned side-on to her, holding the instrument of death out in front of them, turning it over in demonstration.

'Touch it,' the Reaper said.

Sundance trembled. 'What?'

The Reaper took her hand, gently raising it toward the weapon. It was a fascinating thing. Captivating. The blade appeared razor sharp. A barely perceptible field of pure energy sparked around the cutting edge. Sundance felt the pull of curiosity as she extended a finger toward the lightstone held fast in its hilt.

'Touch it.'

At the lightest touch, she jolted. Her muscles tightened, invigorated, long-dormant synapses fired. Breath came easily. She looked at the Reaper with the eyes of a twenty-year-old. 'Moon!'

Bandack smiled from ear to ear, elated at the gift she'd given her parter of the moment.

'It likes you,' she said. 'Now smell.'

Sundance inhaled. Her senses were flooded with new information. She could see trails, distinct paths walked and repeated through the space. She could taste the sex, age, and mood of its most recent visitors. She felt incredible.

The Reaper winked at her, registering her newfound understanding.

Sundance shot her gaze around the space with breathtaking speed, her new instincts driving her. 'This way,' she said.

RENIA GASPED, FROZEN in place, unsure where to look, surrounded by wonders. Curiosities spat light and sound like the chiming of bells, spherical jars with impossible vortices of smoke crackled and flashed like miniature tamed storms, odd-looking strands of metallic rope were bent around toroidal stones that floated above desktops as if detached from gravity, an enormous tuning fork stood erect in one corner, vibrating at a rate that made her tremble with euphoria. Columns of quartz divided the wider triangle of the room into three distinct spaces, each seemingly devoted to a different discipline, or field of research. Unlike the rooms of Avantus Venn, this space was meticulously kept, and not a speck of dust dared to rest within.

'Wonderful,' she mouthed almost silently, her jaw agape.

'Isn't it,' said Venn-Dor.

Her attention was arrested by what appeared to be a floor-standing mirror. At the apex of the triangle, and in stark contrast to the activity of the other wonders, it stood silently in a pool of nothing, a nullifying aura deadening the space around it. She approached with care, unsure of what drove her toward it. The frame was fashioned from a wood of the deepest crimson, the like of which she had never seen. She had encountered the woodwork before, similar patterns to the ornate carvings in Venn-Dor's chambers. More curious were the nine lightstones mounted at the top of the frame. They were positioned around a circle, equidistant from each other but numbered, the nine at the top and the rest following sequentially, clockwise. The three, six, and nine stones were black, the rest white.

She jumped in alarm, finding herself stood an arm's length from the crimson mirror, mouthing words that wouldn't come. In her curiosity, she hadn't looked into the mirror itself, a perfect reflection of the room, without her or Venn-Dor in it. She span around to see the Grand Master staring into the mirror with a concerned expression on his face.

'Best not to touch it,' he said.

'What is it?' She found her breath rushed.

'Chaos, insanity.'

Renia found herself drawn to look again into the mirror, but shook the feeling off. 'This is Istopher Venn's residence, isn't it?'

'It is.'

She took another glance around the room. So many things to look at, rows of books to read. This was truly the life of a scholar. How had it been possible to amass so much knowledge, such mastery, in a single lifetime?

She turned back to the mirror, and cried out in shock at the image she saw. A child stood staring back at her, eyes as black as obsidian, leathery skin, unsettling proportions. She staggered, and fell back into Venn-Dor's arms.

'It's alright, it's alright.'

She looked down to see the child standing by the two of them, looking up at Venn-Dor with the sort of smile reserved for long-lost friends.

Venn-Dor whispered in her ear. 'This is Aevus. Do not be alarmed. He is the keeper of this place.'

She righted herself and watched as Venn-Dor nodded at the child. The Grand Master retrieved an hourglass from a nearby table and knelt beside the black-eyed being that stood watching her intently, so still, so unsettling. She realized what it was that disturbed her: the child didn't appear to be breathing.

'Come closer,' Venn-Dor said. 'You must let him touch you.' He turned the hourglass, allowing the sand within to flow, and placed it on the floor.

She blinked, and the child's hands were outstretched to them, as if they always had been. Renia frowned, and wondered if the vibration from the tuning fork was altering her perception of time.

'Are you ready?'

She knelt and nodded.

She felt a sudden snap, and at once Aevus's hand was around her wrist. Suddenly the child's movements became fluid, natural.

'Doratus,' the child said, his voice as smooth as milk. 'Aevus feels warm to see your face.'

'Hello, old friend.'

Renia couldn't help the flush of embarrassment as Aevus looked deep within her. She felt his awareness leak into her like water flowing over her scalp, probing, soothing. The child lit up, beaming.

'Father…Father lives in girl.'

Venn-Dor looked at each of them in turn. 'That's right'

Dizziness threatened her. She tried to focus, to take in what was happening. The vibration she'd felt before had stopped, the lights had stabilized, and the bottled storms seemed to have slowed almost to a halt. She looked to the hourglass the Grand Master had placed on the floor and gasped upon seeing that the sand had stopped mid-fall.

Time had frozen.

'Not stop,' said Aevus, as if reading her thoughts. 'Very slow.'

'Aevus,' said Venn-Dor. 'Renia has important work to carry out, and little time to do it.'

The child smiled. He rubbed his thumb over Renia's wrist, stood on his tiptoes, and touched his forehead to hers. 'Aevus will help,' he said.

THE JANITOR YELPED as Bandack leaped on top of him crotch first, pinning him to the floor. Tears rolled down his cheeks as the Reaper drummed a merry tune on his chest with the flats of her palms.

'Ha—Have I met my end…Reaper?'

She grinned. 'Not today, friend. Not by my hand, anyway.'

The janitor shot a concerned look toward Sundance as she surveyed the closet with intent. She saw little of interest. Jars of cleaning materials, mops and brushes, and images of a sexual nature. There were some curious tribal markings on the floor and walls: spirals, religious perhaps. Bandack had the man pinned next to a temporary cot by a large sink. He whimpered and muttered prayers under his breath, words of hope, requests for deliverance by the 'faithful'. Bandack shushed him with a slap.

Her eyes widened as she saw the neat pile of notes deposited at the foot of the man's cot, each folded neatly in the middle with an apartment number written on the outside.

She picked the top one up and sniffed it while Bandack restrained the weeping janitor. Her enhanced senses told her that they had been deposited in the last hour, and a familiar scent told her the depositor was more than a mere scribe. She laughed out loud at the gift she'd received. 'Hall Master Pistorious Staine,' she said with conviction.

'Now you understand?' Bandack rested her elbows on the janitor's chest as she spoke. She turned her attention to the captured man. 'What's your name, then?'

'L—Londo,' he said, frozen with shock.

Sundance squatted by them, surprised at the ease with which her joints allowed her to do so. 'How long have you been working with Mister Staine, Londo?'

The janitor fought to regulate his breathing. His breath and the sweet scent of day-old sweat assaulted her heightened sense of smell.

'I never saw him, I swear!' He looked from woman to woman, sweating. 'Months ago, a bunch of notes appeared with a bag of gold. There was a note. It said there would be more pay in exchange for me delivering them. Please don't kill me. I have a wife and two children.'

Sundance opened one of the notes, and read it aloud.

'*Brothers, sisters, we are undone. Remember well all you have learned. Remember that you are not alone, that you may find allies in the darkest corners of the world. Know that they will come for you. If I make it out of this alive, I'll return to you. If I don't, spread my words as far and wide as you can. We can change the world.*'

'How melodramatic,' Bandack said, climbing off poor Londo's chest. 'You're free to go, Londo. Try to avoid taking money from strange men in the future.'

The janitor pressed himself against the wall as he left, stuttering his apologies.

Sundance chuckled as she watched. 'What now?'

'Take me to the wall with the secret entrance.'

THE DEAD OF night was the best time to move around the grounds unnoticed. Sundance wondered twice if she was dreaming. She felt no hint of exhaustion as the hours rolled on, bounding from floor to floor, taking stairs three at a time like an athlete. She felt liberated. It was too good to be real, but she knew it was.

She laughed and giggled like a child as she tried to match the Reaper move for move, leaping silently in minor displays of acrobatics. Like schoolgirls they went, unseen and unheard, an unlikely pairing of assassin and bookworm.

Sundance overtook Bandack with a cartwheel, cringing at her childish glee at the feat. She never imagined she'd be able to do one again, and images from her childhood swam back to her.

She stopped abruptly at the target location, panting excitedly. 'Here it is.'

The Reaper winked and resumed her more serious persona, inspecting the brickwork with her usual sniffing. She licked several of the stones before nodding and unsheathing her dagger. 'Stand aside,' she said, before depressing each of them in turn.

Sundance watched in fascination as the wall depressed and opened into darkness. Bandack used the lightstone dagger as a torch, stalking into the space like a predator. 'It's clear.'

The room was old, circular in shape and perfect for the kind of lectures she guessed Staine would enjoy giving. She imagined the man relishing the attention as his perceived underlings sat and listened to him from the edges.

The current state of the space painted a different picture. A collection of blankets lay on the floor in the center of the room. A single candle for light, and a sack full of books thrown into place alongside. It was obvious that the young master had been hiding out here.

Bandack rummaged through the sack of books, grunting as she pulled out what appeared be a journal. She flicked through it with a speed that made Sundance jealous.

'It's sad really.' The Reaper handed over the journal. 'For all his arrogance, he actually has a way with words. His ambitions though…Unrealistic.' The Reaper cocked her head as she spoke. 'He would never have succeeded in changing anything. He lacks the character, and the common sense.'

Sundance nodded, glancing through the journal. It contained detailed notes on everything: the plan to recruit his followers, their names, reasons he thought they might be sympathetic, the order in which he would reveal his doctrine. Also present were research volumes on the life and deeds of Sanas Inoa.

She had it all, proof of the thinkers' circle's leadership, addresses of its members—

'Well,' Bandack said, slapping her sides. 'That's your mystery solved.'

'I'll have to get this to Jeff.'

'That's for you to worry about. I still have a job to do.'

Sundance looked at the Reaper with genuine affection. 'Thank you,' she said. 'For giving me a night I'll never forget.'

The Reaper shrugged. 'I was bored. And you smell nice.'

Sundance took the girl by the arms and kissed her cheek. It was a risky move, but the urge took her nonetheless. 'How long will it last, this effect on my body?'

'Oh, a good month or so.' The Reaper held out the dagger for her to look at. 'It's quite a rare piece, took me a long time to earn it.'

'I can imagine.'

'You should go now, Sundance. Good luck with your novel. I should like to read it one day.'

Sundance smiled. It was a strange sensation. Hours ago she'd both feared and despised the girl. She left the Reaper to her business with a nod. As much as she'd enjoyed their time together, she was sure she didn't have the stomach for the more serious business to come.

The dawn would break soon, and she had a hall to oversee.

Twenty

Time

Renia placed the candle by the window of her study. With the morning's chores addressed, and Dail settled, she felt the familiar itch of work waiting to be done.

Excitement stirred in her stomach. She'd often fantasized about having a lightstone that could stop time, about how much she could accomplish if only the world would be still, just for her, her own personal bubble of focus. Never had she imagined that the means to do so actually existed, or that it would take the form of a being such as Aevus. How old must he be? How wise? For him, a hundred years must have felt like an age. Astonishing. How lucky she was, to be honored so.

She lit the candle and took a breath, gazing lazily out into the distance. No longer taking it at face value, she saw the landscape as a realm of possibility once more, through the eyes of the child she'd long forgotten.

She turned to see Aevus standing behind her patiently, his arm outstretched. Startled, she laughed, realizing that she should have expected as much. She studied the face of the childlike figure. How long had passed for him in that small moment since the candle flickered into life? How long had he held that innocent smile on his lips?

Renia sat cross-legged on the hard wood of the floor and reached out to take Aevus's small, outstretched hand. In a blink, the world stopped. The void of silence that enveloped her made her stomach lurch. She wondered if the purpose of the tuning fork in Venn's residence was intended to compensate for the sound waves that froze outside Aevus's bubble of awareness.

'Hullo, Renya,' said Aevus.

'Hello, Aevus. Nice to see you again.'

The child smiled, staring at his tiny hand, wrapped in her grasp. The warmth of his touch surprised her. Aevus's lip trembled, and a tear rolled down his leathery cheek. Renia loosened her grip instantly, worried that she had held it too tight.

'Is everything alright, Aevus? Did I hurt you?'

'Aevus fine.' He nodded, and bit his lower lip. 'Let's get to work!'

Renia frowned. 'Do you not want to talk first?'

'Father said, "hot air is for heating water". Usual we start with "Let's get to work!" ' There was an imitation in the way he said it, a bluster that reminded her of Master Petor on his better days.

'Alright then. How does this work? I'll need both my hands.'

'Aevus hold on in different way, can hold from distance, just easy when touch.' The time child looked around the room. 'You can do now.'

She let go of his hand in a slow motion, guarding her breath as an invisible tether flexed between them. Taking a seat at her desk, she cast a last look toward the window and the silent, frozen world beyond.

Aevus sat cross-legged on the floor beside her and rested his head against her thigh. She felt an urge to stroke his hair, so soft and light, and at odds with his defining features. A familiarity fell over her, and she placed her hand over her abdomen and the baby growing within.

She shook the feeling off, focused and ready to begin.

PAGE AFTER PAGE, the work came easily. She lost herself in the words of her ancestor. For the first time in what felt like forever, she remembered what life had been before all of this began, before she'd lost her way. The mysteries of the lightstones unfolded within her, whetting her curiosity, driving her on. From moment to moment, she caught herself pawing at her own stone where it lay on her chest.

'ARE YOU ALRIGHT?' Renia looked down at the child. He hadn't moved for what must have been hours. At first he'd whimpered and mewed, occasionally wrapping his arms around her leg. She hadn't minded; it was just an unusual sensation. She worried that when she'd stopped working to consider this, he'd noticed, cursed himself, and done his best not to distract her.

'Aevus fine. Did distract?'

'No, I was just worried.'

'Why?'

The question left her speechless. She reached down and took his hand. 'Stand up for a while, you'll hurt yourself sitting like that for too long.'

The child stood and stared at her, perplexed.

'Do you want to have a look at what I'm doing?'

'Why?'

'It's your father's work. I'm copying it, see?'

Aevus's eyes flickered toward the open book, but then back again. 'Aevus distracting.'

She frowned. 'I've done almost half a day's work. Let's call it a little break, alright? Let's do something you want to do for a while instead.'

Tears started to well once again in the child's eyes. He shuffled uncomfortably in place, his black eyes glinting. 'Important work, Doratus said.'

'Oh no, Aevus, I wasn't trying to upset you. I just thought we could rest for a moment and refresh.'

He started to calm down. 'Little rest,' he said.

She pulled him close and pointed out the last page of her work. 'You see, this talks about how lightstone seems to absorb emotion, using it to grow.'

Aevus stared at the page with a mixture of confusion and pain. It became clear to Renia that he couldn't read, nor did he seem to think he should be able to. He was ashamed, ashamed of his curiosity and his imagined imposition.

'Here.' Renia pulled a slate from beneath her desk and fumbled around for some chalk. She scratched out the letter A. 'Do you know this shape?'

HOURS MORE HAD passed. The sun had barely moved. Renia felt a special kind of exhaustion that made her body scream. She felt out of sync, adrift.

'Let's sleep for a while,' she said.

'Alright, Aevus will leave.'

'No, no. Can you stay? I mean, can we stay in this time bubble whilst we sleep? I'm too tired to return to normal time right now.'

'Aevus always fast.' He exhaled, a hopeless look on his face. 'Father sleep with Aevus, always. Gone now.'

'It must feel like an eternity to you.'

'Touch is nice. Renya is nice.'

She lay a blanket on the floor where the sun burst through the window. 'Come on,' she said, pulling him in tight. They slept.

'YOU DID IT!'

'Alphabet.' Aevus proudly displayed the slate.

'Now let's work on writing your first word.'

'Any word?'

'Any word.'

Aevus furrowed and bit his lip. 'Father,' he said.

'RENYA, WHAT WRONG?'

'I need to eat a good meal. How long has it been?'

'Three sleeps.'

She looked to where she'd marked a line on the floor. Roughly calculating the point at which she'd have to return to real time and tend to Dail. 'Let's go to the canteen and see what we can rustle up.'

'Rustle?'

'I'll show you, come on.'

THEY SAT IN the canteen.

Statuesque, the few people that had been lucky enough not to be confined to their quarters sat frozen, mid-bite. Renia and Aevus laughed, and laughed at their facial expressions, trying their best to mimic them.

'Your speech is getting better,' she said.

'Aevus is remembering how.'

She placed her hand on his.

'BEETROOT JUICE AND glue. It makes a good dye.' The guard stood frozen mid-stride. They sat cross-legged on the stone floor beside him, mixing the concoction in a bowl they took from the canteen.

'Feels naughty,' said Aevus.

'Oh don't be silly. It'll wash off easily enough. It's plate armor.'

Aevus stood, and rocked on his heels, unsure.

She finger painted a smiley face on the guard's chest plate, whilst Aevus looked on in disbelief, on the edge of laughter. 'Just think of all the joy this will create...It's called a joke.'

The child jumped up and down, before painting a mustache on the guard's helmet. 'Ah ha! Ahahahaha!'

'Perfect!' she announced.

They rolled on the floor, laughing uncontrollably.

THE LIGHT IN the study had finally changed. The sunbeam from the window finally reaching the line she'd drawn on the floor.

'I won't be lon—' She paused, frowning. It *would* be long for him. 'What will you do?'

'Aevus will clean for Father.'

'And then what?'

She thought she sensed a frustration in him. 'Maybe I will try to read.'

'That's good! Remember, there are lots of children's books in the library.'

'Aevus will try.'

'Alright, I'll see you soon.'

He nodded at her, a longing in his eyes. She knelt and embraced him, placing her palm on his face. 'Do it,' she said.

A rush of noise assaulted her ears. Aevus was gone. She stood, and looked at the stack of completed pages on her desk. It was the most she'd been able to produce in a long time, and in all respects, her finest work. She felt the knowledge seep into her, a slow soaking, that came charged with the essence of Venn himself. With it came a sadness, a realization that Aevus had been a tool to him, a means to achieve, and little more.

She rubbed her belly. Childhood for Renia had been short, and the memory of it sat heavy with feelings of guilt, of shame. Her time with Aevus had awoken those old feelings, the joy of play, and mischief. She struggled with thoughts of her future. Perhaps the baby could help to heal those old scars. Could she be deserving of that? Would it really be such a terrible distraction from what she thought she needed? Or could the answer to all the recent turmoil have been inside her all along?

'Renia! Renia!'

Dail.

WITHIN THE HOUR, she'd seen to Dail, laid out fresh linen, and bathed him. Alice came to take over, and with her arrival Renia's thoughts returned to the slow-world and the relief from reality that it offered.

She rushed through the list of things that she had taken care of, and carefully explained to Alice that she could not be disturbed, and not to open the door to the study under any circumstances.

With that, the candle was lit once again, and the work could continue.

'RENYA, NOT WORKING?'

She looked back at Aevus, distracted, carefully balancing a spare candle in the middle of the room. 'Yes. I just want to try something first. Stand back a little?'

Aevus gave her a concerned look, but nodded, retreating to the far wall.

She held the necklace containing her lightstone shard, focusing her will toward the wick of the candle.

'Light,' she whispered.

Nothing happened. She shook her head. *You're overthinking it, feel it, focus.* She closed her eyes, feeling for the world's pulse. She felt the vibration of her being at the base of her spine, and imagined energy flowing up through her body, to her arm.

She opened her eyes and focused once more on the wick. *Light,* she thought.

An acrid smell hit her nostrils and the gentle crackle of sparks filled the air. Tiny lights danced in arcs around the wick, then snapped out of existence.

Renia fell to her knees, her heart pounding. Aevus rushed to her side.

'You're hurt,' he said.

'No. I'm fine.' She swept her hair out of her face and smiled at him. 'I've done it before, I can do it again.'

AEVUS SAT WITH one arm wrapped around her leg. With the other he practiced copying words from a children's book he'd grown fond of, a tale of three children who banded together to save the world from a man made of shadow.

The pages continued to flow, each one carrying the promise of further knowledge and the secret to controlling the current of energy that would allow her to wield her stone. Her mind was flooded with insight, and memories that were not her own threatened to force themselves into her psyche. She needed to rest.

She reached down and stroked Aevus's hair. 'You're getting good at that.'

He turned to look up at her in wonder, his jet-black eyes sparkling. 'This is best part, they escape cave and decide they should stick together forever.'

A mixture of joy and sorrow written on his face, Aevus put down his chalk and stood to face her. 'Father did not allow Aevus to ask about things.' He dropped his head. 'Aevus feels bad, guilty.'

Renia's heart ached. She knew why; she understood Venn's need of Aevus, and what it would have meant for him to have overstepped his purpose. Venn hadn't needed another son, he had needed an escape from the responsibilities that came with already having one. Allowing Aevus a real childhood would have defeated the object.

She placed her hands on his cheeks. 'He's gone now, Aevus. It's time to start living for yourself.'

The child began to sob. 'But what does mean? Aevus promised to keep Father's things. To protect, always.'

'And yet you are here, with me, enjoying yourself.'

'And then Renya will be gone. What will Aevus then?'

Renia felt the tears pooling. She held him close. 'Come on, let's go outside.'

'I CAN'T, RENYA.'

Renia stood on the first step of the main entrance to the Halls of Venn. She turned to look at Aevus where he stood on the threshold, trembling.

'It's alright, come on. You'll love it.'

'I can't leave. I should be with Father's things.'

'Aevus, we'll be back before anyone in real time can take a few breaths. Nothing bad will happen. Come with me.'

He lifted his foot, covering his eyes with his hand as he teased towards the step.

'Aha.' He jumped forward. 'I did it. I did it.'

THE GATE WAS heavily manned. Lifeless guards, locked in their movements, lined the stone archway that gave way to the iron gate barring entry to the outside world.

Renia tested the chain that raised the gate, finding it heavier than she expected. She made a show of leaping up and using her body weight to drag it down, making silly noises as she raised the gate by enough for them to crawl through.

Aevus laughed out loud at the spectacle.

'IT'S CHILDREN,' SAID Aevus.

She nodded, showing as much enthusiasm as she could. 'They are playing kickball.'

Aevus frowned. 'What's kickball?' He moved among the smiling faces, inspecting them, copying their poses. Renia could see the wonder in his demeanor. The promise of a childhood neither of them had been lucky enough to enjoy.

'Do you see the ball there? One team is trying to kick it between those markers, the other is trying to kick it between the markers at the opposite side.'

She retrieved the ball from its position in mid-air and placed it at Aevus's feet. 'You try.'

Aevus bit his lip. 'I can't do that.'

'Of course you can, look.' She booted the ball with a satisfying thud. It flew through the air and bounced off a wall, missing the markers by a wide margin.

They laughed out loud. Acting out the ball's trajectory, and mocking the failure.

'Now, you try.'

He looked at the ball. 'Don't want to.'

'Why ever not? It's fun.'

She studied his face. Indecision stared back at her.

'I can never play like them. With them.'

Renia started to understand. 'Aevus, have you ever tried to speed up your time?'

He nodded. 'Father asked me try, one time.'

'What happened?'

'He said make it opp'sit, so outside Aevus is fast, very fast'. Aevus looked away in shame.

'Aevus,' she said. 'What happened?'

'I failed. It hurt so much, and made my face hard and wrinkle like this.' He sobbed. 'Father was angry.'

Aevus took another look at the frozen children, tears rolling down his leathery cheeks.

'I can never be slow, like them,' he said. 'I will die.'

ANOTHER WEEK IN slow time passed. Renia broke once more to tend to Dail and prepare his evening meal. The duality of the two worlds started to wear on her, and she found it significantly harder to adapt the second time than she had the first, knowing that for the rest of the world less than a day had passed.

Finishing the first book had given them a reason to celebrate, and as such she took the time to teach Aevus how to dance, a waltz that Molan had taught her in her adolescence. Aevus was quick to mention that her singing voice wasn't very good.

All the while, Venn's knowledge unraveled within her like a snake uncoiling. She practiced with the candle regularly, with Aevus watching intently.

'You can do it, Renia.'

She grinned at him. 'Maybe this time?'

He nodded, poking his finger toward the candle. 'Go.'

She once again drew the world's energy within. Allowing it to flow through her, becoming a conduit. She felt her lightstone warm in her palm and rush with potential.

Her hair stood on end, and an arc of static flashed between her hand and the wick. It blazed to life, leaving a perfect flame rocking gently, illuminating the space around it in victory.

'You did it.' Aevus rushed to her side and leaped into her arms. 'You did it. You did it.'

Her heart raced, and she struggled to catch her breath as emotion caught in her throat. The pair embraced, tears soaking into her shirt as they wept together.

'I did it,' she sobbed.

'THIS IS AMAZING,' she said.

'What is it?'

'The old ones.'

Renia hadn't expected to be as interested in her second project. Aevus worked steadily at his own reading and writing skills, making better progress than could be expected of any child.

'Would you read it to me, before we sleep?' said Aevus.

'Of course I will.'

'NO CANDLES THIS time?' said Aevus.

'Not this time. I want to try something different.'

Renia found she was able to use her lightstone with her necklace around her neck; freeing her hands helped her focus.

She held her arms in front of her, envisioning a ball between her hands. Her eyes flickered. Sparks began to form, casting an oscillating glow over her face. She smiled as a swirling ball of energy manifested between her palms. A vortex, much like the ones she'd seen in jars in the residence of Istopher Venn.

Aevus clapped and jumped on one foot, unable to control his excitement. 'You're doing it. You're doing it.'

She smiled and removed one of her hands, attempting to move the miniature storm around her in a clumsy, unpracticed motion.

'And so it would appear that the initial success of Daralar's mission of domination was due to the Aceraceians' strong belief in the preservation of all life, and the significant losses inflicted during the Moonfall. Survivors of the catastrophe often speak of the prowess of the individuals that gave their lives to slow Luna's descent. The old ones, it seems…'

She felt the vibration of Aevus's snoring on her chest, and smiled. *I agree, not the most riveting chapter,* she thought. She pulled the blanket over them and fell asleep with her arm around his shoulder.

'Aevus, why are you crying?'

'I'm not.'

'You are. Come on, tell me what's wrong.'

'I just love having a friend.'

'I'll always be your friend.'

'But you're almost out of pages.'

Renia rested her quill and placed the page on the stack, which had grown thicker with breathtaking pace. She grinned in satisfaction.

'Ready, Aevus?'

Aevus waddled over to place the last candle. He had organized them in a circle, a couple of feet between each. 'Ready!' He retreated to a space behind the desk, peering out from behind the desktop, which came roughly to his eye line.

'Here we go,' said Renia.

She manifested the storm-ball with expert precision, a perfectly contained sphere of energy flashing smatterings of blue light around the room, crackling and whipping. The smell of noxious gases came and went, leaving a tang at the back of her throat.

Renia motioned with her outstretched arm, and the ball of energy mimicked her movements, floating to where she directed it. With the poise of a conductor, she navigated it around the circle of candles, lightly brushing each wick and setting it alight.

She grinned, swelling with pride. She turned the ball around, arcing it back to her, and froze mid-turn as she noticed the door to the study ajar. A pair of frozen eyes stared at her from the opening.

Alice.

The energy ball snapped out of existence. She ran to the door and slammed it closed. 'Aevus! Drop me into real time, quick!'

Panicked, Aevus nodded and closed his eyes.

She descended into real time, suppressing the lurch in her stomach, and rushed to the door. Alice stumbled backward as Renia opened the door and pressed into the room.

'Alice…'

The old woman stuttered, gathering her skirts in an attempt to right herself. 'I, um… well, forgive me, miss.'

'Alice, what did you see?'

'Nothing, miss. I mean, well, it was only for a split second, a small moment.' Alice's eyes glazed over. 'It was… well, then the door was closed, in a blink.' She shook her head. 'Dear, I fear that my mind might be playing tricks on me.'

Renia came to the older woman's side, allowing her to steady herself. She helped her to a chair, and brought her a cool, damp towel and a cup of tea.

'Alice, it wouldn't be wise to open that door again.'

Alice took a long moment to meet Renia's gaze.

'My dear, I'm not sure I could.'

'Aevus, calm down.'

'But what if she saw me?'

Aevus sobbed and spluttered, shaking uncontrollably and spattering Renia with spittle.

'Shhh.' She pulled him in close, resting his head on her shoulder. 'Nobody is mad at you, sweetheart. Father is gone, he's gone. You don't have to be afraid.'

She placed the last page neatly atop the stack and sighed, brushing down her dress. She inhaled deeply and turned in her seat to see Aevus staring at her, a distressed look on his face.

'You're finished,' he said.

'All done.' She smiled at him. 'Hungry?'

Aevus shook his head.

She beckoned him over. 'Come now, don't be sad.'

'I'm not sad.'

'Alright.'

Renia smiled and pulled the child onto her lap. 'We have lots of time.' She tapped his nose. 'Thanks to you.'

A hint of a smile formed on his leathery face.

'Come on, let's go for a walk.'

'AEVUS, WHERE DID you come from?'

'What do you mean?' He scrunched his face, confused.

'I mean, how were you made?'

'Oh. Father said when a man and a woman love each other they have a special cuddl—'

'No, no. I mean where did you come from?'

'Well, Father once said I came from the red window.'

'The mirror?'

'The shiny one.'

Renia rubbed her eyebrow. 'You can enter it?'

'I don't want to go in there, Renia. Don't make us go in there.'

'Shh, it's alright. I won't. I won't.'

SLEEPING IN DAYLIGHT hadn't been too hard to adjust to, but a night that lasted for seven days... *That* was too much.

'It's time, Aevus,' she said.

The child looked down and away, and she felt the pang of guilt she knew so well. Renia knelt beside her friend, conflicted. Not just for the loss of Aevus's company, but for the loss of the sanctuary that it brought, a freedom from the world that had brought her little but pain. She couldn't hurt anyone here, she couldn't draw anyone close enough to be caught in her wake. That was the saddest part. That was exactly what she'd done to Aevus.

'Come,' she said, taking his tiny hands in her own. 'You know I can't stay any longer. Doratus brought us together for a purpose.'

'...'

'Don't be like that.'

Aevus pulled a hand free and wiped his nose, sniffling away his melancholy. 'I'll miss you.'

'I'll miss you too.'

They shared a moment of silence. Renia kissed the hand she still held and ruffled his hair. 'Why don't I read to you tomorrow night?'

'How many sleeps will that be?'

She paused, knowing that the answer wouldn't help.

'Twenty one.'

TWENTY-ONE

Bargain

VENN-DOR STOOD by the glass cabinet that housed his weapon. His staff, the source of both his power and his weakness. How long had it been since he'd felt its energy, since he'd employed his gifts?

As long as it had been. A day at a time; that was how he'd measured it.

After Raellon's death, and the period of grief that followed, he'd found himself questioning so much about his character, questioning so many of his choices. It was easy to blame the weapon—power corrupts, after all—but was it really the weapon? Or was it him?

His failure.

Not the failure to wield power, but to control it. The failure to recognize the point at which it started to control him.

Hubris.

Hubris was his weakness, and each day over the long years since Raellon's death, he'd denied himself any real test of humility by keeping the staff locked in its case. Perhaps he had learned nothing, and all his efforts to control his hubris were *for* nothing. You can't learn to control something by ignoring it. Discarding the source of his power had been easy. It was a simple excuse to lapse into lethargy, and embrace the relative safety of a purely administrative role. Who did that serve? Did it serve his lord, his charges? Did it serve the realm? No. It served him. It served his fears.

This was the Praelatus's intention. This was the lesson that Venn-Dor had refused to hear.

A rapping at the door snapped him out of his thoughts. He'd sent for Renia first thing, eager to know if Aevus had been able to help her complete her task. Time grew shorter. The old ones were stirring and it wouldn't be long before they required a new Shepherd.

'Come!' he commanded, and the doors opened.

Renia strode into the room, two stacks of pages held to her chest. He noted the confidence in her step, the straightness of her back. She'd changed. She had the look of a woman who had herself in order. Her hair was well made, her outfit pressed and clean.

Her footsteps rang on the tiled floor. Colored light from the windows washed over her face as she approached. He smiled at her, already pouring tea for the both of them.

'Grand Master.' She bowed. 'I would submit these pages for your review.'

'I accept your submission.'

They shared a moment of satisfaction. He tried not to grin at the change in her demeanor.

'How long were you gone?' he asked.

'Twenty-one days have passed for me, sir.'

He already knew that. He wasn't sure why he'd asked; perhaps it was the novelty of hearing such a statement spoken with conviction.

'You will need to shed the habit of calling me sir.'

'Sir?'

He grinned. She blushed.

'Shall we sit? I've made tea.'

He took the pages from her and laid them on a counter top. He would bind and finish them personally. It was an exercise he'd missed—good, honest work.

They sipped their tea, regarding each other. The lightstone shard around her neck glinted, reflecting the morning's light directly into his eyes.

It had grown.

'I see you've been busy practicing your sorcery,' he said.

The girl nodded firmly. 'I have. Venn's work was very helpful.'

'How was working with Aevus?'

She smiled. 'He's a wonderful—'

Yes, it is difficult to say it out loud, he thought.

'I think child is the right word.' She nodded again. 'Do you know how he was created?'

Yes, he did. Though it wasn't something he wanted to talk about; hopefully neither did she, and he wouldn't have to. He simply nodded and sipped his tea. They lapsed into silence.

'I would ask something of you,' she said.

'I would ask something of you.' The words rang in his head. Another time, but the same table, the same tea. He swallowed, and lowered his cup. 'Oh?' He felt his eyebrow ride up. 'Go on, then.'

'I would like to try to heal Dail. I mean—I would like to have use of a healing stone, just temporarily.'

Would you now?

There was little he could do to stave off the invading memory. The parallels were too great. Youth, optimism, hunger. The Grand Master found himself torn between distaste and envy. Just as he had when Raellon had sat in that chair, making his own request. He had been in his prime then, whole and brimming with charm.

A twitching sensation in his hand drew his attention back to the present. He spared it a glance, though only for what it was, a curiosity. Renia still sat patiently, awaiting his response.

He should have seen it coming, the strut, the formality of her words. He recognized it well, overconfidence. *A little practice and suddenly you think you're a master sorcerer, able to bend any lightstone to your will.* She wasn't alone in it; he himself had been the same once, as had countless others.

'It would not be wise,' he said.

'I have to try.'

'Did you not read Venn's book well enough? Lightstones are not tools, Renia. They have sentience, they have to *choose* to grant you their power.'

She would not be bowed, even in the face of his dismissal she continued to press. 'But a bargain can be made, it said so in the book.'

'Yes, but the cost is high. If you try to force your will on a lightstone it *will* take something from you in return. Weeks, years, the image of youth, perhaps worse. Do not do this, Renia.'

'You could bring a healing stone here. It is within your power.'

A great many things were. He could summon one of the healing masters to restore Mister Svelt, but he would not. Such gifts were reserved for the few, those on whom the stability of the realm depended. If word were to spread, it would cause unrest, accusations of privilege.

'I could, of course,' he said.

'Then let me do this. I know I can do this. I've taken so much from Dail. I would give some of my life so that he might have his back.'

Was that really what drove her? Or was it her own life she wanted back?

He studied her face for a while, considering the answer.

'I know I can do this. You know I can do this.' His eyes closed as the words pulled on his heart.

Raellon sat with his face to the window, smiling as the light bathed his skin; reflective with the grease of a late night. He sat with his legs apart, one heavy boot tapping at the tile.

'You're late.' Of course he was.

The young man raised an eyebrow and opened his eyes, still smiling. 'I had a late night.'

Doratus fought the urge to huff, and settled for exhaling slowly though his nose. It wasn't that he wanted to disapprove of his adopted son's choice of friends or recreational activities. But he did. How could he not? Had the boy heard nothing of his lessons?

'Please, Father. Spare me the lecture, I haven't the head for it.'

He inhaled sharply, pouring his own tea. 'Very well,' he said.

'I would ask something of you.'

'Oh?'

Raellon grinned. 'It is a strange request. But I need a book that looks a lot like one of Inoa's journals.'

He tried not to laugh, and reciprocated the unrestrained amusement in his son's eyes. 'Looks like?'

They chuckled together. 'A fake. I was thinking the text could be ciphered, blocks of pages could repeat. It can be gibberish for all I care, I just need something that looks the part.'

'And I suppose you're going to ask me not to question what you want it for?'

Raellon winked, and clicked his fingers.

'Well. Now I am truly curious.'

'You're going to refuse, aren't you?'

Doratus shrugged, feigning indifference. 'It does sound terribly laborious.'

'Alright, indulge me a moment.' They laughed again as Doratus waggled his eyebrows from behind his teacup. 'Father, be serious. Look—we both suspect there are agents of Daralar here. I think I have one made, and I think I can use him to root out the rest of them.'

It wasn't the first time he'd heard such a statement.

'I know you're skeptical, and rightly so. But I know I can do this. You know I can do this. So please, just make the book?'

Would things have been different had he refused? Would his son be sat here now in Renia's place?

His every urge fought the idea of humoring her request. The cruelty with which fate imitated the past wore on him. Why? Had providence deemed his choice of penance unworthy? Or was it a more earthly power at play? Was it within the power of the Praelatus to influence events to such parity? A lesson to be learned? He didn't even know if he could, for to let go of his pain would be to unleash it, to relinquish control of it.

'Renia is not Raellon.' He winced at the memory of his master's voice.

'Come with me,' he said.

Renia sat upright, startled by the break in his silence. 'Where are we going?'

'The North Wing.'

PETOR STARTED THE day early. Half a bottle of whiskey sat exhausted on his desk. He talked to his paintbrush, mocking Vedora's words. 'Be the bnest bainter you can bee. Haha.'

He inspected the painting. The image of a rotund woman with large breasts eating a heart stared back at him from the canvas. It was an unlikely choice of subject for him.

He laughed and staggered to the door, dragging the bottle of whiskey along with him. As he stopped, he wondered why he'd risen and burst into tears at the fact he'd forgotten.

The morning had brought with it a soundtrack of chaos from the nearby halls, though he'd lacked the mental acuity to spare it much thought. He opened the door and balked, giggling as the breeze tickled his bare lower half.

A passing guard spared a look at the half-naked drunkard swaying in his doorway and paused, clearly questioning what he was seeing. 'Get back in your home and await further instructions.'

'Fffuuuuckkk ooffff,' Petor replied, waving a raised finger in the wrong direction. 'And shurrup all this basdarrd noiz!'

He slammed the door behind him and fell against it in a slump, being careful not to let his bottle fall over before he passed out.

AS THE GREAT doors to the North Wing parted, Renia stood frozen in awe at the sheer scale of the entryway. Unlike the ostentatious nature of the South Wing's decor, the North Wing had a more brutal appearance. The room was built of large dark stones, expertly cut with hardly any noticeable seam between them. The pillars that supported the ceiling were equally bare, smooth polished stone as black as night. The floor was paved in a lighter shade, but equally as well cut, no decorative pattern, no familiar motif, just a clean functional space.

Multiple corridors broke from the central chamber, archways promising the answers to questions already forming in her mind. She looked at Venn-Dor, who kept his gaze set on the scene unfolding further into the space.

As they approached, the shouting became louder. A handful of people were arguing, and two guards held back a particularly agitated man in simple robes. She paid little attention to the debacle. Instead, she was drawn toward the balcony they stood on, and the huge sweeping staircases either side of it that descended into a dark space filled with dim, flickering lights. It looked like a starscape from where she stood.

She ducked instinctively as something flew past her head.

'So you'll allow these two to waltz in here whilst you keep us prisoner? We've had enough, Ferron. There are hundreds of us and a handful of *you*. How much longer do you think you can control this situation?'

Ferron—she knew that name. The chief of security for the North Wing. Her attention shifted from her surroundings and she began to understand what was happening. Ferron stood with his arms folded across his chest, stern-faced and bored-looking. She let her gaze linger on the scar running down his face as the Grand Master led her toward the staircase.

'Pay them no mind,' Venn-Dor said. 'Ferron is more than capable of handling it.'

As they descended into the belly of the North Wing, they passed doorway after doorway, each unlabeled and nondescript. Utter silence enveloped them and gave no clue as to what lay beyond. Downward they spiraled, the flickering candles struggling against the growing darkness, and a musky, damp smell began to gather at the back of her throat.

'Not much further,' said Venn-Dor.

At what must have been close to the bottom of the pit, the archways began to glow, each a different color. Renia held herself in check, wide-eyed in anticipation. Venn-Dor led her through an archway that radiated white light, and into a footway that forked around a pillar large enough to obscure what lay within.

Renia gasped at the sight that awaited her. They stood in a decent-sized room, shelves and counter tops filled with ledgers and tools for taking measurements littered the space. A tunnel that stretched for what seemed like an eternity began at the end of the room. Inside, rows after rows of brilliant white lightstones sat on specially made shelves with spherical recesses.

'Incredible,' she mouthed.

'Yes,' said Venn-Dor. 'The remains of a civilization.'

For years she'd dreamed of the sight. The stockpiles of lightstone she'd seen gathered in the Wastes as a child. Though she had never imagined such volume.

She tried to focus on the end of the tunnel. 'So much power...'

'Indeed,' said the Grand Master. He frowned at her.

She watched as he shook his head, and walked toward a stone near the tunnel entrance. It had a label: 'Spero'. He reached for it, but then pulled his hand away.

'THIS IS GOING to hurt,' said the Grand Master.

Stubs was a teenager then, gangly and misshapen with the rapid growth of puberty. 'Do it,' he said. 'I'm not afraid.'

'You should be.' The grin-grimace he tried to hide was lost to the boy, who held his incomplete hand flat against the table.

'You said you could do it.'

'I can.'

'Then do it!'

Something that felt like pleasure rose in his chest, a shameful excitement. He admired the boy's bravery, his desire for action. It reminded him of his own youth. The boy had been valuable over the years, immeasurably so, but more than that, he had become something more. Doratus had allowed himself to feel something for the child. It was this that gave him pause, a paternal instinct to protect the boy from the pain he asked for.

'Do it!'

Doratus extended his staff. With a thought, light gathered and metastasized in bubbles around the boy's stunted fingertips. There was a flash, then a deafening clang that gave way to the boy's scream. The light slithered away, and blood shot from freshly cloven stubs. It splashed the walls and ceiling as Stubs thrashed and turned, howling in agony.

He pulled Spero from the large pocket in his robes and began to chant, his gaze fixed on the flailing limb. He felt joy, and laughter began to rock his chest—he lost focus. What was he doing? He returned his attention to the bleeding stumps as the boy held out his arm, pleading. Doratus chanted, and channeled the light into extending cylinders that extruded from the point of severance. Flesh and bone swirled into the real, pushing themselves outward with the boy's reach. Pink, slick flesh slid over the protrusions, and fingernails began to grow.

Doratus remembered both awe and fear in the boy's eyes then, when he stood flexing his new fingers. He remembered the fear he felt at his own reaction. It rose like bile in his throat, and burned. He bit it back. 'You're going to need a new name.'

The Grand Master pulled his hand away from the stone, and lowered his gaze. 'This one,' he said to Renia. 'Take it.'

JEFF SWORE UNDER his breath, looking out over the sea of heads that threatened to crash over him and make him pay for his part in the lockdown.

There is nothing more dangerous than an angry mob.

They shouted and swore. Bottles, mugs, and bars of soap flew through the air at him and the two guards at his side, who exchanged nervous glances and backed slowly toward the door.

They stood in the entrance corridor to one of the staff residential blocks; it housed scribes from the halls that had been closed. The mass had been left in relative peace until this morning, when the deep search had come calling. Mattresses had been upturned, clothes thrown from wardrobes and left in piles, drawers emptied into sinks, every private possession inspected, questioned, in some cases mocked.

If it was possible to smell outrage, Jeff smelled it, though it could have been sweat and the mixture of the contents of smashed bottles. The mob's demands rang in his ears.

'Let us out, bastards!'

'You've done your search, now open the fucking doors!'

'This is wrong!'

Jeff looked to the guards at his side and shook his head. 'Stop backing away, they only need a hint of weakness and we end up like your comrades.'

'There'sh tgoo many,' said Rurghesh. Jeff had spent the morning with him and his partner Shqlaum, searching another block. 'We can't get to them.'

Jeff frowned, he strained to see through the morass of protesting bodies to the guardsmen who had been responsible for keeping the peace on this block. They were tied up with leather belts, and looked beaten and confused, lolling their heads, sat on the floor, surrounded by the mob.

Jeff did his best to project a commanding tone. 'Listen.' He held up his palms. 'I know this is a difficult time.' He eyed as many of them as he could. 'I know it is. But the article we are searching for is important enough to warrant these measures.'

'Bullshit, Jeff.'

'Fuck off.'

Jeff waved his palms. 'Please listen, *listen*.' The crowd settled slightly. 'Many of you know me. You know that I take no pleasure in this. You know that I would not support this unless the stakes were high enough to affect all our lives.'

He lowered his hands. 'Please, consider this. Just a few more days. Let me do my job, so I can bring an end to this, for all of us.'

A murmur began to spread through the press of people. Some exchanged clipped words, others stormed into their dorms and slammed the door behind them. But steadily, Jeff's words began to sink in, and the rage that held the mob together began to die.

Retreating scribes glared at him as they left for their dorms, others thanked him, some apologized, but eventually the path to the defeated guards opened up and the entrance hall fell calm once more.

He turned to Rurghesh and gave him a grim nod. 'Take your brothers back to Garamond. Tell them to be more respectful of people's belongings next time.'

'Yesh, shir.'

Jeff walked slowly back to his office with his stomach growling. *When did I last eat?* That was the second situation he'd diffused that morning. Requests for his help came thick and fast, leaving him little time to take care of himself, let alone focus on his investigation. He'd slept only fitfully in his chair in clothes he'd worn for two days.

There it was again—he turned in a flash. Nothing there. For days now he'd felt a presence following him, watching him. Probably paranoia. Lack of sleep would do that to a man.

He entered the security office rubbing his eyes. His head throbbed.

'Everything alright, sir?' Jinger said, looking up from her desk.

'I could do with a coffee, if you wouldn't mind.'

He slumped into his chair, lifting his leg onto the box that he used to keep it elevated.

What a mess.

Another three envelopes were placed neatly on the desktop. He tore them open, frowning. *Death threat, Sundance—what's this?*

He turned over a strange note.

Jeff, I have something you want.

Marked with the symbol of the moon cult. He knitted his eyebrows in confusion. What was this now? Was this a joke? Was it genuine?

'Jinger?' he hollered. 'Is this Bobb's work?'

She approached, a steaming cup of black coffee in her hand. 'No…' She placed the cup in front of him with care. 'I only left two notes on your desk, sir.'

He studied her green eyes. 'Hmm.'

'Sir.'

Jeff pulled his attention from the note. 'Yes?'

'You smell a bit musky. Why don't you rest a while? Freshen up?'

She was right. It didn't send the right message, looking unkempt. He couldn't take his eyes off the note.

He stood, and put it in his pocket. 'I think I will.'

Jinger called out to him as he made for the door. 'Sundance will be back at lunchtime. What should I tell her?'

To leave me alone?

Another oddity. 'She wouldn't tell you what she wanted?'

'She says it's for your ears only, sir.'

Perhaps he had misjudged the situation.

'Tell her to visit me after work. Send two guards to escort her.'

'Yes, sir.'

He sniffed his armpit and turned to leave.

'Jinger… Thanks.'

The cult. He almost laughed. As if being caught between conspiring colleagues, southern agents, and a protesting mob wasn't enough. Now he was supposed to believe that the trogs were also more than they had seemed to be, more than cave-dwelling, moon-worshiping drones, scavenging scraps of food, preaching their message to the weak-willed from the shadows. What could they possibly have that Jeff would want? The book? Not a chance, surely.

Moreover, what could the 'faithful' want *here*, in the Halls of Venn, far from their beloved 'shade-bringer'? The cultists were little more than savages when he'd left Southgate. Could the rumors be true? Had something changed beneath Luna? Was his father aware of this?

His brain limped to a stop, unwilling to add another layer to the already fragile house of cards in his mind. He needed to rest, to allow his subconscious to filter through the variables.

He needed more time.

RENIA STOOD WITH the Grand Master, her mood determined, focused on the sleeping man that lay in her bed. Dail, the man she'd broken, the source of her guilt, her frustration, the anchor that held her locked between two lives.

In her hand she held the lightstone. Its brilliant surface cast a white light that painted the walls with long shadows. She saw it reflected in Venn-Dor's eyes as he regarded her with a mixture of curiosity and concern.

'I'm ready,' she said.

Venn-Dor inhaled through his nostrils. 'You will not reconsider?'

'I will not.'

He stepped backward. 'Then go ahead.'

She remembered the teachings of Istopher Venn, closing her eyes and feeling for the pulse of the stone, its song. It was a dance. A dance she had never attempted, and she knew she could stumble with the slightest lapse in concentration.

She felt for it, the throbbing of life that existed within it but it jolted her—a threat, a protest to her intrusion. Something had to be offered. She gritted her teeth, and imagined her own blood, her life energy flowing down her arm into the stone.

'Rrrgh.'

Venn-Dor stepped forward to protest, but she waved him back and shot him an irritated look.

The stone drank her energy. She felt it greedily lapping at the life force she'd offered. Her feet began to tingle, a feeling of distance grew between her legs and the ground that supported her. Still she held tight, intent on seeing it through.

Again, the stone rebuffed her advance. She whimpered as it sent stabbing waves up her arm, into her shoulder. *You will not deter me.* The grinding of teeth ran through her inner ear. She realized that tension had taken her. She needed to relax.

Calm. Work with the stone, not against it.

With the thought, her muscles released. She stood taller, still exchanging sensation with the glowing orb.

I wish to heal this man.

Renia opened her eyes, realizing her vision had blurred at the edges. Dail's prone form lay before her; the image ebbed and jarred, unstable in her mind.

The lightstone chimed, and began to suck, drawing Renia's life source into itself. Her limbs grew heavy, her breath lazy and shallow. She began to lose her train of thought, her grounding.

Focus. Heal Dail.

She held on, massaging her will toward Dail. Imploring the lightstone to take on the work of mending him.

Please, heal him.

With a rush, white light began to radiate from beneath his skin. Dail glowed. The room began to vibrate.

'Urngghhh.' Dail writhed, unconscious but animated on the bed. A mess of noise rose from his flesh, hissing and popping, the sound of meat and bone knitting, the snap of dead nerves firing once more.

He screamed, thrusting up into an arch with his arms and legs spread.

Renia held on, her eyes sagging, her limbs losing their weight. She felt the life drain from her, the approach of death. The very world felt numb.

Was this what it was to die? To lose one's attachment to existence itself? To have everything taken from you, and have no will, no energy to try to hold on to it?

'Stop'

What?

'Stop, Renia. Something is wrong.'

Who is that?

'Renia! Stop, you're bleeding.'

I'm...

She snapped into reality—allowing the lightstone to drop to the bed—and fell to her knees. Venn-Dor's arms broke the fall.

'What happened?' she said. 'Did it work? Is he healed?'

Her vision began to clear. She looked into Venn-Dor's eyes and saw the same look she'd seen for most of her life: pity.

'Renia, the baby.'

Something in her heart snapped. The last of her energy drained from her face as she realized her inner thighs were wet. 'No.' She ruffled up her skirt in fury. 'No!'

'Renia, stop.'

Red. Blood. Covered in blood. 'No, no, no.'

She clamored to her feet and stumbled to the bathroom, casting off the Grand Master like an old rag.

She stood, bent double over the sink, holding her belly, feeling for any sense of life.

Nothing.

She looked up into the mirror and saw the consequences of her work. Her skin had sagged, leaving bags under her eyes. The flesh that bordered her lips ran with deep wrinkles. She pulled at her hair and it came loose in her hands. A long streak of gray ran from her scalp to her fingers.

'No.'

She slumped to the floor, and lost consciousness.

* * *

I have to act.

No longer will I stand by and watch you weave this tapestry of chaos and despair.

You've gone too far, Vera. This has to end.

Are you so blind to the suffering? Do you not hear the cries of the innocents that dwell here as they bounce off every wall?

This is not the Reaper's way. Reapers inflict pain by writ, harbingers of justice.

There is no justice here. Only vendetta, only your desperate plea to remain relevant.

I will not have it. I will take your captive. I will take him. And without him, whatever your scheme is, it will unravel. I might not understand your delay, but I understand the writ. I remember the gnawing urgency they bred into us, how it eats away at you, piece by piece, until it is satisfied.

How long do you have before the Reaper loses patience? How long can you hide him from her?

I will act now, and you will have no choice but to stop this.

I will stop you.

TWENTY-TWO

Riot

JEFF HELD HIS watch to his ear. It had been a long few days. Bobb had offered him a bottle of whiskey before leaving his post, and he'd needed it.

All around him the sounds of protesting residents rang, from distant altercations with guards, to the nearby calling of angered prisoners cooling their heels in the cells. He imagined the scene unraveling, private spaces violated by armored soldiers, furniture upended, intimate belongings probed and questioned as innocent people stood horrified at the invasion. He'd seen it firsthand a dozen times that day as he'd been repeatedly called on to restore order.

On and on, his pocket watch ticked. He smiled, allowing himself to drift away into a memory.

'A reminder.'

'Of what?'

'That time is precious. So you won't be willing away the hours, despising everything and everyone. You can be a grim bastard at the best of times, you know.'

'I have good reason to be now.'

'Let me be the reason for you not being, then. Take the watch, remember me.'

So long ago now. He sipped at the whiskey, willing away the hours. *What am I doing here?*

'Pour one for me.' Venn-Dor, *fantastic.*

The *great robed one* sat across from Jeff at his desk. Jeff met his calculating gaze with disdain.

'What do you have?' said the Grand Master.

Jeff shook his head, serving the man a fresh glass. 'Fuck all. I've been dragged from pillar to post all day cleaning up this damned mess.' He indicated toward the holding cells. 'Didn't have you down for a drinking man.'

The Grand Master nodded. 'It's been a challenging day. Renia—' His face paled. 'There was another incident.'

Jeff regarded his superior. 'Is she alright?'

'She'll live. She's resting.'

'I see.'

'You say you have made no progress finding the book at all?'

'I wouldn't be drinking otherwise.'

'Suspects?'

Jeff raised his glass and nodded. 'Just the one.'

'Oh?' The Grand Master leaned forward, raising an eyebrow. 'And you failed to report this to me?'

'You won't like it.'

'Spare me the suspense, Jeff, I'm not in the mood.'

'Pistorious Staine.'

From above flared nostrils, Venn-Dor's eyes widened. 'Interesting.'

'At first I suspected revenge. Petor did a number on his ego with the "Piss-Stain" thing. But these seditious booklets we uncovered…I had a hunch. You should have seen the way he reacted when I accused him of writing them. He's been up to *something*.'

'I assumed you'd kept him in custody to keep him from the Reaper's grasp. To buy some time. A good move. I didn't expect him to be involved with the Inoa.'

'I let him go.'

The glass almost toppled as Venn-Dor smacked it down on the desk. 'You did what?'

'I let him go. I couldn't hold him.'

'Couldn't hold him? Your only suspect, and you let him go on, what, a matter of protocol?'

'Yes.' Jeff blinked, alarmed at the question.

'Have you taken leave of your senses?'

'What did you want me to do? Lock the man up on a hunch? He's a Hall Master.'

'*Yes.*'

Jeff considered his words. He was lying. To protect Bobb, to protect himself and his team. Staine had escaped, with ease, and that reflected poorly on them, but he wasn't sure that he wouldn't have released Staine, knowing that searching his apartment yielded nothing to support his hunch. 'Look. As much as I want to believe that arrogant runt did this, I can't bend the facts to suit my suspicions. I *still* have nothing tying this man to the booklets, let alone the missing book.'

The Grand Master held his anger at a fever pitch. 'I entrusted this task to you, Mister Sothgard, based on the assumption that you were competent enough to understand and act on my instructions. What is it that you have been doing with your time, exactly?'

The tension in the room reached its peak. The two men breathing heavily, silently cursing the other's position.

Jeff seethed. He'd been misled, misdirected, and left alone to piece together this grim charade. All while the Grand Master had concerned himself with Renia, apparently, and little else.

'Perhaps my progress would have been more to your liking had you been more forthcoming with the truth,' said Jeff.

'I told you that the south was behind this, did I not?'

'And offered nothing tangible to support your theory. Why didn't you mention the history? Why was the report on Raellon's death scattered all over the place? It took me forever to learn the truth of the matter. When our enemies are more forthcoming than my allies, what chance do I have?'

The pair sat eyeballing each other, tension rising. Venn-Dor said nothing. Jeff could see the Grand Master fighting his choler.

'You're right,' said Venn-Dor. 'Which begs the question, where is Staine? He is the subject of the writ. If he is dead, then the Reaper has no reason to remain here.'

Jeff lifted his eyebrows. 'Really?' It seemed as if his bluff to the Hall Master during the investigation had been less than hollow after all. Had he inadvertently saved his life?

The pair looked to the doorway as the sound of chainmail and plate gave away the incoming guards.

'Another mess for me to clean up, no doubt,' Jeff said, nodding at the door.

Sundance strode in at the head of a column of guardsmen, each dragging an angry-looking member of staff into the security office. 'No', she said. 'I cleaned this one up by myself. You left me no choice.'

Jeff's eyes widened at the sight.

'What is this?' said the Grand Master.

'This,' said Sundance, standing proudly, 'is Staine's thinkers' circle.'

Jeff shot to his feet. How, by the moon, had she done this? Realization gripped him: all the pestering, the notes, the visits, she had had information all along, and he'd ignored her. 'I, uh…' The words would not come. He stood dumbstruck before the gathered criminals.

'It's quite alright, Jeff. I am partially to blame.'

'I'm sorry, Sundance.'

'No need for apologies.'

The gathered men and women struggled against their restraints, cursing the armored figures that held them.

'Lock them up,' said Jeff.

The guards complied, dragging the thinkers' circle off toward the cells.

'There are two others,' said Sundance, 'Dail Svelt and Tannis Rutger. Dail appears to have left, and I couldn't find Tannis.'

'Tannis died. Fell from the cliffs,' said Jeff.

The older woman paled at the news.

'I see,' she said. 'That—'

'Sundance, how did you do this?'

She told them the tale. How she'd stumbled upon the evidence, her visit with Tannis, the unlikely pairing with Bandack—the Grand Master bit back his opinion on that part. They listened intently, Jeff's respect for the woman increasing with each beat.

'Impressive,' he said.

'Thank you.'

'The janitor lived, then?'

'Oh yes, I imagine he's back to drawing his spirals and muttering prayers as we speak.'

Jeff stiffened. 'What did you say?'

'I said—'

He pulled the note from his pocket. 'Spirals like this?'

Sundance looked at it and nodded. 'Why, yes. Yes, that—'

Jeff bolted from his seat, and charged toward the door, his thoughts alive with a memory: a scruffy looking janitor, scraping away at moon cult symbols and denying he'd ever seen them.

RENIA'S EYES FLICKERED. Her vision was blurred, and the room span from wall to wall. Thick hammerblows of pain assaulted her temples. She groaned and attempted to rise.

She retched. Her nostrils were flooded with the coppery tang of blood, with the stench of mucus, and shit, and piss. Her stomach turned. She rolled away from it instinctively and fell from the bed, landing with a thud that sent tingles up her spine.

Her stomach squeezed itself in knots, mangled. Vomit forced its way up her windpipe. Specks of it sprayed her hands. She cried into the pain—through the acidic burning in her throat, through the mucus and saliva that dripped from her nose and mouth—and spat away the burning filth that clung to her lips.

The familiar shapes of her apartment began to resolve as her eyes adjusted. She pushed herself to her knees. One of them slipped in the mess. Her wrist and the side of her face broke the fall.

She stayed like that for a period of time, though time and urgency had little meaning to her; she felt neither. She shook, and wheezed, and sobbed, and for that moment, that was all there was. She was wet everywhere, wet and cold.

After a while, the urge to use the toilet took hold of her. She forced herself to her feet, braced against the wall, and hobbled forward a few steps before pausing at the foot of the bed.

She saw him, laying there in moonlight, as still as a mortician's slab. His face was pale, calm—

He didn't seem to be breathing.

She staggered toward the bed. He wasn't breathing. She bent over him and her hand sank into the bedding, the blanket soaking into the pooling effluvia beneath it. A sickly warm liquid embraced her fingers before she could retreat. She shook it off and placed her ear by his nose.

Nothing...

Nothing?

White pain speared into her head. She yelped and placed her hands at her temples. She saw herself holding a lightstone, saying words, looking at—

She'd killed him. She did this. She tried to heal him and failed and now he was dead. It was over. It was *over*.

Renia started to cry.

Another flashback, of falling backwards into *his* arms. Of looking down at her thighs and the red mess that left her—

Dail lurched. She jumped in her skin and fell backward. He started to convulse, gurgling and frothing at the mouth like a rabid beast. His head snapped backward, his mouth opened and from it came a scream that pushed her eardrums to their limits. Even her eyes hurt.

She covered her ears and watched in horror as he sat bolt upright and turned to her. She retreated, moving backwards toward the bathroom on her hands and feet. Dail jerked into motion, and swung his entire body from the hip. The momentum carried him off the bed and onto the floor. His head hit first. The sound of it made her wince.

In the grip of raw panic, she paused, watching as Dail flapped his limbs, slapping the floor in jerky motions as if he'd forgotten how to use them. He screamed again and again, the sound of it ripping through her skull.

She stood, ran to the bathroom, and slammed the door behind her.

PISTORIOUS STAINE WHIMPERED into his hands. He fought to contain himself, to stop the trembling, but the fever bit hard, forcing his body into convulsions. Had it been days? Weeks? How long had he been left with nothing but the sores on his back and the dull ache of disused muscle to keep him company? He'd been forgotten. Forgotten and left to rot.

His mind swam with fever-induced visions. Visions of his father, his laughing brothers, a childhood spent in ridicule and shame. He saw the Reaper that came for his blood, a hulking figure cloaked in black, the whites of his eyes and grinning teeth. Over and over he felt the swing of the blade, the touch of its edge on his throat in the moment before his death. Every time, he jumped, rattling the packing crate that had become his home, and risking exposure.

He screamed silently into the darkness, slapping his head in frustration. He'd become lost in the labyrinth of his own fears, alone and sickly, surrounded by vomit and shit, rotting in his own filth. Screams and shouts of a gathering crowd rose and fell as he ebbed between sleep and waking. Phantom or real, they served as fuel to his paranoia. He wept, tears creeping in uneven runs over the salted grime that cracked and pulled at the skin of his cheeks.

He rocked slowly, his knees held tight to his chest, longing to disappear into the darkness of the cupboard he'd folded himself into.

'Leave me alone, please. Just leave me alone.'

Outside, beyond the kitchen walls and out in the gardens, they called for him. His brother jeered, soaking up the encouragement of the other children, reveling in their hunger to see him humiliated. His stomach fluttered and groaned. He fought the urge to swallow as mucus and tears welled against the throbbing lump in his throat.

He felt his heart skip, and then race at three times the pace of the heavy padding of boots on the wooden floor. A step he feared more than that of his brother's. He filled his lungs to bursting, and held tight to the burning air in his chest as the steps grew louder.

No, no, no. Please, no.

The floorboards creaked beneath his father's heavy frame, mere inches from his hiding place. A single board of wood lay between them, a paltry shield. His chest burned. He began to convulse as the footsteps passed him, rattling the cupboard's contents—

He exhaled.

The world stopped.

The seconds stretched like rubber as he waited. Blood rushed to his head, roaring in his ears, puffing the flesh of his face.

A single thud marked the dropping of his heart as he knew he'd been discovered. The cupboard door flew open, assaulting him with light that burned his eyes. He squinted into it, freeing the tears that clung to his cheeks. His vision cleared. His father's eyes latched on his own—cold, uncaring. Tremors shook his tiny frame. He sat in paralysis, arrested by his father's gaze.

Pistorious watched in horror as his father's nostrils flared. Hot air rushed from them, announcing his wordless displeasure.

'Father, p-please. Dorian…He's—'

*A single grunt was the only warning he got. The weight of his
father's hand flew at him. Pain ran down his neck as his hair was
yanked into a knot. He kicked and yelped as his heels dragged along
the floorboards, toward the door to the gardens.*

The packing crate lid slid open. He barely managed to register
it, squinting at the invading light and the frowning pair of eyes
that looked down on him where he lay, huddled in a corner like a
frightened child.

'You stink,' said Londo.

Londo...Yes, Londo. He was the one, the one who had
helped him to hide.

'Here,' said the janitor. He lowered a plate of bread and some
odd looking lumps into the crate. 'Chaga', he said. 'For the fever.'

Staine nodded, but could manage little else.

'The time is coming. I've incited quite the little uprising here.
Try to pull yourself together, eh? The next time I come for you
might be the time you escape.'

PETOR WOKE SUDDENLY after inhaling his own vomit. Night
had fallen, and starlight crept through the kitchen window. He
coughed up the lingering chunks of burning mess and stood,
almost slipping in it.

'Ahm up! Ahm up. Bagg to wurk, the lorra yu!'

He turned, confused at not seeing the expectant faces of his
scribes. His head boomed.

Realizing his condition, he decided the best thing for it was
a cup of coffee. The machine hadn't seen much use since its
restoration. Petor stroked at it lovingly as he dribbled all over the
kitchen floor. 'Schhiny schiny!' His laugh turned into a cough as
he tried to remember how the thing worked. After a minute of
frustration, he gave up, content with mindlessly shoveling coffee

beans into his mouth and crunching on them with the flats of his back teeth.

He staggered over to the display case that listed his achievements, then reached out and placed his palm on the glass, squinting as he tried to make sense of the words. His mumbling was unintelligible save for the occasional recognition of a name, the memory of a scribe he actually liked. He moaned in pleasure as he emptied his bladder against the glass.

Renia comforted herself by humming. She sat with her arms around her knees, rocking gently on the bathroom floor.

Where am I?

She blinked into the darkness and clutched at her sodden clothes—wet, dirty. A ceaseless groaning came from behind her.

Who am I?

Her legs shook as she pushed her body up the door, into a standing position. They throbbed and tingled. She felt weak, nauseous. She turned and rested her weight on the door, numb and confused.

The groaning continued.

Renia? Yes, Renia.

A pain shot from her abdomen; she stiffened and grunted through it.

You stink.

More groaning and knocking came from beyond the door. Intrigued, she turned the handle. The moonlight hit her and she braced, holding her arm across her face. The outline of a man in an awkward heap on the floor, flapping and gargling.

She stared at him in idle fascination from the doorway. Why was he there? What was he doing?

The moonlight lit the room she had been in. She cast her gaze around it, *sink, toilet, bath tub. Bath tub.* Her attention lingered on the invalid man for a moment longer, before she turned her back on him and removed her sodden clothing.

His groans were ceaseless. She hummed over them as the bathwater ran. Its heat felt like heaven between her fingers. She waved her palms through it, allowing the steam to cleanse her nostrils.

'LET ME IN.' Jeff commanded the guards to open the doors to the basement complex. Two armored Mohruscans barred his entry, feverishly looking at each other in indecision.

'Let me in, now.'

'Gshir, you gdon't understand.'

Jeff understood perfectly. The hammering and yelling from the other side of the door told him everything he needed to know. The people were afraid, confused, and angry. Having your questions ignored and being locked in the basement had a way of nurturing that sort of behavior.

'For the last fucking time. Let me in.'

One of the guards relented, and shouted through the door. 'Zstand back! We're opening the gdoor!'

The peace lasted long enough for Jeff to cross the threshold to be received by an angry mob. Before he could open his mouth to speak, they burst into activity, barging him into the wall and cramming themselves into the doorway, screaming and shouting, desperate to reach the open air.

'Let me pass. Let me pass, damn it!'

He was thrown back against the wall repeatedly, the press of bodies deaf to his command.

He pushed on, snaking his way through the morass. One man tried to wrestle him to the ground, but Jeff slipped his grasp and threw him into the moving crowd. It was like wading through treacle. Face after angry face flashed by, rushing out of the doors. The guards must have been trampled.

Strong arms wrapped around his shoulders. He turned to protest, but was hurled aside like a rag doll. He crashed into pipework, shoulder first, and his cry was devoured by a hundred angry voices.

Jeff stuck to the wall, easing his way down the tunnel away from the mob, wheezing and clutching his shoulder.

THE NIGHTGOWN WAS soft and silky against her skin. Renia paused as it fell over her stomach and thighs, intrigued at the skin of her legs, how it felt loose, and tough.

She sang over the groans of the strange man in her room.

Her reflection studied her. The old woman in the mirror looked at her with the hollow expression of the recently bereaved, her eyes lifeless, darkened bags hanging beneath them. She picked up a comb, and began to run it through her damp hair.

Strands broke away from her head. The gray streak that ran from her forehead was coarse, brittle. Clumps of hair gathered in her hands as she inspected it.

She stopped singing, and the groaning man cried out. She locked eyes with her reflection and screamed until her throat ached.

'AH, CHIEF. YOU came.'

The janitor stood squarely in the center of the room, sweating, a predatory grin on his face.

Jeff grunted, rubbing his shoulder. He pulled the note from his pocket and waved it in front of him. 'I take it this is your doing?'

The janitor gave a theatrical bow. 'You've come to hear my offer at last. I was worried you wouldn't come.'

'You could have just put your name on it.'

'And where would have been the fun in that?'

Jeff snorted. 'What is it you think I want?'

The janitor's grin widened. 'Pistorious Staine, of course.'

'You? You kidnapped Staine?'

'Kidnapped is the wrong word.' The janitor approached cautiously. '*Assisted* is perhaps the right one.'

Jeff kept his guard up. He didn't know who this man was, or who he really worked for. 'And what do you want from me?'

'It's not what *I* want, heathen.'

Jeff sighed. 'What is it that you ask in return?'

'Mako Aranomo.'

Jeff laughed out loud. 'What would the moon cult want with a deranged old man?'

'The faithful do not *want!* The faithful are led by the light of the shade-bringer. My place is not to question my calling. I am faithful, and when the time of change comes, I will be saved. Aranomo has been chosen. The reasons are none of your concern. Do you accept the exchange?'

'What do you think?'

The janitor tutted, mocking disappointment. 'Come now, Jeff, old boy. We both know how badly you need a win, things haven't been going very well for you, have they? Sooner or later you're going to have to learn to play the game.'

'So I keep hearing,' said Jeff. 'The thing is, I don't really want to, so why don't we try something else. I'll arrest you for kidnapping, and you'll tell us where you're hiding Master Staine in exchange for leniency.'

'I don't think so.'

'And why is that?'

'You couldn't arrest me if you tried. You're an invalid, and a tired one at that.'

'I've also been dealing with cultists since the days I wore short trousers. Even if you were able to best me in combat, there would be no escape. The gates are closed. We house a company of guards. We would find you, and I would lock you away. *I* would become your shade-bringer. I would lock you away in the darkest hole I could find, where your faith would waste away, serving no one.'

The janitor growled in frustration. 'Have it your way,' he said. 'I only need your keys. The coming riot will provide a convenient distraction.'

'You're welcome to try. Come and take them.'

The janitor rushed toward him, hammer in hand.

CAPTAIN GARAMOND SPAT. Everything she'd told Venn-Dor would happen was happening. She stood before the gatehouse, looking on toward the halls, where a rabble amassed, chanting and shouting, heard by everyone no doubt, due to the hour. By starlight, it was difficult to make a clear assessment of the mob's number: a hundred at least, perhaps as many as three.

Shit.

They were not ready. Barely thirty soldiers stood ready to hold the gate. The rest were still engaged in the search, no doubt making a royal mess of it judging by the demeanor of the lot heading her way.

Her voice cut through the air. 'Light the torches. Bar the gate from both sides. You three, with me.'

She ran to meet them, unsheathing her sword as her soldiers fumbled to match her pace.

'Don't dawdle.' she commanded.

She watched as her soldiers carried out her commands, keeping one eye fixed firmly on the mob atop the hill. 'Faster. Get it done. I want a shield wall up here in sixty seconds.'

The voices began to carry toward them on the wind. Flame light flickered; they had torches, already a hazard she did not want to have to deal with.

'Shield wall, now!'

The quiet rumble of hundreds of feet began. It rolled over the hill and toward their position. She fell in with her men, positioning herself at the center of the line. Steel scraped and rubbed together as they locked their defenses into place.

'Nobody attacks without my command. I fucking mean it. If any of you harm a single one of these people without having a very good reason, I'll kill you myself. Am I understood?'

'Yes, sir,' Mohruscan and Daralarian voices alike rang out in chorus.

'Good. Now hold firm. It's going to be a long night.'

Twenty-Three

Bells

Renia stood before her desk, staring at the wall.

Nothing.

How long have I been here?

Her desk was void of work. A nagging thought pulled at her conscious mind, something she'd forgotten to do, but she couldn't hold it.

Lost.

Memories came flooding back. She'd lost everything: her future, her youth, her *baby*. Oh moon, her *baby*, a baby she hadn't wanted, that she could only now admit to herself she had resented in some way. A stabbing pain struck her in the heart, and she felt the rumble of a groan escape her.

Her baby.

She'd killed her baby, she'd taken its life and given it to Dail. How could she possibly fall any further than that? How could she live with herself, with what she'd done?

She'd failed. Failed to heal Dail, failed to heal herself, failed her child, failed Venn-Dor, failed her parents—

Dail thrashed and groaned from the other room. She entered to find him lying face down, the bed a mess of neglect. The stench made her heave. He struggled and moaned and convulsed, helpless. This was what she'd bought with her baby's life, this was the future she had invited.

The furthest point in the apartment from Dail was the study. It was where she found herself curled into a ball, rocking back and forth in silence. The whispers of the dead pestered her, *Away, away,* itching at her, compelling her to run. She registered a commotion from outside, but couldn't distinguish it from the voices in her head.

Fly away, Renia.

Fly away, Moonpie.

What felt like hours swept over her broken, sobbing soul, torturing her with impossible suggestions, filling her head with ways she could escape her hell.

JEFF DUCKED AS the janitor swung the hammer towards his head, a blow meant to kill. Jeff wasn't carrying a weapon. He was tired, injured, and unarmed, in a fight for his life.

He pivoted on his good leg, narrowly avoiding another hammer blow, buying him a fleeting moment to look for a weapon. The janitor came at him again, unleashing a flurry of attacks that were difficult to avoid. Jeff leaned in to the last one, holding the janitor's arm locked at his shoulder, and head-butted him squarely in the nose.

The janitor rocked back three steps, holding his face and blinking furiously. 'Ha. Hahaha!' He spat, blood slapping at the cold stone of the floor. 'A dirty move for such an honorable man.'

'A hammer is a dirty weapon.'

His opponent grinned back at him. 'I do dirty work.'

In a flash, the janitor charged him again, swinging at Jeff's torso in a blind rage. His eyes were watering, which gave Jeff the edge he needed.

Jeff rolled around and behind the janitor, toward a pile of discarded copper pipe. His knee cracked and gave way as he exited the roll, sending him falling forward toward the heap. He landed on his side, sending offcuts of piping rolling away from him in all directions.

Londo followed the sound, struggling to see through his watering eyes in the dim light of the basement. 'You'll have to do better than that!' He tossed the hammer around in a deft move, then threw it from hand to hand. 'Get up, Sothgard!'

Jeff got up, a length of thick copper piping in his hand. He drew back and held his ground as the janitor came at him again. The hammer came at his face. He felt the rush of air as he pulled his head back and away, felt the iron graze the hairs at the end of his nose. *Too close.*

Another swing. Jeff butted it away with the short end of the copper pipe, then drew back and swung hard, connecting solidly with the janitor's back and ribs.

'Argh!' Londo instinctively straightened, giving Jeff the opportunity to draw back and swing again, putting his full weight into the blow. It connected at the back of the janitor's knee, knocking him off balance and down to the ground. Jeff's own knee couldn't take it; the swing put too much pressure on the joint and he heard it crack and dislocate, sending him tumbling after Londo.

Jeff grimaced, shuffling backward on his arse with his hands and his good leg. He shuffled back as far as he could before he hit a wall, breathing hard and wincing as shards of pain rocketed up his hips and spine.

'Bastard,' said Jeff.

'You wound me,' laughed the janitor. 'Now give me the cell keys.'

'Eat shit.'

Londo stood tall and took a step toward him. 'Give them to me, or I'll kil—Oof!'

A figure appeared at the janitor's side with impossible speed and swung its leg into his solar plexus. Jeff watched as Londo flew across the room like a sack of meat and slapped into the stone wall several feet away.

Bandack.

Jeff made out her darkened figure as the sparse light reflected off her leather leggings. She was fast. *Moon*, she was fast.

The janitor tried to get to his feet, his rib cage moving as he struggled to catch breath that wouldn't come. The Reaper charged him and launched herself through the air knees first, driving him to the floor as she landed, straddling his prone body.

'Well tootle, tootle, toot! Here we are again, little Londo,' she said. 'Did you think I'd forgotten you?'

The winded man heaved, glaring at her with pure hatred.

'Just what were you about to do to my Jeff?' She tapped on his chin. 'Hmm?' The Reaper smiled down at her prey. 'What's the matter? Winded? That's alright. I'll wait.'

Jeff struggled to regain his composure as he listened to the Reaper humming a tune he didn't recognize. He tried not to smile.

'I have…no…quarrel with you…Reaper.' The janitor barely managed the words.

Bandack leaned forward, prodding him in the chest. 'Well, I have one with you. You see, I just heard you admit that you have been hiding a man I have a writ for. And that puts you directly under my knife.'

'If you kill me, you'll never find him.'

The Reaper idly checked her nails, uncaring. 'Don't take this the wrong way, Londo, but you stink. It won't be hard to follow your scent back to him.'

The janitor started to panic, his breathing erratic, powerless under the weight of the Reaper with his arms pinned under her thighs.

'You'll pay for this, you'll all pay. The Faithful are rising! Our leader is stronger than you can imagine. He will dethrone the sleeping king and take Luna Ruinam for all the Faithful. The time is coming.'

'Shhhh,' said Bandack. 'Haven't you heard yet?'

She leaned in close, placing one hand under Londo's neck and the other against his forehead. 'Daddy's dead.'

Crack.

She broke his neck, clean. Londo died instantly. She let his limp body fall back onto the stone. She stood, and casually walked toward Jeff, bending forward to meet his eye level as if nothing had happened. 'How bad is it?'

Jeff grunted. 'I've had worse.'

The Reaper squatted into a slump against the wall beside him. She unsheathed her dagger and held it out toward Jeff. The lightstone in its hilt glowed yellow. The light reflected in her face—such soft features for such a dangerous woman.

'Are you going to kill *me* now?' he said.

'Don't be silly.' Her words took on a more wistful tone. 'That would be a waste of a good man.'

He met her gaze, defeated, and shook his head. *Would it?*

'Touch the lightstone,' she said. 'It won't fix the leg, but it will help for a little while.'

Jeff shook his head. 'Then what's the point?'

She nodded and rested the dagger between her legs.

'Why did you save me?'

'You remind me of someone, a man I admired.' She smiled. 'Charismatic, loyal, singular in his focus, stoic. A born, but hesitant, leader.'

Jeff sighed. 'Sounds like my father.'

'Do you want to know what happened to him? He was torn apart, fighting a battle he had no hope of winning. Out of loyalty, out of duty.' She sniffed. 'A waste. I couldn't save him, but maybe I can save you.'

Jeff met her gaze. 'You don't think I can win?'

She shook her head. 'Not on your own.'

'Reapers aren't like us,' Jeff murmured. 'Ferron warned me.'

'You shouldn't listen to him, he's half the man you are.'

Was that true? Ferron might have been emotional, unpredictable, but he'd held his position for longer than Jeff. He hadn't let his weaknesses ruin him. Years ago, Jeff could have dealt with Londo in his sleep, unarmed and naked, now here he was, useless, sitting on the floor at the mercy of a Reaper.

'You saved my life,' he said. 'I owe you.'

She grinned. 'That's two favors you owe me now.'

'You're going for Staine?'

'I don't have much of a choice in that regard. I gave you long enough to conduct your investigation.'

'What does it matter now?'

'We both know you don't mean that. What was it you really wanted to prevent me from doing?'

'Taking the book,' he said.

'I'm here to kill Staine, not take a book.'

'We both know you don't mean that,' he echoed.

'So if I don't touch the book, I keep my promise. And you owe me two favors?'

Jeff chuckled. *This woman.* 'Sounds right.'

'Maybe one day I'll marry you, take on the simple life. We could live somewhere remote, just you and me. You would work the land and I would slaughter anyone who threatened us.' She grinned and squirmed. 'Mmm.'

Jeff frowned and looked her dead in the eye. 'You're insane, you know.'

'Come now, darling. There's no need for that.'

'I'm not going to marry you.' Jeff shook his head.

'A favor is a favor. You're going to marry me—and there will be sex.'

'I'm not going to marry you, Bandack.'

'Oh, but you are, and then you will still owe me a favor.' She leaned over and swept the hair out of his face. 'Now touch the damned lightstone and get your arse up.'

RENIA FOUND HERSELF standing in the open air, with no memory of leaving the apartment. The thrashing sound of the ocean buffeted her as she became aware of her surroundings.

The bell tower.

The stinging sensation in her feet told her she'd run all the way.

The crystalline trails on her cheeks told her she'd been crying.

The location she found herself in told her what she'd intended to do.

Was this the end of her story? Was it time for her to leave, to release her burden, and put an end to it all? Would it make the slightest bit of difference in the grand scheme of things if she allowed herself the luxury of peace?

Her own voice rattled in her head.

Haven't I endured enough?

You will continue to. It never ends.

How much more can one person take? Who am I doing this for?

...

What do I have to live for? Everything I've ever loved has been taken away.

It's your fault. It's who you are.

Its my fault.

I'm cursed.

You are the curse. Everyone pays the price for your ambition.

I have no ambition.

Then die. What is life standing still if not death?

No. I will fight on.

For what? For who?

For me, for my father.

He's dead. You killed him.

She cried out, the echo spearing into the open air. She stepped closer to the edge. A gust of wind whipped her dress, unsettling her stance. She felt no fear. She willed it to make the choice for her.

You traded away the life of your unborn child, Renia. Your parents died for your mistake. Molan and Carol endured years of servitude because of your mistake. Dail will never live a normal life again, never create anything again, because you were so desperate for a reason to push him away. You couldn't even bring yourself to help him off the floor. Petor lost his position. His life and career lie in tatters because of your carelessness. Hundreds of people suffered under weeks of oppression. There's nothing left of you; you're a withered old hag. Your facade finally reflects what you are. You're disgusting, Renia. The world would be a better place without you in it.

Yes.

PETOR STOOD NAKED on his doorstep. The commotion had drawn him away from burning his journals and guzzling down a mixture of whiskey and his own tears.

He took a step out, staggering into the garden.

'Fugggerz, kee the bast'd noizzz.'

He regained his footing, cooing at the sensation of the wind on his skin.

One foot, two. One foot, two. Just keep going.

JEFF LIMPED OUT into the night, and followed the flattened ground left by the people he'd allowed to escape from the basement. He didn't need to look far; the commotion drew his attention downhill toward the gate, where the mob chanted, shouted, and threw rocks at the defending Captain Garamond and her men.

Shit.

His knee hurt like hell, but the Reaper had been true to her word, and it supported his weight as he hobbled across the grass.

In the darkness up ahead, he made out the figure of a naked, drunken old man, staggering toward the crowd.

'Petor! Petor, stop!'

VENN-DOR STOOD BY the window, watching the scene. He frowned, and looked back toward his study.

When the time comes, you must pick up your staff.

The words of the Praelatus echoed in his mind. Had the time passed? If he'd listened sooner would this debacle be unfolding before his eyes? At what point did the needs of people he'd sworn to direct outweigh his own need for inner peace?

He could have put an end to this already. He could have picked up *Spero* himself and healed Dail, saving Renia the cruel ordeal of losing her baby, her youth, and her newfound confidence.

Shame laid its cold hand around his throat. He had fallen, and could no longer lie to himself. The fear of what he could be had overridden what he knew to be right.

No longer.

The Grand Master marched into his study, determination setting every stride. He opened the glass cabinet and laid his hand around his staff. Its power coursed through his veins, the familiar tingle where the wood rested against his palm, the sharpening of his senses, the definiteness of purpose, it all came flooding back to him.

I will not be afraid.

He struck the floor with the butt of his staff, and in a snap of ear-splitting light, he vanished.

'SHIELDS UP!' THE captain swore at the assault. Bottles of piss and other vile things flew at them. One of her soldiers was down.

'Get that fucking shield up, idiot!'

She dodged a torch, flames licking her armor as she flattened its bearer with her elbow.

'That's enough! Back! Get back all of you, before someone gets hurt.'

She looked around, utterly surrounded by the increasingly angry mob.

'Ring the bells! Ring the bells now! I want everyone back here, right now!'

PETOR FOUND HIMSELF face down in the grass. He lifted his head, groaning. Red light flared in his eyes as he tried to focus on the scene. He struggled to his feet and continued to plod through the night toward the noise.

Bells rang out, drawing his attention upward and disrupting his balance.

His stitches tore. Blood ran freely down his leg. He didn't feel a thing. Onward he went, cock and balls swinging in the wind, mumbling to himself like a madman.

The crowd parted for him. Confused looks and gasps of astonishment interrupted the shouting and jeering from the crowd.

Bells were ringing. He timed his steps to them, slowing, seeking balance with each.

Then he was down, again, face up this time. A jar of piss had hit him in the temple on its way toward the soldiers defending the gate.

The sky was thick with smoke. He coughed up vomit as a sea of faces swirled around him like a whirlpool.

The noise quieted, hushed voices turned into waves splashing, slapping him in the face as he lay face up in the—*lake?*

'Petor! Petor!' The voice was distant.

'Grandpa?' he whispered to the sky.

'Petor!'

'Grandpa, you're dead.' He felt the tears rolling down his face. 'You were the only one who cared, Grandpa. And now you're gone. I want to go with you.'

He allowed the waves to crash over his face, stealing his breath. He longed for it, willed it to take him. 'Let me die.'

'No!'

'I want to die.'

'Petor! Look at me!'

'What?'

'Look at me!'

The clouds parted. A face. A face he knew from somewhere. Not his grandfather, but someone—

'Jeff?'

He heard the bells again.

'Stay with me, Petor! Do you hear me? Petor!'

DEEP WITHIN THE upper levels of the Halls of Venn, in the former residence of Istopher Venn himself, a dozen candles blew out in unison. The slow throb of vibration that emanated from the oversize tuning fork intensified in a moment of temporary discord. Smoke from the candle wicks folded back on itself, trapped, lifeless in suspension, awaiting the arrival of something unnatural.

The crimson mirror squealed, the wooden frame that housed it cracked and reformed a thousand times a second, flickering between dueling states of being. Three lightstones ebbed in its frame, sputtering wisps of aether fire into the fast-cooling space around the glass.

The surface of the mirror grew fat with mercurial potential. A blob of liquid metal forced itself out toward reality. Within it, a face pressed against the boundary between worlds, mouth agape in a silent struggle for escape.

A loud hiss, and a trail of gas burst out of the liquid glass. A child's fingers split the surface, and wrenched open a hole big enough to crawl out.

Aevus's limp body slid through, and hit the floor with a slap. He pulled himself to his knees, wheezing and croaking for breath, shards of ice crystallizing on his leathery face.

'Renia...' he choked.

RENIA PUSHED OFF the ledge and fell toward her death.

High-pitched whining flooded her ears. The sweet, cool air washed her face, blowing her hair out behind her. Her fingers waved joyfully, exploring the resistance of the wind. Her nightgown pressed flat into every curve of her body. It embraced her, as a mother swaddles her child. The cold burned at her forehead, nose and breast.

Exhilarated, she fell. For what felt like forever. Images of her life flashed before her. Her mother smiled at her from across the dinner table. Her father ruffled her hair playfully. Molan and Carol embraced her at her graduation. Sundance showed her to her desk on her first day of work.

Gratitude welled from within her, for the wonderful people that had shared their lives with her and given her so much. *Thank you all.*

Goodbye—

She felt a hand wrap around her wrist and jolted her eyes open. Aevus's face looked back at her. A shriek assaulted her ears. The child smiled back at her, his black eyes intense with adoration. 'Fast,' he mouthed. Renia watched in horror as his flesh began to decay, pieces of hide-like skin peeling away and turning to dust.

'Aevus! No!'

VENN-DOR APPEARED IN a ball of light that dispersed in a single heartbeat. He stood firm on the grass, his arm outstretched, brandishing his staff. He charged forward, forcing the crowd to part before him, stunned faces looked on in horror, irrational fear forcing them back.

He spoke to the earth, commanding it to listen to his call. The ground around him rumbled, inspiring fear in the surrounding rioters. Behind him, Garamond's voice pierced the noise, booming over the ruckus, calling her men back to safety.

Walls of crusted stone emerged from the ground, pushing away dirt and grass, providing the soldiers with cover. Rock dust and debris swirled up around him, coalescing into the rough shapes of men, seven feet tall and almost as wide.

A brave rioter charged toward one of his golems, only to be embraced by its immovable form. Held firm in its grasp, the man cried out and spat in fury.

'Stop this at once!' The Grand Master's voice shook the air, forcing the crowd into a state of shock and confusion. He waved his staff in an arc, willing the molecules of air to vibration, a slow throb that would press down on the collective rage of the crowd.

The riot began to disperse, outliers running back up the hill toward the safety of the halls, lost in the throes of survival instinct, while others fell to their knees in supplication.

A collective gasp rang out, and a woman screamed.

'There! Look!'

Heads began to turn, upward and toward the bell tower.

'Praelatus! He brings us a sign!'

'He is displeased!'

Venn-Dor traced their attention up, and saw what it was that held the crowd in shock.

Hanging in mid air, a woman and a child lay frozen in time, unmoving as if placed there by divine will. The wind ignored them, utterly still, suspended in a bubble.

Renia.

Venn-Dor whipped his head around to Garamond. She swallowed and returned his gaze, her eyes wide in shock. He nodded at her and held out his staff.

The Grand Master vanished, producing a blinding flash and a clang that drove the remaining rioters to their knees.

Twenty-Four

Dawn

A LOUD CRACK jarred her teeth. Renia fell to the floor in a slump, landing awkwardly with Aevus by her side. The impact had been softer than she anticipated, a dull ache in her pelvis and a persistent throbbing sensation in her head were all.

Something felt wrong; she should be dead. As her eyes focused, she saw the familiar stone walls of her study. She was no longer outside, nor was she alone.

Venn-Dor stood in a halo of light, peering down at her and Aevus in consternation. 'Are you injured?'

She shook her head, trembling. How? How had he done this? A whimpering from beside her drew her attention away from the Grand Master and back to the child who had saved her life.

'Aevus?' she said.

What was left of Aevus's face smiled back at her. His skin, stripped back almost to bare flesh, sizzled and steamed, wisps of decaying matter burning to dust in the air. 'Hello, Renia,' he said, his voice coarse.

'Aevus, what did you do?'

'Inverted. Went *fast*, Renia.' He smiled. 'Father would be proud.'

'Aevus, you're dying. Why would you do that?'

The child wheezed, and looked past her to Venn-Dor. 'Doratus, thank you for moving us.'

The Grand Master nodded once, and knelt beside them.

'I don't have a lot of time,' said Aevus. He spoke now with the voice of an adult, transformed within what, for him, would have been the better part of a month, for Renia a single day.

'You have to live, Renia,' said the dying child. 'What you do… What you do for us all, it has to happen.'

Renia shook the tears away. 'What are you talking about, Aevus?'

'I was brave—went into the red window. I spoke with the people there. They showed me what is to come, what I would have to do, to make sure it happens.'

'The mirror scared you, you said you would ne—'

'That was before. Before you came.' His chest started to rattle, his breathing slowing. 'We are alike in many ways, Renia… Neither of us had the childhood we needed. We know what it is to be alone, out of place.

'I never dreamed I would meet anyone like you. So much time passed… I didn't *learn*, didn't *speak*. But you came. You came and changed everything. Showed me new things, taught me not to be afraid—to change. To learn… Laugh.' His gaze moved to the ceiling, his smile serene.

Renia reached out to touch his hand. His fingers crumbled in her grasp.

Aevus's black eyes started to fade to gray. She felt her heart race as panic set in. She clasped at his arm and shoulders, but they turned to dust that ran between her fingers.

'Let him go,' said Venn-Dor, placing a hand on her shoulder.

She took one last look at his smile as the life faded from his little body. Her stomach lurched, and she winced as the rush of the outside world hit them, and time resumed its relentless march.

She opened her eyes to see the last of the dust that had been her friend dissolve into nothing. Her chest tightened and she wailed, floods of tears rolling off her face.

Why? Why hadn't he let her go? He deserved to live far more than she did.

She felt Venn-Dor's arms wrap around her. 'Shhh,' he said. 'It's going to be alright. It's going to be alright.'

Renia fell deeper into his arms, sobbing, where she stayed for what felt like an eternity. She closed her eyes and drifted between waking states, her heart beating in time to the bells that rang outside. Each time she tried to wake, she found her eyes too heavy: She felt a blanket being wrapped around her shoulders. She heard the sound of running water. She heard a man groaning in protest and splashing as the bells stopped ringing. She heard the scrubbing of bristles.

The last thing she heard was Venn-Dor's voice, echoing through her subconscious. 'Please don't do that again.'

DORATUS PULLED THE door closed and placed his hand on the wall. His head sagged, heavy under the weight of emotions he'd kept locked away for what felt like a lifetime.

The rain clawed at him as he emerged into the courtyard. It fell in sheets that obscured his view, though through it he saw the broken form that lay in a heap, staining the paving with diluted gore.

No.

He shook his head, composed and straightened himself against the memory. His eyes burned, and he wiped them with the back of his hand as his gullet rose and throbbed.

Each step brought him closer and yet further away. Like the dream in which you run yet make no progress. His every step shook his vision as if his eyes hung from string in their sockets. Pieces of his beloved son lay scattered around his feet like meat fresh from the butcher's cleaver.

He fell to his knees, surrounded by the remains of the boy he had loved so much. Peeling the sodden flaps of blood-soaked hair from what remained of his head.

The body lay hunched, awkwardly resting atop the book clutched to its chest. He rolled Raellon over, and prised it from his grasp.

Doratus turned the book over, the fake journal that he had so lovingly crafted at Raellon's request. Rain and blood dripped from the pages, rendering them slick and waxy between his fingers. His blood rose. He felt his body shake and rock with rage. He grabbed at the pages, and crushed them to pulp in his fist.

No.

Not now. Not here.

STAINE FLINCHED. THE silence that had enveloped his surroundings only served to further fuel his fever-induced paranoia. He chewed on the block of chaga that Londo had given him. It crumbled into tiny cork-like pieces in his mouth, and tasted like bark. Trying to dry-heave silently was an art in itself.

The bells stopped ringing.

The endless time he'd spent in the packing crate had worn on him in ways he had previously thought himself above, and made him think of all the people his father had condemned to a similar fate, left to rot in the dungeons beneath his palatial childhood home in Verda. On more than one occasion he'd thought of

Mako, his long time friend and mentor, and what must have become of him since the last he'd seen him.

And now, a ray of light. Londo had given him hope that his long suffering would come to an end. The weakness of his body abated in anticipation of release. Did that make his symptoms less real? Had he exaggerated the toll it had taken? Or was it survival instinct? Perhaps it was his body pumping stimulants into his blood that would allow him to undertake what promised to be a long and perilous escape.

Footsteps.

He held his breath—not Londo's footsteps, someone new.

The lid to the packing crate slid open, and a face—one he knew—stared down at him impassively.

'You,' said Staine.

'If you want to live, I suggest you get out of there and follow me, quickly.'

'Wh—what do you—'

'You are about six minutes from being on the end of a Reaper's blade, Pistorious. Now are you coming or not?'

He felt his pupils dilate, and a flood of adrenaline hit his muscles. Shaking, he stood for the first time in what seemed like an eternity, and attempted to pull himself over the edge of the crate.

His unexpected savior spoke in a whisper. 'We're going to have to do something to mask this smell.'

He would have been offended by such a comment before, but the experience had left him with very little of the pride he was known for. 'The bucket,' he said.

What a life he had made for himself. From noble son, to respected scholar, to free-thinker and leader, to this. *The ignobility*, he reflected. The desperate methods of scent-masking that followed would have repulsed him just a few short weeks ago, but no longer. He almost found solace in the depravity of his plight, comparing his situation to the heroes of history who found themselves brought low before ascending to great heights, emerging from the darkness to bring light to the world.

He followed the hooded figure into the depths in silence, his head bowed. The sticky grit of the filth he had lived in lowered him, eroding any sense of pride, or confidence. As they pressed on, he became aware of his malnourished body, and its cries for rest, food, and water.

They passed passageways of dark stone brick, through hidden stone doorways and into a maze of tunnels. This was the true legacy of Daralar, the shared heritage of north and south, an ancestry of burrowing into the earth in defiance of a sun that did not permit their presence.

Fitting.

Fitting that he should find himself walking the path of his ancestors, hiding from his fate.

They reached their destination shortly after navigating the maze, and his escort illuminated the room, revealing a bunker, a place for someone like him to lay in wait. The cave contained a bed, food stores, a writing desk, and other essential items that any hiding scholar might need. He squinted at the dry, cool space, relieved to see fresh linen and clothing.

His voice croaked as he spoke. 'What is this?'

'A place to hide.'

'For whom?'

'Venn.'

He looked his savior in the eye and raised an eyebrow. The chamber must have been over a hundred years old, left here and forgotten, but not to all, apparently.

'How do you know of it? Who are you really?'

His escort looked away and motioned across the chamber. 'After the war, an uneasy peace settled over this land. Trust was in short supply. No one knew how long the treaty would last. Venn, Inoa, they built these chambers into this place to be forgotten, but they are numerous.'

'Forgotten indeed.'

'Venn was a man of many secrets.'

The figure tossed a cloth his way, and motioned toward a bathing tub.

'The water is fresh. Clean yourself. But keep the beard. When the time comes it's better that you aren't recognized.'

Of course he'd become accustomed to hearing such promises, but he nodded nonetheless. What other choice was there? At least here he could rest with some degree of confidence that he would be safe.

He regarded his host with suspicion. Could he really afford to relinquish his trust to a face he knew, knowing well that they were not who they claimed to be?

He inspected the bookshelf, thinking better of his urge to touch them with his grubby fingers. 'These books are old.'

'Antique, forgotten, priceless.'

'You've read them?'

'I've had a lot of time to.'

'Why are you doing this?'

He saw the frown, however masked it might have been.

'I have to go,' she said. 'Be ready, when the time comes. We will have to be swift.'

A thousand questions. Staine opened his mouth to demand an answer only to find her gone.

The air tasted dank, but far sweeter than the filth of the box he'd crawled out of. That part of his journey was over, for now, and he thanked providence for the relief, for the opportunity to bathe himself and wash away the indignity of the past...however long it had been.

At once, he felt the familiar pull of exhaustion as his knees began to give way. He steeled himself against it, looking to the inviting steam that rose from the bath tub. He cast aside his clothing, and staggered toward it, breathing slowly, deliberately, in through the nose, out through the mouth.

The heat of the water stung as it passed over the sores on his legs. It crept up and over his groin, and the sensation made him groan aloud. He sat deflated, beyond humiliated, feeling numb and violated, just like the time his father had thrown him out of the kitchen and into the jaws of his older brother and the other children, allowed them to tease him, threaten him with sharp sticks, scare him half to death.

That was the first time he'd noticed *her*, sat in his piss-soaked trousers, shivering in the shadow of the fountains. After his brother had satisfied himself with Pistorious's shame, after the other children had grown bored of chanting 'pissy pants' and left in search of dinner.

She had remained.

Only *she*.

And Pistorious remembered the look on her face in every waking moment since. *Lilian.* How soft, and pure her skin.

How sweet the smell of her had been. A servant's daughter, a jewel formed under the pressure of his family's house. *She* had remained with him, *she* stood apart from the rest of them, and knelt by his side whilst he wept. Her eyes had glistened in the sun with compassion. He remembered the way her hair shined like gold thread in the light.

They had sat together until the wind blew cold, and his body shivered from the wet he sat in. She had held his hand in silence, until he felt ready to return to the house.

Pistorious smiled, and let the bath water creep up and over his chin, he allowed it to envelop him as he recalled how soft and warm Lilian's hand had felt as she had led him into the kitchen.

Only to find his brother leering at them from the table, chewing on bread and showering crumbs all over the place.

He gasped as the water ran down his nasal passage, and bolted upright, splashing water over the sides of the tub and onto the dirt of the chamber floor.

'Do you want me to call one of my men to assist you?' Garamond peered back at Jeff. His legs were rapidly turning to jelly.

The bells stopped ringing.

'I'm fine,' he shot back.

He was not. His body twitched and spasmed, and screamed for rest. Though he couldn't feel the pain consciously, he had no doubt that it was there. Every step toward the hospital wing was an effort in itself, and Garamond's patience would only last so long.

She stood on a landing between two flights of stairs, peering back at him with Petor held in her arms. The old man was unconscious, but breathing, Garamond lifted him with ease. Such endurance was a distant memory for Jeff.

'You don't look fine,' she said.

Jeff waved her comment off, his breathing labored and his face cold and bloodless.

'Go on ahead. He needs the doctor.'

'So do you.'

'I'll be right behind you, go.'

Garamond nodded, and started up the next flight without looking back.

Come on, Jeff, get yourself moving.

He tested his weight against the handrail. Now alone, there was no need to pretend he could make it without. His legs shook uncontrollably, practically numb and tingling with what felt like a thousand moving pinpricks. The sensation shot up his thigh and into his hip as his foot landed on the next step, and he faltered. His weight swung around where he held the rail. He turned face-up mid-swing, and his shoulder hit the wall.

He lay flat on the stairs, and felt the uncontrollable urge to laugh.

What are you going to do now, then?

Getting up was an impossibility; he had nothing left.

A few minutes' rest here, just a few min…

RENIA WOKE FROM a dreamless sleep to the mild burning sensation of the sun on her face. The calls of nearby seabirds in their morning ritual nudged her awake. She smiled, and stirred against the cool sheets that covered her body. A familiar voice welcomed her.

'Renia.'

Dail?

She opened her eyes, and pushed herself upright slowly as they focused on the man that lay beside her.

'Renia, it's you? Smell like Renia.' He spoke with a slight stammer, but it *was* his voice, his old voice.

'Dail?'

Renia rubbed her eyes, wiping away the sleep. Was this a dream? It didn't feel like a dream, but how could this be? She shot upright, her heart swelling in her chest, and felt the burn of tears and a lump in her throat. It had worked. She had healed him.

Dail's face dropped in confusion. 'Renia. Can't see.' He started to breathe heavily, then twitched and writhed, testing his limbs.

She took his hand. 'Shh,' she said, stroking him soothingly. 'It's alright.'

Dail shook, his whole body trembling. 'Can't see.'

She sat and held his head in her arms, caught between dueling emotions, of guilt, of pride. She swallowed at the cruel reality that she had created. 'You have no eyes.'

He moaned, sobbing into her lap. 'Can't see,' he said, shivering. 'Can't see.'

PART THREE

Kindred

TWENTY-FIVE

Frustration

BENEATH THE HALLS of Venn, under tons of stone, and wood, and dirt, within the hidden network of tunnels and chambers long ignored by the feet of scholars and scribes, a lone quill scratched and scraped its way across page after page. The Hall Master known to all as Vedora winced, and cracked her wrist, then resumed her task, hunched over what was to be a perfect copy of the Arch Traitor's journal.

Sanas Inoa – Journal 26.

Candlelight wavered over exposed rock. The chamber was just one of so many incomplete spaces that riddled the tunnel complex. A complex too vast to monitor, a safe place for a Southern agent to hide.

The woman raised only her eyebrow as the Reaper padded her way into the space.

'A complication,' said Bandack.

Vedora's attention remained on the book. 'Go on.'

'A cultist, posing as a janitor. He had Staine hiding in a box.'

The aging Hall Master lowered her quill and shifted in her seat. 'You killed him?'

'I did.'

'Staine?'

'By the time I'd disposed of the body, he had been moved. I lost the scent.'

Vedora nodded once, a glazed expression on her face. 'Another cultist?'

Bandack shrugged. 'Or not.'

'I know what you are suggesting.'

'I'm getting bored of this plan of yours.' Bandack dusted the dirt from her clothing and propped herself against the wall.

'I'm almost done. I just need a little more time.'

'Why do you torture me? You know as well as I the itch of the writ, how it burns. My *writ* is for Staine's life. The mission is to send a clear message to his father. *This*,' she said, waving her hand toward Vedora's desk, 'is a secondary objective. My orders said nothing of waiting for you to copy the thing. This delay not only paints a dull picture of my competence, it increases suspicion that the book is the *real* reason for my presence. You're endangering the mission out of what? Sentimentality?'

'Those are my terms. I made them clear when I sent for you.'

The Reaper sighed, her frustration plain. 'We may have already lost Staine.'

'You'll find him.'

'She's working against us. You know it, and so do I.'

The two women regarded each other, neither displaying any sign of weakness. 'You'll find him,' said Vedora.

'What makes you so sure?'

'You're my daughter.'

'Another week, that's how long you have before I lose my patience. Make it count, *Mother*.'

WHEN JEFF AWOKE, it was to the sound of chirping birds and muffled sobbing. He prised open his burning eyes in a state of confusion, with no idea where he was, and no memory of how he came to be there.

A staircase, Garamond—Petor.

His eyes slowly filtered away the haze of sleep and focused. He lay in the hospital ward, on his back, staring at one of the knotted wood beams that supported the ceiling.

The muffled sobbing continued. *From the left,* his ears told him. He was not alone; new information slowly trickled into his awakened senses, distant groans of pain, snoring, excited tale-telling.

The ward was busy. *The riot. Of course.*

In the next bed over, Petor lay in a state of calm sleep. Master Vedora sat by his side, his hand in her own, where she rested her head: a bony pillow for her tears. He looked so peaceful, a far cry from the man he'd held to his breast—

When? Last night? How long have I been out?

Jeff made to rise, but found his leg bound and still. Further inspection revealed his nakedness, and he thought better of the attempt.

Where are my clothes?

From behind a curtain wall, a flustered nurse appeared, hunched over an armful of bloodied towels and bedsheets. *Alice,* Jeff recalled, one of the nice ones. The nurse shot a glance toward him as she deposited her spoils into a linen sack and thrust them away across the floor with her foot. 'You're awake. Good.' She stood and placed her hands in the small of her back, stretching out the tension caused by what must have been a busy shift. 'Any pain?'

'Nothing new,' Jeff replied, casting his arm out in a conciliatory gesture. 'My clothes—'

'Filthy. I sent them to be cleaned. And I know what you're thinking, young man, and *don't*. There's no way you're walking out of here without giving all the girls a good look at you in your altogether.' She smirked. 'Although I'm sure they'd all thank me for it.'

'Fantastic,' Jeff grumbled.

'Now get some rest. I'll have some food sent over when I get a minute.' She did her best to appear commanding.

Jeff nodded once and watched her hobble away. He rolled his eyes and sighed, becoming aware of Vedora's watchful gaze. He met it dead-on, his suspicion rising. 'How is he?' he said.

Vedora did her best to steel herself against the question and return her attention to the retired Hall Master sleeping by her side. She stroked his arm, searching for a hint of awareness. 'They say he'll be fine, that he's exhausted, and sickly.' She grimaced. 'That he's trying to drink himself to death.'

Jeff let the comment sit, watching her intently. *Something is off*, he thought. The tears, the body language, *guilt?*

He turned away, perturbed to find himself feeling useless once again. His leg, heavy, dead weight that it was, had become an anchor that bound him to failure. He cursed it, and flared with impatience.

Bollocks to it.

He drew himself up, gathering the bedsheets around him in a makeshift toga, and hopped away from the bed, looking for anything that could be used as a crutch.

Vedora sat staring, incredulous.

After a moment peering around the curtain wall for any sign of Alice, he turned back to the watching Hall Master. 'I know you're involved in this,' he said, his words measured and cool.

'I don't know what game you're playing. I don't know if I care anymore. But I know that you had something to do with all this. I *know* that you're in some way responsible for that man's situation.'

She didn't flinch. No hesitation, no ready defense, no sign of any emotion, only the level stare of a predator stalking its prey. Jeff curled his lip and limped away toward the exit, dragging the sagging sheets along with him.

SUNDANCE HESITATED. SHE stood in the library, her latest reads held to her breast. She watched as Bandack sat in the center of the reading hall, rustling her way through a novel with a pace that made her envious. She had so much to thank the Reaper for: her newfound vitality, a mental clarity she hadn't felt for a decade, a triumph in contributing to the downfall of a seditious group—she could not bring herself to consider the Reaper her enemy, far from it.

Why shouldn't she say hello? After all, her part in the ongoing investigation had led to her being permitted to roam freely despite the lockdown. And now, with a suitable replacement for Petor returning to Hall Three, she had time to engage in pleasantries without the guilt associated with dereliction of one's duties.

Why not?

She shuffled toward the Reaper as quietly as she could.

'You know I could smell you from the hallway,' Bandack announced, obliterating the mandated silence. She offered Sundance a smile, and patted the seat beside her. 'Come, sit.'

'How are you, dear?' Sundance sat, resisting the urge to pat the Reaper on the arm. She spoke in a whisper, keen not to draw attention to the two of them. 'Well, I hope?'

'Why are you whispering?' Bandack said, confused.

A quick glance toward the angry librarian made Sundance flush with embarrassment. 'It's customary to remain silent in the library.'

'That explains a lot,' whispered Bandack, nodding. The Reaper beamed and winked at the librarian, who let out a barely audible shriek before scuttling away behind a bookshelf.

Sundance stole a glance at the open book Bandack had been reading. She knew it well, a tale of a widow and her struggle to find a safe home for her children during wartime. 'A beautiful story,' she said nodding toward the book. 'What a mother will do for her young.'

The Reaper looked down at the book and back at Sundance. 'I never really knew my mother.'

'Oh, dear. I'm so sorry—'

'No, no. She's not dead. I just never really knew her.'

'I see.'

A pregnant silence ensued. Sundance wasn't sure whether to pry further. The distant look on the young girl's face spoke for itself.

'It doesn't bother me,' Bandack said. 'Once, perhaps. But not for a long time.'

'What happened?'

Bandack frowned, and shrugged. It was the most genuine moment Sundance had shared with the girl. She wondered if the bravado, the odd behavior, was all a mask, a way of coping with the loss.

'I always wondered what she might be like. I think all orphans fantasize about the same mother figure: kind, patient, loving.'

Sundance smiled. 'Unfortunately, not all mothers are.'

The Reaper snapped out of her reverie, grinning once more. 'I am terribly bored, Sundance.'

'Don't you have a *job* to do?'

The Reaper blew out her cheeks and leaned back on her chair. The creak echoed through the library. 'Complications.'

Sundance nodded. 'Well,' she said, 'let me pick out some more books for you, dear. I know a few that will get your blood pumping.' She stood, hesitating at the lost look on the girl's face.

'Thank you,' said the Reaper. And at once Sundance understood what it was that had led to their unlikely pairing. She smiled, and placed her hand on the girl's shoulder.

DAIL WALKED AGAIN. As impossible as it was, he walked, and Renia watched and clapped and feigned encouragement as he tentatively made his way toward the bathroom, led by a length of string she had set up for him.

Should she be happy? She should be, *definitely*. She smiled to herself and to the sound of Dail using the toilet unaided for what seemed like the first time in forever, but the smile died on her lips as the doubt crept back into her thoughts.

She felt guilt for the pride at hearing his voice again, at hearing clarity in his words. It wasn't pride for him, it was pride in her own achievement.

She had done it. *She* had healed him.

And then came the guilt, the guilt at the price she'd paid for it. A life. An innocent life, traded away for the life of its father, for the hubris of its mother. It cut like a knife, the selfism of it. What had she bought with her child's life?

Her mind's eye conjured the memory of Aevus. As clear as he had been in the flesh, he shook his head in disapproval and she felt a tear forming. What had she done?

Renia and Dail had spent most of their time talking since his awakening. At first, she'd reveled with him in the triumph of it—him standing, walking, forming complex sentences again. And with communication came confession—the events that had led to their fight, and her unconscious use of her lightstone to fight him off. She'd cried, and he'd held her.

'I was my fault,' he'd said. 'Don't blame yourself.' But how could she not? His words rang as hollow as they always had, and that's when she'd started to realize that nothing had changed.

When she'd told him of the pregnancy and what had happened to the baby he bowed his head, a distant look took him, and several minutes of silence followed. She didn't cry, she didn't join him in his reaction, because she didn't believe it. She didn't believe him at all.

'I'm just happy to live again. Don't blame yourself,' he'd said over and over.

Spilling water slapped at the floor in the bathroom beyond, and the walls rang with the sound of Dail coughing. 'Are you alright?' she called out.

'Fine,' he said between coughs. She heard him hock up and spit in the overflowing sink. He'd been bringing up what looked like clots for the past few hours.

'I'll clean up in a minute,' she said. 'Try to drink some water.'

Should I be happy?

A knock at the door.

Dail pulled his way along the string into the living area. 'Do I look alright?' he asked.

'You look great.'

Renia answered the knocking, exchanging a smile with Venn-Dor before inviting him in. 'You should see this,' she said.

The Grand Master's eyes widened as he entered, fixed on the sight of Dail standing in the middle of the room, straining to hear who had come in.

'Who is it?' said Dail.

'It's the Grand Master,' Renia replied. She didn't take her eyes off him, projecting her mixed feelings at the turn of events.

'Remarkable…' said Venn-Dor, rubbing his chin.

'Oh, Grand Master!' said Dail, attempting to bow without losing his balance. 'Forgive me, my sight has not returned.'

'Please, please. Don't fret.' The Grand Master waved away any formality, appearing genuinely fascinated by his recovery. 'How do you feel?'

Dail stammered a little, but managed to speak with clarity. His control over his thoughts and speech improved with every passing moment. 'Well. Thank you, sir.'

The Grand Master's attention finally shifted to Renia. 'You did it.'

She nodded in response.

Venn-Dor hesitated for a moment and then addressed Dail. 'Mister Svelt. It pleases me to see you making a recovery. I need to borrow Renia for a moment. Please excuse us.'

Dail nodded, though she detected a hint of annoyance in it.

Did you think he came here to see you?

She shook her head and followed Venn-Dor into the quiet of the hallway.

'Are you well?' he said.

She shrugged. 'I don't know. I'm supposed to be happy, or grateful to be alive, to have succeeded…' She lost the thought; what else could she say?

The Grand Master stood mute for a long minute, studying her for a warning of a second suicide attempt, no doubt. The thought made her feel pathetic; how weak she must appear to him, to everyone who knew what happened.

Oh moon, everybody saw. Everyone must have seen her with Aevus when she fell.

'You've been through a lot,' he said. 'I wish I could offer you time to recuperate and endure these feelings, but things are changing quickly.'

'What do you mean?'

'We had word this morning. We have days until your presence will be required elsewhere.'

'Days?'

'A week at the most. It's time for you to consider your future, Renia.'

She looked back at the door, and thought of Dail.

'It's alright. As long as we have each other,' he'd said. 'We'll find a way to work together. With my mind and your pen hand we can be useful here—don't cry. We will try again. We'll make another baby and this time we'll do it right. Things will be fine, as long as we have each other, things will be fine.'

Her stomach turned. She made no attempt to hide her feelings from her Grand Master as she met his eyes. 'What do I do?'

What could she do? Did the fact that she was responsible for Dail's disability, or the loss of their baby, change the fact that all the doubts she ever had about the man were still there? She still felt the unease, the silent, unacknowledged wrestling between them. She still heard hidden meaning in his words.

'Something else you should know,' Venn-Dor said. 'Molan has returned.'

To KILL ME? What is this?

Vedora flicked through the pages of her sister's diary. Except it wasn't Vedora, it was Veralack. Rage bubbled to the surface with each line of text.

'There is no justice here. Only vendetta, only your desperate plea to remain relevant.'

She clicked her tongue, biting back the bile that rose in her throat.

She paced around the hidden chamber, sparing a look at the room they had shared for a decade. Shared. *Everything*, they had shared. She gritted her teeth, finding herself in front of the mirror. The face she knew so well stared back at her with all the anger and malice contained within the diary's pages.

A face with three identities. Vedora, Veralack, Maylack. To the rest of the world, one person. And for a lifetime, the two sisters had split their time here in this old forgotten cavern beneath the Halls of Venn, working to keep the facade that *was* Hall Master Vedora alive.

And now this.

The door creaked open, and once again she turned to see her reflection as her twin entered.

'Where have you been?'

Maylack snarled at her, slamming the door behind her. 'With Petor, where else?'

'And what is this?' She picked the diary up, waving it around like the shit rag that it was.

'What does it look like?'

The twice-born pair stood glaring at each other, several feet apart. It might as well have been the span of the world.

'You're going to kill me, then?'

'I am.'

'What, by the moon, is wrong with you?'

Maylack snarled. 'Wrong with me? How dare you?' She stomped toward her twin. 'Petor almost died!'

'He didn't die.'

'But he *almost* did! And for what? For you and your stupid scheme to buy your ticket home. Have you once asked me if I wanted that? Did it ever cross your mind that I might not *want* to return to Daralar? That I might even be happy here? That I might have something *worth* staying for?'

'Of course it did.'

'Oh really? I suppose that's why you used the man I love, *once again*, to stand as convenient fodder for your goals.'

'He isn't dead.'

'You make me sick.'

'You don't understand, you never understood. How could you?'

Maylack spat at the floor by her sister's feet. 'That's what I think to that. Oh how could I possibly understand? It wasn't me that fell in love with another Reaper, it wasn't me that fell pregnant, it wasn't me that had to hide my children from the Five. But I paid the fucking price anyway, didn't I?'

Veralack grimaced, rushing at her sister and gripping her about the arm. 'Do you think I don't know that—'

'You knew then! You knew what you were doing! You knew what it would cost us if you didn't hand those children over, and you had them anyway. Fuck your sister, *your twin*. Exile or death, that was the choice offered to me for your sins. Do you know I used to dream of seeing this place? Of escaping with you and heading north, to the *beautiful* Luna Ruinam? I used to imagine us looking out over the mountains, visiting the seas, looking down into the great scar. An adventure. What did we get instead? Shipped here in a box, like meat, and left to rot until we made ourselves useful.'

'I had no choice.'

'Don't give me that shit. You had every choice. You just couldn't help yourself around Hosst. Couldn't keep your fucking legs closed—'

'Now see here!' Veralack lunged at her sister, swinging from the hip, but the blow was blocked, and Maylack countered, throwing her to the floor.

'I've had enough!' Maylack spat. She mounted her, pinning her to the ground. 'I'm not your lesser, I never have been!'

'Go on then, do it!' Veralack wrestled her arm free and pulled a dagger from her boot. She flashed it up, stopping a hair from her sister's throat.

MAYLACK FROZE, KNOWING at once that she didn't have the speed to win. Her sister lay beneath her, barely breaking a sweat, piercing her with her eyes.

Veralack pushed the knife into her grasp. 'Do it! Do it, you stupid old crone! If you want it so badly, do it!'

But she couldn't. *She couldn't.*

Tears started to roll down her cheeks. All those years, all that time spent living a lie, watching Petor drift further away from her and her dual personality, knowing that she could never have what her sister had, however brief it may have been, or how bad the consequences. She'd never bear a child, never retire, never be free of her service. Even in exile, she lived by the will of others.

'I can't,' she whispered.

Veralack shoved her off, leaving her in a heap on the floor. 'Of course you can't. You're weak.'

She was right, of course. No matter how much she'd endured, how much she'd fought, studied, trained—Veralack had always been stronger. She'd always been the rock that kept them together.

She took a look at her twin, the both of them sitting on the floor. 'Stupid old crone?'

They laughed.

Maylack snorted. 'You're no spring chicken, yourself.' Another laugh. 'You're stronger. Did you find a lightstone?'

Veralack nodded. 'I do have a plan, you know.'

'Of course you do.'

'Not just for me.'

'Then why didn't you say something earlier?'

'I needed Petor to make it work. You would never have gone along with it.'

That was true enough. 'Probably not,' said Maylack.

'It was you, wasn't it? You have Staine.'

She nodded.

'Good.'

'Good?'

'I need to finish copying the book before he's killed.'

'Copying? That's why the delay. Did you know where he was before?'

'Only that he was here. The cultist did us a favor. It would have been harder to get him out from under Jeff's nose.'

Maylack nodded slowly. 'You want to return the journal.'

'The original. Bandack will take the copy south, present my favor to the Five. Petor will find the original. They'll put it down to his deterioration and you'll get to live on as Vedora, here.'

'This was your plan all along?'

'I'm not the monster you think I am. And I'm not stupid. I know that I'll never have the things I lost, but my place is in Daralar, yours is here. You're still my sister. I wouldn't expect you to come with me.'

'I probably would have.'

'I know. All the more reason not to tell you.'

Maylack looked into her twin's eyes. The rush of a connection almost forgotten struck her, and she flushed at her behavior. 'Forgive me.'

'Always.'

They sat in silence as the thoughts swam.

'It won't work,' she said.

'Of course it will.'

'It won't. Jeff knows. He told me as much earlier on. He'll be coming for us, probably before the sun rests.'

Veralack sighed through her nose. 'Then we'll need a new plan.' She swung her head toward the door. 'Come in!'

Bandack entered, frowning, and looked her dead in the eye. 'Hello, Auntie,' she said.

TWENTY-SIX

Resignation

JEFF BURST INTO the security office, dragging his injured leg along behind him. Whatever Bandack had done, it hadn't been helpful; yes, the pain had diminished but the function had not improved, which resulted in lumbering around with what felt like dead weight.

'Where is Bobb?' He directed the question at Jinger, who sat in shock at his abrupt entrance.

'You're up. Shouldn't you—'

'Where is Bobb, Jinger?'

She recoiled, collecting herself and attempting to mask her upset. 'He's with Ferron, sir.'

'Ferron? Why?'

'Temporary reassignment.'

'Venn-Dor?'

Jinger gulped and nodded once. *That man,* Jeff thought. He stormed across the room and toward the cells. He strode past the bars and oak doors, carrying his anger with him, greeted by empty cell after empty cell, save for Mako, who barely lifted an eyebrow in his direction.

Where is everyone?

'Where is everyone?!' he roared into the dark, his voice bouncing back at him from every brick.

Mako charged at the bars of his cell. 'Keep the noise down! Tick! Branch!'

Jeff shot him a glare and turned on his heel. Charging back into the office toward a shocked and meek-looking Jinger. He stopped just short of her desk.

'What is this?' he demanded.

'Sir, you were incapacitated.'

'What did he do? Where are the thinkers' circle?'

'Venn-Dor came in, with Ferron. They transferred everyone to the North Wing for interrogation. Bobb went with them.'

'Leaving you on your own—'

A loud crack and a flash of light interrupted the exchange, rattling his eyeballs and ears and forcing a welp out of Jinger.

Venn-Dor appeared in a ball of light and strode toward Jeff, concern writ across his face. 'They told me you'd checked yourself out,' he said. 'What are you doing? You should be resting.'

'What am I doing? You've pulled my investigation out from under me, undermined me again!'

Venn-Dor frowned. 'You were incapacitated, chief. The doctor insisted. Might I suggest you adjust your tone.'

'I'll adjust something,' Jeff snapped. 'Bring them back.'

'I will not.'

He slammed his fist on Jinger's desk. She squealed and pushed herself back. 'That's it!' he said. 'I've had enough. This has been a joke from the beginning. You've interfered and undermined me at every turn. You've questioned every road I've taken, withheld information. I need my team back, now.'

'What for? Ferron is capabl—'

'I need them back because I need someone watching Vedora, I need everything—' He swung toward Jinger. 'I need everything you have on her. How she came to be here, family history, everything.'

Venn-Dor sighed and spared Jinger a pitying glance. 'Hall Master Vedora is not a suspect. Her loyalty is not in question.'

'Well, it should be!'

'What do you know? Do you have evidence to support this accusation?'

'I have my gut!'

Venn-Dor paused, his face creased in consternation. 'Your gut is not enough, Jeff. I have already lost two Hall Masters. I'm not going to risk losing another to satisfy your frustration.'

'My frustration?'

His frustration. Is that what he thought this was? *A tantrum?*

Was this a tantrum? For so long he had kept his temper in check. Not even when they had exiled him had he lost it. Why now? Why had he lost his composure so publicly?

It wasn't about Vedora, or the book, or even Ferron. It never had been.

This was about duty, and the bars it had erected around him. It was about the life he'd lost, and his slow march toward uselessness in a place he had no love for: its politics, its internal dramas, all of it a shallow veneer over what life should really be, a fight for survival. For all the progress their species had made, for all the abundance they had created, they had found themselves wanting. These petty games were the plight of the bored, the idle—

'I've had enough,' he said.

Venn-Dor looked to Jinger, who showed no sign of understanding either.

'I've had enough. Consider this my resignation.'

'I won't accept it,' said the Grand Master, shaking his head.

'You will. I have nothing left to give this place. It ends now.'

'*WILL YOU READ it to me again?*'

Pistorious lay on his back. His eyes were heavy, burning from
the strain of reading for so long in low light.

'*Again? Really?*'

He remembered every word. Every glance, every smell, every
touch. He was twelve then, and flooded with the fire of youth and
optimism, spellbound by the girl who had shown him kindness in
a time when he knew nothing of it.

'*Come on, Story, please?*'

That was what she called him, and he embraced it. It made
a refreshing change from 'Pissy'. They were inseparable, and
despite the constant leer of his older brother, who always seemed
to be close by, watching and waiting, and the whistles and jeers of
the other children, they were left—for the most part—in peace.

They spent what felt like a decade together, though it was
at the most a few weeks. It was the longest summer of his life,
the only one that had stayed with him. Hours passed as they had
looked out over the great green city, her hand in his, hot and sticky
with adolescent sweat, her head on his shoulder, his arm around
hers.

'*Don't ever forget me,*' she said.

'*I would rather die.*'

Pistorious opened his eyes and sat upright. He darted to the
desk, opened an empty, abandoned journal he had found, and
began to write.

Is it any wonder that our choices are so influenced by events that happen during childhood? A time when emotion runs as freely as a river after a storm. When love comes without question, and holds on so intensely that nothing else makes any sense. Of course, we don't appreciate it. It's one of time's exquisite cruelties, that creeping erosion of our sensitivities, the hardening of our souls to the world, a skin that thickens with every passing moment, like bark on the sapling that grows into a great oak:

Majestic in mourning.

Beautiful yet stubborn and rigid.

Paralyzed.

THE GUILT TREE: the oldest tree on the grounds of the Halls of Venn.

Renia wasn't entirely sure when the tradition had started. For generations, people had visited the tree, carved out slits and inserted coins into its bark. The massive tree now resembled some sort of ancient reptile, its scales a sea of oxidized copper, a great cyan beast of collective shame.

Renia was no stranger to the guilt tree, having paid it for its comfort many times in her life. There were coins for her father, for her mother, for her adolescence, and now for her baby, Aevus, Dail, and Petor.

Renia had forgotten what it was to feel comfort. She was exhausted. Days had passed like years between caring for Dail and her commitment to completing her project.

Neither had been easy.

Dail's behavior had become more erratic as his ability to move around increased. What should have been considered an improvement had actually worsened his frustration. As he grieved the loss of his sight, the realization that the loss of his sight also meant the loss of his passions had set in.

The sight of him still turned her stomach.

The guilt tree seemed like an appropriate way to avoid the crossroads she now approached. She allowed herself to slump to her knees before it.

Was her life ever truly her own? She walked back through every year since her parents' death. She'd been led, *advised*, mentored. And through her talents, she'd advanced toward goals that had not truly been hers. She was grateful, of course. The path Molan had chosen for her had been the most appropriate for her skills and what he knew of her desires before the tragedy that ended her childhood, but had it been the one she would have taken?

Was she avoiding making choices? Had she willingly traded her own agency for an exemption from responsibility? Had it made the slightest bit of difference?

The last thing she'd truly chosen to do was the choice that resulted in the death of her parents.

The thought wore on her for the duration of the journey toward Hall Three, a gift perhaps, a distraction from the anxiety of facing her peers once again, and whatever they might think of her after her very public suicide attempt and the subsequent supernatural intervention.

Molan was the wisest man she'd ever known. He always knew what to say, or when to say nothing at all. He'd simply been there for her, slowly guiding her through difficulty when she needed him. She was not surprised to find him present again now, in this dark time.

Her footsteps disrupted the near silence of Hall Three, rousing the attention of her former colleagues. Familiar faces greeted her over the sound of pages turning and the scribbling of quill on parchment. Painfully aware of her intrusion, she walked the central void of the hall, nodding as she went. Some returned the gesture with a smile, a nod. Others regarded her with shock, or fear. *Understandable,* she thought.

She paused as she passed her old desk, meeting the nervous gaze of a young intern, her face pocked with the signs of recent adolescence. How long had it been since she'd found herself in the same position? Stuttering through her early days under the stoic gaze of Sundance.

She looked to the next desk, disappointed to find her mentor had also been replaced. Jensen sat there now, a good man, an experienced scribe. He would make a fine mentor for the young girl. He looked up from his work, from Renia to his apprentice, and spared Renia a nod.

'Good to see you,' he whispered.

She thanked him, and walked on.

A member of the janitorial staff struggled to hang a plaque by what was once the door to Petor's office: 'Hall Master Molan', it read. She envied her old colleagues the honor of working under him.

'Close the door behind you, love.' Molan greeted her with warmth as she entered. His embrace was welcome. She rubbed the aging man's back and squeezed him as hard as she could. It made him laugh.

'I'm so sorry I wasn't there to greet you,' she said.

'Don't be.' Molan winked, motioning her to sit. 'Seems you've been busy.' She could feel her adopted father studying the signs of premature aging, trying his best not to make a show of it.

'How much did Venn-Dor tell you?'

'Enough,' he said. 'He's not my biggest fan.' He nodded to himself, pouring her a glass of water.

'How is Carol?'

'Aloof as ever. The Baron finally agreed to let her take off on her hunt for the missing burial grounds. It seems there is no spirit too hard for her to break.' They shared a laugh. 'I have to admit I didn't expect to be back here again, certainly not like this.'

'I take it you didn't have much choice in the matter?'

'Two Hall Masters to replace, lots of staff gone. Someone has to keep the quill moving.' Molan grinned. 'I'm fairly happy, in honesty. I'm getting a bit too old to be digging around in the dirt.' Molan sipped his water, momentarily lost in thought. 'What about my girl? What's next for you?'

'Venn-Dor didn't tell you?'

'No. Above my station, I suspect.'

'Do you know what the Shepherd is?'

Molan rubbed his chin, leaning back into his chair. 'No.' He flashed her an excited look. 'Not definitively. I know it's a Grand Master position. Are they making you a Grand Master?' His grin lit the room.

'I suppose they must be.'

Molan beamed and tapped his palm on the desk. 'My little girl. I'm so proud of you.'

Renia felt the throb of shame, and she looked to her feet. 'You shouldn't be.'

Molan rocked back on his chair, lighting his pipe. It was a familiar sight that put her at ease, made her feel safe. The smell of it filled her nostrils, reminded her of another time. 'Why ever not?' he said.

'The things that have happened…I should be locked up.'

'You're an asset to this place. Momentary lapses in judgment are often weighed against your value.' He leaned in. 'Besides, from what I hear you gave as good as you got.'

Renia shook her head. 'You don't understand. What I've done…I lost control.'

'Well, you've always had a bit of a temper.'

'I'm so ashamed.'

'I had a similar conversation with your father once,' he said.

The thought of it brought sadness. She missed him so much. 'What did you say to him?'

Molan laughed heartily, waving the smoke away from his eyes. 'I spouted some pseudo-philosophical shite that was barely relevant.' He shook his head. 'I was young.'

They laughed together.

'What are you going to do?' said Molan.

'I don't know. Venn-Dor says I will have to leave, head out on my own.'

'How do you feel about that?'

'I don't know. *I don't know.* That's the problem.'

She placed her hands in her lap, laying her weakness before the only man left alive that she truly trusted. 'I just do what I'm told. How am I supposed to make a choice like this? I have a life here, I have responsibilities now. I have to care for Dail…'

Molan nodded once.

'I wish he would just order me to go.'

'That's probably why he won't.'

Renia blinked. 'What do you mean?'

'I think he's trying to teach you something about yourself. And from what I can see, it's working.'

She stopped to consider the words of her adopted father, grateful once more for his insight. 'That doesn't make it any easier,' she said.

'No.' Molan took another puff on his pipe. 'But nothing worth doing is ever easy, is it?'

It was those words that followed her back to her apartment. They had embraced, and promised to meet again out of work hours. She smiled more than once at the thought of the man who'd become the father she needed so badly.

The door was slightly ajar. *Has he been out?*

She could hear Dail coughing again inside, bringing up more of the black mess that seemed to be lining his lungs. The thought of it troubled her. His patience would be wearing thin.

She entered and sat on the edge of the bed, watching Dail work his way out of the bathroom and back toward her.

'You're back,' he said.

She smiled. 'I'm here.'

Dail wiped his mouth and cleared his throat. 'It's still coming up.'

'Dail, I need to tell you something.' She fidgeted. This had to be the time; the longer she kept it from him the harder it would be.

'What is it?'

'They want me to leave.'

Dail scratched his head, a frown forming on his face. He adjusted the blindfold wrapped around his head. 'For how long?'

'Forever, Dail.'

He nodded. 'And they are angry with you for refusing?'

She stared at his lips. They flickered slightly in the moment that passed, confusion creasing his features.

'I didn't refuse, not yet,' she said.

He tilted his head. 'What do you mean, you didn't refuse?'

'You know what I mean.'

'So we'll go together then, you and me. Have our family somewhere new; a fresh start.'

She felt a tear grow by her nose. How could she consider leaving him now? After everything she'd done? 'I have to do this alone, Dail.'

He surged forward a step, then paused, steadying himself. 'Sounds like you've already made up your mind.'

'No. I told you, I haven't made my decision.'

'*Your* decision? What about us? What about the things we said? About trying again, having a baby.'

'I don't want a baby, Dail. I never did.'

'Why are you saying these things?'

He started to rock on his heels. Patting his thighs in restrained aggression.

'It's me, isn't it. You can't bring yourself to be with someone like me, broken, blind.'

'It's not that. I'm trying to explain—'

'You're trying to justify it!'

'I'm not. You're not listening.'

'Why should I listen? Nothing you say makes any *sense*. One minute you want me, you want a future for us, the next you're leaving, going off on your own.' He shook visibly, gritting his teeth. 'You're a cold bitch, Renia, you always have been. Self-absorbed, solipsist!'

She jumped to her feet. 'Solipsist? Dail, that's not fair.'

He clambered over to her, face pink with frustration. 'Come here. Please, come here.'

'Dail, stop, I'm trying to talk—'

'Please, Renia, just come here.' His grasp reached her, pulling at her skirt, bringing her closer to him. His kiss missed, head bouncing off of Renia's cheekbone.

'Dail, stop!'

'Stop fighting me. Just come here.'

He held tight to her clothing as she tried to wrestle free. He'd grown so strong since she'd healed him, it took all her effort just to keep her face away from his.

'Come here, woman!'

'No!' She slammed her forehead into his temple. He shouted out in pain. He held her arms at her side. She could barely move; the head-butt had only made him more angry. She started to panic, her breathing labored. 'Get off me!'

Dail roared and dragged her to the floor, scrabbling about to restrain her. She looked up at his face, to the bandage that had fallen out of place, and the hollow eye socket revealed in the struggle. 'Stop struggling,' he growled.

He started to force his hand between her thighs, under her skirt. 'No!' she screamed. She let loose with her right arm. The hook connected with his jaw and left him reeling.

The moment was fleeting. He drew back and swung his full body weight around in a hook of his own that knocked her into oblivion.

What's happening?

She thought she heard her cheekbone snap from somewhere distant. The pain called to her, though its urgency was absent.

All was black. The stars shone bright above. The wind whipped at her hair, but she saw no land, no foliage. She was floating.

Where am I?

'You're on the floor. Out cold, love.'

Dad?

'You've got to wake up, Moonpie. Get up, now.'

Why can't I stay here with you?

'Because I'm dead, Renia. It's time for you to let go of me.'

Never! I won't.

Silence responded to her. She felt icicles forming on her naked flesh.

You're dead because of me, Dad. You and Mum, and so many others since. It's my fault, all of it. I deserve to die.

'Renia.' A woman's voice now. 'Renia, stop this at once.'

Ma?

'Renia. That's enough. This is not the way we taught you. What did I teach you, daughter? What is rule number one?'

She started to cry, humbled by the command in her mother's tone. The voice she'd forgotten, that she had missed without realizing. *You either happen to life, or life happens to you.*

'Again, girl!'

You either happen to life, or life happens to you.

'Get up, Renia! Get up and happen to life!'

A tear rolled down her cheek. The stars danced around her in a vortex, pushing her upward.

Goodbye, Ma. Goodbye, Dad. You either happen to life—

HER EYES SNAPPED open. Sharp as a knife, her vision locked on Dail as he attempted to pull down her underwear.

'No.' The word came out flat, commanding.

Her awareness surged into her lightstone in a whoosh of energy. A bright orb of lightning snapped around her in a protective bubble that sent Dail flying through the air like a rag doll. His flailing body crashed into the wall, sending the contents of shelves crashing to the floor. He landed in a heaving lump by the door.

She stood, rising with ease. 'I've had enough of being led through life by guilt and shame, Dail. It's time for us to part ways.'

She swept him from the doorway and across the floor with a wave of static energy. He tumbled toward the kitchen counter. The move came so naturally to her, she reveled in it. Static crackled around her like a suit of lightning.

Dail lay winded, struggling to breathe. He held up his hand for her, reaching out, pleading. 'Please,' he barely managed.

She was steel. Her awareness, her confidence, all came together in a beautiful moment of clarity. She stood taller than she had in a lifetime, and at once felt like the self she always should have been, that she was *born* to be.

'I need you,' he said. 'You did this to me. You *have* to stay.'

'You're a weak man, Dail.'

She took one last look at the final reason she had to stay, and shook her head.

I'm leaving.

She smiled.

'I'm leaving.'

VERALACK ENTERED THE stone cavern carrying a tray of food. A dark rain cloak hung loosely over her arm. 'It's me,' she said.

But it wasn't.

Staine couldn't tell the difference, however. He lowered his quill, looked up from whatever it was he had been writing, and met her gaze with a mixture of hope and frustration. 'I thought you had forgotten me, Vedora.'

'Of course not.'

She placed the food on the desk in front of him. He took no pause in devouring it, and she took the opportunity to survey his surroundings, placing the overcloak on the foot of his bed.

'So nice to have a hot meal,' he managed, mouth full.

'I can imagine.'

He swallowed, turning to face her. 'Have they lifted the lockdown?'

'Not yet, but it's coming.'

'When?'

'Soon. You'll need to be ready.'

Staine groaned. 'I've been ready. That's all I am.'

'Good.'

The poor fool had no idea that he might have just eaten his last hot meal.

Twenty-Seven

Initiation

RENIA'S FOOTSTEPS PATTERED into the home of her great ancestor. The respect she felt for him grew in her chest as she looked once again around the private residence of Istopher Venn, the residence she would claim as her own, as was her right as his last living relative.

She winced away the pain in her face. Her broken cheekbone had swollen to the point of blocking her vision. She paid it no mind, supporting her body instead with the energy of her lightstone. The light crackle of static danced on her skin, a molecular circus, probing her muscles in harmony with her intent.

'I will be worthy of you.' She whispered the words, and hoped that somewhere, in whatever realm the echoes of the dead resided, she would be heard. The crimson mirror rippled at her from across the room, as if in sympathy with her message. A reply perhaps? Or just coincidence, a *synchronicity*.

She smiled to herself as she explored the space, examining the relics of his research, running her fingers over shelving and frowning at the dust that had already started to settle in Aevus's absence.

Aevus.

She found his tiny clothing neatly folded into the alcove he'd claimed as a bed. Barely large enough to hold his frame. She imagined his little body curled up there, sleeping peacefully as he had done under her arm.

Renia half expected him to be waiting for her. His face breaking into the warm smile she'd come to love so much. *I will be worthy of you too, little one.* His sacrifice would not be in vain, his warning to her would be heeded.

You have to live, Renia. What you do... What you do for us all, it has to happen.

She swallowed. His bravery, his determination.

I went into the mirror. I spoke with the people there, and they showed me what is to come, what I would have to do, to make sure it happens.

His words. As clear in her mind as they had been in his final, ragged breath.

She looked again to the mirror. Its presence dominated the space around it, playing with the shadows as if mocking the very reality it stood in.

What wonders do you hold? She reached out to it as she asked, holding her fingers just inches from its shimmering surface, glad not to see her own reflection in it. Her sagging, swollen, mess of a face.

A loud knock at the door broke her thought.

'Enter,' she commanded, and the Grand Master did, with a wary expression that betrayed his position.

'Don't worry,' she told him. 'I'm fine.'

He stood in the entrance, considering her. 'You've made your choice, then?'

'I have,' she said.

Venn-Dor cocked his head in wait.

'It's time,' she said. 'I'm ready.'

MAYLACK LAID HER quivering hand on Petor's chest. It rose and fell in slow, collected waves. He slept still. Lost in whatever world he'd created to allow himself to heal.

The night had stolen all the bustle of the ward, and taken with it the facade of normality that had made it easier to believe that he would wake.

But he will wake, wont he?

The gentle purple light of the fallen moon found its way through the window, and rested on his face. The long lines of worry and strain, now just an echo of the animated man she remembered, slack creases in the fabric of his being.

'Soon, Petor,' she whispered. 'Soon it will all be over.'

She ran her fingers through the coarse tangle of his hair. 'I'm so sorry.'

She wouldn't allow tears to come. Not now. She had a job to do, and she had to play her part in the plan.

Her sister's plan.

It wasn't a particularly cunning one. She wasn't even sure it would work. *Desperate?* Perhaps. But she didn't have a better one, and if there was a chance, however slim, that it would work, she would take it.

For Petor. For herself.

Am I fooling myself? She shook her head. To wish, to hope; nothing but the currency of fools. Her rationality told her that she would be caught, imprisoned, or worse. She didn't care.

Would it be so different from the life she had always endured?

Petor had been the only light in it, the only tenderness she'd ever felt. Time would call for her before long, and she'd trade whatever shred of freedom she had left for a chance at spending the rest of her time with him.

'Soon,' she said, and kissed his cheek. 'Not long now.'

PISTORIOUS SAT AT his desk, chewing on a piece of dried meat.

The longer his isolation lasted, the further into his past he probed, and his latest change in surroundings had become a reflecting pool for his unresolved feelings toward Lilian, and where it had all gone wrong.

He snuck out after hours and padded from the main house and into the servants' quarters, raising eyebrows and encouraging silence as he went. He kept his head low, risking the odd wave, the occasional embarrassed smile.

'My lord.' Lilian's mother had opened the door so quickly he'd jumped.

It was at that point he had known that something was wrong. Her eyes were swollen, she shook visibly, and spoke to him in pleading tones.

'Hullo,' he had said. 'Is Lilian home?'

Confusion crossed the woman's face. She shook her head, and a tear rolled off her cheek. It was fear. She was afraid. 'No, my lord.'

'I'm, uh, sorry. Do you know where she is?'

The woman's lip trembled, her voice quivering as she spoke. 'She was summoned, my lord.'

The ground felt as if it had moved beneath him. His heart lay heavy in his chest as he felt tears of his own forming. 'By—Summoned by whom?'

'By your brother, my lord. Young master Dorian.'

Pistorious's arms dropped to his sides and the piece of dried meat fell to the floor. He had been so young. How could he have known? Yet his innocence brought him no comfort. It was his fault. On some level, it was *his* fault.

He'd hardly slept that night, not knowing what his brother wanted with Lilian, or why he had sent for her at such an hour, not fully understanding the grief in the woman's eyes.

The day after, everything had changed. He woke early and ran out toward the well, desperate to see her, fraught with worry he couldn't rationalize.

'Lilian! Lilian!' She did not turn to face him. The girl continued toward the well, walking with obvious discomfort, her head bowed. 'Lilian!' She would not stop, she would not turn. He still remembered how she hissed, and winced when he pulled at her arm.

That sparkle in her eyes never returned.

'Yes, my lord?'

'My lord? It's me, Story. What happened to you? Are you alright?'

She wouldn't look at him, couldn't. If it were possible to feel one's heart tear in two, this moment was the closest thing to it. He knew that his joy, his love, had died.

'If it please my lord, I will return to my morning duties.'

She never looked back. He just stood and watched her hobble away toward the well, trembling and cold with shock.

'WHAT WILL HAPPEN?' Renia followed Venn-Dor into his chambers.

'You'll be initiated, brought into the light.' The Grand Master hurried into his dressing room, searching for something.

She followed him. 'Yes, but what does that entail?'

'I'll talk you through the ritual on the way. You shouldn't struggle to remember the words with your memory.'

Venn-Dor found what he was looking for, a bundle of white robes, perfectly folded and brilliant in their color.

'Ritual?' she said.

The Grand Master checked himself. 'Sorry,' he said. He took her in his arms and cast his gaze over her broken face. 'Are you sure about this? Everything will change after tonight.'

She was, though she wasn't sure that she enjoyed being led around by the nose.

'How can I be sure when I don't know what to expect?'

'You're right, of course.' He inhaled, straightening himself. 'You will appear before the Praelatus, myself, and another Grand Master. Words will be spoken. You'll surrender your body, mind, and soul to the realm, and in return you will be blessed. You'll trade your name for the title of Grand Master and enter into service to your land forevermore.'

'Forever?'

'You will not age.'

She staggered. *Of course.* She looked into the face of her Grand Master—Doratus—and wondered what name he had traded for his apparent immortality. She saw his face anew, a veneer over what must have been several lifetimes of all the things she had endured. *What fortitude he must have, what spirit.*

What face had he worn in her position? All those years ago, preparing for his own initiation. Did he have time to prepare, to properly process the information she'd just been smacked with?

'There is no tuning back from this, Renia. Are you sure?'

Forever.

Imagine what I could accomplish.

'You have to live, Renia. What you do… What you do for us all, it has to happen.'

'I'm sure,' she said.

'Very well.' Venn-Dor nodded and reached for his staff. 'Put these robes on, and wait here. I have to make the necessary preparations.'

She swallowed, and nodded back.

Venn-Dor thrust his staff at the floor, and her ears rang like a bell. White. Everything went white, the shapes of the room around her slowly forming once more to show nothing where the Grand Master had stood.

DARKNESS. SOMEWHERE BETWEEN that dreg-space of half-seen shapes and figures and the bliss of oblivion, The un-timeable moment before your senses get off their lazy arses and start telling you something useful. You're two things at once in that place, two beings, one fighting to stave off the impending barrage of sensory input, the other fighting for control of the physical body, for autonomy.

Petor wasn't sure which he was, only that opening his eyes would come with tremendous effort. Why should he? He didn't owe it to anyone.

What if I don't?

His ears woke up first. Thick with the sound of his own breathing, they forced their way toward his attention.

What is that? Footsteps?

Survival, then. The impulse that always wins. A rush of awareness in his muscles, a jolt of aid, a leg up over the hurdle of waking. His eyes flickered, once, twice, and then open, allowing his growing irises to swallow as much of the sparse light available.

Cold. Whatever sheets he'd been wrapped in were wrenched free. Someone was there. A dark outline at the foot of the bed.

His voice croaked. 'What—' but broke into a cough before he could finish. His legs were raised and stuffed into what must have been some kind of sack. Wrestling proved useless; wherever he had been, it had been for long enough for his limbs to hum and tingle with numbness.

'Oi!' He managed the single syllable before a familiar voice cut him short.

'Quiet, old man.'

'Vedora?' Petor squinted into the approaching woman's face.

She towered over him, and sighed. 'I wish you'd stayed asleep.'

And then a flash of pain in his jaw sent him back into bliss once again.

Renia almost lost her footing. Venn-Dor's arm, wrapped tight around her waist, kept her from falling. She looked out through a bubble of dissipating light into an ornate chamber, a circular, tiled space guarded by statues of long-dead heroes.

'Where are we?' she said.

'The palace.' Venn-Dor pulled her upright. 'Are you alright?'

'I'm fine,' she lied. The creeping anxiety she'd hidden would be ignored no longer. The prospect of standing before the great protector churned her stomach, bled her limbs of heat.

'You remember the words?' said Venn-Dor.

'I do.'

'Then follow three paces behind me.'

The Grand Master led her out of the room, into a hall lined with ancient trees carved from marble, leafless but still majestic, a mourning perhaps.

Focus, Renia, she scolded herself.

Under different circumstances, she would have taken in every detail, studied each work, not the slow procession of the Grand Master's footsteps.

The dryness in her throat threatened her twofold: not only would coughing be inappropriate, her broken cheekbone would make sure that it hurt. She bit her tongue instead, hoping that it might stimulate a sensation she could actually control.

Venn-Dor came to a stop before a throneless dais, and moved to the side, leaving Renia wondering if she should follow.

A voice came from the shadows on the opposite side: 'Kneel.'

A deep, rumbling voice that she didn't recognize. Renia strained her eyes for a glimpse at the face under the hood as her knees came to rest on the marble.

'Avert your eyes,' said Venn-Dor.

A pressure grew, akin to a threatening storm. Light gathered, reflecting from the tile to her lowered face, prickling the hairs on her cheeks. She closed her eyes instinctively, unprepared for the deafening ripple of broken space as Luna Ruinam's lord and savior manifested before her.

She blinked frantically, her eyes struggling to focus on the immense being floating mere paces from where she knelt. There was a word for it, a word from the motherland, an old word—God. An otherworldly intelligence. It was the only term that came close to describing the reverence she felt in that moment.

'Stand,' called out the unknown Grand Master.

Her legs shook, weak under the energy radiating from *him*. It took all her effort to push herself up. She could not bring herself to lift her head, even for a moment.

She caught a glimpse of the moonstones orbiting her great lord in a slow, supernatural dance, and remembered the first time Molan had described them to her.

'Place no barrier between your flesh and the old ones,' said Venn-Dor.

She reached up and cast aside the robe she wore. Exposing her broken, aged body to the light.

The heat of his presence prickled her naked flesh. She stood before her lord as she had been made, free from the confines of shame, or pride.

'Raise your left arm.'

She complied, lifting it above her head slowly, squinting at Venn-Dor as he approached.

'What name do you offer in return for the gifts you are about to receive?'

'I offer the name Collis, as given to me by my adopted father. I also offer the name Stone, the name of my birth.'

'Very well.'

Venn-Dor knelt before her and cupped her left breast in his hand. In his right, a dagger the size of a knitting needle loomed. Pain ripped through her as he pierced the skin beneath her breast, forcing her to stifle the urge to cry out. The blood felt cool in the heat as it ran down her midriff. The second Grand Master came forth, a dropper in hand. He retrieved a drop of blood from the puncture and approached the blue moonstone, carefully dropping her vitae onto its surface. There was a flash of light, and at once her skin was aflame. She tingled from head to toe and felt her head grow light.

Her thoughts settled into a state of clarity, each line of internal direction falling neatly into its own lane. She blinked rapidly as the internal fog of warring wants and needs subsided into unity.

'*Let your mind be soothed by the wisdom of the old ones,*' five voices spoke in unison, the two Grand Masters and a tri-tone voice that had no discernible source.

She looked down at the puncture. The bleeding hole in her flesh glowed brilliant blue from within.

'*Outward into time.*'

Venn-Dor wiped the needle clean, and approached again to claim her blood. Renia bit down the urge to shriek as her skin was pierced again, an inch away from the previous wound. Once again the second master took her blood, depositing it this time on the moonstone that shone with brilliant white light.

'*Let your soul be nourished by the tree of time.*'

She cried out, instantly plunging into a pool of thought, losing any sense of space or time. Her awareness split into a thousand pieces. At once she found herself living an infinity of different manifestations of herself, some of which were experiencing the initiation ritual, others that were far from it: a dream-like life in the Wastes, as a wife to the son of the man who'd pulled her from a window, a hermit living on scraps in the underbelly of a city with two hearts, a cleaning lady at work in the dormitories of the Halls of Venn.

Every possible path she could have taken, every consequence of each choice she hadn't made, concurrent. The depth of her experience and the weight of her choices assaulted her, forcing her to swim upward and out toward the branch that was her own, to reach for *her* anchor to reality.

Breathe.

She gasped for breath, focusing on the eyes of Venn-Dor, who knelt before her. He nodded once, and pulled her to her feet. Renia watched in horror as Venn-Dor cleaned the needle once again.

No more, please. She entreated him with her eyes. Pleading for an end to the assault on her being.

'*Inward into space.*'

Renia cried out in anguish as her body was pierced again, all sense of pride and determination stripped from her naked form.

Once more, her blood was given. To the third, and final, red moonstone. It ignited, bathing the room with firelight.

Gravity gave way. She felt her body rise off the ground. Her swollen cheekbone snapped back into place and knitted together with a curious burning sensation. Her skin pulled itself taut, smoothing out the wrinkles and sagging. Old scars itched as the stubborn tissue gave way to new skin, renewed.

'*Let your flesh be tended by the love of the old ones.*'

She fell slowly to the ground, landing on numb and tingling legs that gave way as she touched the heating marble.

Five voices sang out in chorus: '*All is song.*'

On one knee, she spasmed and heaved involuntarily, one hand held over the three holes in her chest. The punctures sealed themselves, leaving scars of brilliant shining light, each the color of the moonstone that it had nourished. Three crusting lines of dried blood left tracks from her newly taut breast to her thigh.

Rise, Venn-Renia. The command made her wince. The voice of a god. A voice that now came from her very blood. She planted her feet beneath her and slowly pushed herself from the floor, squinting into the light.

Venn-Dor spoke. 'Your names are no longer your own. From now on you are Venn-Renia, Grand Master of the Light, bound to the Praelatus for eternity, and forever a servant of Luna Ruinam.'

She added her own voice to the chorus. '*All is song.*'

Silence.

The light left. As abrupt as a slamming door. She searched the dim space with desperation, retinas burned and scored with the afterimage of a silhouette of a man.

Her body was released, and she landed with a thud by Venn-Dor's feet. She clamored for his robes, wrapping her arms around his leg. 'Is it over?' Hyperventilating. 'Is it over?'

'It's over.' Came the voice of the man she didn't know. 'Rest, sister.' She felt a hand on her shoulder. 'Rest.'

DAIL SVELT. THE blinded man convulsed, spitting an oily black liquid into the gathering pool at his cheek. *I am Dail Svelt.*

He inhaled through a film of flapping viscosity, each breath a gurgle. Laid on his side, he shifted in discomfort, the dead weight of his body pressing on what little volume his lungs had left to accommodate the air he so desperately needed.

More of the metal-laden filth slid from his tongue, rich with the taste of iron and sulfur. He started to cough, splattering wetness around his face and eye sockets.

I am Dail Svelt.

'Sssalt.'

Echoes of laughter danced around him, goading him. The voice of the bitch that had left him here, and the self-righteous despot that had stolen her away.

They mock us.

'Me!' he yelled into the darkness. 'I am Dail!'

Another outburst of laughter. 'Shut up!'

I am Svelt. He dragged his leg up beneath him, and forced himself into a kneel. *I am Dail.*

'Need...salt.'

His face burned, a score of tiny pinpricks that felt like burrowing insects. *What is happening, what is—*

He gasped as the air returned, rushing into his lungs in a wave.

'I am—'

Something, a point of distant light beckoned him. *I can...* It came closer and closer still, growing into a sphere of gray, and again into a cluster of fractal windows. Contrast, shapes resolving.

'I can...'

The blinded man stood. And saw.

TWENTY-EIGHT

Junction

'*WHAT YOU DO for us all...It has to happen.*'

'No!' Renia woke with a start, clawing her way back into the headboard, silk sheets gathered in her fists. She leaped from the bed and staggered into the center of a room she didn't recognize. She heard the sound of racing footsteps, bare flesh against tile, as she whipped her attention from point to point.

Venn-Dor crashed into the room, wearing nothing but a pair of silk trews. 'What's wrong?'

'Where am I?' she said, taking in the details of the bed chamber: the same ornate windows, the hand-carved furniture, a floor standing mirror, a dressing table, clean clothes.

'In my guest room,' said Venn-Dor, rubbing his head. 'You passed out.'

His skin glistened with sweat. She cast her eyes over his lean physique, over his taut musculature. The three scars beneath his pectoral ebbed their colors.

The scars.

Renia looked back to the mirror, to the image of herself renewed. Her heart raced, her flesh: flawless, pert, youthful once again. She approached her naked reflection, reached up to her face, pulling at it, testing its new elasticity. Beneath her breast, the same three colored scars lay, a permanent reminder of the path she had chosen.

Doratus draped a gown over her shoulders. 'Here,' he said, averting his eyes. She turned to him, feeling no shame or inhibition, leaving her gown open.

'It really happened, then.'

'It did.'

She studied his face for a sign of discomfort, but found none. But of course—the man was over a hundred years old, what pause would the vision of her nakedness cause him?

She flushed. Her hand ventured toward him. She laid three fingers on each of the scars on his chest. 'Grand Master, I—'

He cut her short. 'Renia, in terms of rank, we are equals. In private, I would prefer to hear my name.'

She stirred at the heat that radiated from his torso. Her lightstone flickered in response, arcs of static bridging the gap between her fingers and his chest.

Doratus took her shoulders in his hands and smiled. 'Get dressed. You must be hungry.'

THEY ATE IN silence, each lost in their own thoughts. Renia stared out of the window, recalling the first time she'd eaten at that table, and how she'd felt about the man sitting across from her, how he had appeared complacent and superior, knowing and secretive. She turned to watch him as he sipped soup from his spoon, and saw the innocent soul behind the veneer that lived in service to a higher power, no more or less immune to the tides of fate than she. Perspective, it seemed, could reveal a great deal.

Was it her newly elevated position that granted her this insight? Or was it a residual knowledge, a gift from the moonstones? Renia felt powerful, charged, and ready for action.

Yet still she found herself bound to the will of another. Her newfound agency started to ring hollow in her thoughts, and she defied it, she willed it not to be so.

Aevus's ghost still spoke to her, his final words rang like a bell in her ears. What had he meant? What had he seen in the mirror that had made him so sure? If her fate had already been determined, then had all her efforts, her battles to reach this state of clarity been for her? Or providence? She didn't know whether to race toward that fate, or rage against it. Only the glazed eyes of a decaying child met with her defiance, and she swallowed the guilt of it before it began to show.

'I'll send for the airship today,' Doratus interrupted.

She responded with a blank look.

'Time is short. You're ready now.'

'I'm not ready. I don't know the first thing about the mission you're sending me on.'

Doratus nodded slowly. 'You will. It is not my place to tell you.'

'You mean you don't know.'

He lowered his spoon and they locked eyes. 'I know. As do you. It's in there.' He motioned toward her head. 'It just takes time to fully assert itself.'

'Why don't you just tell me?'

'Believe me, I would love to.'

'You're being evasive.'

Doratus sat back in his seat. 'Yes, Renia. I am.' His face creased in effort. 'There is knowledge—' He paused, visibly struggling. 'There are things we can know, because of what we are, things that we are unable to speak of.' He twitched, beads of sweat appearing on his forehead. 'There is a man there, where you're going. He can tell you of these things, if you are unable to reach them.'

'Another Grand Master?'

'No.'

She placed her hands on the table. 'You're telling me that you're physically unable to talk about where I'm going and why I'm going there.'

He nodded. 'To an extent, yes.' Doratus wiped his brow. 'I can say this: at the end of the war there was a negotiation—terms were agreed. The Praelatus sought to protect the Aceraceian people from extinction. Powerful as the old ones were, the Five were slow to accept this notion, and the cost of this clause was high. Every fifty years, a new generation of Aceraceian children are born, far away, in secret, in a place where they pose no threat to the south. The bargain—' Doratus began to shake. He gripped at the tablecloth, veins bulging in his neck, his face flushing with effort.

'Stop,' she said.

Doratus exhaled. He wiped his mouth with his sleeve, panting.

'I'm going there, aren't I? Far away, in secret. To watch over them? To ensure the peace is maintained?'

He nodded.

Renia rubbed her eyebrow. *Caretaker? Childminder?* The surface level reactions were powerful, but not overwhelming. She considered why she had been chosen for the role—her curiosity, her insight. 'I will be free to research there. To study them, learn from them—'

She interrupted herself. 'I will be far away from the library, from here. What if I need something? If I wanted to continue Istopher Venn's work—'

'You will be provided with whatever you require. Venn's belongings are yours by right. If you want them, they will be transported to you.'

She smiled. Doratus nodded again.

'Does this satisfy you, Grand Master?' His lip twisted on the edge of humor.

'I don't feel much like a Grand Master.'

'The scars don't make you feel like a Grand Master,' he said, wistful. 'Time does.'

Satisfied. Yes, the idea did appeal, yet still she found herself in doubt, a slave to the unresolved. She was about to leave, to skip merrily away from her home and the people her actions had affected, leaving a mess behind.

'It has to happen.' Aevus's memory again. A memory that refused to let go, itched at her, forcing her to consider every choice as if it led to some world-changing event that she herself had not foreseen. What if she failed? What if she missed the opportunity to make good on her unspoken promise to the child that gave his life for her.

'What you do for us all.' Didn't she owe it to him, to all of her friends and colleagues to help bring an end to the chaos that had started with her? 'I have to help,' she said.

'Hmm?'

'I can't leave yet.'

Doratus pushed away his bowl, and tilted his head. 'Renia, this isn't the time. I've told you the—'

'I have to help, I have to do something. I can't just walk away and leave things unresolved.'

'What are you talking about?'

'The Inoa, of course!'

The color drained from Doratus's face. 'I see.'

She stood, and leaned over the table. 'You said yourself, the book is dangerous, that is imbued with the essence of the author, that Daralar seek him and his knowledge so that they might learn how to wield their moonstone.'

'I did.'

'That cannot be allowed to happen. I understand now, I have seen the power— *felt* the power of the moonstones. This must be it, Doratus. This must be what Aevus meant.' She started to pace, lost in the thought. 'I will fight the Reaper if I must, recover the book—'

'No, Renia. This is not the path laid out for you.'

'Or better yet, I could use the crimson mirror.'

'Enough.' Doratus slammed his palm on the table. 'Istopher Venn entered that mirror and never came back out. Do you think you know better than him?'

She clamored for common ground. 'Together we could, though. We are strong together.'

Doratus shook his head. 'The book is *my problem,* my duty. I do not believe the Praelatus wished for you to be involved in this.'

'What do you mean?'

He sat back in his chair, speaking as if lost in thought. 'Inoa's journal offers little to you in your new role. I'm starting to think that the Praelatus knew it would be stolen, to distract the South, or perhaps...'

'From what?'

'From you. The realm is weaker without a Shepherd. You are the key to removing the threat to our peace.'

'But people will be hurt before this is over, killed.'

'Peace has its price.'

The comment took her back. 'Do you really believe that?'

'I've paid it. Many times.' She watched as the painful memories assaulted him, and his face became a picture of mourning.

'How do you do it? How do you live with all this death?'

He smiled at her. 'I make friends slowly.'

She sighed.

'Please, do not interfere in this. I do not wish to lose another friend,' he said.

'How can I not? Aevus gave his life because he saw something, something that I am supposed to do that is important enough to make a difference to the many.'

'Your role as the new Shepherd, of course.'

'No, Doratus. I don't think so. He made it sound like a singular event. How can I ignore anything now? For whatever reason, my fate is bound to this book. You can choose to call it coincidence if you like, but I feel it.'

'The will of the Praela—'

'I can't leave until I know I did something. "In terms of rank, we are equals"—you said it yourself. You cannot stop me.'

Doratus sighed. 'You're right. And therefore it will fall to you to explain to the Praelatus *why* you were absent when the next generation awakened.'

She flinched at the thought. She had sworn an oath to the Praelatus. Her soul was bound to him, yet she felt nothing of his displeasure at her thoughts or actions. Was this choice truly hers to make? Did her oath to serve the realm exclude this action? Was she simply to do as she was bid and ignore her own sense of fate? 'How long will it take for the airship to arrive?'

'A day or two, depending on the weather.' He frowned.

She rounded on him, pursing her lips. 'Then we had better fix this before then.'

Doratus inhaled and spread his arms. 'What do you suggest?'

Renia walked toward the window. She looked out into the Wastes and lost herself in the phantom images that pockmarked the surface of the fallen moon. Her thoughts returned to another theft, one that left a ruin, a ruin she'd walked away from, never to return. One that left a hole in her heart that had never been filled. She remembered the morning after her parents' death, and the uncertainty she'd faced. She remembered the faces of the people that made it possible for her to live, and how they made a pact to deliver her to safety.

'Together,' she whispered.

'What did you say?' Doratus called from the table.

'We do it together.'

IT HAD BEEN an interesting week for *Substitute Sundance*.

She chuckled at the nickname she'd given herself. Covering for Petor, covering for Staine, and then most unexpectedly covering for Jeff. And why not? Thanks to Bandack she had the energy for it, though it did irk to be taking such enjoyment from what was, for almost everyone else involved, a bad situation.

Venn-Dor had been most complimentary of her performance in all respects, in his own distracted and condescending way. It was nice to hear, though his approval was secondary to the personal satisfaction of it all.

Plenty of use left in this old girl. She grinned, striding merrily through the apartment block without so much as a challenge from any patrolling guards.

The lockdown had to end soon; everyone knew it. The fear and reverence that had hushed the dissenting voices would not last. The story of the Praelatus's demonstration of power was, to most of the staff, just a story. And though his prowess was a widely accepted fact, stories degraded through retelling. Sundance wondered if this unusual summons had something to do with that inevitable end.

She knocked three times on the door to Jeff's apartment.

'Come,' came his call from inside.

She entered to find the chief lost in a mess of his belongings, neatly folding clothing into a suitcase. He turned to her, surprised to see her face at the doorway.

Jeff was a stoic man. Sundance couldn't help but display her concern at what she saw in him that morning. Anger? Frustration? It could well have been despair, although if it was, it was hidden beneath a veneer of impatience. His nostrils flared before he reluctantly opened his mouth to speak.

'I owe you an apology,' he said, curt and to the point.

'Whatever for?'

Jeff took a step toward her, softening somewhat in his approach. 'I dismissed you, continuously. It appears you had a better handle on the situation than I did.'

Sundance frowned. It brought her no pleasure to see a man such as Jeff displaying weakness so openly. 'I had help,' she offered.

'And I could have taken yours.' Jeff shook his head and sat on the foot of his bed. 'It's frustrating.'

She let the words hang in the air and watched the man from Southgate rub his damaged leg. What was there to say? Men like Jeff were seldom consoled by words; action was the only language they understood.

She nodded to herself. 'We've been summoned,' she said.

'We?'

'You and I. Our presence has been requested by the Grand Master.' She paused in her own curiosity at the words that were to follow. 'And Renia.'

'Renia?' Jeff cocked his eyebrow, now apparently as intrigued as she was.

'I know.'

Jeff frowned. 'I don't answer to Venn-Dor anymore.'

'Clearly.' Sundance nodded toward the suitcase, a slight grin on her face. 'But these are strange times, dear, and this is a *strange* summons. Are you not the slightest bit curious?'

She watched him stew for a moment, knowing exactly what he would do, seeing the internal monologue gently reminding him that he owed Sundance, and then that this wasn't for her, and then the need for action taking hold.

'Fine,' he said. 'I'll hear them.'

'Right you are,' said Sundance. 'Shall we?'

RENIA AND VENN-DOR waited in the security office, enduring the curious stare of a particularly buxom secretary. Renia smiled at the woman, painfully aware of the fact that the last time they exchanged glances Renia had been in chains—not her finest moment.

The door swung open, announced by a bell that stole the woman's attention. Renia grinned as Sundance bounded toward her and into her embrace.

'Dear girl!'

Renia smiled. 'Hello, Sundance.'

'Just look at you. Wonderful, absolutely wonderful.'

Renia blushed as Sundance appraised her attire, nodding appreciatively at the master's robes she now wore, a finery that would take time to get used to. Her mentor's gaze halted at the lightstone pendant around Renia's neck.

'You found it, then.' Sundance grinned.

Renia nodded, turning her attention to Jeff as he skulked into the room, looking less than impressed.

Venn-Dor straightened at the man's entry.

'What's this all about?' said Jeff, shooting a confused look in Renia's direction.

Venn-Dor spoke first, breaking the uneasy silence. 'We are waiting for another.'

'Who?' said Jeff.

'Master Vedora.'

Jeff snorted. 'Of course we are.'

Renia frowned at Doratus, curious as to what had transpired between the two men to warrant such behavior from the chief.

'And Ferron?' Jeff enquired.

'Ferron is busy.'

'Sticking sea monsters to people's heads, I suppose.'

Doratus bit down on his ire. The minutes that followed passed painfully, with only the occasional excited question from Sundance, who seemed entirely impressed with Renia's change in mien.

'She's not coming,' said Jeff.

Renia spoke up. 'Why wouldn't she?'

'Because she's behind all this.'

Doratus shook his head. 'Do you have a shred of evidence to support that accusation?'

'I don't need it, and neither should you, *Dor*.'

Renia waved her hands. 'Enough, enough. Please. I brought us here for a reason.'

Jeff snarled. 'Then speak. I don't have time for suspense.'

Renia regarded each of them in turn. Finding herself emboldened by the events of the previous days. She stood confident, well dressed, and fighting the satisfaction of it all in the face of the task she'd set out to accomplish.

'We're going to get the book back,' she said.

Her announcement invited a display of blank stares.

'What do you think we've been doing?' asked Jeff.

'With respect, bickering.'

Jeff looked to the secretary, who did her best to act distracted.

'We can do this,' said Renia.

She gave Jeff an apologetic look. He sighed and offered his counter argument. '*With respect,* we've been led around by the tail this entire time. Every lead is a dead end. They've been ahead of us every step of the way.'

'The reason for that seems fairly obvious,' said Sundance.

'Oh?'

'Renia is right. We've been working against each other,' her mentor continued. 'Instead of together.'

'I was offered no mastermind group at the start of this investigation.' Jeff shot an angry look at Doratus, who stood collected and silent.

'What do you propose, Renia?' said Venn-Dor.

'Why is the Reaper still here?' she replied.

Her question was met by another silence, with each party looking to the other for an answer.

Sundance spoke up first. 'She sits in the library, reading. For days now.'

'Why does she sit in the library, day after day, reading?' Renia continued. 'Her mission is to carry out her writ and return to Daralar.'

'Something hinders her,' said Jeff.

'Exactly,' said Renia. 'Someone else is interfering. If she's here for the book, then she can't just take it and leave. Her writ is her writ—it is law.'

'You are suggesting that someone is keeping Staine here, hidden from her?' said Doratus.

Sundance flinched visibly at the naming of the Reaper's target.

'Staine's gone,' said Jeff. 'Why would he stay?'

Sundance placed her hands on her hips. 'How would he leave, dear? There are guards everywhere, the gates are closed, to take to the cliffs would mean certain death—he never struck me as the climbing type.'

Jeff nodded, accepting her argument.

Venn-Dor turned to the window, 'We have another player on the board.'

'The Reaper that killed Raellon,' said Jeff with confidence.

Renia sensed Doratus's rage, and she followed his empty gaze out of the window.

'The enemy of my enemy...'

'Is my friend,' Sundance completed. She raised her eyebrows. 'You believe we should ask Bandack for help.'

Doratus rounded on them in fury. 'Outrageous.'

Renia felt no fear at his annoyance, and she stood firm and composed. She turned to Jeff. 'You said yourself, they are leading us by the tail. Maybe it's time for us to start playing by their rules.'

Jeff shuffled, wincing. 'She's not…normal.'

'She's not stupid either,' offered Sundance.

Doratus spoke next, having composed himself. 'Why did she help Sundance?'

The four shared curious glances. Renia stood suspended in anticipation, gaging each of them in turn. Surely they would see the merit in her suggestion. 'Where is she now?' she said.

'The library, most likely,' said Sundance.

Venn-Dor cleared his throat. 'Renia, you cannot be a part of this.'

'What? Why?'

He cast a sparing glance at Jeff and Sundance before continuing. 'You are important to the realm. You have to leave. If the Reaper were to find out who you are, it could put you in danger.'

'We've been through this, Doratus.' She winced internally; it was a mistake to disrespect him with such familiarity in front of the others. 'I won't leave until this is over.'

The two Grand Masters stared at each other in stalemate. She held his look, determined not to betray herself by showing doubt or weakness after making such a bold move.

'A suggestion then,' she said at last. 'Put me in a room with her.'

Doratus raised an eyebrow.

'If your suspicion is warranted, or she wishes me harm, believe me, I will know it.' She bowed her head. 'Does that sound reasonable, Grand Master?'

'And who will protect you?'

'You will. Snap in, and snap me out of there.'

Doratus straightened, regarding her with the same respect she had shown. 'Very well,' he said. 'Grand Master.'

Jeff and Sundance exchanged glances. It would have been the last thing either of them expected to hear.

'Well then,' said Sundance, clearly keen to move on. 'Does anyone want to hazard a guess at where Master Vedora has gotten to?'

Jeff spoke to the secretary. 'Jinger, would you head up to the hospital ward and see if Petor is alone or not, please.'

'Yes, chief.'

Jeff shook his head. 'Just Jeff,' he said. 'Sundance is your chief now.'

Jinger reeled, looking from one chief to the other. 'Yes...Jeff,' she managed before leaving the room.

'Right,' said Sundance. 'To the library.'

SUNDANCE ENTERED THE library with Renia at her side. They stopped abruptly upon seeing Bandack stood on her chair, glaring into a row of bookshelves at the opposite side of the hall.

She shared a sidelong glance with her companion and stepped with caution toward the Reaper.

'I don't like her,' said Bandack.

'Who, dear?'

The Reaper pointed in annoyance to the bookshelf, where Sundance saw the librarian slink away.

'The librarian. She's rude and she smells of old gravy.'

'I see,' said Sundance.

The Reaper turned and laid eyes on Renia, cocking her head.

'Bandack. This is my friend, Renia.'

Renia bowed politely. 'How do you do?'

The Reaper hopped off her chair and rounded Renia, sniffing. 'Your *friend* smells like sorcery, Sundance.'

Bandack took a step back, taking in Renia's clothing. 'Master is it? Grand Master?'

Renia smiled. 'Not yet. But hopefully one day I'll be worthy of the title.'

Bandack returned to the desk and sat, marking the page she'd been reading by crudely folding the corner. Sundance winced.

'I'm sorry, Sundance,' said the Reaper. 'I'm frustrated.'

'No apology necessary, dear. We all have our days.'

Bandack's eyes unfocused as she drifted off into her own world.

'Bandack?'

'Hmm?'

'We were wondering if you'd come with us.'

Bandack leaped to her feet. 'Absolutely. Another mission?'

'Well, you could say that. There's a matter that we were hoping—' Sundance felt her words hitting a wall as she continued to speak. Bandack's attention drifted toward Renia again. The Reaper tilted her head to and fro in curiosity.

'So you want me to attend a meeting then?' said the Reaper.

'Yes.'

Bandack looked at Renia as she spoke. 'You didn't ask,' she said.

'I didn't ask what?' said Renia.

'Every time I meet someone, they ask me if they have met their end,' Bandack said, frowning.

'If I had, wouldn't I already be dead?'

Sundance grinned. They were a curious pair. Renia had always had a way with words.

Bandack grinned back at her. 'I like your friend.'

'AND YOU THINK that this *Vedora* is holding Staine?'

Bandack sat perched on the edge of Jeff's desk, stroking it.

Renia's gathered crew looked on with growing concern at the Reaper's nonchalant demeanor. None had a ready answer.

'Why?' said Bandack.

'We're not sure,' said Renia.

Jeff took a step toward Bandack. 'You wouldn't be here if you knew where he was. Someone is playing us against each other. I questioned a member of the Unseen, who told me a story about a Reaper sent here with orders to retrieve something of Inoa's. He said that they wouldn't be allowed to return home without it.'

Bandack grinned at Jeff. 'Not *sent*, no. *Exiled*.' She nodded her enthusiasm and addressed the group. 'My betrothed is right—'

'I'm not her betrothed,' countered Jeff instantly.

'Don't interrupt me, darling.' She smiled. 'As I was saying, it's a well known story. Although you're missing half of it. First of all, it's not *a* Reaper. You're talking about two people. Second of all, they are twice-born—sisters.'

Bandack adopted a serious tone for the first time since Renia had met her. 'And they are no longer Reapers. They were exiled.'

'What for?' said Sundance.

Bandack met Sundance's eyes, a flat, unconcerned look on her face. 'Making babies.'

The group waited in collective confusion.

Bandack sighed, demonstrating her boredom. 'Reapers are not permitted to create life without the consent of the Five. One of your *guests* broke the rule. She gave birth to twins, and the sisters hid the children from the Five. Naturally, they were caught, and the sisters were held to account—exile or death. They chose exile, and ended up here.'

'What happened to the children?' Sundance asked, shocked.

Bandack shrugged in response.

'And the name Vedora means nothing to you?' said Jeff.

'Nothing at all, my love,' said Bandack.

Jeff rolled his eyes.

Renia looked to Doratus, who kept his gaze fixed on the world beyond the window. Whatever he was thinking, it was powerful enough to render him mute.

'Would you recognize her?' she asked the Reaper. 'If you saw her?'

Bandack flashed a sickly smile. 'I wasn't a Reaper when this happened.'

Venn-Dor spoke at last. 'Alia.' He turned to face Bandack. 'Was she an exile?'

'A legend,' Bandack said. 'Not an exile. But according to the rumor mill, she grew impatient with the Five and decided to take matters into her own hands. She would have faced censure if she'd made it home.'

Venn-Dor seemed satisfied with her answer. 'Two Vedoras,' he said.

'A way that she could have stolen the book *and* been with Petor when she stole it,' said Jeff.

'We find them, then.' Renia spoke with as much conviction as she could muster.

Bandack cocked her head to the side. 'You mean *I'll* find them.'

The room fell silent. Each of them lost in thought, until Jinger bounded into the room, rattling the entry bell. She stood sweating, struggling to catch her breath.

'What is it?' said Jeff.

'Petor,' said Jinger. 'He's missing.'

TWENTY-NINE

Unintended

'NO MORE.'

PISTORIOUS tore the sheet from the bed. Into it he threw what meager supplies he could realistically carry from the stores provided: dried food, a cloth, candles, a piece of old rope.

He looked to his journal where it sat on the desk and considered leaving it there before thinking better of it and racing across the room to retrieve it.

No longer would he sit and wait, no longer would he trust in Vedora and whatever her motivations were for helping him to escape. It made little sense. They were friends, yes. Were they friends? Or had she simply been his colleague? His own desperation to be liberated had clouded his judgment, of course it had. Survival instinct bred all manner of delusion.

No.

He couldn't afford to trust anyone. He had to depend on his own wits to deliver him from this dark ordeal.

He pulled the corners of the sheet around his supplies and knotted them before tossing the sack over his shoulder and striding toward the door. He stopped short, looking back into the safe space that he'd been provided and giving air to the doubts that began to creep in.

He rested his hand on the doorknob.

'We have to go, now!' The memory claimed him:

'Story, I can't. My mother, I—'

'I won't let him hurt you any more, Lilian.'

'I…I can't'

'You must! Come on.'

He practically dragged her out into the gardens, careless and desperate, their steps pounding through the house and out into the black of night, where they ran and ran until they heaved and retched and their legs and lungs burned with exertion.

'I can't go on,' she said.

'We have to, it's our only chance. We'll run away together, as far away as we can, where they'll never find us.' He started to cry. 'Where I can protect you.'

'You can't, Story.'

'I can! You'll see, just a little further. Once we get past the outer walls we can rest a little.'

And so he led her on, fumbling through the darkness, tripping and wrestling with brambles in the overgrowth, to the gate to the woods at the edge of the estate.

And it was locked.

He pulled on it. He yanked and yanked until his arms grew heavy and fell useless by his sides. The sobbing started then. He hadn't the strength to scale the wall. It was late, he was tired, and the adrenaline had started to wear off.

'Story…'

He slapped her hand away.

'Let's go back. It's not your fault, Story.'

'No!' His scream echoed through the surrounding brush and into the night beyond, the sound of searching guards and the

whooping of hounds promising a swift end to their escape. 'No,' he sobbed.

'Hahahaha.'

He froze. The laughter grew louder, and made no attempt at hiding the sheer pleasure it reflected. Dorian. His brother swaggered out from behind a nearby tree, waving the key to the gate in front of him, grinning like a cat.

'What's the matter, Pissy?'

'You.' He felt his rage burn through his tears, burn through any doubts or fear he should have felt at his brother's larger, stronger frame. He cried out and charged, throwing himself at Dorian's face, thrashing wildly and clawing at his eyes. His brother laughed so hard that Pistorious almost got his hand on the key, but quickly ended up in a headlock, panting and wheezing like a dog in the dust.

He remembered the fear on her face, how pale she looked in the twilight, and how frozen she stood as he lay there.

'Over here!' Dorian shouted. 'I've got them, they are over here!'

'I'm sorry,' Pistorious whimpered under the weight of his brother's arm. 'I'm so sorry.'

He released the doorknob, and fell into a slump by the door, numb, weak.

Helpless.

'Vedora.' Petor urged the battered woman to wake through gritted teeth. 'Vedora. Wake up, woman.'

She stirred, testing the restraints that bound her to a chair. One eye opened, a slit in a swollen socket. Was it Vedora at all? After all the years, everything they'd shared, did he even know the beaten woman that sat limp before him, heaving for breath?

He tested his own restraints to little effect. Days spent unconscious had rendered him a useless bystander in the barbarism he'd just witnessed. He could tell himself that, perhaps even believe it; lies come far easier to ourselves than they do to others.

'I'm sorry, Petor'. Her face creased with effort.

The door remained closed. No other exit existed in the barren rock walls of the chamber.

'All this time,' he said, 'there were two of you.'

It made sense; courting her as a younger man had been a distraction he'd quickly discarded. Different from one day to the next, interested, then not, attentive, then not. With hindsight, the answer was obvious but highly improbable. The twice-born were an old legend, from the time before the great exodus. A prophesy that he believed existed solely to give hope to those that hid in caves from the brutal conditions they lived in.

It must have been difficult for them, an expectation too great to meet. How he'd managed to find himself embroiled in this inevitable sibling showdown was the greater mystery.

He grimaced at the door, and then at a bundle of tools that had been left open on the desk. How much worse would this get before it ended? Would he even live through it? How long would it be before the sister started to use Petor as a tool to extract the information she needed?

He had to escape, and soon.

RENIA SAT WAITING. The group had disbanded to prepare themselves for the coming mission. Only Jeff and herself had remained, whilst Sundance retrieved something that carried Petor's scent, Bandack recovered her gear, and Doratus left for whatever mysterious reasons drove him.

She fought back any feelings of doubt, any creeping, nagging voices that told her she'd overstepped, that she would regret this. This was the time for action, not consideration. She wondered what Molan would think of her audacity in that moment. *He'd laugh, probably.*

Jinger's eyes wandered in her direction often, though Renia did her best to act like she hadn't noticed. She focused instead on preparing herself for what might happen. Would Bandack betray them? Would the exile lash out? Would there be blood? Death? Renia would have to steel herself against any outcome to remain effective and justify her presence, not just to the others, but to herself.

JEFF STOOD BEFORE the ceremonial short sword that was pinned to the wall in the security office. He wouldn't be caught unarmed again. He couldn't afford to be. Whatever Bandack had done to his leg had made it worse somehow—not in terms of physical pain, but in its usage. Pain he could use, an awareness in itself. The lack of sensation, however—not useful.

He tried to remember the last time he'd prepared for something like this—for the unknown, with a team of others. A long time ago, back home. At least he knew who he'd be fighting then, and have some degree of familiarity with the enemy. This was different. He trusted his men, trained with them, ate with them. In truth he'd never walked into a dangerous situation quite the way he was about to, with a group of people he barely knew, or trusted.

He reached for the sword. *Not this time.*

He tested its weight in a series of cuts. *Usable, surprisingly.* It would have to do.

The hairs on his arms stood on end, a tingling sensation. He looked to Renia, who quickly covered her ears and shut her eyes.

Oh shi—

The flash blinded him instantly, his vision a sea of white and gray dots. His ears roared, giving way to the high pitched wail of shock. Now *that* was pain. He cursed Bandack and her lightstone for the heightened senses they had given him.

His vision cleared slowly. Venn-Dor stood over him, offering his hand.

'Apologies,' he said. 'Jeff. A word?'

Bastard.

He grimaced, slapped away the Grand Master's hand and rose to his feet. 'In there,' he said, gesturing toward his office, where he led the Grand Master, and closed the door behind them.

'What is it, Dor?'

If his insubordination had any effect on the man, he made no show of it. The Grand Master merely looked past him, seemingly lost in thought.

'I owe you an apology,' said Venn-Dor. 'More than one, in fact.'

'It's not necessary. We do this and then I'll go.'

Venn-Dor turned to him. 'Would you reconsider?'

'No.' Jeff delivered his response with as much finality as he could.

From within a pouch at his hip, the Grand Master pulled a lightstone, as white and as pure as winter snow. 'We don't know what to expect. As such, I would heal your leg. If a battle is to come, I would rather have you with us in full force.'

Jeff looked upon the stone and for a brief moment found himself captivated by it. He felt his heart lift. A phantom pain shot from his knee to his hip, pleading. Such moments in life were few. He knew then that this was a choice he would have to live with for the rest of his days. It was an obvious choice, one his body would have made for him readily. Yet his heart protested at the pull of temptation. For who would he be if he accepted?

'No,' he said.

Venn-Dor faltered, perplexed by his refusal.

Jeff looked him in the eye. 'When we last spoke I laid blame at your feet. In that, I feel shame. You may not understand, but despite doing the best I could with the information I had, the failure was ultimately mine. I was handicapped by your scheming, as I am handicapped here.' He pointed to his knee. 'Yet I never once blamed my knee for failing you, because I believe that a man is more than his weaknesses, more than his handicap. A man is measured in how long he continues to fight, when his body is worn and aged, and broken, when the weight of his choices is crippling, when he feels like all is lost, and wonders if he can go any further—

'It's what he does *then* that matters the most.'

The Grand Master's frown abated. Jeff watched the impact of his words. Silence fell over them.

Jeff looked out of the glass toward the main office, where Bandack had arrived and stood, tightening her bootstraps with one foot on Jinger's desk. 'Enough talk,' he said.

They made their way back toward the group. He nodded toward the Reaper, who returned the gesture.

'Are we ready?'

'Waiting on Sundance,' replied Bandack, who casually turned her gaze toward Jinger where she sat, speechless, watching her. 'What?'

Jinger lowered her gaze.

Sundance entered shortly after and handed one of Petor's shirts to the waiting Reaper. *All of that training*, Jeff thought. *And here she is being used as a hound.*

The Reaper sniffed at the old shirt. 'I recognize this scent.' She turned her head from side to side. 'We should go, now.'

The group nodded their assent and departed, with Bandack leading the way.

THEY DESCENDED QUICKLY toward the basement levels. The Reaper moved ceaselessly, always in motion, probing and sniffing her way toward their target. Renia had never met a Reaper before, but couldn't help but be intrigued by the woman and the way she carried herself.

She'd always imagined Reapers as the stoic warrior types that she had been familiar with in the Wastes. The sort to take a man's hands without hesitation. The sort that had done as much to her father. This woman was not. Focused, yes. Deadly? No doubt, but more than that. If murder had an effect on the psyche, it was not the effect she imagined. It made her wonder if the Reaper in fact had learned to use her own persona as a weapon, and what that might mean for their mission.

She pushed the thought aside as they squeezed their way into the storage levels, through dim light and dust, with Jeff and Sundance bringing up the rear.

'How close?' Venn-Dor asked the Reaper.

'A ways,' replied the Reaper. 'Something stinks down here, it's making it difficult to follow.'

'Something?' asked Renia.

'It's hard to pin down. A rotting smell, seaweed perhaps.'

Venn-Dor turned to Renia. 'Do you smell it?'

She shook her head.

'I do,' said Jeff. 'There's something familiar about it.'

It burned.

It burned in the most sublime way. Every split, every tear, every extrusion brought them closer to perfection. Each convulsion sent waves of ecstasy through them. They writhed and moaned through it, expelling fluids in toe-curling bursts, lost in a realm of searing pleasure.

Stronger.

Silent now was the voice of 'Dail Svelt'. They had become something greater, something divine. A calm fell over them, kin to the darkness, squatting in the corner of the store, surrounded by the spilled salt they had gorged themselves on.

Voices.

They twitched. Through the chittering rattled hushed tones, people, the smell of fear. They latched onto it, sucking the air around them through the body, interrogating it, teasing out its secrets.

The body pulsed, fibers throbbed. *Rrrrr.*

Their laughter took the form of a slow throb, a knocking staccato that died beneath the layers of flesh.

Renia.

They pressed on. Through dark corridors and accessways that seldom heard the patter of feet. Bandack backtracked several times, uttering her discontent. 'What is down there?' she demanded at a cross section, pointing down a corridor large enough to drag a cart through.

'Preserves,' replied Venn-Dor. 'Foodstuffs, herbs, and spices.'

The Reaper nodded in grim determination. 'The stench is there. I'll think twice before eating here again.'

Renia heard Jeff chuckle from behind her. 'Do you still have the trail?'

'Better now,' said Bandack, leading them on.

They continued deeper into the subterranean structure. Exploring depths that Renia had not dreamed existed. For every square foot of space above, there must be several below. In the time after the exodus, when her ancestors had fled the South, she'd assumed that they had abandoned their tunneling ways in favor of life on the surface. The assumption had clearly been incorrect.

Bandack stopped abruptly and took two steps backward, narrowly avoiding standing on Renia's toes. The Reaper turned, grinning at a stone brick to her right.

'What is it?' Renia said.

'Watch,' replied the Reaper. And Renia saw the shock and discomfort on Doratus' face as the Reaper licked several bricks in the wall before depressing them in a sequence that solicited a series of clicks and thumps before the whole section opened before them.

'Moon!' gasped Renia. She span to Venn-Dor, his face a blank.

The Reaper spared the man a glance, and winked as she crouched through the hole, leading them into a tunnel system, bare of brick and awash with stagnant air that bathed them in a cool breeze.

'This way,' she said.

PETOR JUMPED IN his skin as the door swung open. The woman that was not Vedora stalked forward, wearing a butcher's apron over her black leather attire.

'Where is the book, May?' she said.

May. Was that the true name of the woman sitting across from him? The woman he knew as Vedora. He felt his legs begin to tremble as the sister approached the open satchel of tools and retrieved a pair of pliers.

'Where is the book?'

Petor watched in horror as recognition flickered in May's eyes. She gurgled and struggled against her restraints, tears rolling down her swollen cheeks.

'She can't speak, you idiot!' Petor regretted the outburst instantly as the butcher backhanded him across the face, bursting his lip.

'Quiet, you,' she warned. 'My sister deceives us. She can speak as well as either of us.'

'Leave him alone,' muttered May.

The butcher grinned at Petor. 'Now, dear sister. Where is the book?'

The question sat in the air between them, each sister fixed on the other with hatred in their eyes. 'You'll have to kill me, Vera.'

Vera, then.

Vera smiled and knelt before the chair that held her sister. She tested the leather straps that bound her at the ankles and set the pair of pliers under May's toenail.

'I'll ask you again,' she said. 'Where—' She twisted, dislodging the nail from one side. Petor watched in horror. Such barbarism, such disregard.

'She's your sister! Have you no—'

'Is—' Another twist, and the nail broke loose. May screamed, her eyes wide in panic, sweat pouring down her face.

'No!' Petor cried out.

'The book?' She tore the nail off, a trail of gore following it away.

May's shriek rattled Petor's eardrums. His heart beat heavy in his chest. Speechless, he sat in horror, watching the torture unfold.

'Stop, please!' His cries fell on deaf ears.

'Where is it, May?'

She presented the nail to her sister, still gripped in the teeth of the pliers. 'Tell me.'

Through ragged breath, blinking away sweat and tears, May responded in defiance. 'The Five take you,' she whimpered. '*Sister.*'

Vera released her grip on the pliers, dropping the bloody toenail to the floor. 'Have it your way,' she said, bending down again.

THEY HEARD THE scream. Renia's blood ran cold.

'What was that?' she said.

'Agony.' Bandack nodded grimly. 'Move!'

They charged toward the source of the scream, kicking up dust, any notion of stealth abandoned. Bandack pulled away from the pack, picking up incredible speed that none of them could match. A right turn led into a tunnel barely tall enough for them to stand in, forcing them into single file as they hurried toward the tortured screams in the darkness beyond.

A stunned silence awaited them as they burst into the chamber. Vedora whipped her head toward the interlopers, shock written upon her face. Bandack stood with her dagger unsheathed, poised in a combat stance. She didn't look back as the remainder of her group piled in.

The twice-born. One woman stood unscathed, looming over the other, who sat bound to a chair, battered, bloody, but unmistakably the same.

'Help!' cried Petor, who sat similarly bound in a chair to her left, gripped in panic and struggling to free himself.

Vedora charged at Doratus with blistering speed, seeking to make an escape through their group. She failed. In a thought, she flashed from her position to the far side of the chamber and fell from the ceiling, landing with feline grace.

The room reeled with the shock of the Grand Master's sorcery. Doratus merely stood, glaring at the growling woman in her bloody apron.

'So,' she said. 'The sleeping king *does* have his sorcerers.'

Doratus held out his staff, lifting the struggling woman into the air. She choked and cried out as the very building blocks of her body were manipulated.

'You.' Doratus spoke with barely controlled aggression. '*You* killed Raellon.'

An incredible display of magic. The control, the focus required to manipulate matter in such a way. Renia stood awestruck, barely noticing Sundance scurry past her to release Petor from his bonds.

Vedora squealed. A sound that died in her throat as Doratus compressed her body, slowly squeezing the life out of her.

'Renia!' Master Petor's voice. She span toward him in shock. 'Free her,' he said, nodding at the second woman. 'She's innocent!'

Renia struggled to pull her attention from the display. Petor's request went unheard as all present fixated on the floating, constricted woman, and the rage of the man that held her.

Sundance undid the last of Petor's bonds. Renia registered the old man scurrying toward the beaten woman in the chair, frantically fiddling to free her.

'Enough!' Bandack called. 'You have her bound.' She positioned herself between Doratus and the struggling, floating woman.

'I should crush you now.' Doratus ignored the Reaper standing between them.

'We had an agreement, Grand Master. If you kill her now, you interfere with my writ.'

'Ask her what you will.' Doratus would not yield; he held her in his grip his jaw set in determination.

Bandack turned to the suspended woman. 'Where is Staine?'

Vedora grimaced, her face twisted in effort as she wrestled the words free. 'Release…me…' Blood ran freely from her lip. 'First.'

With a gesture, Doratus tightened his hold, baring his teeth. Vedora managed to cry out in pain.

Bandack flared and she span, squaring up to Doratus. 'Release her now. This has gone far enough. You're very close to violating the law.'

Jeff spoke from the rear of the room. 'What is that?'

Sundance turned from the scene to Jeff. 'The smell.'

Renia registered a rumbling. The smell followed shortly after. She turned from Doratus to the door. 'What is that smell?'

Sundance retched. Jeff backed away from the door slowly. The rumbling grew in volume, carrying with it a scraping, and—laughter?

'Something's coming,' said Jeff.

The distraction drew the attention of everyone present. Eyes and ears turned toward the doorway.

'Get back!' Jeff shouted the order, limping back, dragging his injured leg.

Renia stumbled backward, her view through the door blocked. Shock arrested her other senses as an animal fear took hold. Whatever was about to burst through the door, it was big, loud, and smelled like rotting corpses.

The brickwork around the door shattered. Sundance screamed in terror, fleeing to the rear of the room. A second impact fractured wood, throwing splinters into the space.

Doratus and Bandack turned at once toward the source. The lapse in the Grand Master's focus sent Vedora hurtling toward the ground.

The stone around the door frame exploded inward, showering them in dust and rock chips. Long dark tentacles whipped around the opening, swirling masses of jet black larvae, gripping for leverage, hauling the warped and disfigured body of a man into the room.

Renia reeled in horror, watching as a limp body propelled itself inside on countless slimed, sinewed limbs.

Its jaw cracked open, and it laughed, a booming maniacal rhythm that resonated through her core.

'Renia!' the thing called out.

She edged backward, away from the beast. All eyes locked on it, a collective paralysis.

'Dail?'

Thirty

Trull

THE BEAST HUNKERED down on its human legs. Scores of larval xentt, no bigger than a thumb, spiraling around each limb, rushing to bolster the rotting flesh beneath. Bulging, pulsing obsidian muscles formed from the morass. The thing that had been Dail Svelt drew itself upright, bellowing laughter into the increasingly cramped subterranean cavern.

Jeff's ears roared, and the terrified screams and hurried warnings fell mute beneath the splattering, skittering sound of countless rushing sea-spawn. He stumbled back into the wall, jaw flapping, sword shaking in his fist.

'Trull!' Petor's voice. 'Get the women out!'

A risked glance to the rear of the cavern revealed a vision of panic; Reaper, scholar, and sorcerer alike huddled away from the monster, united in fear.

The beast lashed out, each tentacle a community of xentt larvae acting in unison, whipping about the space, slamming into the walls and the floor around them. They broke out of Dail's chest, his back, and worse. The only recognizable parts of the man left uncovered were his face, and parts of his torso.

The thing leaned forward, casting its slow gaze around the room. As it registered him, Jeff recoiled from its empty eye sockets, overflowing vortexes of black slime.

'*Oh, Renia,*' the thing bellowed, its voice a harsh gargle, its breath as foul as decomposing meat.

'Get the women out!' Petor struggled with the last of the straps holding the exile woman in place and pulled her free from the chair. Venn-Dor, seemingly in control of his fears, held out his staff and closed his eyes.

'*Oh no, I don't think so,*' mused the Dail-thing, before lashing the Grand Master around the waist, constricting him in his grip like some great serpent. Venn-Dor yelled, struggling against the combined might of the larvae as they slinked over and around his throat. Another smaller appendage prised the staff out of his hand.

Bandack wrestled with Vedora—the one that seemed to have been doing the torturing. Singularly focused, they traded blows with the finesse of dancers, expertly avoiding the mess of tentacles that whipped around them.

Jeff locked eyes with Sundance, pressed into the wall at the opposite side of the chamber, transfixed in horror. 'Get out!' he yelled. She didn't move, she couldn't. Tears rolled freely down her face.

Damn it. He edged around the rear of the chamber, past the door and toward Sundance as the beast skulked toward Renia, each step a slap that shook the room around them.

'*There you are, my love.*'

They parted around it. The torturer leaped over and through a gap in the beast's appendages, turning in mid-air. Bandack followed, grasping at her foot. Jeff watched the event in slowed time, part of his mind laughing at the absurdity of this seemingly elderly woman flying through the air like a bird while he dragged his leg toward Sundance like an injured dog. Both Reapers landed on their feet, the torturer swinging a back-handed blow across Bandack's face, sending her spinning to the ground. Jeff watched as his twice-born nemesis scurried away through the shattered doorway, into the safety of the tunnel.

'*Come now, don't look at me like that.*'

The thing had its back to them. Bandack shot a concerned glance at Jeff, poised to follow her prey. He nodded at her. 'Go,' he mouthed, and she darted into the tunnels.

'Put him down, Dail!' Renia's shout echoed around the chamber.

Jeff returned his attention to Sundance, and to Petor as he made his way around the rock face. Petor heaved the confused, beaten and tortured woman back and around toward them. Her head lolled from shoulder to shoulder.

'Come on, Petor, faster!' Jeff beckoned, putting his arm around Sundance.

She swung her head up to meet his eyes. 'What's happening?'

'You need to snap out of it, now.'

The older woman shook her head, reeling in shock. Blood trickled around her neck, down toward her clavicle. *Blow to the head.* He slapped her across the face. 'Get it together!'

She blinked frantically, taking in the situation. 'Trull...'

Jeff nodded. 'Take Petor and run!'

She turned, grabbing Petor's outstretched arm and pulling him in, and with him the somnolent woman who had been bound to the chair. Tentacles probed the space between Jeff and the door, vine-thin appendages that skittered around the floor and walls, searching, feeling for their presence.

The four of them huddled together, avoiding the touch of the slimy probes.

'We need a way through,' said Sundance.

'Dail!' Renia shouted, obscured from view by the beast's back, a writhing tangle of xentt. 'Stop this. Put him down!'

Venn-Dor groaned as the Dail-thing tightened its grip.

It laughed. *'Dail doesn't take commands from you anymore, little woman.'*

Jeff gripped the sword in his hand, waiting for an opportunity to clear a path between them and the doorway. 'Get ready,' he said.

The beast recoiled its larger tentacles, holding them up, preparing to strike at Renia. 'Now!' Jeff called.

He dragged Sundance and Petor with him, and they bolted toward the opening.

'No!' cried the tortured woman, wrestling free of Petor's grasp.

'May!' Petor called after her, as Jeff hauled them toward the opening.

May? Jeff risked a look back to see the woman leap in front of Renia, throwing herself between the scribe and the monster. Its tentacles adapted in an instant, grabbing her by the arms and holding her up like a new toy.

'May. May!' Petor wriggled in Jeff's grip, fighting him with every labored step toward the exit.

'Well, well. What do we have here?' Dail inspected the woman with curiosity. *'Master Vedora!'*

'No!' Petor yelled.

Jeff grabbed him around the waist, wrenching him back to the exit and thrusting him into Sundance's embrace. 'Go!'

He watched her wrestle Petor away, down the tunnel, and turned back to the monster, and to his companions, readying his sword.

VERALACK SNARLED. 'GET out of my way.' Her sister was in there. *Her sister.*

'Don't be a fool.' Bandack shoved her back a step, determined not to let her pass.

'She's my sister! She'll die in there with that thing!'

The youngster shoved her again. 'Think!'

She would not. Her instinct had her. She'd always protected her other half. *Always.* Her legs thrust her toward Bandack, willing her back toward the tunnel, but Bandack was faster, blocking and countering her every move.

'Get out of my way!'

'Mother!'

Mother? She faltered, locking eyes with her daughter. Yes, *mother. The mission.*

'Think. This is better. Your plan is certain to work now. They all saw what you did to her. By the time they've killed the trull, they will believe it all. She'll have given them the book—she'll be free to stay. No one will doubt her allegiance.'

A trull. How? Why?

'Are you listening to me, Mother? It *will* work.'

Her daughter held her by the arms. It had been a lifetime since she'd felt her touch. What—

Focus.

'My sister will die in there,' Veralack said, regaining her composure.

'Unlikely,' retorted Bandack. 'They have two sorcerers and Jeff. I'm sure they can handle a trull.' She pointed past Veralack's shoulder. 'We carry out the mission, as planned.'

Veralack turned her body, unable to free her attention from the tunnel and the commotion behind them.

'Now,' said Bandack.

Don't die.

The pair of them charged off into the tunnel system to complete their work.

RENIA WATCHED IN horror as Dail pulled the woman's limbs, holding her cruciform. Her attention darted from the woman she knew as Vedora to Doratus, who also floated in the creature's grasp, wide-eyed and mute, as the slimy creatures covered all but his eyes and nose.

Jeff appeared from behind him, swinging his sword in an upward arc that severed the tentacle holding the woman. Separated larvae splashed upward in a parabolic shower that fell back onto him.

The severed limb began to fall, only to be caught by another and made whole again by the endless charge of oily black spawn.

Jeff cried out, slapping larvae from his shoulders and head as they fell to the floor only to slink back toward the mass at Dail's feet.

'Dail, stop!' she implored him. 'What happened to you?'

The layers of larvae rippled along Dail's body in a wave of reflection. He roared and whipped Jeff with a tentacle the size of a tree trunk. Jeff crashed into the wall and fell onto all fours, gasping for breath.

'*Dail is here, yes. Thanks to you, Renia.*'

She staggered backward, repulsed by his monstrous, alien form.

'*You happened. You made us strong.*'

The thing loomed over her, covering her in moving shadow.

'*We were weak, dying. Mere seedlings, we burned and wilted within the Dail. We almost gave up. But you came. You came with your magic, and made us whole, strong. You will make us stronger.*'

'Dail, talk to me.'

'*We are all Dail, now.*'

The monster pulled on Vedora—no, May's limbs. She shrieked as they popped and cracked. A covering of xentt larvae wormed over her arms, holding them straight.

'*See how strong we are.*'

A larger tentacle that protruded from Dail's tailbone darted toward May's head, grasping it in a wet slap. The woman let loose an ear-splitting scream as the larvae wrapped around her head, invading her ears. Blood started to run down her neck, pooling at her clavicle. Her scream held, as if sustained by the wind itself. It rose and fell in pitch until the larvae settled. May's eyes rolled back in her head. She began to sing with an operatic warble.

Dail laughed.

'Stop this now!' Renia planted her feet. She felt the rise of her power. A growing orb of static burst into life around her. She thrust at Dail with a spear of lightning.

The thing cried out in pain. Hundreds of larvae fell like raindrops from his body. They writhed and flapped on the floor, spasming in time to the residual crack of the blast. But for every hundred that fell, there were a thousand more, quickly replacing the gaps she bored into his living armor.

'*Bitch!*' Dail swept one of his tentacles around her legs. She flew to the ground, landing badly on her wrist. Before she could react, another vine of larvae pulled at the lightstone pendant, breaking hand-forged links of gold that bounced off the floor around her.

He tossed the pendant behind him. A flash of lightning lashed out at them all as it hit the wall. Her vision swam. Disarmed, she looked from Doratus to May, both of them rendered as useless as herself, ensnared like prey.

May's song echoed through the chamber, a terrible, somber melody.

'*You will make us stronger,*' said Dail, advancing toward her.

'WE SHOULD GO back.' Petor insisted, though fear held him in a grip that would not relent.

They had run as far as Petor's legs would carry him, fueled by the rush of adrenaline.

Near-darkness shrouded them. They sat slumped against the rock face of the tunnel wall with ghostly echoes for company, a harrowing singing noise that Petor didn't want to admit sounded a lot like May.

'With respect, Master Petor.' Sundance's voice shook as she spoke. 'Go back and do what?'

He turned to her, though saw only the vague outline of her face. What could he say? They were old.

'We should go back,' was all he could muster, though the words rang hollow, and wrought with defeat.

THE CRUEL OPERA continued. Renia glared defiantly into the monstrosity, recalling everything she'd ever read about the xentt.

'I won't do it,' she said.

The Dail-creature laughed. '*Yessss, you will. You will make us strong, and we will feast.*'

'No.'

'*Then we will feast now.*'

Dail turned his attention to May, and tensed the tentacle that had wrapped around her head. Her neck bent backward, stifling the song she'd repeated over and over. New tentacles began to form from the ones holding her legs, leeching up her thighs toward her pelvis.

'*Let's see if the old girl has any eggs left, shall we?*'

Renia almost heard the voice of the cocksure man that had captured her attention years ago. She despised it. She despised what he had become.

'No!' She charged toward May, and leaped at the tentacle that held her suspended. It was as she wrapped her arms and legs around it that she realized her mistake. The larvae arrested her, slinking around her arms and legs. She flailed her limbs in an attempt to cast them off, only to fall back to the ground.

'*Don't be jealous, Renia.*' What was left of Dail's face grinned. '*I told you we would try again, and we will. We will make so many babies.*'

Her stomach turned as she watched in horror.

'Stop.' Doratus spoke through gritted teeth 'Stop. I'll do it.'

The creature halted, '*Hmm?*'

'I'll do it. The lightstone—in my satchel.'

Dail chuckled, nodding with his entire body. '*Yes, yes. Good.*' The xentt larvae retreated from Doratus's arm, and the satchel at his thigh. '*Make us strong.*'

The lightstone emitted a white glow that highlighted every individual creature colonizing Dail's body. Doratus held it out, closed his eyes, and began to chant. The light in the room intensified, and Dail stretched out his appendages with a roar of approval.

'*Yesssssss. Make us strong!*'

Renia blinked frantically as the light washed over her vision. She heard a wet slap and registered May falling to the ground.

'*Strong!*'

She stared in disbelief. *Why, Doratus?*

The Grand Master smiled.

JEFF STOPPED HEAVING. His cracked ribs snapped back into position. His chest erupted with a burning sensation as his bones sewed themselves back together. Every bruise, cut and abrasion glowed with intense white light. A photonic salve that soothed and erased all his pain.

Venn-Dor smiled at him, continuing his chant. Jeff gasped as the bones of his knee exploded in a tingling wave. Each piece of shattered bone within worked its way back to its proper place.

He started to sweat, grimacing as Venn-Dor finished his work. The sword still sat in his fist. He regarded it with purpose.

Simplicity of purpose.

He grinned.

The beast rippled in annoyance. '*Do it!*' Venn-Dor tensed as Dail shook him. '*What are you doing?*'

Jeff's muscles surged with power. He rose to his feet, his stance as sure as a man half his age. He charged toward Dail. 'Renia!' He flicked the fallen pendant with the tip of his sword, sending it hurtling toward the startled scribe.

He leaped into the air, bringing the sword down through the filth that held the Grand Master, severing it at the midpoint. The beast yelped, and roared in pain. Jeff landed, span on his heel, and drove the sword through Dail's heart.

The monster slumped. Its weight fell over him, showering him in a sea of confused larvae. Jeff gripped the sword and twisted, watching as Venn-Dor's sorcery emitted a glow through the sheet of larvae that slowly enveloped his arm.

'Renia, now!' Jeff cried. 'Now!'

The larvae smothered his torso, working their way up his neck and face. He closed his eyes as they washed over his head.

He felt Renia's hand on his back, and started to convulse as the air trapped in his lungs burned.

'Goodbye, Dail,' she said.

Everything shook. A static shock wave exploded around them. The xentt larvae burst away from his flesh, bouncing and splattering around the cavern.

Dail groaned as the lightning traveled through the sword and seared his insides, reaching out in arcs that burned his every nerve, rendering the xentt inert, a convulsing, steaming mess.

Venn-Dor's chant intensified, protecting them from the electrical onslaught. The beast juddered, steam pouring from its every orifice. What was left of Dail threw back its head and let out a last, harrowing scream as it melted, leaving them standing in a pool of hot, oily filth.

Venn-Dor stood, and nodded. They regarded each other with respect and disbelief as the steam continued to rise around them.

The tortured woman whimpered, laying prone on the ground. Renia knelt beside her and wiped the filth from her eyes.

Petor and Sundance burst through the fractured doorway, pausing to take in the scene, before running to kneel by the fallen woman.

Jeff looked down at his arms, throbbing and taut with renewed vigor. The pain in his leg completely absent.

'Heal her!' said Petor. 'What are you waiting for? Heal her!'

Venn-Dor shook his head. 'I cannot.'

'Of course you can. Heal her!'

Renia laid her hand on the retired Hall Master's shoulder.

'The larvae,' she said. 'Some may survive in her. We can't risk creating another one of those things.'

Petor's bottom lip trembled, his eyes wide in shock. He nodded slowly.

'Desk …' May spoke in a whisper.

'She's trying to speak.' Petor pressed his ear to her mouth. 'Under the desk,' he repeated.

Jeff turned to what was left of the writing desk, one of its legs shattered to splinters, and another snapped in half, its corner now sat on the ground. He flipped it over with ease. Strapped to its underside was a book.

Journal 26 – Sanas Inoa

He stared at it.

'What is it?' said Renia.

'It's over,' he said. 'We won.'

THIRTY-ONE

Legacy

FATHER,

IF YOU are reading this, it is likely that I am dead.

Though I'm sure this news will paint a smirk on your face, I write to you nonetheless in good faith. For you are my father, and although It pains me to admit it, that means something.

I have hated you. My earliest memories hate you. I often dream of your smug face; it haunts me. I wake up sweating, wishing you were dead, praying for the relief I would feel at the removal of the threat that you are, not just to me, but to everything and everyone unlucky enough to even skim the world you created. A world where everything exists only to serve you and your agenda, where no one, not even your children, is safe from the sacrificial altar.

Your throne is built on the scraps of broken dreams, Father, but you don't need me to point that out. Necessity, you would say—unfortunate. Such is the extent of your compassion.

Imagine my disgust, then, to find common ground with you throughout the ordeal that has cost me my position, my life, and my goals. To understand that had I heeded your warnings, learned from your cruelty, none of this may have come to pass.

To find my approach foolhardy in hindsight, to regret the plans I made in defiance.

To realize that my primary motivator was, and has always been, defiance.

I hate you all the more for this. Truly, I do.

Know that you were the last thought in my mind when I died, and that it made me retch.

Reluctantly yours,

Pistorious

PISTORIOUS STAINE: SON of Verda pricked his finger, smeared his blood over his thumb, and pressed it onto the paper. His bloody thumb print would not serve as proof of his death, but it would have to do.

He bound his thumb with a scrap of old cloth and expertly folded his first and last letter to his father, before blowing out the candle that illuminated the desk.

'All those gathered, bear witness.'

All of the servants were present, corralled into a circle, surrounded by the house guard, Mohruscan and Daralarian alike. Fear rose in waves from the empty space in the center, dozens of eyes shifting awkwardly from it to the bound and gagged woman where she knelt by her lord and his sons.

Pistorious had already tried to run, and he stood apart, held by the scruff of his neck by Arthus, his father's first sword. He couldn't look, but his ears would not indulge his cowardice. Muffled cries and stifled sobbing made him painfully aware that Lilian was suffering, stood several paces away, awaiting her mother's punishment for the escape attempt.

It wasn't fair.

The poor woman had no idea. It wasn't her fault, it was his. Why did she have to be punished?

He would never forget the sound of torn fabric as the guards ripped the dress from her back, the way his lecherous brother smiled at her exposed breasts, the way his father stood like a statue, showing no sign of feeling anything at all toward her or the sheer injustice of it.

His father nodded to Arthus, and Pistorious leant backwards against every step as he was pushed to his side. Those gruff hands once again reached for the back of his neck, knotted his hair. You, watch. The intent was clear.

A single lash of the whip. That was all it took to floor the woman. Her skin split from shoulder to pelvis with a shriek that died in her throat. She fell onto her face, her arms bent awkwardly. Pistorious was sure she had died.

'Take her,' his father said.

And the gathered servants complied, silent in their fear. Only Lilian screamed. She screamed for her mother, she screamed at Dorian, she screamed at Pistorious so hard that streams of spittle flew from her mouth. It took two grown men to hold her back. Everything happened so slowly.

The gathering dispersed. First the servants, then the guards, and then his brothers. Pistorious glared at Dorian as he skipped away laughing, enthused. One by one they left, leaving him alone with his father, the two of them staring at the disturbed earth where the woman had fallen.

'Why, Father? It was Dorian. He started this. He took Lilian to his room, he hurt her.'

'He did.' His father's voice shook him, the deepest voice he had ever heard.

'How can you let him do these things?'

'One day, you will understand.'

*'I'll never understand! It's wrong. It's wrong and you know it.
It should have been Dorian that got the whip.'*

'Be silent, boy.'

*He couldn't help but obey. He looked up into his father's face
and saw nothing of himself. His lip trembled.*

*'You will understand because one day you will rule over this city.
You will face challenge and deception from every corner, and when
that time comes you will need to know that you have the right set of
tools to meet those challenges. This world cares nothing for justice,
or sentiment. Never forget that, Pistorious.'*

*He cared. He cared for those things. He might have been too
young to truly understand them, but he knew what he knew to be
right, and just. He knew that a world without compassion was no
world at all. Who would want to live in a world without it?*

*'There is no justice, son,' his father continued. 'There is only
will. And the strongest will, will always win.'*

'I hate you.'

'Good.'

'Why is that good?'

*His father looked him in the eye for the first time he could recall.
'Love is for the led.'*

The door to the chamber opened.

Vedora entered his sanctuary, her clothes scuffed and her face
bright with the sheen of urgency. 'It's time,' she said. 'Quickly.'

He stood, half of him still lost in the memory, and swept
down his robes. This was it. His moment. The end of a long and
confusing chapter in his life. Everything hung on what happened
next.

Vedora's face creased with impatience.

For the led...

He smiled. 'Lead on, Master Vedora.'

They raced through the tunnels, pushing his atrophied body to its limits, ignoring the falling dust, the cold, and the harrowing noises that carried on the scant air that flowed around them.

'What is that?' he said between labored breaths.

Vedora did not pause, nor did she look back. 'A distraction,' she said, pressing on, turn after disorienting turn.

They stopped at the end of a long tunnel where the stagnant air gave way to the smell of civilization and the first sight of a brick wall. The woman expertly worked the combination lock that would allow the hidden hatch to open, casting only a glance in his direction as he held the candle that was the only source of light.

'Your hood,' she said.

He nodded, and pulled it over his head.

With a clunk and a thud, an outline appeared in the stonework, and Vedora pushed at the hidden door, which swung inward into the familiar surroundings of the basement. She led him through, throwing a cautionary glance in both directions as she moved. They pressed on, back through the corridors, past storage rooms and pipework, onward and further into the basement.

They turned abruptly, darting into a food storage area. Pistorious gawked and held his hand to his nose as the smell assaulted him, putrid, sulfuric. 'What happened here?' Barrels of preserves lay smashed around the room, and salt crunched under his shoes as he slowed to a halt.

'Why have we sto—'

She turned.

'Oh.'

Pistorious smiled at her; it was all he could do. Of course it was *her*. He lowered his hood, closed his eyes. *The end, then.*

Footsteps from behind; he turned and laid eyes on another woman, clad in black, wearing a mask formed from the skull of a reptile. She approached with grace and stood between him and the exit, her arms folded across her chest.

He should have felt fear, the urge to run, to save himself. He would have, only he wasn't the same man. He was no longer confused, no longer angry. He realized that everything he had been, everything he had done up until that point—none of it told the story of a selfish, arrogant, power-hungry man.

He wasn't his father.

It was love: love for his people, his culture, the very land that nurtured and nourished them, that was his anchor, his reason to push on. Yes, he had erred, he had lost his connection to that love somewhere along the way, but he knew it now, and that was all that mattered.

'Vedora,' he said. 'Would you be so kind as to deliver this letter to my father?' He held it out. She nodded and took it.

'Goodbye, Master Staine.'

'It has been my pleasure, Master Vedora. Farewell.' He surprised himself at the sincerity of his words.

The woman nodded again, and walked away, past the waiting Reaper and into the darkness.

The Reaper stalked forward. A bizarre, double-toned voice assaulted him, a strange song that grated at his senses. He couldn't move. He couldn't move anything. The air in his lungs set hard like a boulder he couldn't shift.

A rush of air sent his hair flapping, and he expelled the contents of his lungs as he felt something split. A dagger's edge shimmered, protruding from his chest. He coughed, leaking from the mouth, as he fell backwards into the Reaper's embrace.

'Shhhhh.'

She held him. Fixing his hair with her free hand. He felt his life slipping away in the silence that followed. His vision faded. A white light beckoned him from afar.

He closed his eyes, and a single tear rolled off his cheek.

'I would hear your last words, Master Staine.'

Lilian?

The light came closer. He floated toward it, onward toward the green vista, the summer that had changed him forever. *Last words?*

'S—Story,' he said. 'Call me Story.'

The wind struck him as he turned into the light. He found himself sitting on the hill, brimming with emotion. Embraced from behind, her touch, her smell.

'I would hear your last words, Story.'

He exhaled. 'Love, Lilian.' He started to laugh. 'Love is the answer.'

There were worse ways to die. It was fitting that he should spend his last moments with her, watching his own memories replaying, two children hopelessly in love. Running, laughing, dancing.

Those were the thoughts he died with.

And they didn't make him retch.

'LOVE IS THE answer.'

Bandack sighed. She closed her eyes and smiled as the itch of the writ faded and waves of pleasure cascaded over her, her task completed at last.

The aftermath of the trull's unlikely appearance surrounded her: splinters of wood, scattered salt caught in a web of foul-smelling mucus.

What a mess.

All was calm. The basement fell silent, without care for her, or the empty vessel that had been Pistorious Staine. How valiantly he had accepted his fate. Perhaps she had misjudged him. She would commit his last words to memory, and add them to the others in that place within her where she kept the echoes of the souls she had claimed.

She inhaled. The stink of effluvia filled her lungs, the true face of death, free of the romance, or fanfare. A humble end—a fitting end.

'Is it done then?' Her mother's voice. She raised her head and turned toward it. Veralack stood with her arms folded, a mirror of herself, a glimpse of what she might become if the years were kind to her.

'It is done.'

'We don't have much time. They will pass through here soon.'

Bandack nodded. 'They all live?'

'It sounds like it.'

'Quickly, then.'

The menial staff would find Pistorious in the food storage area, laid with his hands over his eyes, and the Reaper's writ pinned to his chest.

Smiling.

Thirty-Two

Departure

ONE BOX. JEFF had to wonder what it said about him that the entire contents of his desk could fit so easily within a single box. A reflection of his lack of investment, perhaps. He wasn't sure how to feel about his resignation. There were regrets. He regretted that his lack of passion had in some way contributed to the chaos, and to some extent he held himself responsible. He'd realized this as he'd watched Petor *almost* die in his arms during the riot, kneeling in a pool of blood and piss, surrounded by chaos. He would have done what he did for anyone, of course. But in that moment he had caught a glimpse of his own future, what his own life might become if he continued to serve out of duty alone. It was in *that* moment that Jeff resigned his position, that he knew his time in the Halls of Venn had come to an end.

He spared a glance toward his old, neglected office, where Sundance busied herself with the business of decluttering, shaking her head in disapproval. He found it hilariously funny, but kept the sensation to himself out of respect for the woman. She had a lot on her plate.

He found a lot of things funny of late. Even Bobb had had him laughing out loud on a few occasions. It made him wonder how close the two of them might have been if Jeff had allowed himself to be content in his situation.

'I can help you carry that if you'd like?' Bobb appraised the paltry collection of personal effects.

'You might have to carry it for me, Bobb. I've got this bad knee, you see.'

The two men laughed.

'It won't be the same around here without you, you know.'

'Well, you'll have to actually work.'

That earned him a slap on the shoulder.

'I was thinking.' said Bobb. 'Before you head out, you might want to stop over in Venntown and have a pint with me in the local.'

'I think that sounds like a good idea. Thank you.' He'd never been invited to the pub before. It felt good.

Jeff checked the empty drawers for a third time, hesitating before lowering himself to one knee, only to realize that those habits were now useless to him. He knelt as easily as a man of twenty, and had a final check for anything that might have fallen under the desk.

That was it.

His career as security chief had ended, ready for someone else to inhabit. He smiled at his colleague before heading toward his old office.

'SETTLING IN ALRIGHT?' Jeff smiled at being able to find a chair to sit on.

Sundance smiled at the younger man. 'Not bad, dear. How are you?'

'Very well, thank you.' He fumbled around in his box, retrieving a smaller gift-wrapped one and presenting it to her. 'A parting gift.'

'Oh, you shouldn't have.' Sundance hadn't expected the visit, let alone this. She was surprised to have been given Jeff's job at all, but accepted it instantly. She respected the dignity with which he'd handed over his responsibilities. It was a quality she would have expected in a man much older.

She watched him as he took in the view. He seemed to approve of the renovations she'd made. How he'd managed to operate in this space for so long had baffled her entirely.

Unwrapping the gift revealed a beautiful pocket watch. She had half a mind to refuse it, feeling it a disproportionate gesture, but thought better of insulting him. 'It's beautiful.'

'It is. It was a parting gift from someone very special to me.'

'When you left Southgate?'

'Actually,' Jeff said, grinning, 'I was outcast.'

'Oh, you devil. How dare you tease me with a morsel like that.'

A moment of laughter filled the room. 'Would you like to know how I ended up here?' Jeff said.

'More than anything in the world.'

'Very well.' Jeff leaned in and slapped his knee, still grinning, as he looked for the right place to start. 'Southgate is an odd place. To me it was always just home, and obviously one day, I was told, I'd replace my father and spend my adult life fending off cultists and barbarians from the South. It was painful, in honesty, listening to the same old lecture over and over. In my adolescence, I found myself rebelling against him, only in small ways, but the short of it is that I fell in love with someone that I shouldn't have, a situation that would have embarrassed the family.'

He nodded and winked for effect. 'There was a nobleman, very self important, who enjoyed flashing his wealth before the common folk. He'd spend days at a time drinking in the tavern, flirting, groping the barmaids, telling his stories. Nobody liked him, but nobody liked him less than his suffering wife, who'd grown tired of having to justify his behavior. I'm sure that after hearing of her husband's latest affair with a very curvaceous young girl of seventeen, and the resulting pregnancy, she decided to get her own back.'

Sundance poured him a glass of water as he went on, shaking his head and laughing.

'So one night, I'm sneaking off to visit my lover and there she is: the wife. I've been selected as the rod with which she intends to beat her husband, and she's making a pass at me, pinning me to the wall and whispering in husky tones.' He imitated the movement, much to Sundance's delight. 'I let her know in as gentle a way as possible that I wasn't interested. That she wasn't my "cup of tea." To which she took great offense, and slapped me so hard I can still feel the heat on my cheek to this day. I shrugged it off and went about my night.'

Jeff drained his glass and continued. 'Several hours later, I returned home. I heard a disturbance and realized that something wasn't quite right, that I'd better sneak around it. I popped my head around the door to the banquet hall and saw our friend the nobleman leaping from table to table, swinging a woodcutter's ax around his head like a madman. He was demanding justice!

'At first, I didn't put two and two together.' Jeff nodded, mouth agape at the retelling. His enthusiasm lifted Sundance's spirits. 'I'd completely forgotten the incident with his wife after spending hours with my lover. And then he turned to me, pointed the ax directly at me, and charged. Of course he was that drunk that I found it easy enough to avoid the sharp of the ax, but as fate would have it, I lost my footing on a runaway cup, and as I turned, he managed to clip me with the flat of the blade.'

Jeff shook his head, tapping his bad knee. 'Shattered my knee. Of course, the fact that this nobleman had crippled me meant that my father had to step in. He beheaded him later on. But the wife, keen to save face, insisted that we'd slept together.'

He paused momentarily taking a breath. 'I had no alibi. Other than to reveal where I had truly been that night, and who I had been with. It would have ruined my father, damaged his credibility even further, to admit the truth. Furious at my indiscretion, and at my diminished ability to replace him, he banished me.'

He ended the story with a single clap. 'And here we are.'

Sundance sat dumbstruck. She'd never heard Jeff speak more than two sentences. The animation and charm with which he'd told his tale had surprised her to the extent that she fought not to laugh.

Jeff looked at her and cracked up. The two of them laughed for minutes, slapping their legs and wiping away tears.

'The best thing about it was, I never touched her. Everyone thinks I'm some sort of gigolo.' Jeff spoke an octave higher than usual, wiping his the laughter from his eyes. 'Oh well. What can you do?'

Sundance held out the pocket watch. 'So this was a gift from your lover?'

Jeff nodded.

'Don't you want to hold on to it?'

'It's taught me its lesson. Besides, I have a feeling I might see them soon enough.'

Sundance nodded in understanding. 'Where will you go?'

'North. Toward the mountains. I've enquired about a vacant blacksmith's forge. I thought it might be poetic to live out my days making axes.'

They laughed.

'Goodbye, Sundance.'

'Take care, Jeff.'

RENIA CLIMBED THE stairs, lifting her Grand Master's robes so as not to sully them. She emerged into the embrace of a breathtaking sunset. Birds called to her in the cool evening air as she crested the top step and walked out onto the roof, toward the proud smile of Molan.

'Dear girl,' he said, taking her in his arms.

She blushed, but kept his gaze. She hadn't sent for him, but knew he would be there for her, like he always was, like he always had been.

'You're here,' she said.

'Where else would I be?'

He stroked a stray strand of hair from her eyeline. 'I'm so proud of you.'

'Thank you,' she said. 'For everything.'

'It is, and has always been, my pleasure. I'll miss you, love.'

'I'll miss you too.'

A gust of wind kept the idle conversation at bay. She simply stood, determined, proud of how far she had come.

'I'll write to you.' She nodded at him. Molan nodded once, kissed her on the forehead, and walked away.

She wiped away the tear that had crept into her eye, and made for the dock.

Time slowed. She froze in place at the sight before her. A mighty dirigible bobbed and swayed in the gentle breeze, tied off with a rope the width of her thigh. It loomed over her like a celestial bubble, proudly expressing its presence with the grace of a star as the evening sun reflected off its envelope.

A stout figure in a brown leather jacket fussed over the ramp leading to the airship. He rustled his white beard in confusion and shouted something to Doratus. The two men laughed, smiling as she approached. Doratus stood in his ceremonial robes, his staff strapped to his back.

The little man lifted his bug-eyed goggles.

'Master Venn-Renia?'

She kept her gaze locked on the looming airship, slack-jawed in awe. The little man, thinking she hadn't heard him, raised his voice.

'Venn-Renia?'

She fought back the tears, and nodded. 'Yes.'

'You'll be glad to know, the weather has cleared up nicely. Should be a smooth run.' He approached her. 'I'm Bruce. Pleasure to meet you.'

She laughed, bending down to shake his hand. His grip was firm despite his height. The leather jacket did little to conceal his muscular frame.

'Shall we be off then? Before it gets dark.' He looked around her. 'No baggage?'

A hundred things passed through her mind in that moment. The weight that had held her down for most of her life. The sisters that had come to end her childhood, the man who saved her from the hound, her mother, her father, Dail, Aevus—where every one had been a source of shame at some point, she found herself freed, accepting of their fate and her part in it, knowing that she'd narrowly avoided making their hardships worthless, that she had to live, to look forward, and thrive.

Her hand wandered to the pendant around her neck. She held the lightstone shard and fought to prevent her voice cracking.

'No,' she said. 'No baggage.'

'Fair enough.' His eyes wandered toward the ever-patient Grand Master. 'I'll see you aboard then, Venn-Renia.' He tipped his head toward Doratus. 'GM.'

Doratus grinned and nodded him away.

He turned to her with the softest of looks, and placed his hands at her shoulders. 'Ready?'

She sighed. 'I am.'

She spent a moment to take him in. Remembering the first time they had spoken. He was no more the same person than she was, though he hid it better.

'Lost for words?' said Doratus.

'Quite.' She laughed.

He let go of her and took a step back, casting his eyes over her attire.

'The robes suit you,' he said.

She blushed, but held her silence.

'I have something to say.' His face became taut. 'You, uh. I…'

She laughed. 'Lost for words?'

'Let me finish.' He chuckled. 'I am grateful to you. For the longest time I've lived a solitary existence, closed off to the touch of another.' He shifted uncomfortably. 'It's difficult for me to say, but you have enriched my life in more ways than you could know. I no longer hide from my heart, or my power. What I'm trying to say is, that I'm proud to call you friend, Renia.'

She almost cried. She outstretched her fingers, and placed them over his chest, one for each scar she knew was there. 'You'll write?'

He bowed his head and met her eyes, before nodding toward the staff strapped to his back. 'Faster to visit.'

They shared a final grin, and he stepped backward.

'Grand Master,' he said.

'Grand Master.' She nodded in mock formality, then turned, walked up the ramp, and stepped over the open air onto the deck of the airship.

VERALACK NAVIGATED THE sewer with feline grace. She left little in her wake as her feet penetrated the running water.

The echoes of crashing waves bounced around the walls of the cylindrical space, bringing with them the relief of cool, salt-laden air. The smell of freedom, adventure.

She needed no lantern to navigate the space; years of lightstone exposure had heightened her senses beyond any hint of difficulty with the dark. Not that it mattered; she knew all the hidden tunnels and chambers within the grounds as if she'd built them herself.

She thought of Pistorious as she went. His family would come for his body, and the message would be felt. It should keep them in line for a time, remind them of their loyalties.

She followed the bend far enough to see the dark outline of her approaching daughter, who stopped to await her advance. Bandack stood before her, hands on hips, the image of impatience.

Veralack grinned at the younger woman. 'Have I met my end, Reaper?'

'Not today, Mother.' She sniffed. 'The preparations are complete?'

Veralack nodded.

'And you planted the box?'

'I did. It wasn't easy. We're thin on the ground here now. We'll have to import fresh blood.'

Bandack shook her head. 'Our numbers are depleted. There is much you don't know.'

That didn't sound good. 'Our last operative rots in a cell, slowly losing his mind.' She sniffed. 'Poetic, no?'

'Perhaps.' Bandack turned her head toward the sound of the waves. 'Maylack?'

'Safe. Venn-Dor retired her. She'll live with Petor on the grounds, but her use as an asset will be limited. They bought the whole charade. You were right, of course; the trull fiasco played a part in it, made it feel *earned*, I suppose.'

Bandack shook her head and sighed. 'Strapped to the bottom of a desk—I can't believe that worked.'

'Oh ye of little faith.'

'It puzzles me, Mother. Why go to all this effort? She wanted to kill you.'

Veralack raised her head, smiling. 'We shared a womb.'

Bandack frowned, seemingly none the wiser.

'We shared everything, every moment, every tear, every triumph, every failure. Whatever rage she felt at my actions, I shared. Do you understand? How could I leave her behind and pursue my happiness, knowing I would share in her misery? This way, I leave safe in the knowledge that she will be happy.'

Bandack stood in thought, nodding. 'Good.'

Veralack studied her daughter's face. 'Sentimentality?'

'You're surprised?'

Perhaps she was. She knew what her daughter must have been through, what she'd been through herself as an initiate, as an orphan, as a sister. Though Veralack had always *had* her sister, and something of her sentimentality had survived with their bond.

The thought frightened her, and she wondered what she would become without her.

Veralack held out the copy of *Journal 26*, eager to be free of its weight.

'No,' said Bandack. 'You keep it.'

'Your mission was to retrieve it, was it not?'

'It was,' said Bandack. 'But I made a promise. I won't touch it.'

The girl could be strange at times. Veralack thought better of pushing it, and changed the subject. 'I was surprised that they sent you.'

'Well,' Bandack said. 'I was the only one in the area.'

'I see.'

The tension between the pair rose. Neither knowing what to say.

She broke the silence. 'What now?'

'We can't leave together. Head west, for the Halfway, wait for me at the Three Sisters Inn. We'll sail home together and I'll vouch for you, for whatever that is worth.'

'Your achievements are their own merit.'

'It was *your* plan, Mother.'

Veralack nodded. 'Wait for you?'

'I have something to do before I leave. A favor to call in.'

'I see.'

Bandack turned to leave.

'Will you tell me of them? Your brother?'

Her daughter stopped in her tracks, and she turned, puzzled at the question. 'I do not know him.'

The revelation hit her like a brick. To be one of two, and to be separated, the pain must have been unbearable. She studied her daughter's face and saw nothing but indifference. 'Your father?'

Bandack turned away, and lowered her head.

'Dead,' she replied, already walking off.

Veralack shed a tear as her daughter walked into the light. So many years she'd waited for a second chance to complete her assignment, unable to return home, trapped in the prison of a cover that became her life.

It had cost too much. She couldn't help but feel sympathy for those hurt in the fallout of her mission. She wrestled with the idea of returning south to a home that had moved on without her, to the uncertainty that awaited her.

Three lives, two women. A lifetime of service to two opposing forces.

Who knew what the future would hold. She resigned herself to her fate, secure in the knowledge that both her and her sister had what they wanted.

'Home,' she whispered.

As THE SUN began to set, Sundance dropped into her office chair, exhausted. She'd done her best to settle in as quickly as possible, painfully aware of the amount of work she had yet to do.

The lockdown was over, the gates open, and life had returned to normal. The toll had been high, the strain too much for some, and it had resulted in the highest loss of staff in recorded history. There was no sign of Bandack; the discovery of Staine's body had cut the question of her absence short. The whereabouts of Vera remained a mystery. Perhaps Bandack had killed her. Perhaps she lived on, stalking the grounds in shadow.

She hefted the satchel she'd kept her research and writing materials in with half a mind to spend an hour or so on her manuscript, only to find another gift left inside. It was a small wooden box about the size of a pencil case, decorated with black lace tied in a bow.

She raised her eyebrow, slowly unraveling the bow. A gentle yellow glow crept out as she opened the box. Inside lay a small decorative dagger, clearly designed to be concealed. The beauty of the thing took her breath away, the small lightstone shard in its hilt held in place by winding brass vines.

She read the note left in the box.

Dear Sundance,
Never stop doing cartwheels.

MAKO SLEPT PEACEFULLY. His gentle snoring was the only sound save the slow dripping of distant pipework. Sundance stood before the bars to his cell, conflicted, wondering if his past deeds ever haunted him in the dream realm, as they did her.

He woke suddenly, one eye opening before the other, and rose, coughing, before lumbering toward her.

'You came back,' he said in a whisper.

She didn't speak. He could rot for all she cared. Her only hesitancy in taking this position had been him, and she'd quickly made her terms clear.

'You've thought—tick, tick, branch!' He hunched over, cursing himself. 'About what I said?'

'No.' She grinned. 'Not for a moment.'

She enjoyed the confusion on his face as he tried to resolve her presence and her words. 'Then why—'

'I'm the chief now.'

Mako's eyes widened. His pupils flickered from left to right. He fiddled with his thumbs, lost in thought and mumbling to himself.

'As such, it is no longer appropriate for you to be here.'

'What do you me—'

'I'm having you moved.'

'Where?'

'Aradinn,' she said. 'I'm sending you home.'

THE DECK OF the airship was wider than it looked and resembled the sailing vessels Renia had seen once whilst visiting Aradinn with Molan and Carol. Every surface was clean and well maintained, the crew clearly dedicated and well led by Bruce, who shot her a wave from the bow.

Deck hands made their preparations, testing knots and stowing away loose items, shouting their confirmations from mouth to mouth. She smiled at a pair of books strapped tightly beneath a covered plinth, her own work, newly bound and finished. *Doratus, no doubt.* Ever humble, it was no surprise that he'd made no show of presenting them to her.

The envelope loomed above her, an enormous volume of gas imprisoned in a patchwork of brilliant white and green. She almost choked on her saliva as she gawked at it, and stumbled backward as the ship lurched into action.

She laughed, waving away the captain's concerned look and the approach of a flustered worker, and lost herself within the bustle of the crew, looking for a safe place out of the way.

She beamed from ear to ear as the wind began to rise, whipping her hair wildly behind her head. She whooped as the ship was released and clutched the railing as the upward motion pushed down on her.

They rose. Higher and higher. The open ocean spread out before her, boundless in its mystery, it called, begging her to adventure.

Bruce leaped past her with a grace betraying his stature. She had to shout to be heard over the rushing wind. 'Where are we going?'

He smiled at her, directing his finger toward the tallest rock formation the world had ever seen, the defining act of the Praelatus, torn from the earth by his will alone.

The spire.

Its sheer majesty pierced the heavens. For all anyone knew, it had no end.

'All the way up,' he shouted. Bruce motioned to a spyglass by her side. 'Good time to take a look back. It's quite the sight from up here.'

She nodded, flushed with enthusiasm, and complied.

She saw her home, complete in its brilliance, each tower a work of art, each window, each stone—to take it in from the sky was to truly appreciate the sheer scope of its construction.

Locating her old apartment, Doratus's chambers, Hall Three, filled her with childish glee, and she whipped the spyglass from point to point, watching the grounds and the bodies within going about their daily chores. She followed the cliff line, and watched the waves crash up against the rocks, how the ocean spray burst into prismatic rays of colored light as it faded. Then to the left, to the south and the—

A figure stood watching from the rocks, hooded and clad in black—a woman. Renia moved back from the spyglass and saw with her own eyes.

The Reaper, Bandack. She was waving.

Renia laughed. A satisfied smirk crossed her face. She thrust her arms into the air.

And waved back.

PETOR TWISTED THE lid back on the tube of oil paint. His intention was to depict the great building at sunset. And in that moment, he knew this was to be his greatest work.

A beautiful sunset. Breathtaking.

The sweet smell of evaporating water carried on the wind. Petor inhaled, smiling at the simple pleasure of it. He considered himself lucky, grateful to be able to experience and capture this moment of glory.

'Lovely, isn't it?' said May. The blanket she wore over her lap rippled in the wind. Petor hurried to secure it, and checked over her bandages. Her voice was hoarse, and she'd slept much since the unfortunate incident with the trull, but Petor had insisted that he take care of her himself, and she'd been wheeled to the cottage and entrusted to him.

'Isn't it?' he said.

The angle of the sun crept into place, its timing perfect. He'd been delighted to see the arrival of the airship, and eager to make it an addition to his piece. He started to lay down the oils, acting quickly to capture the best of the light whilst it danced off the windows and the slick stonework of the ancient building. The airship rose, heading north toward the spire. He hurried to sketch its form, burning the rest of the image into his memory to come back to.

'Renia.' May nodded, a picture of serenity.

Petor grumbled. 'Good riddance, eh?'

'Oh, you are insufferable, old man.'

'Well. What a fuss.' He shook his head, sporting half a smile.

They watched together as the airship faded into the clouds.

'Will you miss it?' she said.

'No. The days of booting snotty youngsters into action are over for me. I've done my bit. Besides, I'll have more time to think about the things that *actually* matter.'

'Such as?'

'Such as why we are here at all.'

May blinked, shocked at his sudden philosophical outburst.

'I love you, you know,' she said.

'I know,' he replied, feeling every word like warm honey poured over his heart. He cleared the lump in his throat and blinked. 'You're a pain in my arse.'

Through the laughter, he painted. And when laughter faded it was replaced by steely focus. The art took over. The piece painted itself, as if some unseen force guided his hand.

He pressed on through the hours, grinning into the canvas like a lunatic. Stroke after stroke, he continued, unyielding, until the work was done.

DORATUS SLID *JOURNAL 26* back into its resting place on a shelf in the restricted library, at the end of a long line of its siblings— back where it belonged, in a darkened room, untouched and left to be forgotten. He ran his fingers down its spine and smiled to himself, a small chuckle left his lips.

He thought of Renia and what she must be feeling, flying through the air toward her new life, free of all the memories she'd left behind. How she had surpassed his expectations, and proved him wrong. How she had *defied* his expectations, and his fears, lived, and thrived in the end. He looked forward to seeing her again, and watching her grow into her title, a new equal, someone with whom he could share his burdens.

He tore his gaze from the spine of the journal that had caused him such turmoil, and looked away to the right, where a display cabinet held the remains of the imitation he had created, the book he had prised from Raellon's body.

'Goodbye, son,' he said, with his palm resting on its cover. The lightstone in his staff pulsed white light from behind his head, in sympathy with his emotion. It made him smile.

The leather cover of the fake book had aged well. He ran his fingers over it, thinking back to the days he spent making the copy, how long it had taken to match the color, and how he'd debated with himself over whether it even needed to match the original at all—

And then he thought of how long had passed between the real book being stolen, and recovered, and how obvious its hiding place had been.

And he frowned.

Thirty-Three

Dusk

ABOVE THE CLOUDS, the wind gently swirled and heaved, carrying dancing winged insects of fantastic color, scattering seed pods, and creating ripples in the sea of trees that towered larger than any Renia had ever seen.

Color. So vivid. It stole her breath. Not even in her dreams could she have imagined such a sight. Even with the sun's light dying, the foliage proudly displayed its green brilliance, highlighted in the soft blue and yellow glow of mushrooms that grew in large colonies at the forest's feet.

The rushing of nature hissed and croaked, a cacophony of life. The very air sang, its breath rich with the scent of pollen and sap. It flowed over her like a river, rendering her knees weak and her jaw slack.

She blinked as the dust of life came on the wind to welcome her to her new home.

The airship swayed and bobbed beneath her feet. The crew bellowed over the sound of the forest, preparing to heave-to.

'We'll have her docked and ready for you to depart shortly, Venn-Renia.' Bruce stood with his hands tucked into his trousers, sticking his belly out in a display of satisfaction.

She turned to him, exuding wonder. It seemed to please him.

'That won't be necessary, Bruce. I'll depart on my own.'

The man looked up at her, confused. 'And how do you intend to do that? Jump down?'

She simply grinned, and planted a kiss on his cheek. She lingered long enough to watch his cheeks flush, then picked up her books and held them tight to her chest.

She burst toward the railing, taking three strides at a time, vocalizing her triumph, and threw herself over the side. The sound of shock and concern rose in chorus around her, but she paid it no mind. Her lightstone fizzed gently at her breast and responded to her unspoken command.

She descended gently on a cascading blanket of static. Her feet crackled as they touched down on the soft dirt of the Sanctuary.

She turned back to the ship. Most of the crew stood gawking over the edge. Some laughed, others exclaimed their disbelief. There was a roar of approval as she waved back at them.

And then she walked into the fading light, into the forest canopy, led by a lightly beaten path between trees and slow-flowing streams, lit by a star-scape of bioluminescence. Small creatures watched her approach with curiosity from the treetops. They followed along, rustling with her, calling out to their kin to come and see. She whistled and sang to them, in friendship, with love.

From the darkness came light. She followed it through the last of the trees and emerged in a small village. Dwellings sat dormant, fashioned from the shells of giant snails, long extinct. Others made from fallen tree trunks, or giant mushrooms. She laughed out loud, exhilarated by the raw simplicity of it, each sight distinct from the rest, but nothing out of place.

Through the dwellings and closer to the light, she saw what it was that shone so brightly. A tree, flawed, crooked, but majestic. It stood within a pool of brilliant liquid that glowed white in the dusk, silently beckoning her, inviting her to be judged.

She placed her hand on the soft, gently glowing bark. It stole her breath, and her lightstone tingled in response, purring with ecstatic resonance.

Giant seed pods, each large enough to hold her entire body, surrounded her. Each pod sat heavy in the pool, pulling the branches that nourished them into long arcs. Dim light gave away motion from inside them, swaying gently from beneath what could have been veins, or vines, within the crust of the pods.

She knelt, and placed her hand on the closest. It shuddered at her touch. Liquid within sloshed and churned, and the smallest of cracks formed. The dark shape inside the pod resolved itself into the shape of a humanoid child, its limbs outstretched, testing the shell of its mysterious egg.

She leaned in closer, desperate for a peek at—

She froze.

A hand lay on her shoulder.

'You must be the Shepherd.'

EPILOGUE

THE CRYPT WAS kept cold, deep within the heart of the Halls of Venn, close to the ocean. Seven men stood in silence, armored and armed, illuminated by candlelight, all awaiting the word of one man.

Their lord stood before the body of Pistorious Staine, his face taut in restrained fury. His hands trembled as he carefully swept his dead son's hair from his eyes.

'You dressed the body well,' he said.

Glorian Staine. Lord of Verda and Master of Commerce for all of Luna Ruinam. His voice, devoid of its usual melodic tone, was glacial. His honor guard lowered their collective gaze, united in fear.

The Grand Master of the Halls of Venn bowed, a carefully calculated movement that showed respect without reverence.

'When did you find the body?'

'Thirteen days ago,' said Venn-Dor.

'Where?'

'In the basement. A food storage area.'

'And the name of the Reaper?'

Venn-Dor's hesitance to answer lasted for a fraction of a second. A detail that would not be forgotten.

'Bandack, Lord Staine.'

The Lord of Verda set his face in stone. He turned and inclined his head to the Grand Master. 'Thank you, Grand Master. Arrange for the body to be moved. We'll take it with us presently.'

Venn-Dor repeated his bow, and turned on his heel.

His exit was watched by all, with suspicion, with anger. Glorian Staine reached into his pocket and pulled out the note, the last words of his son. He glanced at the sheet and flared his nostrils before folding it neatly away.

'Arthus,' he said, beckoning to his first sword.

'Sir,' replied the warrior.

'Find me the Reaper that did this. Do it quietly.' He fixed the warrior with a cold stare. 'Do not fail me, Arthus.'

The warrior gulped and nodded once. 'Sir.'

'They dare to spill my blood.' He lay his hand upon the chest of his dead son. 'The time for patience has passed.'

He fixed his warrior with a molten gaze. 'Bring me this "Bandack", and send for Locrian.'

A Thank You

Dear reader,

I thank you. Wherever you are, whatever you believe in, whichever side of the political divide you stand on. You chose to engage with this story, and to support the human being who wrote it, despite the cost of living, despite the rate of inflation and multitude of stresses modern life presents. You took the *time* to read it, despite the constant chiming of hand-held devices and the pull of social media applications that bombard our senses with an endless rush of dopamine.

I salute you.

The past few years have been challenging for every human being on this planet. We live in uncertain times, conflicted and divided, at odds with each other over issues both great and small. Writing this book, in part, was an escape from that. Now it's time to let it go, so that it might live its own life. If it offers even one person a fraction of the relief it has given to me, I'll be happy with that.

My mother always said that books were the greatest escape.

She was, and is, right—*thanks, Mum.*

If you made it to the end, then it means I wrote something worth reading. I can't begin to tell what a feeling that is. I sincerely hope that you enjoyed the journey, and that this story and its characters—in some way, will stay with you.

I have plans for many more stories set in the world of Luna Ruinam. It is my hope that I've done enough with this debut that you might want to see that happen. If I could ask just one thing of you, that would be to take a few minutes to rate and/or review this book on Amazon, or Goodreads (or both if you are feeling generous).

Sharing your thoughts and making recommendations is a tremendous help to every writer you enjoy reading—particularly new and self-published ones.

You can also find me on Twitter:

@lunaruinam

Or visit my website. Buying directly from the author almost *always* results in more money ending up where you intend it to go—to the writers. Please feel free to join the mailing list for exclusive offers on future books, special and signed editions, and pre-orders.

@karlforshaw.co.uk